Outstanding praise for *The Only Suspect*!

"Stylish and suspenseful . . . will give readers
everything they want in this gripping tale."
—Jan Burke

"Impressive."
—*The San Francisco Chronicle*

"Absorbing reading."
—*Mystery Lovers Bookshop News*

"Jacobs has written a crackling, fast-paced whodunit,
filled with devious turn and lots of possible solutions,
making it hard to tell the good from the bad
until almost the final page."
—*The Orlando Sentinel*

"Eerie and provocative, this is an intensely
suspenseful novel."
—*Romantic Times*

THE ONLY SUSPECT

JONNIE JACOBS

PINNACLE BOOKS
Kensington Publishing Corp.
www.kensingtonbooks.com

PINNACLE BOOKS are published by

Kensington Publishing Corp.
850 Third Avenue
New York, NY 10022

All Kensington titles, imprints and distributed lines are available at special quantity discounts for bulk purchases for sales promotion, premiums, fund-raising, educational or institutional use.

Special book excerpts or customized printings can also be created to fit specific needs. For details, write or phone the office of the Kensington Special Sales Manager: Kensington Publishing Corp., 850 Third Avenue, New York, NY 10022. Attn. Special Sales Department. Phone: 1-800-221-2647.

ISBN 0-7860-1669-8

First Hardcover Printing: October 2005
First Mass Market Paperback Printing: August 2006
10 9 8 7 6 5 4 3 2 1

Printed in the United States of America

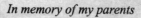

In memory of my parents

Acknowledgments

I am indebted to everyone who answered my questions and offered encouragement during the writing of this book. In particular, I'd like to thank retired police officer and investigator Robin Burcell for generously sharing her insights about police work; Camille Minichino and Margaret Lucke for their perceptive and very helpful comments on the manuscript; and my husband, Rod, for always being there. I'm grateful, too, for the support I've received from my publisher, Kensington Publishing Corp.; my editor John Scognamiglio; my agent Deborah Schneider; and all those readers who've taken the time to write.

CHAPTER 1

I had been dreaming of Lisa. It was late spring and we were strolling through Boston Common as we did so many Sunday mornings back then, wrapped in the simple pleasure of being together. I was pushing Molly in the stroller. Lisa circled her arm around my waist and told me she loved me. The joy I'd known—so fresh and boundless—was tempered, even in my dream, with the sorrow of what followed.

I clung to the memory as an intrusive ringing tugged me toward waking. It had been a long time since I'd felt Lisa's presence so vividly.

The persistent chirping of the phone finally won out. When I groped to retrieve it from the night stand, my hand found nothing but air. In an instant, I was fully awake. I opened my eyes and realized I had not the slightest idea where I was.

Okay, I was in a car; I figured out that much. My car, in fact. In a ditch by the side of some narrow, dusty road. I'd probably spun out in the process of getting here, since the car was facing backward and tilted at an angle. I had a hammering headache and a mouth that felt like the bottom of a bird cage.

I examined myself quickly: limbs intact, no significant

wounds or contusions. As far as I could tell, I wasn't injured. Not badly at any rate. That assessment held even as I became aware of fresh aches and pains, most notably through my back and neck.

Not injured, maybe, but damn addled.

What day was it? What day did I last remember? I struggled to pull anchor points from my cottony brain. They came slowly, when at all.

The sky was clear, with only a few high clouds. That was a good sign, because it felt familiar. I ran a hand along my jaw, discovering yet another spot that hurt. But the stubble from my beard was barely a day old. That was also a good sign. Whatever had happened, I hadn't been out of commission for long.

The phone, which had stopped ringing before I was fully awake, now started in again. I reached into my jacket pocket and checked the number. My answering service.

"Dr. Russell? I have a call for you. A woman by the name of Sherri Moore. She's says she's not a patient but she needs to talk to you."

Sherri was the mother of Molly's best friend, Heather. I was relieved to feel the bits and pieces of my life slowly coming back to me. "Put her through."

"I'm sorry to bother you, Sam, but it's almost noon." Sherri sounded as though she was working at not being angry. "Where are you?"

"I'm, uh . . ." I glanced at the dry, rocky terrain around me. I hoped I was somewhere close to home, though I couldn't be sure. But I knew that wasn't what she meant. "There was an emergency," I offered by way of explanation. Not entirely untrue.

"I figured as much. I wouldn't have called, but the other girls have left and Molly was getting worried." Sherri paused. "Maureen said one of you would be by to pick her up at nine."

"Be by . . ."

"Heather's slumber party, remember? Molly spent the night here." Sherri's tone was one I'd heard before from Maureen's friends. *Men, what do they know?*

When it came to Molly, I usually did know. But not this time. My mind was in a fog. "Where's Maureen?"

"I don't know. That's why I finally called your service. I tried the house all morning, and no one answered. She's not picking up on her cell number either."

Was I supposed to have picked up Molly? Probably.

Although Maureen and Molly were getting along better than they had in the beginning, none of us lost sight of the fact that she was my daughter and not Maureen's. Out of necessity, my wife oversaw Molly's social calendar, but I was often the one who did the "hands-on" stuff. Not that I was complaining. Molly was the center of my universe.

"I'm sorry, Sherri. I think Maureen and I got our wires crossed. I can be there in . . ." I looked around again. The terrain was steep and rocky, covered mostly with scrub. Where was I, anyway? "In an hour," I concluded. It was better than admitting I hadn't the foggiest idea how long it would take.

"No hurry really. We were just worried. Here, let me put Molly on."

"Where *are* you, Dad? Did you forget me?" Her tone was plaintive and maybe just a bit accusing.

"I didn't forget, honey. I got tied up at work. You know how that happens sometimes." Unfortunately Molly knew all too well, and I was disgusted with myself for lying to her. For being in a situation where I *had* to lie. I thought I'd put all that behind me. "I'll make it up to you this afternoon."

"It's already afternoon," she replied with the cutting clarity of an eleven-year-old going on eighteen.

I ignored the jab. "I'll be there soon," I told her. "I love you."

"Me too. Bye."

* * *

My Audi was at an angle, tail down in the ditch, but the grade wasn't much. I was able to push the door open and step out. I'd hoped the fresh air would clear my head. Instead, the movement sent my stomach roiling. I leaned over, gripping the car to steady myself, and tasted the bile that rose into my throat. Another sledgehammer blow pounded at my temples.

Jesus, what had I done? Even when I'd been hitting the bottle 24-7, I'd managed to make it home most nights. And I'd rarely had a hangover.

I'd never been a sloppy drunk either. A functioning alcoholic, to use the lingo. Only I'd not been functioning as well as I thought.

I'd been sober now for almost five years. Ever since I'd returned to California. I'd escaped the black hole of anger and despair that descended after Lisa's death. I had a new life. A different life, but a good one. How could I have been stupid enough to risk losing it?

Because I figured that was what must have happened. Somewhere, probably in the last twenty-four hours, I'd slipped up and taken a drink. And one drink had led to another. And another. And I'd ended up on a hell of a bender.

It wouldn't have been the first time I'd slipped up, but it was the first since I'd met Maureen.

I wiped my mouth with my sleeve and tried again to pull some memory of what had happened into my consciousness. Nothing. I checked the date on my watch. Sunday, May 5.

Yesterday, being Saturday, I'd have seen patients until noon. But yesterday was a complete blank.

One of the attractions of returning to my hometown of Monte Vista and stepping in when my dad retired had been the chance to practice medicine the old-fashioned way. I knew my patients. I knew their families. In some cases, three generations of family. So why couldn't I conjure up just one name, one face I'd seen yesterday? Try as I might, I couldn't.

I must have shown up for work. If I hadn't, Ira would

have sounded the alarm. Ira Kincaid was one of my oldest friends. He was also my partner, formerly my dad's associate, and he oversaw the day-to-day operation of the practice with the eye of a military sergeant. Sometimes it got on my nerves, but mostly I was grateful I didn't have to worry about the administrative stuff myself.

With the work hurdle cleared, all I had to do was find a way to explain last night to Maureen. The truth was always an option, of course. Maureen would probably even understand. Oh, she'd be pissed, and disappointed in me—hell, I was feeling those same sentiments myself—but I didn't think she'd hold my feet to the fire.

Then the significance of the date hit me. May 5. Yesterday had been our wedding anniversary. Only our second. Of all nights to screw up. How could I have *done* something so stupid?

As terrible as I felt physically, the self-loathing was worse. If my head hadn't already been pounding, I might have slammed it against the car in disgust. I settled for kicking the tire.

One day at a time.

The words had steered my course over these last few years. I'd dismissed them at first as overly simplistic, but I found they worked. The fact that I was starting over again at day one didn't make them any less meaningful. I was going to move forward.

And the first thing I needed to do was get out of there and pick up Molly.

I felt wretched, but the chances of that improving without a shower, and probably a heavy dose of aspirin, were slim. I surveyed the damage to the car—not as bad as I'd expected—and the angle at which it was perched. The ditch wasn't deep. Unless there was damage that wasn't readily apparent, I thought I'd probably be able to get out without calling a tow truck.

I'd started to ease myself back into the driver's seat when

I noticed my hands. My fingernails, to be precise. They were darkened with what looked to be dried blood.

Taking slow, deep breaths, I tried to ignore the queasiness in my gut, the pounding in my head, and the rising tide of questions that added to my discomfort. I got out of the car again and looked at my reflection in the glass. Disheveled, yes. The top three buttons of my shirt were undone and the left hem had come untucked from my trousers. I had a swollen eye, a bruised lip, and a scratch along my jaw, but nothing that would account for much bleeding.

So why was there blood under my nails?

I gave fleeting thought to driving directly to Sherri's to pick up Molly, but I realized that in my rumpled, and perhaps rank, state, that was probably unwise. I figured it would also be prudent to approach Maureen first, without Molly around.

The car's engine started easily, and I breathed a sigh of relief. All things considered, I was damn lucky.

It took a bit of wheel-spinning, but I managed to get the car out of the ditch and back onto the narrow dirt road near a rugged outcropping of rock. The country was steep, mostly scrub mixed with oaks and tall pines. There wasn't a landmark anywhere that I recognized, but I headed in what I thought was a westward direction toward flatter terrain. I bumped along the rutted road for a good ten minutes despite relentless protests from my head and stomach. Finally, I saw a field of cows and beyond that a truck whizzing along on a crossroad.

Turning north, I meandered another ten minutes or so, through ranch land that was only generically familiar, until I stumbled onto a sign directing me to Highway 193. At last, I was able to orient myself. It took only another twenty minutes for me to reach home, even stopping at the flower stand along the way to pick up a large bouquet of pink and purple tulips for Maureen. I pulled into the garage, nervously rehearsing my apologies. I hadn't settled on a story yet, figuring it might be best to gauge her mood first.

Maureen's yellow Miata was in the garage, but I knew as soon as I stepped into the house that Maureen wasn't there. The stillness was almost palpable. There was no note either, which wasn't all that surprising given that I hadn't even come home last night. Pissed probably didn't begin to describe her mood.

I stripped off my clothes and studied myself in the bathroom mirror. The damage assessment remained the same: except for my face and a bruised shoulder, I wasn't hurt. I scrubbed my nails hard with hot water and a nail brush and watched with a nagging sense of misgiving as the pink-tinted water swirled down the drain.

Years ago, I'd taken a swing at a guy who was coming onto Lisa. I'd gotten the worst of it and stayed clear of scuffles ever since. Even when I was drinking heavily. Sometimes I would get loud and obnoxious, but when it came to physical confrontation, I was a wimp. Still, if the blood under my nails wasn't mine—and after examining myself, I couldn't see how it was—then it had to have come from someone else. That bothered me as much as anything.

After I'd showered and changed into fresh clothes, I put the flowers in a vase on the kitchen table and left a note. *Sorry doesn't begin to cut it. Can you ever forgive me? I love you. Sam.*

Then I went to get Molly.

"You look like you could use some coffee," Sherri said as she ushered me through the tiled entry and into her granite and chrome kitchen. Sherri lived in one of the posh new developments at the edge of town.

"That bad, huh?"

She poured me a cup without asking if I wanted one. "What happened to your face? You run into a door?"

I rubbed my jaw and laughed self-consciously. "Yeah, what a cliché, huh? Sorry about the confusion over getting Molly."

"Not a problem. The girls were having a good time." Sherri brushed a strand of honey blond hair from her face. "I hope you and Maureen made good use of your evening."

I hesitated before answering. Sherri might know something of our plans for last night. That would be a place to start in reconstructing what had happened. But did I dare ask? It would mean admitting I didn't remember a thing. I finally decided I couldn't do it. Not given my personal history, and especially not with Sherri, who would undoubtedly spread the word in short order. I offered a generic nod instead.

"Good. I know Maureen was looking forward to it." Sherri paused, as if she were about to say something further, then smiled. "I'll go tell Molly you're here."

My life had changed radically and forever the day Molly was born. Not on the surface so much, though there were changes there too: diapers, interrupted sleep, and armloads of baby paraphernalia everywhere we went. But the most significant changes weren't so readily apparent.

From the moment she first nestled in my arms, I'd been totally swept away by the tiny, helpless bundle of a human being who was my daughter. It was beyond anything I'd expected. The intensity of my feelings **still** surprised me sometimes. And it spooked me to remember how close I'd once come to losing her. It was Lisa's parents and their efforts to gain custody that had finally shaken me free of booze.

Now, inexplicably, I'd teetered on that same brink again. What had I been thinking?

Molly appeared in the doorway, her backpack slung over

one shoulder. She had the same rich auburn hair and brown eyes as her mother. Only, Lisa's hair had been straight while Molly had inherited my cowlicks and kinks.

"Ready to go?" I asked her.

"I was ready at nine."

"It's my fault. I'm sorry."

She flashed me a mouthful of braces that passed as a smile.

I waited until we were in the car to offer a full apology and, if necessary, an explanation, but by then she was on to other things. My failure to show up that morning took second fiddle to tales about the furry black puppy who belonged to the boy next door. I realized early into the story that the boy was the main attraction, not the dog. Not so long ago, I thought with a pang of nostalgia, it would have been the other way around.

It wasn't until we'd been home some time that she asked, "Where's Maureen?"

"I'm not sure. I think she's probably out with a friend."

"Shopping?"

"Maybe." It was as good a guess as any; Maureen *did* spend a lot of time shopping. And her purse was missing; I'd checked that already. "Did she say anything to you about who she might have gone with?"

Molly shook her head.

Though I tried not to show it, I was becoming increasingly worried. If Maureen was angry, she'd have been more likely to let me have it than to simply ignore me. The cold, silent treatment wasn't her usual style. But neither could I discount the possibility that she'd told me where she'd be and I'd simply forgotten it, along with everything else about the previous day.

Molly looked at me suspiciously. "Did you two have a fight?"

"What makes you ask?"

"I don't know. It's weird is all. Both of you forgetting to come get me, then she's not here and you look . . ." She lowered her gaze. "You look like you got beat up or something."

I gave her a hug. "Maureen and I didn't fight, and no one beat me up. Like the klutz that I am, I ran into a door. That's all. It looks worse than it is."

She hugged me back, then gave me a skeptical look. "You'd tell me if something bad happened, wouldn't you? I'm not a little kid anymore, you know."

"I know you're not a little kid, Sweetpea. Not by a long shot. And everything's fine."

I'm not sure Molly believed that any more than I did.

CHAPTER 2

Sunday evenings we usually had supper at my dad's, in the old two-story house I'd grown up in. Most often he barbecued, but sometimes he'd whip up tacos or pizza. Those were his specialties even when Mom was alive. And they were the only times he got anywhere near the kitchen. Since her death he'd learned to cook a few other meals out of necessity, but he never ventured from his standbys on the Sundays he cooked for us.

As five o'clock approached and Maureen still hadn't returned, I debated calling Dad and bowing out. But I knew he'd be hurt, so Molly and I went anyway.

My brother, Chase, was already there, settled in front of the television with a can of beer. Since it was early in the month, he probably hadn't yet hit on Dad for a handout. On those rare occasions when I'd suggest maybe he shouldn't be asking at all, Chase was quick to point out he'd been around during Mom's protracted fight with cancer. I, on the other hand, had been living the golden life—that was his expression—in faraway Boston. To his mind that counted for a lot. I couldn't say I disagreed.

He greeted us without rising from the sofa. "Hey, Molly

By-Golly. Come give your old uncle Chase a hug. I swear you get prettier by the day."

She wrapped her arms around his neck. "You say that every time."

"It's true every time. You're getting to be the spittin' image of your mama." Chase offered Molly a sip of beer in spite of the fact he knew I disapproved.

He looked at me and grinned. "It's not going to hurt her, Sam. It's just a sip. Hell, Dad used to give us nips of his whiskey when we were growing up. Remember that?"

And I'd ended up an alcoholic. I knew, though, it wasn't Dad's fault.

"Where's your better half?" Chase asked, more as a conversation filler than out of any real interest. Chase and Maureen had never really hit it off.

I'd spent a good part of the afternoon playing out scenarios of Maureen's possible whereabouts in my mind. The most likely was that we'd gone out—it was our anniversary, after all—I'd gotten smashed, and we'd argued. Or maybe we'd had one hell of an argument, and that's why I'd started drinking. In any event, she was royally pissed and wanted nothing to do with me for the moment.

What I desperately hoped, though, was that she'd long ago made plans to go off with a girlfriend and I'd simply forgotten about it.

A third possibility played at the back of my mind, and that was that something really bad had happened. I had visions of some street thug demanding my wallet, then slugging me in the jaw and running off with Maureen. It might explain the blood under my nails, but it didn't ring true. I still had my wallet for one thing, and you can be sure I'd have had no qualms about handing it over.

None of this was anything I wanted to get into right then. "She couldn't make it," I told him.

"Smart woman. These Sunday dinners get mighty tedious, if you ask me." Chase looked at me more closely. "What happened to your face?"

"I ran into a door." It seemed easiest to keep the story consistent.

"Sure." He grinned like he didn't believe a word of it.

"I'd better go say hi to Dad."

"You ever want to talk about it," Chase called after me, "I'm here. I'm something of an expert when it comes to woman troubles."

Only if personal experience made one an expert. Chase had a history of bad relationships, but whether he'd learned anything in the process was unclear.

We had steak that night, cooked to perfection as usual. The rest of the meal, which in better times had been my mother's duty, lacked the same expertise. The frozen fries were still a bit soggy in the center, though they improved vastly with catsup, and the salad was nothing more than a bowl of iceberg lettuce. You'd think, since my dad had been a doctor, he'd pay more attention to nutrition, but I doubt he'd eaten a true vegetable since the day my mother had become too sick to cook.

"Debbie tells me you and Ira are redecorating the waiting room," Dad said.

Debbie was our nurse and my dad's main pipeline for office gossip. She worked for him for nearly twenty years and still took his advice over ours. It bothered Ira, more now that he and I shared the practice than when he was my dad's associate, but I didn't have a problem as long as she did her job.

"We're thinking about it," I told him. "Probably some fresh paint and carpeting, and maybe new furniture. It depends how much it costs."

Dad frowned, his bushy eyebrows knit together like an

iron gray ledge above his eyes. "It'll cost plenty, believe me. Nothing's cheap anymore."

"Your patients aren't going to care," Chase said. "They come to you because you're a good doctor and you care about them."

But mostly because I was my dad's son. Still, it was nice to hear Chase stand up for me. Chase was two years older, and when we were growing up he was everything a boy could want in a brother. He taught me to fish and shoot baskets, and pretty much everything I knew about sex before Lisa. Anyone crossed me on the playground, they heard about it from Chase. For years, just the unspoken threat of Chase was enough to keep most people off my back.

Things changed after Chase got out of the army. Maybe it was because he wasn't a hero anymore, or maybe it was the fact that he burned through one job after another, either being let go or quitting over some petty disagreement with his superior. Chase had yet to land on his feet, as my dad was fond of saying, but he never seemed to begrudge the fact that I'd enjoyed successes while he floundered.

"We're not going to do anything for a while," I told them. "Ira's got to pay off his credit cards first."

"He maxed out again?" Dad asked.

I nodded. Ira didn't believe in denying himself any of life's pleasures. And his pleasures were expensive ones: golf, cars, gambling, and women.

"Makes me look like a saint, doesn't he?" Chase burped then shot Molly a sly grin.

She giggled while my father glowered.

After dinner, I excused myself to Dad's den and phoned my home number. I hoped Maureen would pick up, but I reached only my own voice on the outgoing message of the answering machine. I tried her cell phone next. The connection went directly to voice mail. My stomach churned with the eddy of worry I'd been trying so hard all evening to ignore. Where was she?

While Chase and Molly did the dishes, I helped my father set up his new computer. He'd been slow to embrace the electronic revolution, but once he'd succumbed, there was no stopping him.

"I'm sorry Maureen couldn't make it," he said when we were just about done. "I know these family meals can't be her idea of fun, but she's a good sport about it."

"I think she enjoys them." I knew she enjoyed not having to cook.

"It's sad she doesn't get along with her own family. She never talks to them at all?"

"Doesn't talk, doesn't write. As far as she's concerned, they don't exist. I gather they must feel the same way."

"Any idea what happened?"

I shook my head. Maureen didn't talk *about* her family any more than she talked *to* them. *That part of my life is over*, she'd told me at one point. *I don't want it infecting who I am today.* Personally, I think the past is never really over, and in any case, it's something you share with the person you love. But Maureen didn't agree, and she'd made me promise not to keep pestering her about it.

My father stood up from his chair. "Well, you tell her we missed her tonight."

"I'll do that." I looked at my watch. "Molly and I had better be heading home."

"Take some firewood with you. The Feed and Fuel was clearing out what was left from their winter supply. The price was a real bargain. There's a tarp in the garage you can use to protect your trunk."

"Thanks."

With Chase's help, I carried two loads of wood from the side of the house to the driveway, where my Audi was parked. Chase went to get the tarp.

"What happened to your rear bumper?" he asked when he returned.

"I wasn't paying attention and backed into a tree." If I'd

been thinking straight at the outset, I'd have come up with a single story that covered both the bumper and my face. Now I was stuck with two "accidents" that sounded lame at best.

Chase seemed not to notice. "Even a little ding like that will cost a bundle to get fixed."

"I know. I've been kicking myself for my stupidity." That part was true, at least. "Car's old enough I may just forget about fixing it."

"Seems a shame though. It's in pretty good shape otherwise." Chase unloaded an armful of logs and went to get another. The sky had darkened, and the first star of the night glimmered in the twilight. If Maureen were here, she'd close her eyes tight and send a wish to the heavens. She never told me what she wished for. "That would spoil it," she explained. But she'd invariably kiss me on the cheek at the same time.

Suddenly I felt like something inside me might burst.

When Chase returned, I leaned against the car with a sigh. "I need some advice."

His expression grew serious. I hadn't asked him for advice since high school. "What is it?"

"What I said about Maureen . . . It wasn't just that she couldn't make it tonight. She's gone."

Chase dropped the logs into the trunk without stacking them. "What do you mean, gone?"

"I don't know where she is." I choked on a well of emotion. Worry, guilt, fear, loss—they were all mixed together.

Chase touched my shoulder. "She left you?"

"I don't know. Her car's there, and her clothes. Only thing I know for sure that's missing is her purse. I'm worried something has happened to her."

"Have you notified the police?"

"You think I should?"

Chase looked confused. "Why wouldn't you?"

"It might be nothing. It's only been a day. Less than that even. I don't want to make a big deal if it's just . . . you know, nothing."

Chase regarded me in silence.

"Maybe she told me where she was going and I forgot. Or maybe she just wanted some time away from me."

"She's mad at you?"

"I'm not sure."

He rubbed his bristly chin. "Something tells me there's more to this than you're saying."

I hesitated. I didn't want to speak the words, to admit I'd been weak and stupid. But I clearly had been, and admitting it was an important step. I nodded.

"I think I had a drink last night."

"You think?"

"Right. I don't . . . I don't remember. Anything."

Chase waited for me to continue.

"I woke up this morning in my car, in a ditch. With a pounding headache. When I got to the house, Maureen wasn't there. She hasn't been home all day."

"You think she might have been in the car with you last night?"

"The doors were still locked when I came to this morning."

"Jesus."

I nodded again. "I really fucked up."

"You think that's why she took off?"

"That's one theory. To make it worse, yesterday was our anniversary."

Chase shook his head. "Swift going, champ."

"There are other possibilities, though," I added.

"Like something bad happening to her?"

"Right." I looked at Chase, and I could tell he was thinking about Lisa, same as I was.

"It's not the same," Chase said.

"But you can see why I don't want to bring the police in unless I have to."

He was quiet a moment. "I hate to tell you, Sam—I think you have to."

On some level I'd known that all along, but Chase made it seem obvious.

"And you might want to call Jesse as well."

Jesse Black was my sponsor at AA. "That's like closing the barn door after the cows are out, Chase. When I should have called him is when I was thinking about taking that first drink."

"I wasn't thinking of AA," Chase said quietly.

I felt a knot form in my chest. I knew what he was getting at. Jesse was also a former defense attorney. That Chase would assume I'd need Jesse's help wasn't at all encouraging.

I held out some hope that Maureen would be home when Molly and I returned. But she wasn't. The house was as still and empty as when we'd left.

By now it was obvious to Molly that something was seriously amiss. "Where's Maureen?"

"I'm not sure."

"What do you mean? How can you not be sure?" She folded her arms and glared at me.

I could tell she was troubled. But I didn't know if she was concerned for Maureen or simply reacting to the fact that there was something unusual going on. Maureen and Molly hadn't hit if off the way I'd hoped. Maureen had come on too strong in the beginning, expecting, I think, to waltz into a ready-made, Hallmark-perfect family. Molly, understandably, had resisted. Though their relationship was improving, it was far from ideal.

"There are a lot of places she could be," I said reasonably.

"Dad! What is going on?" Molly's voice was close to strident.

"I don't know, Molly. Honestly. Maureen wasn't here when I got home . . . from, uh, visiting a patient this morning." I cringed at how easily the lie rolled off my lips. "She didn't leave a note."

My daughter eyed me suspiciously. "Are you sure you guys didn't have a fight?"

I smiled stiffly. "Not that I remember."

"Aren't you worried?"

"Yes, I am. I thought she'd be home by now, that it was all some big mix-up. She didn't say anything to you about her plans, did she?"

"No."

I touched Molly's cheek. "You go on and get ready for bed. Tomorrow's a school day, remember? I'm going to call some of Maureen's friends. There may be some ladies' thing going on that I've forgotten all about."

"Does Maureen *have* any friends?" Molly asked with a bite of sarcasm.

"Molly, that's not—"

"Okay, I'm sorry. But at least you won't have to spend all evening on the phone."

Maureen complained that she had nothing in common with the other women in town, and in many ways that was true. Except for the increasing number of retirees drawn to the area by reasonably affordable housing, Monte Vista was family oriented. People moved there from Sacramento, and even the Bay Area, because they wanted a quiet, safe place to raise children. The town's social structure revolved around schools and kids' sports, and most women found friends in the mothers of their children's friends. In that regard, Maureen was at a disadvantage. For one thing, she was younger than most of them. For another, motherhood was a role she had donned, rather than a fierce commitment of the heart. But I felt certain if she'd only put a little energy into making friends, she'd find women she was comfortable with.

She hadn't reached that point yet, however. Molly was right. With three or four phone calls, I would exhaust the pool of people who might know where Maureen was.

"Off to bed now," I told Molly. "I'll come say good night when I'm finished here."

* * *

I waited until Molly was asleep before I called the cops. Part of me kept hoping if I waited long enough Maureen would come home. But I knew that was foolish. She hadn't simply taken off. I was growing more certain of that. Finally, I called and spoke with an officer named Hannah Montgomery.

"Have you checked with the highway patrol for accidents?" she asked.

"My wife's car is still in the garage."

"And her friends?"

"None of them know where she might be."

"People take trips," the detective said, "get held up in traffic, forget to call home, that kind of thing."

She paused, maybe waiting for me to jump in and agree. But I couldn't. The innocent explanations didn't ring true.

"There's a good chance everything will work out, but if you'd like I can come take a full statement and pick up a photo. That way we can be on the lookout for her."

"Thank you. I'd appreciate that." I didn't realize how tightly I'd been gripping the phone until I hung up. My fingers were white from the pressure.

CHAPTER 3

Hannah Montgomery pressed her fingertips to her throbbing temples. It didn't ease the pain or the tension. What she needed was a cigarette, and for that she'd have to wait another two hours. She didn't know if she'd make it.

As part of her get-your-life-in-order campaign, Hannah had resolved to stop smoking. Again. This time she was going for the gradual approach. Everyone told her it was easier to go cold turkey, but she couldn't swing that. She'd already tried several times and failed. Not that cutting back was so easy either.

She glared accusingly at the phone, although she'd had the headache long before the call from Sam Russell. Since the guy had waited all day before reporting his wife missing, why couldn't he have waited another forty minutes? Hannah would be off duty by then, and the next shift could have taken it. She wasn't supposed to be on tonight anyway. She'd only agreed to fill in because she was still trying to establish herself as a team player within the department.

Hannah had been with the Monte Vista Police Department only a little over a year, but she'd been a cop for thirteen years, seven of them in LAPD robbery-homicide. When it came to solving cases, she was sure of herself. In the realm of department politics, she was less so. Though politics was only a small part of why she'd left LA, she'd hoped a smaller department like Monte Vista's might be an easier fit. She hadn't decided yet if that was true.

She'd handled her share of missing persons investigations too. If that's what the Russell case actually was. More often than not, these things worked themselves out on their own. There'd been an argument. Sometimes, an accident. Or the missing party had gone to visit relatives. Eventually he or she showed up with no help from law enforcement.

The cases where that didn't happen were another matter altogether. They inevitably ended badly, if there was any resolution at all. Sometimes it was years later before the body even turned up.

Hannah figured she'd have a better idea which way the Russell case might go after she'd taken the report.

In LA, where she'd worked most of her career, Hannah would have told Sam Russell to come in to the station and file a report, or she would have taken the information over the phone. But this was Monte Vista, where law enforcement was as much community relations as by-the-book police work. It was a quiet town, far enough north of Sacramento to be somewhat insular, and fairly bursting with civic pride. The police were there to serve.

Hannah took one last, longing look at the pack of Marlboros in her desk, then grabbed her keys and coat and went to meet Sam Russell.

The Russell home was in one of the older residential neighborhoods, with tree-lined streets and manicured lawns. The houses there weren't as large as in the new developments at the edge of town, but to Hannah's mind they had infinitely more charm.

Sam Russell opened the front door before Hannah had a chance to ring the bell. He hustled her into the kitchen, shutting the swinging door that separated the rest of the house behind him.

"My daughter's asleep," he explained. "I don't want to disturb her."

"I'm Detective Montgomery," Hannah said. She realized she was whispering and felt foolish.

"Sam Russell." He smiled. "Molly won't hear us with the door closed. It's just that her bedroom is right off the hallway."

He was only a few inches taller than Hannah's five-eight, and his dark, unruly hair was thinning slightly at the crown, but his hazel-brown eyes were warm and punctuated with a fan of laugh lines. She found him attractive in the way Robin Williams was. Not classically handsome, but comfortable. In fact, he reminded her a little of Malcolm, who was not someone she wanted to be thinking about right then. Malcolm was part of the life she was trying to put behind her.

She noted a slight purplish swelling near Sam's right eye. Birthmark or bruise? She mentally filed the information away for later.

"How old is your daughter?" Hannah asked. An infant would suggest a different family structure and issues than a rebellious teenager. And family dynamics were always an issue when one of the members went missing.

"She's eleven," Sam told her.

"Does she know her mother is missing?"

"Maureen is actually her stepmother, but Molly knows she hasn't been home today. I tried not to make too much of it because I didn't want to worry her, but I know she senses something is wrong."

Moving a vase of purple and pink tulips out of the way, he gestured for Hannah to have a seat at the kitchen table. It was a rectangular farm table made of pine, and took up most of the open space in the kitchen. Hannah noted the country motif, complete with gingham valance and ceramic cookie jar in the shape of a cow. Not her style at all, but it spoke of a hominess that she begrudgingly found appealing.

"My first wife died when Molly was four," Sam added.

"I'm sorry. That must have been hard for both of you."

He nodded. "It was. Still is. But we're moving on."

Hannah had walked that road herself. Not with a child, which she tried to convince herself was a blessing. Still, she couldn't help feel a twinge of envy that Sam Russell had managed to find love again.

She pulled out her notepad and pen. "What's your wife's full name?"

"Maureen Judith Brown Russell."

"Brown was her maiden name?"

Sam nodded.

"How old is she?"

"Twenty-eight."

Close to ten years younger than her husband by Hannah's estimate. She made a note of the fact, though she wasn't sure it would prove relevant.

"How about a physical description."

"She's five foot six, about a hundred and thirty-five pounds. Light brown hair, a little longer than chin-length. I have a recent photograph for you." He slid a color snapshot across the table in Hannah's direction.

It showed a woman sitting in an upholstered chair next to a fireplace, smiling at the camera. Maureen Russell wasn't beautiful, but she was an attractive woman, and it was clear she worked at looking her best. Her hair was professionally streaked and stylishly cut. Her beige sweater and white slacks looked expensive, as did the diamond pendant at her neck.

"It was taken last Thanksgiving," Sam said.

Hannah put the photo aside for the moment. "Tell me again why you think she's missing."

"Her car's in the garage, but she hasn't been home all day."

"Could she be with a friend?"

Sam frowned. "All day? Besides, I called them. No one's seen her."

"What about hospitals, have you checked there?"

He nodded, ran a hand through his hair, and took a deep breath.

"When did you last see her?"

"This morning." Sam seemed agitated. He pushed his chair back from the table and rose. "Can I get you some water or anything?"

"I'm fine, thank you."

He ran a glass for himself and drank it in one long gulp before answering. "Early this morning. She was still in bed when I left to check on a patient. I'm a doctor," he added as if the reference to *patient* might not be clear. "My daughter was spending the night at a friend's. When I picked her up and came home, Maureen was gone."

"What time was that?"

Sam hesitated. "Actually, I dropped by the house first, very briefly, before picking up my daughter. That would have been a little after noon. We both returned home about half an hour later."

Hannah's headache hadn't subsided any. Neither had her craving for a cigarette. She took a moment to refocus her mind. "No sign of your wife either time?"

"No. I didn't think anything of it at first, and I was in a hurry to get Molly."

"Was the door locked? Any indication the house had been broken into?"

"I came in through the garage," Sam said. He seemed to be replaying the morning's sequence in his mind. Then he shook his head. "I'm sure I'd have noticed if the front door wasn't locked. And nothing appeared disturbed."

"How about your wife's purse and wallet?"

"They're gone too. And she's not answering her cell phone."

"Any of her clothing missing?"

"The closet looks pretty full. I wouldn't know if everything is there though."

"You sure she didn't say anything to you about her plans for the day?" Hannah asked. There was a good chance the woman had ventured off voluntarily.

Sam looked a little sheepish. "Not that I recall. But she might have and it slipped my mind."

Some men *were* that nonattentive. Hannah had no idea if Sam was one of them, but she would have guessed not. "Has your wife ever left without telling you?"

He hesitated. "Once. But she knew how worried I was that time. I can't believe she'd do it again."

All it took was the right provocation, Hannah thought. "When was that?"

"About a year ago. We had an argument, and she left in a huff. She drove into Sacramento and got a hotel room for the night."

"Did you argue recently?" Hannah asked.

Another hesitation, only this time his eyes avoided hers. Finally, he shook his head. "No, there was no argument."

There was something about Sam Russell's response that gave her pause. "Do you and your wife argue a lot?" she asked.

"Nothing out of the ordinary."

"What's ordinary?"

He shrugged. "Household chores. Money. Living here."

"Living here?"

"In Monte Vista. Maureen wanted to live somewhere more urban. San Francisco or the Bay Area, preferably, but she'd take Los Angeles too."

Hannah felt her pulse skip a beat. She looked at him. "Why did you use the past tense just now?"

"Past tense?"

"You said your wife 'wanted' to live somewhere else."

Sam started to smile then seemed to think better of it. He seemed unfazed by the question, however. "We'd more or less worked that one out. My practice is here, my family is here. Molly is settled here. I can't move. Maureen knew that when she married me."

"When was that?"

"Two years ago. Not long after I moved back. I grew up here, but I lived in Boston for a while."

Okay, so maybe his use of the past tense wasn't a slip of the tongue. Still, there was the discoloration in his cheek that might be a bruise. She wondered if Sam and his wife had worked things out or if Sam had simply put his foot down. That might explain why Maureen had up and left. If that's what had happened.

Sometimes when a person went missing, Hannah knew there'd be no good outcome. It was a sixth sense of sorts, something she could feel in her bones. A woman leaves a bar with a man she's just met and is never seen again. Or her car is found abandoned by the side of the road, her emptied wallet on the front seat. But that wasn't the case here.

"For what it's worth," she told Sam, "this isn't the typical scenario of a disappearance under suspicious circumstances. At least not on the surface."

His brow furrowed. "What do you mean?"

"The doors were locked. Your wife's purse is gone, as if she took it with her. It looks like she left the house voluntarily."

"But it's almost ten o'clock at night," Sam protested. "Wherever she went, she'd be back by now. Or she'd have called."

Unless she didn't want to be found. "Have you checked your accounts to see if she withdrew money recently?"

"I'll call the bank in the morning."

"It would be helpful if you could get me a list of names and phone numbers. Family, friends, other people she might have regular contact with."

"Sure. She doesn't have a lot of friends. She's kind of a private person. And she hasn't talked to her family in years."

A motorcycle roared past the front of the house, going much too fast for the neighborhood. Where was a cop when you needed one? Hannah thought wryly. "Does your wife work?"

"Not any more. She used to work in my office. That's how we met."

Maureen Russell, a decently attractive woman, younger than her husband, with no job and few friends. Was Monte Vista maybe a little too quiet for her? Or was it something much worse?

Real crime was rare in the town, but that didn't mean it never happened. Shortly after Hannah came to Monte Vista, a woman had been raped by a drifter who climbed into the house through an open window, and only a couple of months ago an elderly couple had been accosted in their own garage. Could something terrible have befallen Maureen Russell? Absolutely. But Hannah wasn't convinced it had.

"Do you want me to process this as a missing persons report," she asked, "or would you rather wait a day or two?"

Sam studied his hands. His mouth was grim. "I think you'd better go ahead."

"I'll get her description out on the wire," Hannah told him. "And I'll contact the local paper. They're usually pretty good about covering this type of thing. You might want to print up fliers too and get them distributed around town. The more people looking for her, the better."

"Yeah, I'll do that."

"Here's my direct line." Hannah handed him a business card. "Give me a call if you hear from her or think of anything that might be useful." She wanted to add something encouraging, like *Try not to worry.* But that was silly; anyone in his situation would worry. And whether his wife was in trouble or had simply left him, the news would not be welcome.

When Hannah returned to the station, she completed the paperwork and faxed Maureen's photo to key law enforcement personnel in the county. Then she checked with the local taxi service. No cars dispatched to the Russell residence.

The sheriff's department had dogs and a wonderful handler named Rick Thompson. Hannah would contact them in the morning. If the dogs could pick up Maureen's scent, they'd at least have some idea if she'd left on foot or by vehicle.

It was almost midnight by the time she finally made it home, if a sparsely furnished two-bedroom bungalow could be considered home. She opened a bottle of Anchor Steam then lovingly extracted the much-longed-for cigarette from its cellophane pack. She lit it, leaned back on the sofa, and inhaled deeply. It did wonders for her mood. Maybe she should forget about quitting. So what if smoking shortened your life? Hannah wasn't so sure she cared about those extra years anyway.

She had a second bottle of beer and half a cheese sandwich then crawled into bed and turned out the light, hoping that sleep would come easily for a change.

She curled on her right side and then her left. She lay diagonally across the mattress just because she could, then kicked a leg out in front of her.

Having a king-size bed to herself was not all bad. Hannah would admit to that much. But it made her feel an aching loneliness she couldn't explain. Which was why she so often filled it in what she knew were unwise ways.

* * *

Monday morning Hannah was still bleary-eyed when she sat down at her desk with her second cup of coffee. She hadn't fully engaged her mind with the work at hand when her partner, Dallas Pryor, slapped a sheet of paper down in front of her.

"What's this?" he asked, leaning his palms on her desk. He was enveloped in a cloud of aftershave that made Hannah pull back.

"Missing persons report. The call came in last night when I was filling in for Jack."

"Maureen Russell. Wife of Dr. Sam Russell?"

Hannah nodded. She could tell from the tone of Dallas's voice that she was missing something. Some petty high school grievance most likely. Dallas had grown up in town, gone to school with many of the folks who lived here now. It often worked to his advantage, but Hannah thought it sometimes clouded his judgment as well. Dallas seemed to forget that high school had been a long time ago.

"You talked to Sam?" he asked.

"First on the phone, and then I went out there and took a report. Why?"

"How'd he seem?"

"Worried. Perplexed." Hannah wasn't sure where Dallas was going with all the questions. "It doesn't strike me as having the earmarks of a suspicious disappearance, but I figure it's better to err on the side of doing too much than not enough."

Dallas ran a hand over his head of thinning blond hair. "Sam Russell's story seem credible to you?"

"Yeah, I guess so. He didn't really have much of a story, just that his wife was missing. Do you know something I don't?"

"Did he happen to mention his first wife?"

"He said she'd passed away."

"She was murdered," Dallas said. He stood back and folded his long arms over his chest.

"What?" Hannah was sure she'd misunderstood.

"Sam Russell killed her. He's a free man today only because of a hung jury."

CHAPTER 4

Molly was in tears. Not about Maureen but because her favorite pair of pink tights had a tear in them. At least that's what she claimed.

"You must have another pair," I suggested naively. We were already running late. In light of all that had happened, I found it hard to get worked up about a pair of tights.

Molly jutted out her chin and glared at me. "You don't know anything, do you?"

Not about fashion, certainly. But I had a feeling that wasn't the real issue. I took a breath to stifle my impatience.

"I know you must be worried," I said.

She didn't respond.

"I'm worried about Maureen too."

I worried that she was hurt. Or dead. Or the victim of some sadistic and depraved rapist. I worried she'd left me. I worried that, whatever had happened, I was in some way answerable. Worry had about gnawed me raw.

Nonetheless, for Molly's sake, I wanted to sound reassuring. "The police are looking for her," I said. "And we don't know for sure anything bad has happened. She might just have gone away for a while."

"I don't care where she is," Molly snapped, turning her back to me. "I don't care if she ever comes back."

I squeezed my eyes shut and took another deep breath.

"She's not my mother," Molly added.

"That doesn't mean you can't be worried about her."

Molly looked at me a moment. "Do you think she ran away?"

"What makes you ask that?"

She shrugged. "I don't think Maureen likes me very much."

That caught me like a punch from out of nowhere. "Honey, that's not true. Not at all true."

Molly twisted the ripped tights into a ball.

"What makes you think Maureen doesn't like you?"

"It's just the way she acts."

I'd thought Maureen and Molly had been getting along, but maybe that was because I *wanted* them to get along. "Acts how?" I asked.

"Like I'm a big disappointment to her."

"That's not so. She thinks you're terrific." But a part of me understood what Molly was feeling. Sometimes Maureen acted like I didn't quite live up to her expectations either.

Molly scowled. "I *told* her I needed new tights."

"Do you want me to help you find another pair for today?"

She sighed dramatically, grabbed a pair of jeans from the floor, and stomped into the bathroom. "Never mind, I'll wear something else."

While she finished getting ready, I went into the garage to unload the firewood from my trunk. I stacked the wood along the side of the house then pulled up the tarp I'd used to line the trunk and shook it out. I was folding it to return to my dad when I noticed a shoe in the trunk next to the wheel well. A dressy black sandal.

I picked it up and turned it over in my hands. Had Maureen been wearing it Saturday night? That wouldn't explain how it had gotten into my trunk though. I tried to remember what trips we'd taken recently, thinking it might have fallen from her luggage. A trip to the snow two months ago was all I could come up with. She'd hardly have packed sandals for that.

Molly appeared, backpack over her shoulder. "Okay, I'm ready."

I dropped the shoe back into the trunk and shoved it out of view.

But the image stayed in my head. A lone shoe, a woman's shoe, in my trunk. Inexplicably. I felt like the air had been squeezed from my lungs.

It was nearly one when I finished with my last patient of the morning. That left me about twenty minutes of my allotted ninety-minute lunch break. I wasn't hungry—my stomach was so knotted I couldn't have swallowed a bite—but I did need time to regroup. I went into my office and closed the door.

Molly's fifth-grade school portrait smiled at me from my desk. There was also a snapshot of her as a toddler with a head full of springy curls. Lisa had taken the photo while I jumped up and down like a clown to make Molly laugh. The bittersweet memory of that moment brought a lump to my throat. Sometimes the pain of losing her was so fresh it took my breath away.

The most elaborately framed photo on my desk was of Maureen. It was a formal studio shot she'd had taken as a gift for me shortly after we were married. It was a good picture of her, and Maureen did not generally photograph well. She looked happy. Sparkly. Like a woman with an intoxicating secret. I loved the photo, though in truth I'd never seen her look quite so enticing in real life.

What had happened Saturday? I tried again to pull up even a single thread of memory about the day. Sometimes I'd get close—a nanosecond glimmer that vanished into nothing the moment I tried to grab hold of it. But the harder I worked to remember, the more even those sparks were extinguished.

The anguish lodged in my chest like a stone. I loved Maureen. Maybe not with the intensity and steamy passion I'd felt for Lisa, but with something equally gratifying.

Maureen had reminded me a little of Lisa at first, which might have accounted for my initial attraction. They had the same fair complexion and chiseled cheekbones, the same full mouth. The similarities were superficial though. Maureen lacked Lisa's spontaneity and outgoing manner, but she did make me laugh, which was something I hadn't done much after Lisa's death. And she kept me on an even keel, another thing I'd had trouble with on my own.

Our marriage wasn't without problems, but I told myself it was simply the fabric of making one life out of two. It took time.

We didn't fight so much as shuffle our way around our differences. For the most part, it worked. Occasionally, when things didn't go Maureen's way, she would grow quiet and give me a look that I took to mean, *Why did I ever marry you, anyway?* But I was guilty of similar transgressions. There were moments when I silently blamed her simply for not being Lisa.

There was a knock on my door, and Ira poked his head in. "You got a moment? I'd like your opinion on the best course for . . ." He'd reached the chair opposite mine at the desk. "Sam? What's wrong?"

I'd done a pretty good job of keeping it together all morning, but suddenly it was too much. "What isn't?" I said. My voice broke midsentence.

Ira closed the door then sat down.

"You want to talk about it?"

Ira and I went way back. Fourth grade, is what I remember, though supposedly we'd started kindergarten together. We'd been best friends all through high school. Although we went in different directions for college and med school, we kept in touch. Ira had come back to Monte Vista when I went east to practice, and he eventually went into partnership with my dad. When I returned five years ago, we'd tried to pick up where we left off at eighteen, but we'd changed in too many ways. I had Molly and a hole in my heart that had once been filled with the love of my life, Lisa. Ira and his first wife, whom I'd barely known, were divorced, and by the time I moved back, his second marriage was already failing. He wanted to party; I preferred to spend my evenings reading Dr. Seuss to Molly.

We were still friends. We talked about lawn mowers and trends in the stock market, but we no longer had a bare-your-heart kind of relationship. *Personal* simply wasn't a realm we explored.

I'm sure Ira was as uncomfortable at that moment as I was.

"Maureen is missing," I told him. I could feel tears prick at my eyes, and looked away.

"What do you mean?"

I told him I'd gone by the hospital Sunday morning and come home to find her gone. I didn't tell him about waking Sunday morning with my car in a ditch and no memory of the night before, or about the blood under my fingernails and the shoe I'd found in my trunk. I wasn't sure either of us was ready for that kind of confidence.

"You've called the cops?" Ira looked like a doctor from central casting, the kind nurses and patients go gaga over. Dark hair and eyes, and a mouth that curled into a perpetual smile. Even now, with concern clouding his face, he managed to sound reassuring.

I nodded and filled him in on some of the details.

Ira was silent for a moment. Then he shook his head slowly. "My God, Sam. This is . . . unbelievable. I'm surprised you even came to work today."

"I almost didn't. But I figured there wasn't much I could do staying home. I'm not putting in a full day."

He seemed to be searching for the right words, finally settling on, "What are you going to do?"

"I'll probably print up some flyers or something. The detective I talked to suggested it."

Flyers might help, but they didn't guarantee results. For every high-profile missing persons case, like Chandra Levy or Laci Peterson, there were countless others with stories just as compelling that never made a dent in public awareness. I'd checked the statistics the night before on the Internet. Last year, 35,142 adults had been reported missing in California alone, some 4,346 of them under suspicious or unknown circumstances. Most had received scant attention, despite efforts by family and friends for broader coverage.

"I already checked with the bank," I told him. "No activity on our account. I guess it's a matter of waiting. And praying."

"If there's anything I can do, just let me know."

"Thanks."

Ira checked his watch. "I hate to do this, Sam, but I've got a patient waiting. You'll be okay?" He was clearly uneasy about leaving me, yet I thought I read relief too. Ira had never been one to embrace other people's troubles.

"No, I understand. I've got patients myself."

In the five minutes remaining before my next appointment, I called Detective Montgomery to see if she'd learned anything new.

Instead of answers, she tossed back a question of her own. "Why didn't you tell me you were arrested for your first wife's murder?"

The question caught me off guard, as she'd undoubtedly intended. I'd known the arrest would come up—it was a major reason I'd been reluctant to sound the alarm on Maureen—but I hadn't expected it quite so quickly.

The harsh light of scrutiny was damned uncomfortable.

"Is it relevant?" I asked.

"I don't know. Is it?"

"No," I said, "it isn't." And then I hung up.

Of course it wasn't relevant. I hadn't killed Lisa. I couldn't honestly believe I'd done anything to harm Maureen either, though the uncertainty of not knowing was agony.

But to the outside eye, nothing spoke louder than the fact that I'd been charged in my first wife's murder.

Lisa and I were soul mates. You know those sappy movies where a man and a woman look at each other across a crowded room and the sparks start flying? The stories where they fall instantly in love and never look back? That was us. We were so in tune with one another it was almost scary.

We met as undergraduates at Brown. I sat behind Lisa in Southeast Asian Civilization, and she took copious notes. I was too busy staring at her to write a word. I finally worked up the nerve to ask her out for coffee the second week of classes. She grinned and said, "I was beginning to think you'd never ask."

I went to Boston that summer to meet her parents. It was clear from the outset they weren't happy about our relationship.

The Pattersons were blue bloods, descendents of the early patriots. Hal Patterson was the CEO of a major investment banking firm and sat on the boards of such celebrated companies as Ford and General Electric. I was a scholarship student who didn't play golf, ride horses, or sail. I'd never been out of the country except to walk across the border into Tijuana. I was a Democrat, and my grandparents had immigrated to this country from Russia. But most important, I wasn't Julian Broward, Lisa's high school sweetheart, whom they adored and whose family went back about as far as the Pattersons'.

They didn't like me, but they tolerated me with cool reserve then tried with everything they had to convince Lisa she was making a big mistake. The crowning blow came when she put aside her own plans for graduate school in order to follow me to St. Louis, where I enrolled in medical school. She was wasting her life, her parents told her, throwing away her future, and all for some small-town bumpkin with whom she had nothing in common. The fact that we loved each other wasn't important. That I was studying to be a doctor didn't cut it either. As far as they were concerned, I might as well have been going door to door selling brooms. After we were married, and especially after Molly was born, they softened a bit, but only on the outside. If they'd thought there was any chance they'd succeed, they would have driven a wedge between us in a heartbeat.

We'd been married six years, and living in Boston for two, when Lisa was killed. We had plans to go out together that night, so Molly was with her grandparents. But during the day, I went biking, alone. Lisa was pregnant with our second child and wouldn't have been able to join me even if she'd been into biking, which she wasn't. I spent the day drinking in the fresh air and exhilaration of being outdoors after a long, cold winter. My mind was filled with thoughts about Lisa and Molly and the new baby, and how blessed I was to have them in my life. When I returned home, Lisa was gone.

No note. No sign of a struggle. Nothing missing but her purse.

Her body was found a week later in a nearby woodlands park. She'd been strangled and stabbed, her body dumped into a ravine. It took the police two months to decide to arrest me, but almost from the start there was speculation about my guilt.

If not for my powerhouse attorney and a single holdout juror, I'd be sitting on death row. Which was why I was loath to put too much faith in the system now.

CHAPTER 5

My last patient for the afternoon, eighty-three-year-old Cy Bennett, was escorted into my office by his grown son. Although the senior Mr. Bennett was suffering from dehydration, vertigo, and a dry, hacking cough, he refused to acknowledge that he was sick. Not surprisingly, he balked at the idea of being hospitalized. In the end, his son and I prevailed, but not without some heavy cajoling.

It was only three o'clock, but it had been a long day. I was ready to head home and confront my own demons.

They came sooner than I expected, in the form of Detective Montgomery.

She was waiting for me in the parking lot as I left the office. Her face bore the practiced lack of expression I'd noticed among police personnel following Lisa's death. It was a big change from the sympathy I'd seen the previous evening.

My gut tightened. News of Maureen? *Please,* I prayed, *don't let it be bad news.*

"Short workday for a doctor," the detective said.

It didn't sound as though she was about to deliver bad news. Relief washed over me. "Well, I—"

"But a long one," she added pointedly, "for a man whose wife is missing."

A beat of silence while my relief gave way to wariness. I had a pretty good idea what she was getting at. "What was I supposed to do," I asked, "sit home wringing my hands?"

"It wouldn't be unheard of."

I started to respond but thought better of it. For one thing, I'd learned through bitter experience that arguing with a cop wasn't smart. For another, there was an element of truth in what she said. Perhaps I was trying to convince myself that nothing had changed. Or maybe I was trying to make it so, as if by sticking to my routine I could alter reality. To some degree, I'd taken the easier path—denial. In that respect, the elder Mr. Bennett and I had a lot in common.

"I called the bank," I told her. "No activity at the ATM or on our charge card. I contacted our cell phone carrier too. No outgoing calls since Friday, and she hasn't checked messages."

Detective Montgomery frowned.

"That's not good, is it?" I knew it wasn't good—the information had been sitting in my stomach like a lead weight all morning—but I guess I was hoping the detective would cast it in a more hopeful light.

Instead, she ignored the question completely. "We'd like to go over your report again."

"We?"

"My partner and I."

I looked toward the car she'd stepped out of. I didn't see anyone there.

"Down at the station," she explained.

"Why there?"

Again, I knew the answer. They saw me as a potential suspect. They wanted me on their turf, and they wanted me to feel uneasy.

In the latter regard, they were succeeding.

"And if I refuse?" I asked.

She gave me that blank look again. "Why would you do that, Dr. Russell?"

"I've got to pick up my daughter soon."

"We won't keep you long."

I followed her in my own car, wondering for the whole six blocks of the trip downtown if I was making a mistake. But refusing to cooperate wasn't the best choice either. I thought about calling Jesse then dismissed the idea. He wasn't practicing law anymore, and in any event, I didn't want to feed their suspicions.

We walked into the station together. Detective Montgomery showed me to a small interview room. The table was metal, as were the chairs. Along one wall there was a mirror, presumably one-way for monitoring what went on inside. The overhead lights were bright and glaring, the air stale. The room was nicer than the ones I'd been treated to seven years earlier in Boston, but it wasn't about to win any awards for comfort.

"Can I get you some coffee?" the detective asked.

"No, thanks." I could barely make my lungs work. My palms were sweaty.

"Make yourself at home. I'll be right back." When she left, the door snapped shut with a metallic clink.

An invisible steel band gripped my chest. In a flash, I was back in Boston facing Detective Frank Donahue and his peppermint breath.

You have the right to remain silent. Anything you say can and will be used against you.

I shook my head, clearing the memory. *This is different,* I told myself. *Maureen is missing, and the police are going to help me find her.*

The door opened again. I was expecting to see Detective Montgomery. Instead it was Dallas Pryor, who I guessed right away must be her partner. That explained why she knew about Lisa already and why I was a suspect. I found the clarification both reassuring and frightening.

"Hello, Sam," Dallas said, offering the same phony smile

I remembered from high school. "I hear you've got another missing wife. You're a dangerous man to be married to."

"Cut the crap, Dallas."

"It's Detective Pryor."

"Despite what you seem to think, *Detective* Pryor," I emphasized the title, "I had nothing to do with Lisa's death. Or with Maureen's disappearance."

He smiled again. "That's good to hear."

I'd run into Dallas only a couple of times since my return to Monte Vista, and each time he'd managed to bring Lisa's murder into the conversation. Chase said it was because Dallas was a cop, and cops hated to see anyone get off, even if it wasn't their case or jurisdiction. But I thought it was more personal.

Detective Montgomery returned carrying a cassette tape, which she slipped into a machine on the table. She looked at Dallas. "I thought you were going to wait for me."

"We've just been catching up on old times. Sam and I went to school together."

Detective Montgomery shot him a funny look. She was an attractive woman. Mid-to-late thirties, chestnut hair cut short and feathery. She was trim and athletic, whereas Dallas had put on twenty pounds or so since high school. He'd been skin and bones back then, so the extra weight wasn't all bad, even though it was more flesh than muscle.

I tried to gauge the atmosphere between them. If I'd had to guess, I'd have said they weren't the most compatible of partners.

"Do you have new information?" I asked.

"Nothing relevant." Montgomery pointed to the tape recorder. "Okay if we tape this? That way nothing slips through the cracks."

I wondered what would happen if I objected. "Fine."

"We checked with your neighbors this morning. Nobody remembers seeing any strangers in the vicinity yesterday, or anything out of the ordinary."

"No one remembers seeing your wife yesterday either," Dallas added.

Detective Montgomery put a sheet of paper on the table in front of me. "These are the names you gave me last night, your wife's friends. Anyone else you can add?"

I scanned the list then shook my head.

"How about civic activities, social clubs, that sort of thing?"

"She used to play tennis with a group of women at the club," I said.

"The Vista Heights Country Club?" Dallas asked with a barely disguised sneer.

"No, the Swim and Racket Club in town." A decidedly less sophisticated, and less pricey, alternative to the toney country club a few miles west of town. Maureen had been pressing to join Vista Heights, but since money was tight and neither of us played golf, I didn't really see the point.

"Can you give us their names?"

"Terry something. And a Joanna." It was an arena of Maureen's life I knew virtually nothing about. "I don't know their last names."

"Anything else?"

"Last winter she took a ceramics class through Adult Ed. Thursday evenings."

Montgomery scribbled something on her pad. Dallas looked bored.

The detectives led me again through the events of Sunday morning and my discovery that Maureen was missing. Dallas pressed me about the last time I'd seen her. A trickle of sweat ran down my chest. I knew I'd made a mistake not thinking through my answer earlier, but now I was locked into the story I'd already given. If I started backtracking, it would look bad. At least what I told the detectives jibed with what I'd told Sherri.

"You left the house before eight yesterday morning?" Dallas asked.

"Right."

"What did your wife say to you before you left?"

"She was still asleep. I got dressed and slipped out quietly so as not to wake her."

"And then went by the hospital to check on a patient?"

"Yes."

"Who was the patient?"

This time I was prepared. "Mary Conrad," I told them. Mary was indeed in the hospital, and unlikely to remember which days I'd been in to see her, assuming she was even awake during my visit. I felt horrible using her to cover a lie—Mary Conrad was eighty-six years old and a lovely woman. I made myself a silent promise to make it up to her by visiting often in the future.

"There'll be a notation on her chart?" Dallas asked.

I shook my head. "Dr. Becker is her attending physician at the hospital. He's a cardiologist. I'm not directly involved in her care there."

"Then why did you go see her?"

"She's still my patient."

Dallas shot Detective Montgomery a meaningful look. I tried to pretend I hadn't seen it. The story seemed transparent to me too, but there was no way they could prove I *wasn't* there.

"And you got back home at noon?"

"A little after."

"That's a long time," Dallas said, "for looking in on a patient who isn't even under your care at the moment."

"I spent some time in town too. Got myself a cup of coffee, did a little window shopping." For just a moment, I hesitated. My simple lie about Sunday morning was becoming an impenetrable maze and might even hinder their ability to find Maureen. I wanted to go back and start over, but I couldn't.

Detective Montgomery was rubbing her thumb over the metal clip of her pen. "I've arranged for the sheriff's department to lend us their dog handler."

"Dog handler?"

She nodded. "Dogs are amazing. If they can pick up your wife's scent, it may help." She seemed to be waiting for a reaction from me.

"Fine," I told her.

"We'll also want to inspect the house and yard," Dallas added.

"Looking for what?" Though having been down this road before, I knew. They would be looking for evidence of a crime, and more to the point, evidence that suggested I was the perpetrator.

"Whatever we find," Dallas answered. I swear I saw a smirk on his face. "Anything to head us in the right direction."

"The right direction is that she's missing," I said, aware of the rising anger in my voice. "Lost, or hurt, or being held captive. What you should be doing is *looking* for her, not wasting your time trying to make me look guilty."

"You're awfully defensive, Sam," Dallas said.

I knew I was overreacting, but Dallas grated on me. I could tell that already this was personal for him. He'd like nothing more than to be the one to slip the cuffs on my wrists and read me my rights.

Hannah Montgomery rose from her chair and leaned on the table between me and Dallas, blocking our line of sight. "We *are* trying to find your wife, Dr. Russell. But without something more to go on, we have no idea where to look."

"There's got to be a—"

"There's no sign of a break-in," she added. "No sign of struggle. Your wife left with her purse."

"Or whoever took her, took it too."

"Is that what you're suggesting happened?"

I'd spent the last twenty-four hours sifting through conceivable scenarios. Bottom line was either Maureen had left of her own volition as the detective suggested, possibly after an argument with me. Or she was the victim of foul play.

My inability to recall yesterday morning or most of Saturday opened up a frightening corollary to the latter—that I'd been the one to harm her. And since I could remember nothing, I had no idea what witnesses might eventually come forward.

My throat constricted. I dropped my head to my hands. "I don't know what happened. It's not like her to just disappear."

"Except she did it once before, you said."

"Just overnight. And it was after a big blowup."

Dallas stood and stretched, signaling an end to the questioning. "I'll ride with you, Sam. Hannah can meet us there."

"Meet us where?"

"At your place. The search, remember? And the dogs?"

"Right now? I've got to pick up Molly."

"Fine. We'll get her on the way."

In the end, I arranged to have Sherri pick up Molly.

"Of course I can do it," she said. "I should have thought to offer earlier. Molly can stay here and hang out with Heather for a couple of hours. And, Sam, I've already lined up half a dozen people to help distribute flyers."

"That's great, Sherri. Thanks."

I'd stepped away to make the call on my cell phone. I pocketed it and met up with Dallas in the parking lot.

"Nice car," he said. "I've always liked Audis. Of course the price is a little steep for someone on a cop's salary."

I didn't bother to point out I'd had it for ten years. Dallas and I had been at odds since sophomore year in high school, when he and his mother moved to Monte Vista from somewhere in Texas. Not that I was alone in that. Dallas had it in for half the male population in our class. With the wisdom of maturity, I'd come to understand that he'd probably felt pretty insecure and uncomfortable with himself, which is why he acted the way he did. I wasn't convinced that had changed.

Dallas walked along the side of the car, admiring it. "Shame about the bumper. That dent looks fairly recent."

"Yeah, I backed into a tree."

"Man, an expensive car like this, that must hurt."

"It's not a big deal." We got inside, and I started the engine.

Dallas turned on the radio and played with the dials until he found a station he liked.

"I never met your current wife. What's she like?"

I was sure the *current* was deliberate, especially since he'd used Maureen's name throughout the interview. And he'd never met Lisa either. "What kind of question is that?"

"Just trying to get the picture is all."

"She's a wonderful person."

"You knew her in Boston?"

"No, we met here."

We pulled up to my house before Dallas got in any more questions. Because the garage was blocked by police vehicles in the driveway, I parked on the street.

Hannah Montgomery and a uniformed officer were standing on the walkway leading to the front door.

Dallas greeted them then gestured to one of the men. "Check out the car too, Herman." He turned to me. "You don't mind, do you, Sam?"

In a panic, I remembered the woman's shoe, still in the trunk. And I'd had enough of Dallas.

"In fact, I do mind."

He feigned amazement. "Why is that?"

"Because I'm tired of your innuendo, for one thing." I locked the car and led the detectives toward the house. I hoped I wasn't slipping a noose around my own neck.

CHAPTER 6

Hannah was in a rotten mood. She wasn't sure whom she was most upset with—Dallas for being such an ass, Sam for having been arrested for the murder of wife number one, or herself for caring.

Sam hadn't been convicted, she reminded herself. But that hardly mattered. The attractive, nice-guy image was tarnished.

She watched Sam as he slipped the key into the lock to let them into the house. Not nervous exactly but not entirely comfortable with having them there either. He was holding back something, but people were less than truthful for all sorts of reasons. It didn't follow that Sam was necessarily implicated in his wife's disappearance.

Dallas stepped to the side. "I thought you'd have one of those fancy new houses outside of town," he said to Sam. "Being a doctor and all."

Sam's expression was stone. "Guess you thought wrong."

Just then a white sheriff's cruiser pulled up. Rick Thompson and his four-legged partner, Holmes, got out and started toward the house. Hannah went to greet them.

"Thanks for coming out on such short notice," she told him.

Rick nodded. "That's what we're here for."

The German shepherd sat at Rick's side, alert and eager to work. Then a neighbor's cat scampered across the lawn and Holmes tugged at his leash. Hannah bit back a smile. For all his training and skill, Holmes was still a dog.

"We've got a missing person?" Rick asked.

"My wife," Sam answered, joining them.

Hannah sketched the details of Maureen Russell's disappearance. "Last seen in the house Sunday morning. Purse is gone, but her car's in the garage. There's no obvious sign of foul play," she added.

"Let's see what Holmes can do." Rick turned to Sam. "I'm going to need an article of your wife's clothing. Something she would wear close to her skin. A nightgown maybe, or T-shirt."

"Sure. I'll be back in a minute."

When Sam was gone, Dallas said to Rick, "It's possible the husband had something to do with it."

"That's pretty much always the case, isn't it?"

"Yeah, but this one killed his first wife seven years ago."

Rick let out a low whistle. "So why isn't he behind bars?"

"Hung jury. Eleven to one for conviction."

Rick whistled again. "What a system we got, huh? Sometimes I think it's a wonder we got anybody behind bars."

"We could certainly streamline the process," Hannah offered with sarcasm, "if we tossed out presumption of innocence."

Dallas shot Rick a glance that said, *See what I have to put up with?* Rick had the decency to look embarrassed.

Sam returned with a sleeveless, ankle-length cotton nightie. "This was on the hook in the closet, so I know it's not freshly laundered."

"Is that what she was wearing Sunday morning?" Dallas asked.

The question seemed to catch Sam by surprise. "I . . . I'm not sure."

Naturally unobservant, Hannah wondered, or was there something about the question that gave Sam pause? Maybe Maureen hadn't been wearing anything at all. Hannah quickly reined in her imagination but not before she'd caught a mental glimpse of Sam Russell in bed.

Rick held the nightie for Holmes to sniff. He uttered a few short commands, incomprehensible to Hannah. She'd been surprised to learn that Holmes, like many K-9 dogs, had been trained overseas. In his case, Czechoslovakia. Accordingly, Holmes responded to commands in Czech, which had the added benefit of foiling bad guys who might try to confuse the dog with a command of their own.

Holmes roamed the yard, nose to the ground. He could have been any dog out sniffing fresh territory, but he moved quickly, with a purpose and intensity that spoke of work rather than play.

Hannah kept an eye on Sam, who seemed intrigued by the process and understandably anxious. What she couldn't tell was whether the anxiety sprang from uncertainty about his wife's fate or from certainty borne of guilt.

Finally, Rick shook his head and called the dog. "He's not picking up anything here. Let's try inside."

"If she'd gone for a walk," Hannah asked, "would Holmes have been able to pick up her scent?"

"That's the theory," Rick said.

They entered through the front door. It opened into a small hallway that led to the living room. After a few false starts, Holmes headed for an armchair to the left of the fireplace.

"That's where Maureen usually sits," Sam explained.

Rick said something to the dog. The words meant nothing

to Hannah, but she could tell the tone was warm and encouraging.

Holmes made another tour of the room then moved down the hallway and into the kitchen. He circled the center island, hesitated, then headed for a door near the refrigerator. He pawed the ground there and began barking in quick, short yaps.

"Where's this go?" Rick asked.

"Into the garage. That's how we usually leave and come into the house."

Rick opened the door, and Holmes trotted into the two-car garage, making a pass at a yellow Miata, which Hannah assumed was Maureen's car, then returning to the spot where Rick was standing at the kitchen entrance. He let out a series of short barks.

"What's it mean?" Dallas asked.

"Looks like the freshest scent leads from the kitchen to the garage."

"You sure about that?" Dallas asked.

"No, not sure. But Holmes had a good scent at the door leading into the garage. He didn't have one at the front door."

"But her car's still here," Hannah pointed out.

Rick shook his head. "Holmes wasn't interested in her car. My guess is she left in a different car."

"Let's open the garage door," Dallas said, at the same time hitting the button to raise the door.

Rick laughed. "Holmes is good, but he can't follow the scent of someone in a moving car."

"What if that car's still here? Would he pick up her scent inside?"

Rick looked confused. Sam, who had momentarily paled, now turned livid.

"You can't honestly believe I had anything to do with this."

Dallas responded by walking toward Sam's car. "Why shouldn't I believe it?"

"How they ever let you be a cop—"

Hannah cut him off. "Does anyone regularly use your garage besides you and your wife?" she asked.

Sam shook his head, his eyes still on Dallas.

"No cleaning people, gardener, delivery folks?"

"No." After a moment he added, "I suppose she could have had a friend pick her up."

"In the garage? Is that something that's happened before?"

"Not that I'm aware of." Sam ran a hand along the back of his neck. His expression was drawn. "The door into the house is never locked," he added after a moment. "Someone could have broken in through the garage."

"You've got an automatic garage door opener," Dallas noted. "They'd need a transmitter to open it."

"If you fool around with frequencies," Sam said, "you can sometimes hit the right one. I've even seen it happen by accident."

Hannah knew that was possible, though it was unlikely someone who hit on a frequency by accident would then decide to enter the house and abduct its occupant. But someone who had the intent first, that wasn't as hard to fathom. Not that it brought them any closer to finding Maureen Russell.

"Bring the dog out here," Dallas called to Rick. He was moving in the direction of Sam's car. "See if he can pick up her scent on Sam's Audi."

Sam looked like he was ready to throw a punch. Hannah wondered if that's what Dallas wanted.

"Of course, he can pick up her scent there," Sam snapped. "Maureen rode in the car. She sometimes drove it. So what if he finds her scent?"

"Well, if it's not a fresh scent . . ." Dallas shrugged. "It might clear a few things up if you let us take a look."

The muscle in Sam's jaw twitched. "You haven't changed at all, have you?"

"Does that mean you're refusing to let us search your car?" Dallas didn't even try to hide the smirk.

Sam walked back toward the house. He turned and pointed a finger at Dallas. "You can forget about looking around the house too. You want anything more from me, you'd better have a warrant."

"Good going," Hannah said as they drove away.

Dallas ignored the comment, and the sarcasm. "That mutt's truly amazing."

Hannah was at the wheel, which was reason enough to keep her eyes on the road. "Holmes isn't a mutt," she said.

"No reason to get technical. You know what I meant."

Hannah regretted many things about her move to Monte Vista. She reminded herself that her new partner was only one of them.

"He did it," Dallas said after a few minutes' silence.

Hannah felt like arguing with him simply for the sake of voicing disagreement. But she didn't want to interact with Dallas any more than she had to right then. And as much as she hated to admit it, she knew the odds in situations like this. There was a reason the spouse was always suspect.

"Aren't you jumping the gun?" she asked. "We don't know for sure she's even missing under suspicious circumstances, much less dead."

"You think she just walked away?"

"Possibly."

Dallas shook his head. "Whatever happened to the second Mrs. Russell, it isn't good. And my bet's on Sam."

"You don't like him, do you?"

"He's a smug bastard, always has been. Thinks he's better than everyone just because he got all the lucky breaks."

"I'd hardly call having his wife murdered a lucky break."

"It is if Sam killed her and then walked because some

damned bleeding-heart juror refused to believe the evidence."

If, Hannah repeated silently. But clearly eleven people had been convinced of Sam's guilt.

"We need to get a warrant," Dallas said. "We want to get our hands on the evidence while it's fresh."

"Yeah, we do need to get one," Hannah replied irritably. "No thanks to you."

"Hey, I did what any cop would do. You know we've got to search the house and grounds. What's out of line about that?"

"Do you ever think about trying a less confrontational approach?"

Dallas grinned at her. "Where's the fun in that?"

"The fun is in the payoff, which at this point is zip." Hannah was reasonably sure that if she'd been there alone, Sam would have allowed her to conduct at least a cursory search. "We're going to get nothing without a warrant, and we're not going to get a warrant without probable cause. I doubt Sam's prior arrest is enough to convince a judge."

Dallas had the good sense to drop the subject. He leaned back in his seat and closed his eyes while Hannah drove back to the station.

As soon as they'd gone, I opened the fridge and poured myself a Diet Coke. What I really wanted was a beer. Make that a vodka martini. I yearned for the icy bite on my tongue, the warmth in my veins, the easing of the fear in my chest. I wanted it. I needed it. And for a moment, I actually considered it.

Then I pushed the thought away as fast as I could. But the seed had been planted. The challenge now was to ignore it.

I'd really screwed up dealing with Maureen's disappearance. Right from the start. If I'd just told the truth about what had happened . . . No, that would only have made things worse. Damn, why couldn't I remember what had happened?

Had Maureen and I left the house together? That would explain her car being there and the dog's tracking her scent to the garage. I racked my brain for some memory, anything that might help me recall what had happened Saturday night.

At least the dog hadn't made a beeline for the trunk of my car. I should have tossed the shoe the minute I found it.

That was the trouble with lies. They never stayed simple. They grew and took on a life of their own. One lie led to another and another, and before you knew it, you'd wrapped yourself in a tangle of deception that was bound to trip you up sooner or later. I didn't even know what witnesses there might be. I could well have already backed myself into a corner from which there would be no escape.

In disgust, I set my soda aside. I went out and and moved the Audi into the garage. Then, safe from prying eyes, I retrieved Maureen's shoe from the trunk. I stuck it in her closet, noting with distress that its mate was nowhere to be seen.

How had the shoe ended up in *my* trunk?

I felt like a character in one of those horror films who is tied to a conveyor belt moving steadily toward the gnashing teeth of a powerful metal-crusher. I sensed danger ahead, but there was nothing I could do to stop it.

Again, the vision of an iced martini flashed in my mind. The sharp, tangy punch of the first taste. The relief of tension. The muting of worry and fear.

One drink. I could handle it. It had been five years, after all.

The phone rang, and I reluctantly let the vision go.

"Hi, Sam," Sherri said. "Just checking to make sure you were home before I brought Molly over."

"I'm home."

"Do you have a flyer made up yet? There's a bunch of us meeting down at the school this evening to distribute them."

"I started to work on it, but—"

"Do you have the photo you want to use? Tell me what you want to say and I'll have Bill put it together for you. You know how quick he is on the computer."

Actually, I didn't know. In fact, I didn't really know either Bill or Sherri, aside from conversations at kids' soccer games and an occasional school function. I was filled with gratitude for her willingness to jump in. "Thanks, Sherri. I appreciate this."

"I want to help," she assured me. "We all do. It's so terrible. Things like this don't happen in Monte Vista."

I told her I'd have the photo for her by the time she delivered Molly then thanked her again. I'd started to work on a flyer myself late last night, but there was something so chilling, so irrefutably real about it that I couldn't get beyond the word "missing." I knew, though, which photo I wanted to use—not the glamorous one that greeted me every day from my office desk but one I thought captured the *real* Maureen much better. It was taken several months after we were married at a gathering Ira hosted in the backyard of his new home.

Maureen saw only her flaws—her mouth was a bit too large, her eyes too deeply set. And her hair, which always looked fine to me, was, according to her, impossible. But she had an engaging smile and a way of looking at me that made me feel like a million dollars. And those were qualities that came across in the photo.

I wrote out text for the flyer. *Maureen Russell. Missing. Last seen . . .* Here I hesitated, then wrote down yesterday's date. Saturday or Sunday, I reasoned; it wouldn't make a difference in terms of the flyer, and I'd already committed to the story of Sunday. I added a brief physical description and concluded with, *Five-thousand dollar reward for information leading to her safe return.*

I considered the amount. Five thousand seemed a paltry sum for the safe return of one's wife, but I wasn't sure where

I'd get even that amount. I was still paying off legal debts from my defense in Lisa's case, and I'd depleted my meager savings to buy out my dad's share of the practice. Moreover, frugality was not among Maureen's virtues. I figured our precarious finances were a temporary situation that would improve as soon I paid off my dad and, hopefully, built up the practice.

True, there was the life insurance payout from Lisa's death and a small inheritance she'd received from her grandmother, but I'd put all of it into trust for Molly. I didn't even have access to it except indirectly.

Still, I felt cheap and uncaring to offer so little.

Finally, I scratched out *five* and wrote in *ten*. I'd cross the bridge of finding the money if and when the time came.

CHAPTER 7

Sherri not only brought Molly home, she brought me lasagna as well.

"I had it in the freezer," she said. "I figured you wouldn't feel like cooking tonight."

Or even eating. But I thanked her. "I've got something written out for the flyer. Are you sure you don't mind putting it together?"

"Not at all. I'm happy to be able to help." She moved into the kitchen with the lasagna and set it on the counter. "This feels so strange, being here without Maureen. The police are taking this seriously, I hope."

"They seem to be."

"I would guess that sometimes they don't. With an adult, I mean."

I nodded. I'd decided I needed information that Sherri could give me, but I found myself hesitating. Finally I just blurted it out. "When did you last talk to Maureen?"

Sherri gave me a funny look. "Saturday, when she brought Molly over."

Okay, so it was Maureen, not me. That was a place to start. "I meant, what time? I'm trying to put together a framework of her activities in the days before she vanished." At least that wasn't a total lie.

"Early afternoon. She called and asked if she could bring Molly over earlier than we'd planned because she wanted time to get her nails and hair done. It wasn't a problem for me, and Heather and Molly get along so well. I know if *I* was being taken to Pietro's for my anniversary, I'd want to look especially nice too."

Pietro's, our special-occasion restaurant splurge. One more piece of the puzzle fell into place and, with it, the first glimmer of my lost hours. I remembered making the reservations. I'd asked for a table by the window.

"She sounded a little frantic, trying to fit it all in. I told her to relax, that she'd look lovely no matter what." Sherri's voice broke with emotion. "And now she's missing. God, I hope she's okay."

Chase called. Dad came by. So did Jesse. As word spread, I heard from friends and neighbors and recapped my version of Sunday so often I almost came to believe it. The evening news out of Sacramento carried only a brief mention of Maureen's disappearance. The account they gave was the same one I'd relayed to the police. Now, mixed with my worry about Maureen, was the worry that someone out there would see the coverage and know my story was a lie. I expected the police to show up at my door any minute and haul me in.

Later that evening, I was sitting on the couch staring into space when Molly came and sat next to me.

"Maybe she just took a trip and forgot to tell us," Molly said.

"Maybe."

"You're not going anywhere, are you, Daddy?"

I put an arm around her. "No, honey, I'm not. I'm going to be around for a long, long time."

"And you'd tell me before you left?"

"Not only that, I'd call you every day."

Molly was silent a moment. Then she snuggled closer. "I'm sorry about what I said this morning. About not caring if Maureen came back. I shouldn't have said it."

"We all say things we don't mean sometimes."

"It wasn't very nice though."

I stroked Molly's hair. "I want you to feel you can tell me the truth, always, even if it isn't 'nice.'"

"She's okay," Molly said. "Really."

I remembered the other part of what Molly had said. "And Maureen does like you," I added. "She likes you a lot, which is why she tries so hard to make you like her."

Molly looped a finger into the neck of her T-shirt and exposed a heart-shaped locket on a gold chain. "She gave me this," Molly said. "It was hers from when she was little."

I was touched by Maureen's generosity. The gesture was all the more meaningful because Maureen never talked to me of her past. "That was very nice of her," I said. "Did she tell you how she got it?"

"Only that it was part of her lost childhood. That's how she said it—lost." Molly scrunched up her face, whether at the idea of a lost childhood or the gift of a locket, I couldn't tell. "I didn't wear it before because . . . I guess because I didn't *want* something of hers. But now I think maybe it's like a good-luck charm or something, and it might bring her home. Do you think?"

I kissed Molly's forehead. "I think you're the best daughter in the whole universe, and I love you very much."

"And wearing the locket?" She looked at me with the same amazing brown eyes her mother had. I felt a pang of loneliness. Ironically, Lisa would have been the one person in whom I could have confided the absolute truth.

"It will definitely help," I told Molly.

* * *

Without the benefit of drink to ease my mind, I turned to
ice cream and TV. I'd had way too much of both by the time
I finally went to bed. But I wasn't able to sleep.

The empty space on Maureen's side of the bed left me
feeling unbalanced, as if I were perched on the edge of a
vast, dark pit. My mind raced with unanswered questions.
My chest was tight with worry.

*Maureen, please be okay. Whatever our difficulties, I
want you home. I want you safe.*

No matter how hard I tried to pull up the filament of a
memory from Saturday, my mind wouldn't cooperate. It was
like trying to remember an elusive dream. Sometimes I'd get
almost to the edge of an image, and then it would vanish.

How could I not remember?

I gnawed on those long, dark hours like a dog with an old
bone. Where had I gone? Who had seen me? And most important, of course, what had I done?

The dried blood under my nails. Maureen's shoe in my
trunk and its missing mate. I touched my bruised lip and
hoped I'd gotten it defending her, not hurting her.

The anguish of not knowing was terrifying.

I tossed and turned, throwing the covers back in the heat
of panic one moment and pulling them around me to make a
nest the next. Mind and body equally tangled.

And then a thought flashed through the jumble. Maureen's
car had been in the shop last week. She'd driven me to work
so she could use mine for the day. I sat bolt upright in bed.

There it was, a simple explanation. Maureen must have
taken the shoe with her the day she had my car. To the shoe
repair, maybe. Or she'd wanted it when she was shopping, to
see if it would go with a dress or match a handbag. There
were any number of reasons her shoe could have ended up in
my trunk. Reasons that had nothing to do with her disappearance.

I felt the weight in my chest lift.

But other, more sinister explanations tugged at me as

well, mocking my eagerness to embrace such an innocent interpretation.

I had no doubt that Dallas regarded me as a suspect. I
worried what he would find when he pursued that avenue
further. The shoe, for example. It now sat in our closet without its mate. Who knew what he'd make of that? It would be
wisest to simply toss the shoe. I promised myself I'd do so in
the morning.

I checked the clock. Two A.M. I got out of bed and walked
to the window. The night was dark, with only the sliver of a
moon for light. Across the road I noticed a shadowy figure
partially obscured by a hedge. A neighbor walking his dog,
most likely. Or a teen headed home after sharing a six-pack
with his buddies. Nothing I hadn't seen a hundred times before. But tonight it made me nervous. I double-checked the
doors and windows then looked in on Molly. I noticed the
framed photo of Lisa that she usually kept on her dresser had
been moved to the bedside table. I prayed that Maureen
would not become the second major loss in her life.

By the time I went back to check the window, the figure
was gone, but my uneasiness remained.

I gave up all hope of sleep. I pulled on jeans and a T-shirt
and turned on the light. I'd let panic take the place of logic, I
decided. Not only was it counterproductive, it was unlike
me. If I hadn't harmed Maureen, and that was going to be
my working premise for the time being, I'd better find out
what *had* happened. After today's experience with the cops, I
didn't have a lot of faith they would make finding the truth a
priority. Instead, they'd nail me.

I opened the drawer to Maureen's bedside table. I didn't
know what I was looking for, but I was hoping that something would help me make sense of what had happened.
Short of that, I needed to prepare for what the cops might
find. I was certain it was only a matter of time before they
came back with a warrant.

The bedside drawer held no surprises. A copy of *Cosmo-*

politan, a Sandra Brown paperback, and a Walkman. Her
dresser drawers were equally uninformative. Underwear, pantyhose, nighties, and T-shirts. Maureen kept her things neat,
compulsively neat I'd sometimes thought. Panties and bras
folded and arranged in rows separated by quilted dividers.
Knit tops and sweaters stacked so tidily they could have passed
for new. I'd always felt uncomfortable breaching her carefully
ordered space, even when she'd asked me to. It felt worse now.

At the back of the pantyhose drawer, I found a snapshot
of me and Lisa, and I felt my throat grow tight. We were sitting on an outdoor bench eating ice cream. It must have been
late spring or summer, given our clothing and the surrounding foliage. I didn't remember seeing that particular photo
before, but the memories it evoked were vivid. We'd spent so
many afternoons in that crazy joy of simply being together.
There were times still when I would see the sun glinting off
water a certain way, or listen to the soft buzz of a bee gathering pollen, and turn, expecting to find Lisa beside me.

I hadn't the foggiest idea what the photo was doing in
Maureen's drawer. Was she jealous? Except for the photos in
Molly's room, I'd moved pictures of Lisa to a box in the
closet for that very reason. I'd thought Maureen might not
welcome constant reminders of my former wife.

I took the photo into the study and put it with the others
from my marriage to Lisa. No sense in giving the cops fuel
for speculation.

I checked the desk drawer, the household files, and all the
spots I thought the cops might look. There was absolutely
nothing out of the ordinary. Since I was feeling wide awake,
I turned on the computer and typed up a draft press release
on Maureen's disappearance.

Earlier that evening I'd called a couple of newspapers.
The response was so similar at each I figured it must be
something they taught in beginning editorial management
class. Fax a press release, they all said, include a police contact, and they'd see what they could do. The uninterested

tone at the other end of the line led me to believe they wouldn't do much. Apparently, a plain-vanilla adult disappearance wasn't newsworthy.

But press coverage would help. The more people looking for Maureen, the better the chances of finding her. Of course, if she'd gone away of her own volition, I'd look like a fool.

I could deal with it.

And if I'd harmed her myself . . . The thought knocked the air from my lungs. I didn't want to go there even in the privacy of my own mind.

Press release completed, I logged onto the Internet to check my e-mail. A horde of spam and a couple of professional newsletters. I deleted them all. At the top of the page was a note from Hal Patterson, my former father-in-law, asking if Molly could visit this summer. It had been sitting there, unanswered, for two weeks.

When I'd been arrested for Lisa's murder, the Pattersons had taken custody of Molly. It was a temporary, informal arrangement at first, but they'd fought to make it permanent. After the trial, when I'd been released, I'd had to go to court again to argue for my parental rights. The law was on my side, and in the end I'd won, but it was a contentious hearing that left a lot of bitterness on both sides.

After the custody battle, I'd refused to let Molly go to Boston. The Pattersons had stopped in California once on their way to Tahiti and taken Molly to the circus. They'd come another time and taken her to dinner at their hotel. They sent birthday cards, and packages at Christmas. In return, I sent photos and Molly wrote them thank-you notes. The contact had been minimal, but I knew they had a right to see her, and lately Molly had been showing renewed interest in her mother's side of the family. She'd probably love the trip, but the thought of sending her to them terrified me.

I hadn't been able to bring myself to answer. And tonight was no different.

Instead, I started a short note to a colleague and friend in

Boston. When I began to type in his name, I hit a wrong letter. Instead of prompting with my friend's e-mail address, one I didn't recognize popped up.

Redhotsugarbear@hotmail.com.

Redhotsugarbear? I scanned sent messages and found nothing. Ditto when I checked the trash. I was certain *I'd* never sent a message to someone by that name, and Molly didn't have access to my computer. That left Maureen.

Is that where she'd gone? Was she with Redhotsugarbear?

I was overreacting, I told myself. It was probably a spam address that got loaded accidentally into the address book. But my mind kept returning to the possibility that she'd left me for someone else.

By the time I logged out, the sky was growing light.

After I dropped Molly off at school later that morning, I pulled into the parking lot of a nearby 7-Eleven store. On my way inside, I tossed the plastic grocery bag containing the shoe from my trunk into the garbage can by the door. Although there were only two other cars in the lot, I could feel the heat of at least a dozen imaginary eyes watching me. Clearly, I was not made for a life of crime.

I bought a can of soda and a muffin and returned to my car. Only then, as I was setting my purchases on the seat beside me, did I think to wonder if there'd been a grocery receipt inside the bag with the shoe.

No one was going to be rooting through the garbage, I told myself, so it didn't matter one way or another. But I knew that if someone did, for whatever reason, and there was a receipt in the bag, my name would be on it. Such was the fallout of Safeway Club Card savings.

I debated whether to retrieve the bag, which would be a relatively easy though highly conspicuous thing to do, or leave well enough alone. Figuring I'd worry endlessly about the receipt if I didn't do something, I got out of the car to fetch the bag from the trash. Just then the mother of one of Molly's classmates pulled into the lot and waved at me.

"Morning, Sam. I'm so sorry about Maureen. Any news yet?"

My mouth was dry. "No news."

"Maybe this will help." She waved a flyer with a picture of Maureen in front of me. "I got a stack from Sherri Moore. A lot of volunteers showed up. The flyers will be all over town before the day is out."

Maureen's photo took up half the space; the words I'd penned yesterday, the other half. MISSING and REWARD, in large, dark print, jumped off the page.

"That's good of you. Thanks."

"Just wish there was more I could do. Are you holding up okay?"

"About as expected, I think."

"My prayers are with you."

I returned to my car. The window for garbage retrieval was closed. But I was already rehearsing how I could explain the shoe in the event the cops came asking.

CHAPTER 8

Hannah was an early riser. She always had been, even though Malcolm had complained when she slipped out of bed at sunrise. She loved morning—the quiet, the freshness of the air, the promise of the day ahead. And she was most productive in the morning, unlike Malcolm, who did his best work at night.

There, she was doing it again, thinking of Malcolm. She'd hoped to leave all of that behind in Los Angeles. Wasn't that the reason for the move? Well, part of the reason. Her sister, Claire, was the other part.

Hannah threw back the lightweight comforter and padded into the tiny bathroom with its horrible turquoise and black tile. When she'd first seen the house, she'd known the bathroom would be a problem, but the landlord had agreed to knock thirty dollars a month off the rent, and she really had liked the rest of the house, so she took it anyway. It wasn't a room for pampering oneself, but with the hooks and baskets she'd added for storage and the soft, cream-colored rug, it was adequate.

She took a quick shower, decided her hair could go another day between washings, and toweled herself dry. At her right breast—her only breast—she hesitated then began methodically pressing her fingertips against her flesh in search of the lump she expected to someday find.

"You need to be positive," her mother admonished when Hannah had once spoken of her fears aloud. "Think of yourself as cured."

Cured. It wasn't a term her doctors ever used.

But her mother had always been a Pollyanna. That was another reason Hannah had wanted to leave LA. Her mother was adamant that she and Claire could "work things out" if only Hannah would make an effort.

When hell freezes over, Hannah said to her reflection in the steamy mirror. *And maybe not even then.*

She was at her desk and logged onto the Internet by seven A.M. She'd already heard Dallas's version of the earlier case against Sam, but she wanted to read the newspaper accounts as well. It was slow going because there was another Sam Russell who was a marathon runner and whose name popped up on an amazing number of sites. Narrowing her search, she finally found a string of citations about the arrest and trial, and clicked through them.

Many of the links were no longer operational, but she found enough to piece together the bare bones of what had happened. Lisa Russell had been reported missing by her husband, who claimed to have come home from a biking trip and found her gone. Their four-year-old daughter was with her grandparents at the time. Suspicion centered on Sam almost immediately when Lisa's mother confided to police that she'd noticed bruises on her daughter's arm and reported that Lisa had seemed agitated when she came by to drop off the granddaughter that morning. She noted further that Lisa had grown withdrawn in the weeks preceding her murder and had stopped confiding in her parents.

Lisa's clothed body had been discovered eight days later,

dumped at the bottom of a ravine in a wooded area outside of Boston. She'd been bound and stabbed.

Police found rope and duct tape in Sam's garage similar to those used to bind Lisa. At trial, there was conflicting expert testimony, with the state claiming the rope ends from the garage and from Lisa's body were a perfect match and the defense expert refuting this. The prosecution also pointed to the life insurance Sam had taken out on his wife only six months earlier and the heavy debt Sam faced from medical school loans.

The defense called several character witnesses but was able to produce only one witness who could corroborate Sam's alibi—a homeless man who claimed to have had a brief conversation with Sam in the area where he was biking the day of the murder.

After the trial, which ended in a hung jury, Sam's attorney was quoted as saying that while he'd hoped for an acquittal, he was at least heartened that an innocent man had not been found guilty. There were several angry quotes from Lisa's father and a grim prediction from the lead detective, Frank Donahue, about snowballing violence from perpetrators who escape justice. Hannah made a note of Donahue's name. She'd call and see if he could add anything that might help them with their case.

On one of the links, Hannah came across a photo of Lisa Russell. She was an attractive woman with straight auburn hair and a wide smile. Prettier than Maureen and more Sam's contemporary in age. But the two women had similar coloring and the same high cheekbones. It was funny how people were so often attracted to the same type time and again.

Hannah thought instantly of Malcolm and wondered how much her initial reaction to Sam had to do with the fact that he reminded her of Malcolm. She found them both attractive, but so what? Malcolm had been strong, sexy, funny. A charismatic guy who was also a louse.

And Sam? She had the feeling he shared Malcolm's better qualities. It was the other part she was having trouble with. Was Sam a louse or, worse, a killer? He wasn't being entirely straight with them, but standing trial for a murder you didn't commit was bound to make anyone cautious about dealing with the police. Maybe he hadn't been as cooperative yesterday as they'd have liked, but that didn't mean she was ready to haul him in.

Not yet, anyway.

CHAPTER 9

Frank Donahue jabbed a fork into the egg-white omelette his wife had prepared for lunch. Two egg whites with green peppers and mushrooms. No cheese. No salt. She had frowned when he squirted on the catsup but didn't say anything. How was a man supposed to get through the afternoon with such a skimpy lunch? Oh sure, he could have some cantaloupe and a spoonful of nonfat cottage cheese for an afternoon snack, but none of it took the place of a cheeseburger and fries or the hot turkey sandwich at the Alibi.

It was his own fault. He'd made the mistake of telling her what the doc had said—lose fifty pounds or risk another heart attack. Frank wasn't planning on ignoring the advice, he just wanted to lose the weight his own way. But Millie, God bless her soul, had a calling, and her calling was keeping Frank alive and healthy. She'd watched over him with an eagle eye ever since the heart attack seven years ago that prompted his retirement from the force. Twenty-five years as a cop, and then overnight he's got nothing to do but twiddle his thumbs.

"Take up golf," his doctor suggested. But Frank didn't have the patience for golf. And he didn't enjoy traveling all that much, although he and Millie had taken trips to the South and the West and a one-week tour of England. He'd never been so happy to be home. Bad food, warm beer, air so damp and cold he'd taken to wearing long underwear on a daily basis.

Frank still hung around the Alibi, near the station in Boston, when he could. He liked talking to the guys on the force, sharing in the jokes and the gossip, though he was feeling increasingly like an outsider.

The phone rang, and while Millie answered it, Frank poured more catsup on his omelette. Catsup was a vegetable, wasn't it? President Reagan had said so.

"It's for you, dear. Some detective from California. Do you want me to have her call back?"

"I'll take it." He wiped his mouth with the paper napkin. Even if it was only a fund-raising solicitation, it might be the peak of his afternoon excitement.

"Sorry to bother you," a female voice said. "This is Hannah Montgomery, a detective with the Monte Vista police department in California."

A current pulsed through Frank's veins. If memory served him right, Monte Vista was Sam Russell's hometown. He'd moved back there after that joke of a trial he'd skated through. "How can I help you, Detective?"

"I understand you were the lead investigator on the Lisa Russell murder. I was hoping you could give me an overview of the case."

"Why, has something happened?"

There was a pause. "Sam Russell's wife is missing."

Frank felt his blood start pumping—in a good way. The kick was probably as good for him as a game of golf. "He reported her missing?"

"Right, and we're thinking maybe there are some parallels with what happened before."

"You think Sam had something to do with it, then?"

"We'd be crazy not to look at that angle, wouldn't we?"

The Lisa Russell homicide had been the last of Frank's career. His heart attack and forced retirement followed within weeks of Sam Russell's arrest. It left a bitter taste in his mouth that his last case had gone south at trial. Maybe this time, Sam wouldn't be so lucky.

"Sam claimed he was on an all-day bike ride," Frank said. "When he got home, his wife was gone. Her car was parked on the street, where it usually was. There was no sign of forced entry."

"And her purse?"

"It was missing too. Turned up a couple of days later in a Dumpster not too far from the house."

"Where was his daughter when it happened?"

"The baby? She was with her grandparents. I thought that weighed against him pretty heavily. He waits until he knows his kid is out of the house before taking his wife."

"What about motive? Were they not getting along? Or maybe he had someone else on the side?"

"Well, that's where the lawyers got creative. She was pregnant, you know."

"No, I didn't know that."

"Yep. Only a couple of months. The prosecutor argued that Sam didn't want another kid and that he and Lisa argued about it. Her mother testified to seeing bruises on Lisa's arm a couple of weeks before she was murdered. She also said Lisa was upset and distraught but wouldn't tell her mother what was going on."

The detective must have picked up something in his voice. She said, "It sounds like you've got some doubts."

"Motive was always a weak part of the case to me," Frank replied. "But her parents were sure it was Sam from the beginning. It just about killed them to see him walk." It had rankled Frank too, and everyone else who'd worked the case.

"I was more convinced by the evidence," he continued. "The knife she was stabbed with was found at the scene—it was a knife from the Russells' kitchen. And she was strangled with a piece of rope that matched what Sam had in his garage. He said he was out riding his bike when it happened, but there wasn't a single reliable witness who came forward to say they saw him. And there was one woman, a neighbor, who testified she saw Sam and Lisa leaving the house together about noon."

"Were there any other suspects?"

"None that we took seriously. Lisa Russell was well liked and got along with everyone. The defense made a big deal about unidentified fingerprints found in the house and the fact that there were two cans of soda in the trash. That was their lame attempt to show there was some mysterious third-party killer."

"At least one juror bought it."

Frank humphed. "Yeah. The guy was a total doofus. It was like he had his mind made up and didn't even look at the evidence."

"Why not retry him?"

"Good question. Lisa's parents were certainly pushing for it, but the DA decided not to. There were a couple of other big cases in the news about then, and he was running for re-election. I think he didn't want to take a chance of losing a second time."

Millie reached for Frank's empty lunch plate and then pointed at her watch to remind him of their afternoon bridge game with friends.

"I don't know if any of that helps," Frank told the detective. "But feel free to call me if you think of anything else. And keep me posted, if you don't mind."

"Will do. Thanks for your time."

When he hung up, Millie raised a curious eyebrow. "Something new on the Russell murder?"

"Not directly, no. But Sam's current wife is missing."

"And the police suspect he might be involved."

Frank nodded.

"Are you going to let Lisa's parents know?"

Frank supposed he should. That had more or less been his tacit agreement with the Pattersons when they'd hired him after the trial to find new evidence against Sam. Nothing had turned up, but he'd told them he'd keep them informed if anything new did.

"There's no rush," he said, "but I think they'd want to know. If nothing else, it might give them some leverage in getting custody of their granddaughter."

CHAPTER 10

Yesterday at the office I'd been a pillar of strength, at least outwardly, but today I couldn't pull it off. After leaving the 7-Eleven, I called Debbie and had her cancel my appointments for the day. Then I tried retracing my path to the lonely country road where I'd woken Sunday morning and my nightmare had begun.

I took a few wrong turns, but eventually I recognized the unusual outcropping of rocks I'd noticed that morning and pulled onto the shoulder. This stretch of road was winding, and the drop-off in spots steep. It was lucky for me I'd gone off the road to the left, where the terrain was fairly level.

I knew there had to be houses somewhere in the vicinity, but none were visible. What in God's name had I been doing here anyway? If I'd gotten lost, which seemed the only logical explanation, where had I been headed?

I closed my eyes, listened to the rustle of wind in the dry grass, and tried to remember. The waking and confusion of Sunday morning came easily. I'd been over that ground many times in the past two days. But the hours leading up to that were a blank.

Anger and frustration built inside me. In disgust, I started the car again, ready to leave, and then I heard the whistle of a train in the distance. I held my breath.

I remembered a whistle. I remembered it being dark, hearing the train, and feeling oddly comforted by the sound. It was just a fleeting memory, but I mined it for everything I could. It was like remembering a dream. I was afraid if I let it go, I'd never get it back again. Train, whistle . . . head-lights. I remembered headlights. Mine or another car's? And the vague memory of a lemony scent.

But that's as far as it went.

Had someone run us off the road then left the scene? Had they taken Maureen, or might she still be wandering the hills in a daze? Or had I been traveling this road alone?

I got out of the car and examined the ground. I thought I found the spot where my car had been, though it was hard to tell for sure. No glass or flecks of paint or, thankfully, blood. Once again, I regretted my story to the cops. But I was locked into it now, and maybe it was just as well. I couldn't imagine the truth would make me any less guilty in their minds.

I drove back into town, stopped at a car wash, then went to the garden center to see if I could find Jesse.

Jesse was not a big guy. He was about my height and on the slender side except for the love handles at his waist. But with his crooked nose and gold front tooth, he looked like someone you didn't want to mess with.

In his former life, Jesse was a San Francisco public defender, a dyed-in-the-wool soldier for justice. Drugs and alcohol were his downfall. And screwing a prosecutor's wife. He was fired, and his license was suspended. Although he was finally reinstated, the law had lost interest for him. He moved to Monte Vista, traded in his briefcase for a shovel and a rake, and now owned a nursery. The legal training must have done some good though, because the Latin names for plants roll off his tongue effortlessly.

We met through AA, where Jesse was my sponsor. He had since become a good friend.

He was taking delivery of a shipment of aspen when I got there, so I poked around the potentilla and viburnum until he was finished. I knew next to nothing about plants, but hanging around Jesse had at least made me familiar with a few of the names.

He came to join me the minute he was free. "There's news?" he asked.

"No, except the cops have their eye on me."

"That's not unexpected."

"I just worry that they aren't doing enough to find her. I keep thinking of her being frightened and in pain, and I feel so helpless."

Jesse put a hand on my shoulder. "This might be a good time to come back to meetings, Sam."

Jesse was a regular; I'd stopped going a couple of years ago. "That's not my style," I told him, though we'd had this conversation in the past. "That fellowship and sharing stuff. I'm just not comfortable with it."

We moved into the shade of an overhang and sat on one of the cement benches he had for sale. Jesse offered me a Reese's peanut butter cup. They took the place of all his former vices and probably contributed to the roll around his middle.

"No, thanks."

He unwrapped one for himself. "I guess if you can get through this without taking a drink, maybe you really don't need AA."

Elbows on my knees, I dropped my head to my hands and found myself shaking. "Oh God, Jesse, I'm in big trouble."

For a moment, he leaned back and didn't say a word. When he spoke, his voice was soft and even. "What did you do, Sam?"

"I don't know."

"What do you mean?"

"I lied to the cops, for one thing."

"About Maureen?"

I nodded. "Are you still an attorney?"

"I'm a member of the bar, but if you're in trouble you need someone other than me."

I pulled a dollar from my wallet and gave it to him. "That makes it official, right?"

He took the dollar and shoved it in his jeans pocket. "What's the matter, Sam? What's going on?"

I told him about waking up in a ditch Sunday morning and not knowing how I got there, about discovering Maureen wasn't home and then telling the cops I'd left her in bed Sunday morning.

I felt the need to talk about what had really happened and to get an objective reaction to it. I'd been so obsessed with my own doubts and fears, I felt like I'd lost my bearings.

"Now I'm stuck with the story I told the cops, and I'm worried that they'll see it's a lie. I don't know what happened or who's going to come out of the woodwork and tell the cops something that undercuts my whole story."

Jesse unwrapped another peanut butter cup and popped it into his mouth.

"The cops think I'm involved," I told him. "Maybe I am. I can't remember a damned thing."

"Were you drinking?"

Despite the warmth of the day, I was shivering. I folded my arms across my chest. "That was my initial thought, but now I'm not so sure. I mean, why would I suddenly start drinking again? And not to remember anything . . . Even when I used to have blackouts, I'd remember *something* about what went before."

"So if it wasn't booze, what do you think caused you to forget?"

"Amnesia's a funny thing. It could be physical trauma

like a whack on the head. Or emotional trauma. I suppose too that someone could have slipped me a drug."

"Which would mean that Maureen is most likely in the hands of whoever came after you."

"But I *might* have been drinking," I pointed out. "Could be Maureen and I had a fight, and I went on a bender."

Jesse raised an eyebrow. "You haven't been getting along?"

"We haven't *not* been getting along, but she's been kind of distant lately, like I've disappointed her in some way. She gets short with me, then I get short with her. It escalates for no reason."

He nodded, as if I'd described familiar territory. I knew Jesse's wife had left him when he started drinking heavily, but we'd never talked about it in any detail. "She'd have called by now though," he offered.

"Unless she's hurt." Suddenly I felt the need to be totally straight. "There's more," I told him.

"More?"

"More that I haven't told you." I took a breath. "When I came to Sunday morning, there was blood around my finger-nails."

"If you'd been struggling with your attacker—"

"And I found a shoe, a woman's shoe, in the trunk of my car."

He opened his mouth and shut it again before asking, "Maureen's?"

"I assume so. It's her size."

A woman with a toddler came into the nursery and looked around. Jesse watched her until he saw that Carlos, who worked for Jesse, was asking if she needed help.

"What about Saturday?" Jesse asked.

"I was at work. I don't actually remember that, but Ira says I was there, and I made notes on a couple of charts. It was our anniversary, and Maureen and I were going out to dinner that night. I didn't remember that either until her friend Sherri asked about our dinner at Pietro's. Then I remembered making the reservation and asking for a table by the window."

"Do you remember what you ate for dinner? What you talked about?"

"I don't even remember *having* dinner."

Jesse stood up and brushed the seat of his pants with his hands. "Come on, it's almost lunchtime."

I looked at him, confused.

"We're going to find out if you made it to the restaurant Saturday evening." He told Carlos he was leaving then grabbed his car keys from the drawer near the cash register.

"Where are we going?"

"You're buying me lunch at Pietro's."

I was half-afraid to show my face there in case Maureen and I had made a scene Saturday night. But Jesse pointed out it might be better to know that than not.

The restaurant was on the outskirts of Sacramento, a longer distance than either of us typically drove for lunch, and the traffic was heavier than expected. It was close to one o'clock, and the height of the lunch hour, when we arrived.

"Do you have a reservation?" the maitre d' asked, eyeing Jesse's cargo pants with disapproval. Sacramento is casual, but we were pushing the limits.

"Afraid not," I answered.

"Just a moment. Let me see what I can do." He went off to seat the couple that had been ahead of us.

Jesse stepped behind the podium and flipped the pages in the reservation book.

"What are you doing?" I asked.

"Seeing if I can find your name." He ran his finger down the page. "Here it is, Russell. Highlighted in yellow."

"What does that mean?"

"Danged if I know. Your name is the only one though."

The maitre d' returned as Jesse stepped away from the

podium. "It will be about forty minutes," he said, checking his list.

"What does the yellow highlight on a name mean?" Jesse asked.

The maitre d' pinned us with his narrow gaze. "It means the party was so late we could no longer hold the reservation. We try to accommodate people when we can, but that's not always possible. I'm afraid we don't have any no-shows for lunch, however. Now, if you'll give me your name."

"Sorry, we don't have time to wait," Jesse said. "But thanks."

The maitre d' didn't seem disappointed to see us leave.

We ate at Taco Bell instead.

"Think of the money you're saving," Jesse said as we filled our soda cups from the machine.

I nodded glumly. I didn't have much of an appetite anyway.

"Lunch at Pietro's would have been nice," he added, "but the important thing is we learned that you and Maureen never showed up at the restaurant."

Unfortunately, I'd led Sherri to believe that we had.

"Do you think I hurt her, Jesse? Could I have harmed Maureen and not remember?"

Jesse washed his bite of burrito down with Dr. Pepper. "Could you have? I suppose it's possible. Do I think that's what happened? Not a chance."

I wanted to believe him. But there was simply too much I didn't understand.

CHAPTER 11

Hannah was washing her hands, her mind still processing the information she'd gleaned about Sam's earlier arrest for murder, when Carla Adams, one of the uniformed officers, entered the tiny women's restroom. Carla was attractive in a wholesome, freshly scrubbed way, with thick, honey blond hair she often wore in a single braid down her back. She was younger than Hannah by almost ten years, but Hannah had thought they might find kinship since they were the only two women on the force. Hannah couldn't have been more wrong. She wasn't above trying again, however.

Hannah nodded a greeting. "Looks like it's shaping up to be a warm day."

"About average for this time of year." Carla checked her teeth in the mirror.

"Perfect kind of day to curl up in a hammock with a good book. Instead"—Hannah rolled her eyes—"I'm going to be talking to people who knew Maureen Russell."

Silence.

Hannah realized Carla was close to Maureen's age. Maybe she had some insights that Hannah didn't. "What do you think happened?" Hannah asked. "You think the husband was involved in her disappearance?"

A shrug. "I'm not working that case."

"I know, I just thought—"

Carla addressed Hannah's image in the mirror. "You can cut the chummy stuff, Detective. Just because we're both women doesn't mean we're going to be friends."

Hannah blinked. "No, I guess not."

She finished drying her hands and left without another word. *Well,* Hannah thought, *I guess that cleared things up.*

In the interest of time, she and Dallas had divvied up the list of people they wanted to interview. Hannah was glad they were going their separate ways for the day. Dallas wasn't a bad sort really, and he had a solid reputation for clearing cases, but they had very different styles.

Carla. Dallas. Was there anyone in Monte Vista Hannah felt comfortable with? Yes, she reminded herself, there were many. Neighbors, shopkeepers, one of the women at the gym, her dentist of all people, but Hannah hadn't reached the point where she felt like a member of the community in any meaningful sense. She wondered again about the wisdom of her move to Monte Vista.

She looked at the list of names in front of her. First up was Ira Kincaid, Sam's medical partner. Hannah smiled. For once, a doctor's visit she didn't have to dread.

She was shown into Dr. Kincaid's empty office by a pleasantly plump, fifty-something nurse named Debbie, who expressed sympathy and concern for Sam.

"A good man and a good doctor," she said, stopping just inside the door. "He's already had more than his share of trouble, if you ask me."

"You're referring to his first wife, Lisa?"

Debbie nodded. She shifted the chart she was holding from one arm to the other. "I was working for the senior Dr. Russell then, worked for him for years. It just about broke his heart what Sam went through—first losing his wife, then to be accused of being the one that did it." Her tone made it clear her sympathy for Sam was matched by her inability to understand how anyone could think he'd been culpable. "I've known Sam since he was a boy."

"Did you know Lisa?" Hannah asked.

"I'd met her. She and Sam came home to visit every summer. They were a cute couple, affectionate and playful. And very much in love. Anyone who'd seen them together would know that Sam would never hurt her."

"What about Maureen? Do you know her too?"

The nurse nodded. "She worked here. That's how she and Sam met."

Hannah leaned against the back of the jade green visitor's chair. "She's a nurse?"

"No, she scheduled appointments, did some of the filing, filled in as needed. We're a small office, so there's a lot of overlap."

"How long did she work here?"

"A year maybe. She did a fine job, but it was clear she wasn't interested in making a career of the position. In fact, I suspected she had an eye on Sam almost from the start. I used to tease him about it, but it took him a while to see it for himself."

"Did she continue working here after they were married?"

Debbie shook her head. "No, she quit once they were engaged. The poor man must be worried sick. Do you have any ideas about where she might be?"

"I'm afraid not," Hannah told her. "That's part of the reason I want to talk to Dr. Kincaid. We're hoping to find someone who might point us in the right direction."

"Time was, I never worried about predators and serial

killers finding their way to Monte Vista," Debbie said. "Not anymore. I lock up tight every night." She headed for the door. "I'll tell Dr. Kincaid you're here."

Alone in the office, Hannah couldn't quell the familiar sense of dread. It had been in a similar office that she'd first heard the words *suspicious lump* and then, later, *cancer*. She pushed the memory from her mind and took a seat.

Dr. Kincaid's office was tidy and neat: wide desk, papers in a single stack on the left, telephone and notepad on the right. Behind the desk was a shelf of medical texts and a plastic model of the human ear. Diplomas hung on another wall. Ira Kincaid was a graduate of the UC Davis School of Medicine and of several specialized post-degree institutes. Hannah looked for family photos and found none. The only photograph she saw was of a man she assumed was Dr. Kincaid himself, standing in front of an expensive silver sports car. He was a good-looking man, with dark hair and a winsome smile. The kind of man she'd gravitate to in a bar because she knew she'd never fall for him. Conventionally handsome didn't appeal to her.

Ira Kincaid burst into the room a few minutes later. He wasn't as tall as she expected from the photo, and his face was a bit fleshier. He looked harried and tired though the day had barely begun.

"Sorry to keep you waiting, Detective. What can I do for you?"

"It's about Maureen Russell's disappearance."

Kincaid's face clouded. "Any leads?"

"Not yet. I was hoping you might be able to help."

"In what way?"

"How well do you know Mrs. Russell?" Hannah asked.

He shrugged. "I see her and Sam socially, though not often. I wouldn't say I know her well."

"But she worked for you at one time, didn't she?"

He nodded, checking his watch. "She worked in the front office."

There'd been a time when Hannah found doctors intimidating. Not anymore. And she resented the fact that Dr. Kincaid, however unconsciously, conveyed the impression that his time was more valuable than hers.

She sat back in her chair. "Does that mean you didn't have a lot of contact with her?"

"I'm with patients all day," he explained. "There isn't a lot of time for small talk." Then he softened. "Sorry to sound so brusque. I guess this whole thing has me on edge. I feel awful for Sam."

"How's he doing?"

"Yesterday he came to work. It wasn't even until after lunch that he told me what had happened. But then he was . . . not distraught, because Sam keeps his emotions in check. But he's understandably very upset. Today he's not even coming in."

"You talked to him?"

"Debbie did. He called and asked her to reschedule his appointments."

Hannah wondered if their interview with him yesterday afternoon had rattled his composure. "What's your assessment of the Russells' marriage?" she asked.

"Good," he said, almost too quickly.

"No problems at all?"

Kincaid hesitated.

"I realize Sam is your partner—"

"And friend. We grew up together. My dad died when I was a kid, and the senior Dr. Russell was like a surrogate father to me."

Hannah nodded. "I understand your loyalty, but if you have information—"

"No, nothing like that."

Hannah rephrased her question. "What issues were they dealing with?"

"Not issues, really, but . . . well, there didn't seem to be much spark between them either."

"You think he might be involved with someone else?"

Kincaid looked surprised. "I doubt it."

"How about Maureen?"

He held up his hands and smiled. "I wouldn't even venture a guess. I have a long track record of being wrong about women."

A fact in which he seemed to take some pride, Hannah thought. "How are the Russells doing financially?"

The question seemed to catch the doctor off guard. "Fine, as far as I know. I mean, all of us could use more than we've got, right?"

"Anyone who might be upset with Dr. Russell? Have there been lawsuits or complaints?"

"No, Sam's a good doctor. And we have a general practice. We don't have to worry as much as some of the specialists."

Hannah leaned forward. "Did you know Lisa?"

"Yeah, I was at their wedding."

"Were you surprised when he was arrested for her murder?"

"Yeah, I was. Though by then Sam and I weren't as close as we'd been growing up."

"And now? Do you think he could have anything to do with Maureen's disappearance?"

Hannah could see a battle at play behind Ira Kincaid's eyes. That in itself was telling. More telling than the words that followed.

"You suspect foul play?"

"She is the second wife of his to disappear."

He fingered the edge of a paper on his desk. "I guess we never really know what a person is capable of, but Sam's a doctor. He's trained to save lives, not take them."

A sufficiently vague answer, Hannah noted. She stood and thanked him for his time. "Let me know if you think of anything else."

* * *

Sherri Moore was, as far as Hannah knew, the last of Maureen's friends to speak with her before she disappeared. She greeted Hannah's knock on the front door with a cordless phone pressed to her ear. As soon as she realized Hannah was a cop, she told her companion she'd call back later.

"Another of the fifth-grade mothers," she explained to Hannah, inviting her inside with a sweep of her arm.

Sherri had shoulder-length hair streaked with several shades of honey blond. She was slim and perky, with perfectly manicured fingernails and sparkling white teeth. The kind of woman who always made Hannah feel inadequate.

"You're here about Maureen Russell, right?" Sherri said as she led Hannah into a spotless, upscale kitchen.

Hannah nodded. "I understand you're a friend of hers."

"Yeah, mostly because of the girls. My daughter and Molly are"—she made quotation marks in the air with her fingers—"'best friends.'" Sherri dropped the phone back into its cradle. "Can I get you anything to drink?"

"I'm fine, thank you." Hannah slid onto one of the high stools at the granite-topped counter. "Do you have any idea where she might be?"

Sherri shook her head, started to walk toward the sink then apparently changed her mind and took a seat at the other end of the counter.

"Maureen wouldn't just walk away though," she said. "For one thing, she'd take at least two suitcases." Sherri tried to laugh, but the sound caught in her throat. "I'm sure something terrible must have happened to her."

"Any ideas along that line?"

Sherri wrinkled her nose. "I've been asking myself that, but nothing comes to mind. Maureen is just . . . I was going to say average, but that sounds wrong. She's just a regular person. She wouldn't hitchhike or go off with a stranger or anything like that. I can't imagine what could have happened."

"Was anything bothering her?" Hannah asked. "Or anyone? Maybe some odd experience she'd had recently with a deliveryman or someone in town?"

"No, she never mentioned anything like that." Sherri twisted the gold mesh bracelet on her wrist. "And she was upbeat, always. It would bug me sometimes, because to listen to her, she never had a bad day. But I realized that some people, that's just their way."

"What about bad habits?"

Sherri frowned. "Oh, no. She's . . . very polite."

"I was thinking more along the lines of drugs, gambling, hanging out in bars."

"Not that I know of. But we aren't superclose. Maureen is younger than me, younger than most of the other fifth-grade mothers, in fact. And she's not Molly's real mother. I mean, she tries hard to fit in, but I'm not sure her heart's in it."

Hannah felt some sympathy for Maureen. Unless you had kids or were retired, Monte Vista wasn't an easy community to fit into. "What about her and Sam?" she asked.

"Great. She likes being"—again, Sherri punctuated her words with quotation gestures—"'the wife of a doctor.' And Sam's a sweetheart."

Hannah looked for a hint of anything more in the remark about Sam than the words indicated, but nothing jumped out at her. "Molly spent Saturday night at your place?" she asked.

"Yeah. Heather was having a slumber party. Only four girls, but it felt like forty. Maureen and Sam were going out for their anniversary. Big night on the town. That's why I wasn't too worried at first when no one showed up to get her. I figured they'd just slept in. But then Molly was getting worried, and I couldn't reach Maureen, so finally I called Sam's service."

Sam hadn't mentioned the anniversary date with his wife. "Going out where? Did they say?"

"Pietro's. Down near Sacramento. Have you eaten there? Expensive but really good."

"I'll have to give it a try some time," Hannah said. Assuming she ever had what might pass for a normal social life again. But she made a mental note to check with the restaurant. Maybe the Russells had had a lovers' spat.

"What time did you try calling them Sunday morning?"

"Gosh, maybe around ten, ten-thirty. I tried back a couple of times, then tried Maureen's cell too, before trying Sam's work number."

"What time did you finally reach him?"

"It was almost noon."

"What did he say?"

"Something about a medical problem or a patient. I don't recall exactly. But he got here within the hour."

It was almost three by the time Hannah met up with Dallas back at the station.

"How many of the names did you reach?" she asked. Hannah had talked to all of her four, and several others she'd been directed to in the course of her interviews. She'd come away with a slightly clearer picture of Maureen, the woman, but had picked up nothing that would help them trace her whereabouts.

"I was able to reach all but one," Dallas said.

"What did you learn?"

"Nada."

"Give me the gist of it anyway."

"The second Mrs. Russell has no bad habits and no enemies. On the other hand, she doesn't have any close friends either. By choice, it seems. Ms. Personality, she's not. Her life pretty much revolves around Sam."

"That's the picture I got too."

"There *was* one thing though." Dallas paused. There was a glint in his eye that Hannah recognized. It was the *gotcha* glint. Dallas often withheld morsels of information so that he could serve them up like a mouth-watering confection at just the right moment.

Hannah waited for him to continue. She wasn't going to play his game.

"One of the women she played tennis with told me that Maureen had asked her for the name of her divorce lawyer."

"Maureen was thinking of leaving Sam?"

"It's certainly an avenue worth looking into."

"Sherri Moore told me Maureen liked 'being married to a doctor.' Her words."

Dallas shrugged. "Maybe she liked the idea but not the man."

"Saturday was their anniversary. They had plans to go out to dinner at a place called Pietro's. It's worth following up on."

"Good discovery."

"You get the name of the attorney?"

"Myrna Edwards. She's got an office on the outskirts of Sacramento."

A safe, twenty-mile distance from Monte Vista, Hannah noted. Just like her own forays into the world of pickup bars and anonymous sex.

CHAPTER 12

Hannah turned to Dallas as they approached Myrna Edwards's law office the following morning. "Let me take the lead on this, okay?"

"Because of the woman-to-woman thing?"

Try human-to-human, she thought. A tactic she suspected was alien to Dallas.

"That," she replied, "and since I made the initial contact, it might be best if I followed up." Hannah had talked to the secretary rather than the attorney herself, who'd been in court when she called, but she wasn't about to point that out.

"Fine by me," he said. "Never met a lawyer I could stomach anyway."

She thought immediately of Malcolm then pushed the memory away. It wasn't the lawyer part she had trouble with; it was the husband part. Or, rather, the not-so-husbandly behavior.

The divorce attorney's office was on the second floor of a two-story stucco building that also housed a dentist's office, a real estate office, and a barber shop. The adjacent parking lot was striped for maybe twenty cars, but only a handful of the spaces were taken.

Hannah gave the secretary their names then sat in one of the green tweed chairs while Dallas stood at the window looking out at the parking lot below.

Myrna Edwards greeted them a few minutes later. She was a large woman, weighing close to two hundred pounds by Hannah's estimation. She had on a flowing, teal blue tunic, accented with lots of chunky silver jewelry. A far cry from the power-suit attorneys Hannah had known in LA.

She led them to her office, which looked as though a tornado had recently blown through, and gestured to a pair of chairs facing her desk.

"You're with the Monte Vista police department?"

Hannah made the introductions. "We're here about Maureen Russell." She paused, waiting for a reaction. When none was forthcoming, Hannah asked, "Was she a client of yours?"

"I'm afraid I can't answer. It's confidential."

"She's missing," Hannah explained.

"I read that in the paper this morning."

"We're hoping you might be able to shed some light on what's happened."

"How's that?" Myrna Edwards's skin was a lovely alabaster marred only by deep frown lines in her brow. Given the intensity with which she was now scowling, Hannah could understand how the lines had become permanent.

"We have reason to believe she might have contacted you," Hannah said.

"In regard to what?"

Hannah shrugged. "Divorcing her husband, I guess. That's your line of work, isn't it?"

"And now that she's missing, you suspect he might have harmed her." It wasn't really a question.

"That's one possibility," Hannah said. "Another is that she was unhappy or scared and decided to simply leave."

Myrna Edwards folded her arms across her ample chest. The band of bracelets clanked on her wrist. "I'm afraid there's nothing I can tell you."

Dallas rocked forward. "Not even whether or not she contacted you?" He sounded incredulous.

"Not even that."

Dallas grunted with disgust. "This is a police investigation."

"So you said."

"I understand about attorney-client privilege," Hannah said, trying for a less confrontational tone. "But this isn't an instance where a client needs protection from the law. The law's on her side. We'd like to find her and, if she's come to harm, to punish those responsible."

The attorney nodded. "Unfortunately, I'm bound by the rules of ethics, not common sense. I'm sorry you wasted your time by coming here, Detectives. There's nothing I can tell you." She rose from her chair. "I've been without a regular secretary for several months now, making do with temporary help. Anyone familiar with my practice would have told you up front that coming to see me would be useless."

Hannah left her card on the attorney's desk. "If you find there's anything you *can* tell us, please give me a call."

Getting back in the car, Hannah slammed the door. "Well, that was helpful."

"She's way over the top with this confidentiality stuff. Must make her feel important or something."

"Still, if Maureen Russell *hadn't* contacted her," Hannah reasoned, "she'd probably have said so."

Dallas shrugged. "People like that get a kick out of pulling the strings."

A description that fit Dallas himself, Hannah thought. "Maureen Russell asked that friend of hers for the name of her attorney," she said. "I think there's a good chance she contacted Ms. Edwards."

"Makes sense. Let's say the marriage was on the rocks. Maureen wanted out and Sam wasn't any too happy about it. Maybe it was the idea of paying alimony, or maybe he didn't want to let her go. Or maybe it was an assault on his ego. In any case, he was pissed, so . . ." Dallas made a shooting gesture with his fingers. "Pow. No more wife."

Hannah started the engine. "Is that what you think happened with his first wife?"

"Basically. She wasn't shot though. She was strangled and stabbed."

Hannah winced. She tried to picture the mild-mannered Sam Russell angry enough to stab his wife. It was an image that didn't form easily.

"Maybe Maureen was sleeping around on him," Dallas added, still theorizing. "That would really push his button."

"Did you pick up any indication of that from the friends you talked with?"

"Not really." Dallas craned his neck to the right to check traffic as she backed out of the parking space. Like she couldn't manage without his help.

"I didn't get that impression either." Though that didn't mean it wasn't so. Malcolm had managed to keep his infidelity a secret, hadn't he? Hannah had never suspected a thing. It was only when she was cleaning out his closet after he died that she discovered the notes from Claire. She wished she *had* known before so that she could have asked him why. Not knowing how she fell short made her doubt herself even more.

"Do you think Sam could have been having an affair?" she asked after a moment. "If Maureen found out and they argued . . ."

Dallas grinned. "Now there's a thought. Sam always did have a lost-puppy-dog way of attracting the girls."

Girls. She realized Dallas was talking about high school again. "People change," she said. She had only to compare who she was today with the timid, mousey thing she'd been in high school.

But it brought her up short to realize the germ of truth in Dallas's comment. Hadn't Hannah herself found that very quality in Sam attractive?

"What if the attorney actually has information from Maureen that warrants confidentiality?" she asked. "Something about Sam, maybe. His past, his medical practice, some hidden vice. Or something that involves both Maureen and Sam."

"So he offed Maureen to keep her quiet?"

"Not necessarily," Hannah said. "Could be he had nothing to do with it. Not directly, anyway. But I get the feeling he knows more than he's saying."

"I've been telling you that from the beginning." Dallas adjusted the air vents on his side of the dash. "Let's pick up lunch before we head back."

"It's only eleven."

"So what? I'm hungry."

Nothing unusual there; Dallas was always hungry. And if they didn't stop to eat soon, he'd only grouse about it until they did. Hannah sighed. "Okay, what'll it be?"

They settled on McDonald's because it was quick and Hannah could get a salad with low-fat dressing. Dallas ordered a double cheeseburger and fries.

A man who looked to be in his early thirties, five or six years younger than Hannah, was in line ahead of them. Broad shoulders, Hannah noticed. Good muscle definition— the kind that came from everyday hard work rather than hours with a trainer. His butt was firm, his hair long and soft enough to invite a finger-combing. Hannah felt a familiar jolt of electricity somewhere deep inside her. Too bad she was at McDonald's and not one of her regular evening haunts. Although she might have been able to handle the setting, having Dallas along put a definite damper on things.

She stared hard until the stranger turned, then caught his eye. She smiled, and he smiled back. Damn, but he was a good one. What rotten timing.

Oblivious to all but his lunch, Dallas handed her a fistful of paper napkins and a plastic fork. "You want a knife too?"

"Fork is fine." She bit her lip to keep from laughing. She'd come close to saying, "Fuck is fine." She wondered if Dallas would have noticed.

They grabbed a table by the window, where she had a full view of the restaurant. She was hoping for a little more eye flirtation, if nothing else. But the stranger took his food out to his pickup truck and left.

Dallas ate half the burger before he broke for conversation. "You think that pooch got it right about Maureen leaving the house by way of the garage?"

Hannah's mind had followed the stranger into his truck. Reluctantly, she brought it back. "We shouldn't rule out other possibilities, but yeah, the garage is a good bet."

"You realize that implicates Sam?"

She nodded and chewed on a bite of salad. She was sure Sam recognized that fact as well.

Suddenly Hannah had a thought. "What if it was a rental car?" she asked.

"What if *what* was a rental car?"

"The car she left in. If she had a rental car, she might well have parked it in the garage."

"You're still thinking she might have gone of her own free will? Without leaving a note and without telling anyone?"

"If she was running away and didn't want anyone to find her, she might. And if that was the case, she couldn't very well take her own car."

"You watch too many bad movies." But he pulled out his cell phone then popped a couple of french fries into his mouth before punching in the number. "It ought to be easy enough to find out," he said. "There's only one big rental outfit in town." Then into the phone, "Lucy, it's me, Dallas."

Hannah listened to several renditions of "What d'ya mean?" "Of course I did." "No way." He had the same soft, flirtatious tone to his voice no matter what the words.

"Listen, Lucy, I need some information for a case we're

working on. Can you check to see if a Sam or Maureen Russell rented a car in the last couple of weeks? Sure can." He put his hand over the mouthpiece and smiled at Hannah. "She's checking."

"If Maureen wanted to cover her tracks, she might have rented it someplace besides Monte Vista," Hannah pointed out.

Dallas took another bite of burger. Catsup dribbled down his chin, and he wiped it with the back of his hand. "Yeah, that's the one."

Hannah caught his eye, and Dallas shook his head. He mouthed, "She read about Maureen's disappearance in the newspaper." Into the phone again, "Okay, thanks Lucy. Yeah, we will. Sometime soon."

"No record of a rental?" Hannah asked when he'd disconnected.

"Nope. We can try the nearby towns when we get back to the office. But I don't think you're going to find she rented a car. In fact, I don't think she went anywhere voluntarily."

They spent the afternoon on the phones. No record of any rental car and, despite nearly a dozen calls to the tip line, nothing in the way of useful information.

"How about we ask Sam to take a lie-detector test," Dallas suggested finally.

"You know he's not going to agree to it. It wouldn't be admissible in court anyway." She checked her watch. Twenty minutes until cigarette time.

"Wouldn't let us look around the house, wouldn't let us look at his car. Refuses to take a lie-detector test. Does that sound like an innocent man to you?"

"Doesn't sound *unreasonable,* given his history," Hannah said.

"We need to search his house and car."

"Any luck finding a judge who'll give us a warrant?"

"Not yet." Dallas was tapping his pen on the desk. Metal on metal. The sound was tinny and annoying. "You believe Sam's story about going by the hospital the morning she disappeared?" he asked.

"He's a doctor."

"There's no way to confirm that's where he was though. The daughter was away at a friend's house. The woman who was watching the daughter . . ." Dallas checked his notes. "Sherri Moore. She said Maureen brought the girl over Saturday afternoon, right? That's the last time anyone besides Sam saw her."

"Meaning?"

"Meaning, we don't actually know what happened after that. All we've got is Sam's word about what happened."

Hannah took her cigarette break six minutes late. She felt virtuous, maybe even a little smug. She'd kick the habit yet.

She took the case file with her, got a can of diet soda from the machine, then went outside—the only place you could smoke these days aside from your own home. She sat on the concrete bench in the plaza across the street from the police station and reviewed the reports. A neighbor had seen Sam come home around noon on Sunday, just as he'd said, then leave again about half an hour later. Another neighbor remembered seeing Maureen sometime on Saturday but couldn't say when. No one had seen anything suspicious around the house the entire weekend. No strange cars, no door-to-door solicitors, no unusual deliveries. There'd been reports of a plumber's truck and a Sears delivery van in the vicinity Sunday morning, and both had checked out as legitimate.

If Maureen Russell had come to harm at the hands of a stranger, he'd managed to slip past a lot of eyes. On the other hand, Hannah had trouble fathoming a woman just up and walking away, even from a rocky marriage. Much as she hated to admit it, she was beginning to think Dallas just might be headed in the right direction.

CHAPTER 13

The call came at ten Wednesday evening. Maureen had been missing for four days. With all the scenarios that had played through my mind, and there'd been plenty, you'd think I wouldn't have been surprised. But this was one possibility I'd completely overlooked.

Molly had gone to bed. Not willingly, but I'd insisted. The uncertainty and worry were taking their toll on her. I thought she'd slept as little as I had in the last few days.

I was nursing a Diet Coke, longing for a stiff martini. And wondering again if I'd been drinking last Saturday. The television was on—a new reality show set somewhere in the tropics—but I wasn't paying attention. I had too much reality in my own life right then.

When the phone rang, I almost didn't answer it. The local paper had run a front-page story about Maureen's disappearance, and it had been picked up yesterday by the evening news out of Sacramento. The calls had been coming steadily all day—psychics, well-wishers, people who had missing loved ones of their own. I'd resorted to screening the calls by letting my answering machine kick in before I picked up.

There'd been three calls in the last half hour with no message. Clearly, someone didn't want to talk to the machine.

Finally, on the fourth ring, I caved in and answered.

"Listen to me and don't interrupt." The voice was toneless and mechanical. It took me a moment to realize it was electronically altered. "I've got your wife. If you want to see her alive, do exactly what I say. Nothing more, nothing less. Do not contact the police. Do not tell anyone about this call. I'll be in touch again in forty-eight hours. Be at the pay phone outside the Washhouse at eight in the evening. Bring two hundred fifty thousand in cash. Nothing bigger than hundreds. No dye packs, no transmitters, no tricks."

The ground rocked. My heart skipped.

Maureen was alive!

That was my first thought. Relief and joy flooded through me. The second thought was the staggering amount of the ransom.

"I don't have that kind of money. I can't—"

The voice overrode my own. "You bring in the cops, and your wife dies." The line went dead.

A recording. Not a live person on the other end. There was no way to plead with a recording.

I stood frozen in place, gripping the phone as if holding on to it might keep the possibility for dialogue open. Finally another recording came on. "If you want to make a call, please hang up and try again. If you need help, call the operator."

I needed help big time. Unfortunately, it was beyond what the operator could provide. I hung up.

Maureen was alive, I told myself. I'd be able to hold her again and tell her how much I loved her. She would come home and everything would be fine.

A huge weight had been lifted from my shoulders. Maureen was alive.

I didn't want to think about what she must be living

through, but the images came anyway. Maureen bound and gagged. In a filthy basement with beady-eyed rats. Or in a box. I'd read about someone who'd been held prisoner in a buried coffin.

Hold on, Maureen. Just a bit longer. Don't despair. Everything is going to work out.

But how?

Two hundred fifty thousand dollars in forty-eight hours. Impossible. I didn't have that kind of money, and I sure the hell couldn't borrow it. Between the loan I'd taken to pay my defense attorney and what I owed Dad for the business—not to speak of what I still owed for medical school—my net worth was in the negative numbers. Even a loan shark would brush me off.

My heart was racing, my palms sweaty. Should I contact the police? The message had been clear, but what alternative did I have? I'd never be able to come up with the money.

I felt sick to my stomach.

The phone rang again, and I almost jumped from my skin. I picked up right away.

It was Chase. "Don't you hate back-to-back calls?" he asked.

"What?"

"You just got off the phone, right? I tried your line a minute ago, and it was busy. I hate that."

"It was a short call."

"Anything new about Maureen?"

Yeah, she's alive, in the hands of kidnappers who want a quarter of a million dollars to let her go. I swallowed the urge to tell him about the call. "Nothing."

"Did you catch the ten o'clock news?" Chase asked. "They did another short piece about Maureen. Showed her photo again."

"That's good." Only now I wasn't sure if it was good. Wouldn't publicity put pressure on the kidnappers?

"It was only a minute or so," Chase added. "Same stuff as before. They mentioned the reward though. That should help."

The reward. I'd stretched to offer ten thousand, and now I had to come up with more than twenty times the amount. My stomach rolled over again.

"You okay?" Chase asked. "You sound kind of . . . funny."

"Of course I sound funny," I snapped. "My wife's missing."

"Hey, I'm not the enemy here."

"Sorry. I'm tired and my nerves are shot."

"I bet." Chase didn't seem put off by my outburst. He'd received enough flak from me over the years that he'd probably stopped paying attention. "You sure you don't want company? I can be there in—"

"I'm sure. But thanks."

"It wouldn't be any trouble."

I felt bad taking my frustration out on him. "I appreciate it, Chase. Really. I'm going to go to bed soon anyway."

"I'll be around if you change your mind."

I *was* tired. Exhausted, in fact. I climbed into bed but didn't sleep. Too much was on my mind. The money, of course. And whether to tell the cops about the ransom call.

The law-abiding citizen in me said *Yes, tell them.* I'd had the lesson hammered into me since I was a kid—walk away from trouble and let the law handle it. But I'd also seen first hand how often the law totally fucked up. And in this case, with the law being Dallas Pryor, I wasn't sure I trusted it at all.

Okay, so no cops. Several hours into sleeplessness, I finally decided that. Which meant I had to come up with the money. Sure. How was I going to do that?

I tossed back the covers and padded into the bathroom for a glass of water. Idiot kidnapper. Why target us? There were people with more money, lots more, even in Monte Vista.

There were people who were better known or who lived a more extravagant lifestyle. So why kidnap Maureen?

There had to be some reason. Some connection to us, or more likely me. An angry patient? A jealous colleague? Someone I'd managed to royally piss off for some obscure reason?

And then another thought hit me. What was to say the kidnapper was for real? Couldn't someone who'd read about Maureen in the news simply have decided to play the situation to his own advantage? The caller had offered no proof he was holding Maureen. No proof that she was even alive.

What if it was a hoax?

It was as though I'd been punched hard in the gut. For a moment, I couldn't breathe, and then I started trembling. The elation I'd felt hours earlier at knowing she was alive turned to lead.

I ended up on my knees, clasping the counter for support. And I sobbed.

I got to the bank almost as soon as it opened. I was greeted by Maureen's face. A flyer with her photo and the reward information was posted on the glass door at the entrance. Another was in the window by the ATM machine. Sherri and her team had been busy. I would have to make a point of thanking her.

Most of the employees worked at the teller counter or from one of the four desks positioned out in the open, but branch manager Bob Twomey had his own office. I was grateful for that.

He shook my hand by way of greeting then patted my shoulder sympathetically with his other hand. Bob was a contemporary of my dad's and had a son who'd been a couple of years ahead of me in high school. Bob had been with the bank for as long as I could remember.

"Sam. I'm so sorry about your wife. What you must be going through." He had a face like a bulldog's, with deep creases and heavy jowls. He shook his head, and his flesh shook too. "Awful. Just awful."

"I wouldn't wish it on anyone."

He gestured for me to sit. "What can I do for you today?"

"I need to see about a loan."

"A loan." He nodded, but his expression was puzzled. With a missing wife to worry about, why would I be sidetracked by something like a loan?

"Expenses," I explained. "Costs associated with publicizing Maureen's disappearance, special investigations, that sort of thing."

"Yes, of course. How much were you thinking of borrowing?"

"Two fifty." I tossed the number out like it was no big deal. As though I were right at home in the world of high finance.

"Two hundred and fifty dollars?"

I cleared my throat. "Two hundred and fifty thousand."

Twomey stared at me without responding.

"I was thinking a home equity loan might be the answer."

His fleshy face looked pained. "I'd like to be able to help, Sam, but your mortgage is already pushing the limits. I might be able to swing twenty or thirty thousand, but nothing near the amount you're asking."

His answer was hardly a surprise. We'd stretched to buy the house because Maureen loved it. Not as much as she'd loved the fancy new ones outside of town, but even stretching, those had been out of our price range.

We had roughly seven thousand put away in savings for a rainy day. I could cash out my IRA, pay the penalty, and come away with maybe another twenty thousand. With a cash advance on my VISA, I might be able to come up with another five thousand.

Even with the loan Twomey was suggesting, that left me two hundred thousand short.

"What about the practice?" I asked.

"What about it?"

"Is there a way to borrow against that?"

Twomey pressed his fingertips together. "It's not really yours yet, is it?"

"No, but it will be."

"When you finish buying out your dad."

I paid my father a monthly sum toward our agreed-upon price for the practice. I had a long way to go before it was actually mine, but neither of us really cared. With his savings depleted by my mother's illness, the monthly income was what he wanted.

"We could set up a special fund," Twomey suggested. "I imagine there are people in town who would be happy to contribute. The bank will donate its services, so it won't cost you anything."

But it wouldn't get me the ransom money either. I stood to leave. "That's an idea," I told him. "I'll think about it."

"I'm really sorry, Sam. My hands are tied."

"I understand."

"You think of anything else, come see me. And don't forget the special fund idea. People in your situation do that all the time."

I left the bank feeling I was moving through molasses. Short of stealing the money, I couldn't possibly meet the ransom demand.

I could steal it, I thought suddenly. Not really steal it, but borrow it.

Molly's trust fund.

The money from Lisa's life insurance and the inheritance from her grandmother. It was invested through a Boston brokerage in trust for Molly. I was listed as the trustee, though I'd turned the whole thing over to the investment company.

They maintained actual control, but I could request funds for her benefit. I'd only done so twice—once to get us moved to California and then again last summer when she wanted to go to a very expensive horse camp. Mostly the money was for college and her future, and I'd promised myself after last summer that I wouldn't touch it again.

But the money was technically, if not morally, within my reach.

I had only seven patients that morning. I didn't know whether Debbie had canceled the rest or they'd canceled on their own, but I was grateful for the lighter-than-usual load. And Ira had covered morning rounds for me at the hospital. Although I liked to think I was a conscientious doctor, I doubted I could have handled anything more complex than a cold right then.

When I'd finished with the last patient, I went into my office and called Mr. Garweather in Boston. I'd met him only once in person. A thin man with a receding chin and a pale complexion. His manner was terse and formal.

"I want to close out the account," I said.

"Completely?"

"That's right."

"And what is the reason for that?"

I thought for a minute. "I'd like to move the money out of the market and into something more . . . something less volatile."

"We can handle that for you. A bond portfolio perhaps, only high-grade municipals. But over the long haul, stocks are your best bet. Perhaps you could invest some—"

"I'd also like to put it with someone here on the West Coast."

A beat of silence. Finally he must have sensed this was not the moment for salesmanship. "Certainly. We'll need written authorization, notarized, and a completed substitution of trustee absolving us of further responsibility."

"Okay. How do I get that?"

"I can fax you a form."

I gave him the office fax number. "And then can you wire the money to my local account?"

"Technically it ought to go into a separate account. These are trust funds, and they shouldn't be comingled with your personal funds." He paused. "Though we could certainly do that, if you wish."

"For now, that would be easiest."

"Once you return the paperwork to me, I'll put in a sell order. You ought to have the funds at your disposal by early next week."

"Next week?" I felt like the wind had been knocked out of me. "I was hoping to have them by tomorrow."

It was the closest I'd come to hearing Mr. Garweather laugh. "I'm afraid that is impossible."

We finished going over the particulars—I'd had enough of Garweather and wanted the money elsewhere no matter what—then I hung up and stared at the wall. I could feel the prick of tears in my eyes.

Dad would help if he could, but he had little to spare. Chase didn't have a nickel to his name, and Ira lived so far beyond his means he made the federal government look frugal. Lisa's parents were the only people I knew with money, and asking them was out of the question.

What was I going to do?

I'd failed to protect Lisa, and now I was going to fail Maureen.

The bitter taste of despair made me ill.

I dropped by Ira's office to tell him I was leaving for the day.

"Any news?" he asked. It was the same question he'd asked me first thing that morning.

"Afraid not," I said. Ira had a chart open on his desk, and Debbie had just ushered another patient into one of the examining rooms. He was taking on an extra load because of me, and that made me feel worse. "I'm heading home. I really appreciate your covering for me."

Ira shrugged. "It's no big deal."

I knew he was busy and didn't have time for socializing, but there was a coolness to his manner that hadn't been there before. Probably he did mind that my problems were causing problems for him. But I sensed that he was also trying to distance himself from me. Was it any wonder the cops thought I might be guilty when my oldest friend harbored doubts?

I drove home, wondering how it would feel if our roles were reversed. Would I step in for Ira? Sure, but on some level I'd probably also resent it. Would I stand up for him? Certainly in public, unless I had proof of his wrongdoing. But privately? You can't banish doubts by telling yourself you're going to ignore them.

And what would Ira do in my place? Despite having the trappings of a more elegant lifestyle, Ira's financial situation was as bleak as mine. Worse, in fact, thanks to a vindictive ex-wife and a weakness for high-stakes poker. But Ira would never find himself in my position. He had no one in his life to be kidnapped, nothing he cared passionately about.

I was beginning to envy that.

CHAPTER 14

Frank Donahue sipped the glass of sherry Sylvia Patterson had handed him. It was probably excellent sherry— he couldn't imagine the Pattersons serving anything that wasn't top of the line—but Frank wasn't big on sherry. He'd have preferred scotch or a beer, or even a cup of coffee, but four o'clock was apparently too early for a real drink and too late in the day for coffee. He'd remembered this from before, the Pattersons' strict adherence to formality. It always made him a bit uncomfortable.

He set the etched crystal glass on the coaster in front of him and waited for Sylvia to take a seat. She was in her early sixties, a tiny, birdlike woman with carefully coiffed hair and several large diamond rings on her fingers.

Hal Patterson, on the other hand, was a large man, six feet at least, with broad shoulders and substantial girth around the middle.

"How have you been?" Hal asked, settling himself into an oversized leather armchair.

"I can't complain," Frank replied. Although, of course, he did all the time. Millie had hoped that without the pressure

of work, he'd relax a bit, but Frank suspected he was geneti-
cally programmed for discontent. "How about you?"

Hal shrugged. "It's been hard. Lisa would have been
thirty-seven next month. The ache never goes away."

"Not only did Sam murder our daughter," Sylvia added,
"he's keeping our granddaughter from us. We get a photograph now and then, but that's about it. She's grown up so
much, and we've missed it all."

"Meanwhile he's walking around free as a bird, poisoning
our Molly against us." Hal was bitter, understandably so, but
Frank sometimes thought if he'd handled things differently
he might still have had a relationship with the kid. "We've
invited her for the summer," Hal added, "and Sam hasn't
even had the courtesy to respond."

"She looks so much like Lisa did at that age," Sylvia said
wistfully.

Hal leaned forward, addressing Frank. "Do you have
news? Is that why you wanted to see us?"

"Nothing about your daughter, I'm afraid." Frank had intended to pass the information along in a quick phone call,
but Hal had insisted he come by in person. And truth be told,
Frank didn't mind. The Russell murder had been the last big
case he'd handled, and staying connected with those involved made him feel like he still had something to contribute.

"I did get a call from a detective out in California, however. Sam's remarried, did you know that?"

Sylvia sucked in her breath. "We'd heard. He gets to go
on with his life like the past never happened, while we . . .
we are left with nothing."

"That's what you came to tell us?" Hal asked. "That he's
remarried?"

"And that his wife is missing."

Hal's expression morphed from confusion to understanding. "Just like with Lisa. My God, the man's a monster."

Sylvia set her sherry on the table. "Poor Molly." She

turned to her husband. "It can't be good for her living in a home like that. We've got to protect our granddaughter."

"It's not clear yet that he had anything to do with her disappearance," Frank pointed out. "Or that there's even foul play involved."

"But the police contacted you. They must think—"

"I'm sure it's crossed their minds. I thought you'd want to know."

"You bet we do," Hal said emphatically. "Sam got away with murder once. He can't get away with it again. You'll do what you can to see that doesn't happen, won't you?"

"It's not my case. Not even my jurisdiction."

"But you might be able to help. We'll hire you, like we did before. I'd like you to take another look at the evidence against Sam anyway. There are new techniques in forensics I've read about. Maybe we'll get him yet."

"I asked the detective from California to keep me in the loop," Frank said. "As for the other, let me think about it. A case as old as this one—"

"It's only been seven years," Sylvia said, setting her empty sherry glass on the side table. "I've read about cold cases, isn't that what they're called? Cases that were solved years after the crime."

"Solved, yes. Usually through a DNA match. That's different than bringing the same suspect to trial a second time."

"But if you found new evidence . . ."

It wasn't going to happen. New evidence didn't suddenly spring to life seven years after the fact. Still, Frank could feel his blood pumping. It was a good feeling.

"I'll give it serious thought," he promised.

"And let's make sure no one in California forgets what he did to Lisa."

CHAPTER 15

In the end, I told Dad about the call. I didn't have a choice. He may not have had much money, but he had collateral and a solid credit rating. If I was going to get the ransom money in time, I needed his help. But asking for it was one of the hardest things I'd ever done.

He was mowing the lawn when I pulled up in front of the house. He idled the engine as I walked toward him. The newly cut grass smelled sweet and fresh.

"You got a minute?" I asked.

"Sure." He turned the mower off and gave me his full attention. That's the way he was. For as long as I could remember, he'd been there whenever I needed him.

"I have to ask a favor, Dad. A really big one."

"What is it?"

I cleared my throat. "Money."

"Sure, if things are tight—"

I shook my head. "It's not that easy." I told him about the phone call and the ransom demand, and my attempts to raise the money myself. "I can't get my hands on Molly's trust money until after the deadline."

"Oh, Sam." His tone was anguished. He leaned against the mower. "I hate to see you take Molly's money."

"What else am I going to do?"

"No, I'm not criticizing. I understand." He rubbed his palms on his pant legs. "What about calling the cops?"

I shook my head. "If something goes wrong, I might never get Maureen back."

"That's the important thing, keeping her safe."

"I need the money tomorrow night though. I hate putting you on the spot like this. I wouldn't do it except there's no other way."

He nodded then hugged me. "Of course, Sam. I'll do whatever I can."

I felt myself choke up. I was grateful beyond words. "I'll repay it all, with interest."

He waved his hand. "Don't worry about interest. I'm glad I can help. I'm not sure how much I'll be able to pull together though."

"Dad, you're the greatest. I feel awful asking you this, but I'm so—"

He squeezed my shoulder. "Try not to worry, Son. We'll get her home."

After leaving Dad's, I picked Molly up at school, and we stopped for ice cream. I suggested it, though I didn't know why. I had no appetite at all, much less interest in anything sweet. Molly didn't greet the suggestion with her typical enthusiasm either. Still, it was a mark of everyday life, and I think we both needed that.

We got cones—cookies and cream for Molly, orange sherbet for me—and sat on the bench in front of the store to eat them. Molly was still wearing the heart-shaped locket Maureen had given her.

"Does it open?" I asked.

She lifted it from her neck and showed me. "There's room for two photos, but it was empty."

"Whose pictures are you going to put there?"

"I guess one should be Maureen's."

"That would be nice."

"But I think I won't put anything there for now."

"That's fine." I knew Molly was struggling with ambivalent feelings about Maureen. She was frightened that Maureen was missing and felt it might somehow be her fault. But she'd never really warmed to Maureen. I could imagine that on some level Molly was glad to have her out of the picture, and that only made Molly feel worse.

"She had a nickname when she was little," Molly told me several licks later.

"What was it?"

"Elf."

The Maureen I knew was a force to be reckoned with. More titan than elf. "How did she get the nickname?"

Molly shook her head. "She didn't tell me about it. It's what it says on her locket. Do you think that's what her parents called her?"

"Probably."

"I like Sweetpea better."

That was my nickname for Molly, though I'd gotten enough grief over using it in front of her friends that I'd tried to break the habit. I was surprised to hear she liked it.

"Why don't we know them?" she asked. "Are they dead?"

"Her parents? I'm not sure. She doesn't get along with them though. She hasn't talked to them in a long time." I'd given fleeting thought to trying to track them down for help with the ransom money, but in light of Maureen's antipathy towards them, I'd quickly discarded the idea as a fantasy at best.

"Like us and Mom's parents."

"You talked to them last Christmas," I pointed out. From

what I heard of Molly's end of the conversation, it had been filled with awkward silences.

"But we don't talk, talk. I hardly know them."

Someday I would have to give Molly a full account of my relationship with my former in-laws, but not now.

"I bet they have pictures of Mom when she was my age," Molly added.

I nodded. "I'm sure they do."

"I wish I'd known her."

"You did know her. Don't you remember your stuffed dog, Whoof, and how silly Mom was when she tried to feed him?"

"Yeah, but that's not what I mean." Molly paused. "I'd like to visit her grave someday."

We had visited it, Molly and I, the day we left Boston. I'd asked for Lisa's blessing and felt she'd given it. But it was a cold, bleak November day, and I remembered feeling that I was betraying Lisa by moving west and abandoning her. I'd almost decided to stay.

"We'll do that," I told Molly. "You finished?"

She'd more or less stopped licking her cone, and the ice cream had begun to melt down the sides.

"I'm not really hungry," Molly said.

"Me neither." We tossed what was left of our cones in the trash. I handed Molly a clean napkin to wipe her sticky hands. "There you go, Sweetpea."

She wrinkled her nose at me.

"I love you," I told her.

She hugged my waist. "I love you too. You're the best dad in the whole world."

The same thing I thought about my own father. How sad that Maureen had missed that in her own family.

The light was on in the kitchen when we got home. I was pretty sure I'd turned it off before we left that morning. I was careful about that. It was a bone of contention between me and Maureen, who seemed incapable of flipping off a light switch.

For an instant, I thought maybe she'd returned home. "Maureen?"

The house was still.

"She's here?" Molly asked hopefully.

I shook my head. "No, it's just that for a minute there I thought . . . she might be."

It didn't *look* like anyone was inside, but still . . . Once you get an idea like that in your head, it's hard to put it to rest.

"Stay here," I told Molly. "I want to check the house. If you hear a noise, run next door."

"I want to come with you."

I shook my head. "I need you to stay by the door."

I glanced around the living room and dining room. They seemed untouched. Then I headed up the stairs toward the bedrooms. From the top landing, I caught a flash of movement below, heard heavy steps running toward the kitchen. My heart leapt to my throat.

I screamed, "Run, Molly." And sprinted back down toward the kitchen.

He was twenty feet in front of me. By the time I got there, he had Molly in his grip and was holding a knife at her throat.

Fear surged through me. I was frantic, but I didn't dare come any closer.

"Let her go!" I yelled.

He wasn't a tall man, but he was powerfully built. His face was hidden by a ski mask. Molly's was white as a sheet and wore a look of pure terror.

"Daddy!"

The intruder pressed the knife against Molly's flesh. "You keep your trap shut, kid."

"If you hurt her, I swear to God I'll—"

He cut me off. "I'm a friend of Eric's," he said.

I had no idea what he was talking about. "Please, whatever you want, it can't involve her."

"You *know* what I want."

"I don't—"

"I'll be watching you." He held the point of the knife under Molly's chin. "You don't want to follow Eric," the man said. "You or your kid."

"Who's Eric?"

Molly swung an arm up, reaching for the intruder's face, and missed. He grabbed the arm and yanked it hard behind her back. She yelped in pain. He shoved her hard in my direction, and she collapsed against me.

The man was out the door in a flash. I didn't even look to see which way he went. My focus was on Molly, who was sobbing hysterically.

I held her to me while I called the cops with shaking hands.

CHAPTER 16

Officer Dickey looked barely old enough to be a cop, but he'd been quick to respond. He arrived at the house no more than five minutes after I called 911. As I explained what had happened, he went through the house, looking for the intruder's point of entry.

"What did he look like?" Dickey asked me, pulling a notebook from his shirt pocket.

We sat down at the table in the kitchen. Molly pulled her chair close to mine so that she was half lying in my lap. I put my arm around her shoulders and could feel her trembling, like a kitten who'd narrowly escaped the jaws of a ferocious dog.

I wasn't so steady myself.

"He was wearing a ski mask," I said.

"How about physical build?"

"Five-seven or so. Around a hundred and seventy pounds." Even though I routinely looked at height and weight notations as part of my work, I had trouble estimating when a given individual was concerned. "He was stocky," I added. "Muscular."

"Anything about his voice? Or any distinguishing marks or tics?"

"Not that I noticed."

"You're sure he wasn't a neighbor?"

I looked at him like he was nuts. "My neighbors don't hold a knife to my daughter's throat, among other things."

He ignored the sarcasm. "Nothing familiar about the man?"

I thought for a moment then shook my head. My memory of the event was less visual than emotional. I could see the knife at Molly's throat and recall with absolute clarity the instant panic that had roared to life inside me. But I didn't remember much about the man himself.

"Who has a key to your house?" Dickey hadn't found any jimmied doors or windows, though he pointed out that with sophisticated thieves it was sometimes hard to tell.

"Only my dad and my brother."

Molly squirmed into my lap, and I wrapped an arm around her. The intruder's knife might not have broken the skin, but not all wounds bled.

"And my wife," I added. "She might have had one with her when she disappeared."

I wanted to tell him about the kidnappers. They certainly could have gotten their hands on her key. But even with the memory of the knife at Molly's throat still vivid in my mind, I couldn't risk telling him.

Just then I heard a car door slam out front. I got up and looked out the window to see who it was.

Hannah Montgomery was walking toward the house. Thankfully, Dallas wasn't with her.

With Molly shadowing me, I went to the door to let her in. Dickey followed us.

"I heard there was an intruder," she said.

She'd addressed me, but Dickey answered. "Call came in at"—he checked his notes—"at 15:06." He filled her in on what had transpired, more or less repeating what I'd told him.

Detective Montgomery looked at me again. "Anything else?"

"That's it. The whole thing probably lasted only a couple of minutes, although it seemed to go on forever."

"It must have been terrifying." She turned to Dickey. "Did you dust for prints?"

"Where am I going to dust? We don't know where he got in."

"I think he was wearing gloves," I told them.

"Do the doors, just to be sure," she said. "Even if he had gloves, he might not have put them on until after he was inside."

Dickey went to his patrol car to get his equipment. Detective Montgomery asked me to repeat, in my own words, what had happened.

"It has be related to Maureen's disappearance," I said when I'd finished running through the events a second time.

"What makes you say that?"

It seemed obvious to me. "We lead a simple, low-key life, then suddenly my wife is . . . missing, and a couple of days later an intruder breaks into the house. And not your common house thief either, but a masked man with a knife. Doesn't seem like a coincidence to me."

She nodded but didn't voice agreement. "This Eric he mentioned—you're sure the name doesn't mean anything to you?"

"I'm sure." Suddenly I saw a ray of hope and grabbed at it. "You think maybe it could be a mistake? Like he got the wrong house or something?"

"I suppose it's possible, though not likely." She turned to Molly, who was still cowering at my side. "You okay, honey?"

Molly gave a silent nod.

"You must have been very frightened," the detective said.

"I know I would have been. But the man is gone now. You understand that, don't you?"

Another nod. Molly's eyes filled with tears.

Detective Montgomery's voice grew softer. "Did he hurt you?"

Molly rubbed her throat while shaking her head.

"Tell me what happened."

"He had a knife," she said softly. "It was really sharp. He held it right here." Her hand stopped at a spot just under her chin.

"Can I have a look?"

Molly lifted her chin, and the detective stooped down so that they were at eye level.

I realized then that Dickey had completely ignored Molly. She might as well have been a family pet for all the attention he paid her. Detective Montgomery's concern raised her several notches in my estimation.

She examined Molly's neck, tracing a finger along the imaginary line Molly had indicated. The detective's fingers were long and tapered, with short, rounded nails. No rings. Why I noticed wasn't clear to me. Rings weren't generally something that jumped out at me.

"I know it hurt," she told Molly, "but he didn't break the skin. You're going to be fine. And we're going to find him."

Dickey returned and began dusting for prints. Detective Montgomery ignored him.

"What did you notice about the man?" she asked Molly.

"His shoes. They were heavy, with thick soles. Like boots." She was no longer shivering or clinging to me quite as intensely, but she was still breathing hard.

"Anything else?"

"He smoked."

"You saw him light a cigarette?"

She shook her head. "He smelled like it."

The detective did a bit of a double take. "That's good, Molly. You're very observant."

"You smoke too. But you're not as stinky."

A smile played at the detective's mouth. "Well, that's good, I guess. I'm working on quitting, so pretty soon maybe I won't smell at all."

Molly pursed her lips. "I didn't mean you smell bad," she offered diplomatically.

"How about I make some hot chocolate?" Detective Montgomery suggested. "You have some mix or cocoa powder in the house?" The question was so unexpected it took a moment for the words to register.

I wanted the cops gone. Both of them. But before I opened my mouth to decline, Molly said, "Yes, please."

"I'm going to need some help," she said to Molly. "You think you're up to it?"

Molly nodded and left my side to get the cocoa from the cupboard.

With Molly helping her to find supplies, the detective busied herself with heating milk and measuring chocolate. "Do you think your wife knows Eric?" she asked me over her shoulder.

I was sure the intruder, and therefore Eric, were somehow connected to Maureen's kidnapping. It was all I could do to keep from telling the detective about the ransom call. But I wanted Maureen home. I wanted her safe. I didn't want to mess this up.

"She never mentioned him," I said.

"Does she have a PDA or personal address book?"

"Our address book is the old-fashioned paper kind. The two of us share it."

"What about e-mail?"

"We share an account there too." I thought of the contact for Redhotsugarbear in our address book and wished there weren't so many things I was afraid to mention.

Detective Montgomery opened the cupboard and took out three mugs. "Shall we take a look?"

So all this nice behavior on her part was nothing more than an end run around the warrant. "I'll check it out later," I told her. "I'll let you know what I find."

She gave me a hard look. "I'm interested in finding your wife, Dr. Russell. I should think you would be too."

"I am and you kn—"

She leaned close so Molly couldn't hear her. She did smell of cigarettes, but she smelled of apricots too. A very nice smell.

"If you're hiding anything," she whispered fiercely, "we'll find it eventually."

"I'm not."

"Good." She sounded like she meant it.

She dumped the hot milk and cocoa into the blender and frothed it, then poured it into the mugs. "Do you like cinnamon in yours?" she asked Molly.

"I've never had it that way."

"It's good." She found ground cinnamon in the cupboard, sprinkled some into all three mugs, then set one in front of Molly and handed me another. "You look like you could use this," she told me.

I felt momentarily dizzy and took a breath. The ransom call, my blackout, the dinner reservation we'd failed to make, the single shoe in my trunk. I was hiding so much, I was afraid the truth would spill out of its own accord.

"How long have you been in Monte Vista?" I asked suddenly. Anything to turn the focus away from Maureen's disappearance. And myself.

"A little over a year. I was in LA before that." She moved to the sink and began washing the pot. "You've been back how long?"

"Almost four years."

"And you were in Boston before. That's where—" She looked at Molly and stopped. Our eyes met.

Where I'd stood trial for the murder of my first wife. I was sure that's what she'd started to say. I appreciated her not pursuing the matter in front of Molly.

"I was born in Boston," Molly said, wiping the milk mustache from her lip. "We moved because my mother died and we couldn't live with the sad memories."

Words from my mouth to hers. I dreaded the day I would have to give her a fuller explanation.

"I'm sorry to hear that," the detective said and didn't push the matter. Again, I was grateful to her.

"I'm finished here," Dickey said, brushing the knees of his trousers where he'd been kneeling while dusting for prints.

"Did you get anything?" Detective Montgomery asked.

"Some partials. No saying they came from the intruder though."

"Call me as soon as you've got them run." She turned to me. "Might be smart to have your locks changed."

I nodded. "I'm planning to."

We walked toward the door. The detective gave me an appraising look. "You haven't asked me if there've been any new developments in your wife's disappearance."

"Have there been?"

She pinned me with her gaze. "We're pursuing every lead."

It was, I thought, an oddly oblique response. But I focused on the fact that if all went according to plan, Maureen would soon be home safely.

CHAPTER 17

Hannah found Dallas in the break room, pouring creamer into his coffee. "There was an intruder at the Russell house this afternoon," she told him. "A man in a ski mask."

Dallas looked up. "What?"

She gave him the details she'd gleaned from her interview with Sam and Molly. "Joel Dickey took the call. He'll get us a copy of the report."

"Anything taken?" Dallas had slopped coffee from his mug onto the counter and hadn't even made a swipe at wiping it up. No wonder the place was always a mess.

"It doesn't appear that way," Hannah said. "Sounds more like he was making some sort of threat."

Dallas frowned. "Nothing taken, no sign of forced entry. All we've got is Sam's word that it happened."

"Come on. You can't be suggesting he made the whole thing up."

Dallas leaned against the counter and took a gulp of coffee. "What's so far-fetched about that?"

"The daughter was pretty upset, for one thing." Hannah had wanted to fold the girl in her arms. She picked up a cup, eyed the sludge at the bottom of the coffee pot, and poured herself water instead. "The daughter was the one who noticed the guy's shoes and that he smelled of cigarettes. I doubt Sam would enlist her as a co-conspirator."

"It wouldn't be hard for him to have a friend play the part."

"But why—"

"No one was hurt, right?"

"Not hurt, no." But Molly had been traumatized. Would a father use his own child in that way? Some fathers, no doubt about it. But Sam? Hannah had trouble wrapping her mind around that one.

"What about this Eric?" she asked as they wended their way back to their desks. She nodded to Carla in passing and got only a stony glare in return. "Sam claims he doesn't know any Eric."

"That's another reason the whole thing raises red flags," Dallas said. "Sam's probably hoping we'll go off on some wild-goose chase instead of staying focused on him."

"It's Maureen Russell we should be focusing on," she pointed out.

He dismissed the distinction with a sweep of his hand. "One and the same."

"Maybe, maybe not."

Dallas looked at her over the top of his coffee mug. He offered a smug smile and slid a sheet of paper onto her desk. "This came in through the tip line."

He'd been following up on the calls that had come in. They were pitifully few in number, and it was clear right off the bat that most of them weren't going to lead anywhere. But they needed to follow up on all of them. Too often, the one that was overlooked turned out to be critical.

"Guy runs a flower stand along the highway," Dallas said. "He says he thinks Sam stopped by Sunday morning and bought a bouquet."

Hannah couldn't find much sinister in that. "I saw a vase

of tulips on the table Sunday evening. It was their anniversary."

"Saturday was their anniversary, not Sunday," Dallas pointed out. "He says Sam was acting antsy, and his appearance was disheveled. He also remembers seeing what could have been a spot of blood on Sam's shirt."

Doctors and blood kind of went hand in hand. "So Sam stopped to pick up flowers on his way home from the hospital," she said, flipping through message slips on her desk. Maybe he hadn't thought to get flowers on Saturday.

Dallas leaned across the desk. "The flower stand is on the other side of town from the hospital."

She looked up, messages forgotten. "Not on his way home, in other words."

"Not even close."

Hannah felt a prickle of irritation. She wanted to believe Sam had nothing to do with his wife's disappearance, but he was making it damn difficult. "Why would Sam buy flowers for his wife if he'd just killed her?" she asked after a moment.

"Maybe it was another thing to throw us off, like the supposed intruder this afternoon. Anyway, it undermines his story about spending the morning at the hospital. Where, I don't need to remind you, we have yet to find a single soul who remembers seeing him."

Hannah's perspective on hospitals was different than Dallas's. He hadn't been inside one since the day he was born, except on police business. Hannah, on the other hand, had spent way too much time in hospitals, both as patient and visitor. She knew that faces blurred and days blurred and that you might know you'd seen someone and not be able to say for certain whether or not it was on a particular day.

"The fact that no one remembers seeing him doesn't mean he wasn't there," she pointed out once again.

"Sam lied to us, Hannah. And here's something else. Sam and Maureen were no-shows at the restaurant Saturday night."

"Didn't even call to cancel?"

"Right."

It might not mean anything, Hannah reasoned. Maybe they'd decided on a romantic evening at home. Or indulged in frenzied afternoon sex that left them exhausted. Or maybe Hannah was just looking for excuses because she didn't want Sam to be involved. And that annoyed her as much as his fishy behavior.

Dallas drummed his fingers on the desktop. "I say we bring him in for questioning."

She looked up. "Yeah," she said with a sigh. "I guess we should."

Discrepancies usually fueled Hannah's optimism about a case. They were like chinks in a wall that could be worried and picked at until the entire structure crumbled. Sometimes inconsistencies were all cops had to work with. But instead of excitement, what Hannah felt this time was a dim ember of disappointment.

Dallas stood. "Let's go then."

She hesitated. "Sam's upset about the break-in. The little girl's upset. Talking to him now wouldn't be productive."

"All the better if he's upset."

On this point, Hannah felt strongly. It was better to wait. She looked at her watch. "You going to put in for overtime," she asked Dallas, "or do it on your own time?"

"You are such a pain in the butt sometimes," Dallas said, but he said it with a smile. "Tomorrow it is."

Hannah parked her Camry in the gravel driveway, grabbed the mail from the box, and went inside. Despite the new coat of paint, the cottage still had the musty smell of age she'd noticed when she first looked at the place. It had been dark and dim then. The previous tenant kept the drapes pulled and the house closed up tight. But Hannah liked the setting with its southern exposure and sunny patio, and the rent was right. The landlord had painted and put in fresh carpeting, and Hannah had pulled down the draperies—there were no neighbors close enough to see in anyway.

Now the house had a nice, light feel to it. And also the stark bareness of someone yet to fully move in. She had the necessities: bed, dresser, table, and couch, all new. She'd sold her old furniture in Los Angeles along with the house. Most of her boxes, however, were still stacked along the wall of the spare bedroom. Initially, she'd put off unpacking until the painting and cleaning were done. Then she'd gotten busy, first with a rape case and after that a string of residential burglaries. Now she wondered if it wouldn't be wiser to simply leave the boxes where they were. If she wasn't going to stay in Monte Vista, she'd only have to pack everything up again.

Hannah dumped the mail on the kitchen counter.

"Yes, yes, I know you're there." She addressed her comment to the tabby cat circling at her feet then put out food and fresh water for him.

He'd come with the house. Not that taking on the cat had been part of the rental agreement. But he was there. The landlord thought the animal probably belonged to the prior tenant but took no responsibility for getting rid of the creature. What else was she to do but feed it? She hadn't, however, got around to naming it.

She checked her phone messages. One wrong number— didn't people ever listen to the announcement that gave her name?—and a message from her mother. Hannah's niece, Melissa, Claire's daughter, would be celebrating her sixth birthday in a month. It would be really nice, her mother said, if Hannah would make an effort to come to the party.

She felt a pang of regret. In cutting Claire from her life,

Hannah had lost Melissa too. And Melissa was the closest thing Hannah had—would probably ever have—to a child of her own.

But even that couldn't make her forgive Claire.

Hannah flicked on the television, hoping to catch the local news, and noted with smug satisfaction that it was half an hour past her permitted smoking break. A real milestone.

But only a very small one because as soon as she thought of the cigarette, she was overcome with the urge to smoke. As soon as she lit up, she felt the tension ease from her body. Times like this she wondered why she'd ever decided to quit.

The lead story involved a tragic drowning in the river. A young child who'd wandered in too deep and been caught up in the current. It was followed by a story about a big-rig accident that closed the Interstate and another about a wildfire near Placerville. Nothing more about Maureen Russell. Not that Hannah was surprised. Without some newsworthy twist, it was rare that a missing adult generated extensive public interest.

It was strange, Hannah thought, that she still had no real sense of Maureen. In cases she'd worked previously, Hannah had felt a personal connection with the missing person—even when that person was an eighty-year-old man or a twelve-year-old girl. She'd talk to enough loved ones, hear enough stories, that she'd develop an affinity with the victim.

But Maureen Russell remained a name and a few tagline descriptions. A pleasant though reserved woman with few close friends. Not unlike herself, Hannah thought. She'd heard no negative comments about Maureen but no heartfelt admiration either, which was interesting in itself. When tragedy struck, people were inclined to speak in superlatives.

And Sam? That was strange too, because Hannah felt she did have a sense of the man, and it didn't fit at all with the way the case appeared to be shaping up.

She turned off the television and contemplated dinner. A

tuna sandwich maybe, or a bowl of cereal. Anything that didn't involve cooking. She wandered into the kitchen in search of inspiration.

Would Sam even be a suspect if not for his previous brush with the law? Sure, they'd look at him. Spouses and boyfriends were always on the radar screen. But they'd found no hint of affairs, domestic violence, threats, anything that would lead them to look more closely.

Except Dallas was right—Sam was holding out on them. He was cooperating, but only up to a point.

She opened the refrigerator then closed it again. Suddenly sick of it all, she decided to skip dinner. Time to prove to herself that she was still a desirable woman. Someone worthy of love, if only for a few hours. She changed into jeans and her red silk shirt and headed out for the solace of hard bodies and the anonymity of a town thirty miles away.

CHAPTER 18

I volunteered to spend the night in the spare bed in Molly's room and promised we'd keep the hallway light on. Neither of us seemed in any hurry to close our eyes. We talked about the intruder again and how scared we'd been.

"I thought he was going to kill me," Molly said. "And I was afraid it would hurt."

"I think it was probably the scariest moment in my whole life."

"Because you would miss me?"

"Oh, honey, I'd miss you so much my bones would ache."

"Do you miss Mom that much?"

I nodded. "I do. But having you helps make it better."

Molly traced a circle on her bedspread. "How did Mom die?"

"A bad person killed her, remember?" That was the explanation I'd given Molly when she was five, and it had sufficed until now.

"But *how*? Did he shoot her?"

"No, he choked her." I debated adding that she'd been stabbed too. Brutally. But considering the ordeal Molly had been through that day, I decided to leave it at choking.

"Do you think it hurt?"

I imagined the terror must have been worse than any physical pain. I didn't tell Molly that either. "I think it happened very quickly," I said.

"Still . . ." She shuddered. "Did they find who killed her?"

"No, they never did." The time was coming when I would have to tell her everything. I knew it would be easiest if I did it in stages.

I took a breath and jumped in with both feet. "There were some people who thought I was the one who did it."

"But you didn't?"

"No, honey, I didn't. I loved your mom more than anything on earth. Except you, of course. I would never hurt her."

"So why would they think you did it?"

"It's complicated. The police often suspect the husband when a woman is killed."

"That's not fair!"

"Often they're right. But not in this case."

She was quiet a moment, no doubt contemplating the alien concept of a world where love could change so unequivocally to rancor. "They finally believed you though. They know you didn't kill Mom?"

In truth, I doubted I'd won anyone over to my side except the single juror who stood in the way of my conviction. Certainly not my former in-laws. And chances were, even the juror wasn't convinced of my innocence. Reasonable doubt was an amazingly amorphous concept.

"Right," I told her. "They finally believed me." There were times when truth was an equally fluid concept.

I had just finished with a patient the next day when Dallas showed up and asked me to come with him down to the station.

"Did you get him?" I asked, wondering how I'd identify the masked intruder. Maybe they'd do a voice lineup.

"We've got a few more questions," Dallas said.

"So ask. I haven't remembered anything new though."

"I'd rather you came with me."

It wasn't about the intruder, I realized suddenly. It was about Maureen.

"What about the guy who broke into my house? He held Molly at knife point!"

Dallas rocked back on his heels. "It's not an MO that's come up in any other reports."

"What the fuck is that supposed to mean? So what if he's not breaking into every other house in Monte Vista? He wasn't a common house thief, Dal . . . Detective Pryor. He wanted something from *me*."

"And you have no idea what he was after, or who Eric is?"

"Right."

Dallas smiled. He had unusually thin, flat lips, and maybe that was why the smile seemed insincere. "So what is it, exactly, we're supposed to be doing?"

"Whatever it is cops do to solve a case."

"Come on down to the station, Sam. Let's talk there."

"Are you going to arrest me?"

Dallas shook his head. "We just want to talk, Sam."

"Forget it."

Dallas perched on the corner of my desk, shoving a stack of papers aside to make room for himself. "How was your anniversary dinner Saturday night?"

So that was it. They'd discovered Maureen and I hadn't made it to Pietro's. I waved the question aside. "We decided not to go out after all."

"On your anniversary?"

I flashed an intentionally patronizing grin. "Dallas, I know you've never been married, but believe me, you can have more fun at home than by going out."

He met my grin with one his own. One that said he didn't believe a word I was saying. "You got her something, at least? Jewelry, flowers, something to mark the day?"

"Flowers."

"Where'd you buy them?"

Zap. I'd walked into a trap of my own making. That's why attorneys always warned people to keep their mouths shut.

I glanced at the clock.

In less than twelve hours, the kidnappers would contact me again. With my dad's help, I could get Maureen back. Once she was safe, I would tell the cops everything.

"Sorry, Dallas. I don't have time for this."

"So you're refusing to cooperate in helping us find your wife?"

I hesitated. "That's your interpretation."

"We're onto you, Sam. You may think you've covered your tracks, but you're wrong."

CHAPTER 19

I leaned against the stucco wall by the Washhouse, a few feet from the pay phone. The tension of waiting was unbearable. I checked my watch for the third time in as many minutes. Twelve minutes past eight.

What if they never called?

Afraid of missing them, I'd arrived early and had been pacing the tiny strip mall for the past half hour, never venturing far from the phone or my Audi. Locked in the trunk was a brown grocery bag of cash—nothing larger than a hundred, just as they'd instructed. A tenuous lifeline to my wife's safe return.

I hadn't been able to raise the full two hundred and fifty thousand, but by cashing out my IRAs and borrowing from my dad, who in turn had drawn on his line of credit at the bank, I had close to half of what they wanted.

I'd also put a note in the bag asking for more time to deliver the balance. I spent hours on the note, writing and rewriting and then starting over again from scratch. Was it better to beg or be tough? To offer a lengthy explanation or a cursory excuse? In the end, I settled for what I hoped was a personal and heartfelt plea for understanding.

If the kidnappers were at all reasonable—a big if—they had to know it would take longer than forty-eight hours to raise all the money. If they were unreasonable, or simply nuts . . .

My throat tightened, and I fought a wave of nausea.

A young woman emerged from the laundromat, a blue denim laundry sack slung over one shoulder. A heavily pierced couple, both of them long and lean, entered the QuickStop next door. The German shepherd in the minivan a few cars from mine began to bark.

All around me, life went on as usual.

I could barely breathe.

The evening was cool, but my skin felt clammy with sweat. I checked my watch again. Fourteen minutes past eight. Had I misunderstood? Gone to the wrong laundromat? Had I, despite everything, screwed up? Maureen would wind up dead, and it would be my fault.

I stared at the phone, willing it to ring. When it did, it caught me by surprise. The harsh noise shattered the night air like an explosion. I grabbed the receiver on the second ring.

"I'm here," I said, sounding surprisingly calm. Inside, I was churning.

A soft breath. "Sam?"

Maureen! My heart did a double backflip.

"Honey, are you all right?"

"Oh God, Sam. Help me." It sounded like she was crying.

"Have they hurt you? Are they—"

There was a shuffling sound on the other end of the phone. "Just do what he says. I want to come home. I want—"

More shuffling, and then another voice came on. Not mechanical like the last time but still distorted. "I'm going to give you the directions only once, so listen up."

I scrambled for the pen and paper in my pocket.

"Turn left onto Hawthorne when you leave the shopping center. Go six blocks. Turn right onto Hess. At the second stoplight is a Shell station. And a phone booth. Wait for my call there. Make sure you aren't followed. Any sign of the cops, and your wife dies."

"About the money," I said. "I have—"

There was a click, and the line went dead.

My mouth was so dry I could hardly swallow. I got into the Audi, started the engine, and backed out of the parking spot. I looked around the lot as I left. No one else left when I did.

The directions were easy. I drove with one eye on the rearview mirror. I was going to be damn sure it didn't even *appear* as if someone might be tailing me. I was taking no chances.

How would he know if I *was* being followed? Was he watching?

I found the Shell station and the phone. It was in an old-fashioned enclosed booth, probably the last such relic in the county. A broad-shouldered man was inside, the phone pressed to his ear.

Panic began to build inside me. What if the kidnappers thought the busy phone was a ploy on my part? What if they thought I was in cahoots with the guy? Then I thought, maybe it *was* a ploy—something the kidnappers had planned. I couldn't think straight. I had trouble breathing.

I gave it three minutes. Then I moved closer to the booth. The guy inside had his back to me, and his black leather jacket filled the window. His head was shaved, making it hard to miss the snake tattoo on the right side of his neck. Not someone I wanted to mess with.

But I had no choice. I knocked on the window. He turned slightly, and I caught the glint of metal from a pierced lip.

"Sorry to bother you, but I'm expecting—"

He opened the door a crack. "Wait your turn, dickhead."

"How long do you—"

He turned his back on me.

I checked my watch, gave him another three minutes. He

wasn't talking, but he put more coins in the slot. He had to be on hold, or maybe waiting while the person on the other end looked for something. That could take forever.

Finally, I heard mumbled conversation on his end. Talk and then more talk. I could feel the pressure building inside me. I knocked on the window again. He ignored me.

At last, he hung up and opened the door. The phone rang immediately. He picked it up.

"No," I yelled out. "Don't touch it." I scrambled for the phone.

"You expecting a call? A special lady friend, maybe? Someone you don't want your wife to know about?" He seemed amused and held the receiver to his ear.

Please, don't let it be them, I prayed. *Don't let this go all wrong.*

"Give me the phone. Please." I sounded like a kid begging the school bully for the return of his pilfered lunch.

The man grinned and hung up. "Musta been a wrong number." He climbed into a dented El Camino and roared off.

Jesus, what now? Would they call back? I stepped inside the booth to claim it for my own. It reeked of piss and rancid grease.

I waited for what seemed like forever before the phone rang again.

"What are you trying to pull?" demanded the voice.

"There . . . there was someone using the phone when I got here," I stammered. "It wasn't my doing. I tried to get him off."

"I like things to go according to plan."

"Me too." I gulped. "Listen though, about the money . . ."

Silence. But I could hear breathing on the other end.

"I've got it. Not quite all, but a lot. The rest I can get—"

He hung up on me.

I collapsed against the wall. I'd lost her. The woman who'd brought laughter back into my life and made me whole again.

I'd failed her when she needed me most. In the back of my mind, I could hear her crying, *Help me, Sam. I want to come home.*

The phone rang again. I grabbed for it.

"Take El Dorado Avenue past the railroad tracks to Buckey Road. A half mile past the speed-limit sign, you'll see a drive on the left. Take it. A quarter mile in, there's an old barn. Park in front, go inside, and place the bag in the center. Back out and leave."

"What about Maureen?"

A stretch of silence. "I don't know, Sam. You're only giving me part of the money, maybe I'll give you part of Maureen."

My breath caught.

"Which part would you like, Sam? A thumb? An arm? A breast?"

Bile rose up in my throat. "No, please. Don't hurt her. I'm going to get the money. I just need until Monday."

Silence. I thought he'd hung up on me.

"The banks are closed over the weekend," I pleaded. "Please, I'll have it on Monday."

"I'll give you until Monday, Sam. But I'm charging interest. Ten percent. That's ten percent of the total. Another twenty-five thousand, in case you can't do the math."

Monday. A balloon of hope rose in my heart. By Monday Molly's trust money would be in a local account under my control. I could pay the kidnappers the rest of the ransom. Maureen would be safe.

I wasn't stealing, I reminded myself. I was saving Maureen's life. And I was going to repay every cent. Both to Molly and to my dad.

But at the same time I made that promise, I wondered how I'd manage it.

"I'll be in touch," the voice said. The line went dead.

My entire body was drenched in sweat. My limbs were rubbery. But I'd gotten a reprieve.

Slumped against the side of the phone booth, I took a minute to pull myself together. Images of Maureen's imminent homecoming cycled through my mind. I could feel the warmth of her skin, taste the sweetness of her kiss. Whatever petty grievances we'd fought about in the past, we'd put them behind us. We'd be together again. That was all that mattered.

CHAPTER 20

Despite the encroaching darkness and the remote location, I found the barn without difficulty. It was a tilting, weathered structure that stood near the charred remains of what must once have been the main house. There wasn't a soul in sight.

I pulled onto the packed dirt in front of the barn and extracted the brown paper sack from my car's trunk. Somewhere in the distance an owl hooted. Then a twig cracked.

An animal, I told myself. Still, goosebumps rose at the back of my neck. What if it was an ambush?

But he wanted the rest of the money, didn't he? There was no reason for him to harm me.

Not yet, anyway.

Carefully picking my way over strands of fallen barbed-wire fence, I walked the short distance across a field to the barn door. The soft gray twilight had deepened to the cusp of night. I could still make out shapes and shadows and find my way without stumbling. But it was dark enough that those same shapes and shadows toyed mercilessly with my imagination. I wanted to deliver the money and be gone.

The barn door was massive. It creaked and groaned when I pulled on it but swung open more easily than I expected.

I heard a rustling inside. The band of tension around my chest tightened. I listened harder.

A faint squeaking, like a mouse. And then a rush of movement overhead. I dropped the bag and crouched forward, protecting my face with one arm.

Bats, I realized a moment later. Only bats. I almost laughed with relief and stepped inside.

The barn looked as if it hadn't been used in years. Except by bats, and probably rodents and spiders. And kidnappers.

I wondered if Maureen was anywhere close by. She loathed creepy-crawly things. Even flying creatures like birds and butterflies made her nervous if they didn't keep their distance.

I placed the sack on the floor as I'd been instructed then backed out the way I'd come in. I kept waiting for something to happen, though I wasn't sure what.

Nothing did.

Feeling oddly hollow and let down, I got into my car and drove away.

I retraced my route, taking Buckey to El Dorado. There, I turned right and pulled off onto the shoulder about a hundred yards from the intersection. It wasn't a real shoulder, just a wide, flat space on the side of the road partially obscured by manzanita and willow.

Jitters built inside me. I was anxious and at the same time unwilling to put the evening behind me. It felt surreal to leave all that money in an abandoned barn. I couldn't simply head home.

I turned on the radio, listened to a talk show host spar with callers about religion and government, but the angry voices got on my nerves and I switched to soft jazz. I didn't have a plan, not consciously. But I'd made contact with the kidnappers, and I wasn't ready to let go.

I waited for over an hour. Plenty of cars passed by on El Dorado, going in both directions, but no one entered or left Buckey.

Then, suddenly, I saw lights in the distance approaching from the direction of the barn. Had they been there the whole time?

When the car turned right onto El Dorado, I waited until it had rounded the bend then started my engine and followed.

I could see that it was an SUV. Dark, but I couldn't be certain of the color. Nor could I tell the make. I thought I saw two people inside.

I was afraid if I got too close I'd give myself away, so I hung back until we got to town. There, the vehicle stopped at a red light. I was one lane over, two cars back. I peered at the car, which was covered in dust, and was able to make out the first three digits of the license plate. *5TY.*

I debated what to do next. Should I call Detective Montgomery directly? She wouldn't be on duty at this hour. If I called the general number, they might brush me off. If I was lucky, they'd take me seriously and respond . . . in time to do what? Pull the SUV over? I might get my money back, but I'd never see Maureen again.

No. Calling the cops wasn't an option.

Maybe the car would lead me to Maureen. *Then* I'd contact the police.

My heart was pounding. My hands were so sweaty I had trouble gripping the wheel. I followed the SUV through town and out past the high school. Suddenly it sped around a slow camper and ran a red light.

I jammed my foot on the accelerator, intending to pass the camper myself and stay on the SUV's tail. A pickup truck was barreling toward me from the other direction. He flashed his lights. I hit the brakes hard and swerved back into my own lane. The car behind me honked ferociously.

Stuck at the busy intersection, I smacked the steering wheel in frustration. How could I have lost them after all this?

But I had part of the license and a general description of the vehicle. As well as a three-day reprieve. On Monday, I'd deliver the rest of the money. Once Maureen was safe, I'd turn the information over to the cops.

I sent a silent prayer to Maureen. *Don't give up, honey. A couple more days and it will all be over.*

And then I added one to a god I'd long ago stopped believing in. *Please let her be okay.*

The message light was blinking when I got home. The first call was from Dad, who wanted me to let him know that I'd made it home safe. Molly, who was spending the night at his house, added her own good night at the end. The second message was from the kidnapper.

That was stupid, Sam. Didn't I warn you not to play games? You fuck with me, I fuck with you. That's the way it is, Sam.

CHAPTER 21

Hannah leaned back in her chair and pressed her eyes shut for a few seconds. The squad room was stuffy. Worse than stuffy. It reeked of the pepperoni pizza the evening shift had shared several hours earlier. All except for Hannah, who wasn't part of the shift, and Carla Adams, who as far as Hannah could tell never ate at all.

"You put up with this every night?" Hannah called to Carla across the open expanse of desks.

"Put up with what?"

"The lingering odor of dinner."

Carla shrugged. "Goes with the territory. Tonight's not as bad as some nights. Sausage and sauerkraut is the worst."

"Ugh." Hannah located the offending wastebasket and dumped its contents into the large trash can at the back of the coffee room. "They do takeout every night?"

"Pretty much."

Hannah made a face.

"What, you had catered gourmet when you were with LAPD?" There was no disguising the caustic undertone.

Hannah was ticked. Why did Carla go out of her way to be unfriendly?

She turned her attention back to the papers on her desk. She hated filling out forms, which was pretty laughable since paperwork was a big part of her job. It wasn't as bad here as it had been in LA—score one point in favor of Monte Vista—but there was more than most people imagined. More certainly than Hollywood let on.

She finished typing up the last of the investigative reports then tackled the cramped application from Human Resources that had been floating in her in-box for the past week. Now that she had a year on the job, she qualified for supplemental life insurance. It wasn't as if her life had financial value to anyone but herself, but the policy was a perk of the job and she'd be damned if she was going to pass it up.

She zipped through the family history—her father had been healthy as a horse until the plane he was piloting lost power and crashed during her senior year in college. Her mother, at sixty-two, suffered only mild hypertension. Hannah's own health history wasn't as clean, of course, but she noted the date of her mastectomy three years earlier, along with those for the follow-up chemo and radiation, then moved on. The question about smoking gave her pause. She did smoke, true, but in another month she wouldn't. She hoped. She checked the no box, then scratched it out and opted for yes.

So many questions that didn't lend themselves to the simple, checkbox answers. She hesitated again when she came to marital status. Malcolm was dead, and she'd been his wife, albeit not much of one apparently. That made her a widow, but she didn't feel like a widow. Widows were elderly women who played bridge with "the girls" and spoke affectionately of their departed husbands. Hannah didn't fit any part of that. And if she was a widow, what was Claire?

The Rock of Gibraltar, she'd have said at one time. As much friend as sister. When Claire's husband ran off and left her with a one-year-old and no money, Hannah had willingly helped out. In turn, Claire was someone Hannah could turn to for solace. It was Claire she'd called when she first got the news of Malcolm's accident, Claire's shoulder she'd cried on when the doctors pronounced him brain-dead. Claire's fingers that had wiped the tears from Hannah's cheeks after the funeral.

Despite the stormy years of their teens, when Claire's perky good looks and popularity with boys had been a thorn in Hannah's side, she and Claire had found common ground as adults. Hannah laughed at the irony. She couldn't have invented a more common ground if she'd tried. Malcolm. They'd been sleeping with the same man.

Across the room, Carla Adams was cleaning off her desk.

"You leaving?" Hannah asked.

Carla glared back defensively. "I came on early today."

"What I meant was, you want to get a drink or something?"

Hannah was in the mood for company, but she wasn't up to trolling for a good time. She'd done that last night. Josh was his name, if she recalled correctly. A curly-haired cowhand with broad shoulders and a tight butt. Cute as could be and dumb as dirt. She'd woken this morning with a headache and a sour mouth, but at least she'd been in her own bed, alone.

"Sorry," Carla said, "I'm beat."

"Another night, maybe."

"Sure, whatever." She'd have to have been dead to manage a less enthusiastic response.

Carla had been with the department longer, but as a detective, Hannah had senior rank. It made for tension. Hannah had hoped things might be improving. Clearly, she'd been wrong.

Carla slung a leather satchel over her shoulder, waved at the dispatcher, and left without another word.

Hannah made sure no one was looking, then stuck out her tongue at Carla's departing figure. A childish gesture to be sure, but one that offered a small degree of satisfaction.

The empty squad room was oppressive. Hannah decided

to shelve the paperwork for another day and hit Slippery Rock on her way home instead. It was Friday night, after all.

The air inside the bar was heavy. A pungent mix of booze and sweat. Infinitely better than rank pizza, though maybe that said something about her own priorities. There was a band playing on the small stage at the back. Local talent, no doubt. That was all the Slippery Rock attracted. Two young guys on guitar, a drummer, and a skinny, skimpily clad girl on bass. They looked barely old enough to be playing at an over-twenty-one establishment.

Hannah headed for the bar. "Sierra Nevada pale ale," she said. "In a bottle."

The female bartender, whom Hannah had never seen there before, slapped the beer on the counter without looking at her.

"Charlie around?"

"It's his kid's birthday." The bartender gave Hannah a pointed look.

"Just asking. He's a friend, is all." Did the woman really think Hannah had the hots for an overweight guy ten years her junior?

She turned to survey the room. Lots of couples, which was to be expected on a weekend. A sprinkling of lone women, including four in the far corner shrieking wildly at whatever funny story one of them was telling. Several groups of guys. No one who caught her eye though, which was just as well. She had to watch herself this close to home. She wanted to keep her personal life personal and well away from the rest of the department.

She turned back to the bar and saw Sam Russell sitting alone at the far end. A martini, straight up with a twist, was in front of him. The glass was full, but that didn't mean it was his first one. His shoulders were rounded, and his expression was glazed. She thought he must be either half-asleep or totally drunk.

"Hey," she said, sliding into the empty seat next to him.

He didn't acknowledge her.

"Sam?" She touched his shoulder lightly. He flinched.

"Hannah Montgomery," she said. "Monte Vista PD."

"I know." He seemed to focus, finally, and turned in her direction with a look of apprehension. "There's news about Maureen?" His voice was thin and tight.

Hannah shook her head. "I'm off duty."

His whole body sagged forward.

There was a stretch of silence. "Do you come here often?" she asked. She was hoping the line might evoke a smile.

Sam's response was dead serious. "First time."

Interesting, Hannah thought. His wife had been missing not even a week and he was already hitting the night spots. Except he didn't look like a man on the prowl. All he appeared to be doing was slouching at the bar in a daze.

"How about you?" he asked after a moment.

"Now and then, when I can't stand my own company."

His expression softened. "I should think you'd be fine company."

Hannah felt an unexpected tingle of pleasure at the compliment.

"I want to thank you," he said, after a moment. "You were really good with Molly yesterday. She was terrified."

Hannah's heart had gone out to the girl who, despite her ordeal, had tried so hard to be brave. Her frustrated maternal instincts, she supposed. "It's part of the job, but I'm glad I could help."

Even in the darkened room she could feel the warmth of Sam's gaze. She felt a familiar flutter inside her. *Sam Russell. Now wouldn't that be something.* She quickly banished the thought from her mind.

"You have a nice way with your daughter," she said. "It's clear you two have a good relationship."

"I hope so. For a while there, it was just the two of us. Even now, Molly's my priority."

She rested an elbow on the counter. "Is that a problem for your wife?"

He sighed. "Sometimes." The glazed look slid over his face again, like a mask dropping into place.

Hannah had never felt close to her father. Claire was his favorite. Hannah didn't know if this was because Claire was the baby or because Claire was Claire, but she felt she'd missed out. Growing up, Claire had been cute, Hannah tall and gangly. Claire had been, and still was, a flirt, while Hannah was often tongue-tied. Even before she was old enough to be interested, Claire had boys beating a path to her door, while Hannah had never felt attractive or lovable until Malcolm. And then Claire had taken that away from her.

"How's your daughter doing? The department has a list of counselors, if you think it might help."

Sam nodded.

The silence between them grew. It wasn't that Sam was cool so much as simply not there. He'd drifted off again to whatever private place he was inhabiting when she first sat down.

"She's not home alone, is she?" Hannah asked after a moment. Given Sam's state, she wasn't sure he was thinking clearly.

"She's spending the night with my dad." He managed a weak smile. "She loves to stay there. He spoils her like crazy."

"It's nice that you have family close by."

"That's mostly why I moved back to Monte Vista. I didn't want it to be just me and Molly."

"What about her maternal grandparents?" Hannah asked. "Does she ever see them?"

"Not very often." He hesitated. "We're . . . not on the best of terms."

"Because of what happened with Lisa?"

Sam gave a humorless laugh. "That was certainly the crowning blow. They were never very fond of me though."

"Because?"

"Because they're assholes," he said flatly. "But I try to remember they're Molly's grandparents. And she has a right to know her mother's side of the family." He paused. "They spoil her in a different way."

"Different how?"

"Gadgets, toys, clothes. Material things. She eats it up, I'm sorry to say."

"Girls are like that," Hannah said. "I was the same way at her age." Not that anyone was tossing toys and clothes her way.

Hannah finished her beer and ordered another. She looked at Sam and nodded toward his untouched glass. "You okay there?"

He swirled the liquid and nodded.

Another stretch of silence.

"I was reading about the trial," Hannah said after a moment.

"The trial?" Recognition dawned. "My trial? Why?" Then he shook his head in disgust. "Never mind, I know the answer. You think there's a parallel between what happened with Lisa and what happened with Maureen."

"It's an odd coincidence, don't you think?"

"Odd?" He laughed bitterly. "To say the least. But it's not the same."

"What's that mean?"

He didn't answer.

Hannah's beer arrived, and she took a sip.

Sam hunched over his drink. Silence stretched between them.

"I got a call," Sam said finally, in a voice so soft she wasn't sure he'd actually spoken.

"A call?"

He turned to look at her. "A ransom call. From whoever has Maureen."

"You're saying she was kidnapped?" Hannah's pulse began to pound. She could hear it in her ears. "Why didn't you tell us?"

"He told me not to. That I'd never see her again if I did."

"But you reported her missing."

He nodded. "I didn't get the ransom call until two days ago."

Hannah tried to bring order to the questions spinning inside her head. The beer she'd drunk on an empty stomach wasn't helping. Thank God she'd only had one.

"What did they want—money?

Silence.

"How much?"

"It doesn't matter. I fucked it up." Sam brought the glass to his lips.

"What do you mean?"

"I only paid part of the ransom. It was all I could get my hands on."

She choked. "You gave them money?"

"Not as much as he wanted. I promised to get the rest."

"Oh Jesus." Hannah leaned forward, elbows on the bar. She wanted to throttle him for not telling them sooner. She thought about taking him in right now, but he was talking freely and he might not if she went into cop mode.

She shifted her position on the stool to give them more privacy.

"When was this?"

"Tonight. Then I got another call. An hour or so ago."

"From the kidnappers?"

Sam's hands were wrapped so tightly around his glass, his knuckles had turned white. The glass shook, spilling liquid over the side. He nodded. "Because I followed him."

His voice was so low Hannah was having trouble hearing. "You followed the kidnapper?"

"I made a fucking mess of it." He pushed his drink aside and put his head in his hands.

"Tell me what happened," Hannah said. "The whole thing from the beginning."

"It doesn't matter." His voice broke with an odd guttural sound. "It's too late."

Hannah spun around to face him. She pulled his hands from his face so that she could look him in the eye. "Listen to me, Sam. It's not too late. He's going to contact you again, right? For the rest of money? We'll put a tap on your phone. We'll station officers at your house. If we're lucky, we can trace the call. And we'll come up with a plan for the drop."

"You don't understand. He told me I'd pay for messing up. He's going to kill her. I know it."

Hannah's mind was racing as she tried to fit the pieces together. "When you followed the car, did you get a glimpse of who was inside?"

"It looked like the driver was male. Thin. There might have been a second person in the car as well. I lost them on the highway."

"What about the vehicle itself?"

"A dark color SUV is all I know. But I got part of the license plate."

She felt a surge of adrenaline. "That's good, Sam. Give it to me." She wrote down the numbers and letters he recited, as well as his meager description of the vehicle. "I'll put this out on the wire right away. And we'll run the plate. We'll find them."

"Not in time." He pressed a palm to his forehead. "They put Maureen on the phone, just for a few seconds. She sounded so scared. I can't bear to think what he's doing to her."

"You've got to focus, Sam. You've got to help us find her." Hannah signaled for the bartender. "Coffee, please. Black."

Sam studied his martini then pushed the glass away. "Make that two," he said.

Hannah turned again to Sam. "In most cases, kidnappers turn out to be someone connected to victim. In this case, either you or Maureen."

"You think I haven't thought about that? But anyone who knows me would know I don't have the kind of money they're after."

"Someone with a grudge against you, maybe?"

"The only person like that is my former father-in-law."

Hannah blinked. "Is that a possibility?"

Sam shook his head. "The guy's a hotshot businessman. Wealthy, with friends in high places. Kidnapping isn't his style. And he certainly doesn't need the money."

"He must resent that you've remarried though."

"Assuming it's even registered with him."

"You don't keep in touch with them?" Hannah asked.

"Only about Molly."

Revenge, greed, and lust. Most crimes could be traced back to one or more of the trio. Sam seemed ready to discount the first two. That left lust.

"Are you involved with another woman?" she asked, almost casually.

He gave her an icy look. "No, I am not."

"What about your wife? Could she be involved with someone?"

He shook his head, but his expression was ever so slightly guarded. "We've only been married two years. Maybe we're past the honeymoon phase, but we're still in love."

That's what Hannah would have said about her own marriage. And she'd been completely off base. Could Sam be as much in the dark?

She felt bad about kicking him when he was down, but she didn't see that she had a choice. "Maureen asked a friend of hers for the name of a divorce attorney."

For a moment, Sam didn't speak. "You're lying," he said finally.

"No, I'm not."

His expression had gone slack. "Who's the friend?"

"I can't tell you that."

"Maureen could have been asking for someone else," Sam pointed out.

"True." Hannah let him have that. "But if there's something you know that might help us find her . . ." She let the sentence trail off and waited for a response.

Sam looked like he might be about to say something then shook his head. "There was never any talk of divorce," he said at last.

"The important thing now is to find your wife. First thing tomorrow morning I'll have someone at your house to rig your phone so that we can monitor incoming calls."

"It won't make any difference," Sam said glumly. "I keep telling you, I fucked up."

Hannah agreed, but not in the way Sam was thinking. What he'd done wrong was not notifying the police as soon as he'd gotten the call.

Saturdays at the station were generally chaotic, but with this morning's hastily called meeting on the Maureen Russell kidnapping, the sense of urgency was greater than usual. Hannah had called Lieutenant Morrissy at home last night to tell him about her conversation with Sam, and he'd given the okay for electronic surveillance and personnel overtime. Now he and the four officers assigned to the case were crammed into the largest of the interrogation rooms, balancing notebooks with Styrofoam coffee cups and muffins. The muffins had been Hannah's peace offering since she knew all of them had places they would rather be on a weekend morning.

"How does Sam know they actually have her?" Carla

asked. She was drinking her own special blend of tea and hadn't even glanced at the muffins.

"They put her on the phone during one of the calls," Hannah explained. "Just long enough for Sam to hear her voice."

"And he actually paid them part of the ransom money?" Brian Murphy whistled softly. The sound was muted by the muffin crumbs still on his lips. "That's a gamble."

Carla brushed back a wisp of hair that had escaped from her long braid. "I'm surprised the kidnappers agreed to two drops. It doubles the risk for them."

"So maybe we're not dealing with the sharpest tools on the bench," Hannah said.

"The whole story sounds phony to me." Until now, Dallas had been tinkering with his watch, seemingly uninterested in the discussion around him. Hannah hadn't been sure he was even listening. But now he had the attention of everyone in the room.

"How so?" Brian asked.

"The guy runs into Hannah in a bar—I understand he's a recovering alcoholic, by the way. He's been through the whole AA thing, so you got to wonder what he's even doing there."

So that was why he hadn't touched his drink, Hannah thought. Or maybe he'd already finished off a couple by the time she arrived.

"And then he just drops this ransom thing on her," Dallas continued. "Like an afterthought. Why not call us directly if he's going to involve the cops?"

Hannah felt the eyes in the room shift in her direction. "I don't think he planned on involving us," she said. "He was kicking himself for messing up. The words just came out."

Dallas shook his head. "Don't let Sam fool you. He knows exactly what he's doing."

It wouldn't be the first time Hannah had been hood-winked into buying a story that wasn't true. But Sam's desperation had seemed genuine. "I'm willing to err on the side of believing him. Especially since there could be a woman's life at stake."

Dallas ticked off points on his fingers. "First there's the guy who supposedly broke into his house the other day. And now it's a ransom demand. Sam knows we're onto him and wants to muddy the water. He wants us looking anywhere but at him."

"If that's what he's trying to do," Carla observed, "it seems like he'd do a better job of it."

"He's scared," Dallas said. "He's not thinking clearly."

Morrissy ran a hand along the back of his thick neck. "Dallas could be right. But for the time being, we're going to treat this as a legitimate abduction." He turned to Hannah. "Do we have anything more on the intruder?"

She shook her head. "No prints, nothing that points to his identity. Forensics found the lock that was jimmied though. It was a professional job. Not the kind of break-ins we're used to seeing around here."

"You think Sam and his wife are mixed up in something bad?"

It seemed, on the surface, to be an obvious explanation. And it fit with Sam's reluctance to cooperate fully. But at the same time, Hannah had seen Sam right after the break-in. He'd been frightened and angry, but he'd also seemed genuinely perplexed.

"We need to explore that line of thinking," she said. "But I'm not convinced it's right."

"What Sam's mixed up in," Dallas muttered, "is getting rid of his wives."

Morrissy glanced at the notebook in front of him. "Brian, I want you at the Russell home within the hour. Think of a pretext to get in without calling attention to yourself, in case the kidnappers are watching. Once the trace line is in place, you and Carla can alternate covering. Dallas, check to see if

Russell actually withdrew funds, as he claimed." He turned to Hannah. "What have you got on the partial plate?"

"Seven possibilities once we narrowed it to cars that fit the description he gave and that are registered locally."

"Fucking waste of time," Dallas muttered.

Morrissy ignored him. "They need to be checked out immediately. Dallas, why don't you take the lead on that, along with the money angle. You can get some help from the patrol unit if you need it."

Dallas didn't say anything, but he reached for the sheet of registrations.

"And another thing," Morrissy said, "let's keep the media off this."

"They know she's missing," Carla pointed out.

"Fine. Nothing about the ransom though. It's important for our investigation, and maybe for Maureen's life. Let's not forget that Russell was warned about bringing in the cops." He jotted something on the page in front of him. "Hannah, I want you and Carla to go out to the drop sight. Look for evidence that might help us track the kidnappers, as well as evidence that either corroborates, or doesn't, Sam's story."

It better corroborate it, Hannah thought, or she'd look like a damn fool.

CHAPTER 22

I woke up Saturday morning feeling so wrung out my first thought was that I *had* succumbed to the temptation of drink. Then a clear memory of the evening slammed into me with the force of a two-ton truck, making me long for the simplicity of a hangover.

What had I been thinking? Why hadn't I simply dropped off the money and left? *You fuck with me, Sam, I fuck with you. That's how it goes.*

And then I'd topped it off by telling the cops.

If there'd been any chance in hell the kidnappers would overlook my stupidity in following their car, I'd blown it by doing the very thing they'd warned me against.

I was sick with regret. Sick with guilt. Sick with self-loathing.

From the beginning, the cops had suspected me of killing Maureen, and now I'd done just that. I'd made a mess of everything.

I knew something of the cruelty people could inflict on others. I'd seen more than enough examples during my residency at Mass General. Unwanted visions of torture and suffering filled my mind. I felt nausea rise in my throat.

Rolling over, I reached my hand to Maureen's side of the bed. The sheet was cool and taut. My eyes filled with tears as I remembered the soft, warm imprint of her body. On the days she got up first, I would sometimes slide over to her side just to wrap myself in her fragrance. Now, the emptiness overwhelmed me.

How could I live with myself, knowing what I'd done?

I finally dragged myself out of bed when the doorbell rang. I would have ignored it except that I remembered the police were coming to wire my phone.

As if it would make any difference.

Even if the kidnappers called, it would be from a pay phone. As far as I could see, the police could do nothing but screw things up. And that would be my fault too.

I threw on a pair of jeans and a T-shirt, and opened the door to a man from the cable television company.

I frowned. "I didn't call—"

"I'm Brian Murphy with the police department." He held out a clipboard with his photo ID and badge. "I'm here to work on your phone."

I looked at the panel truck in front. "But it says—"

"I know. We wanted to be careful in case the kidnappers were watching."

I hadn't thought of that. I had a moment's panic as I wondered if they might have been watching me last night.

Reluctantly, I let him in. I didn't really have a choice. "What do you need? Any help from me?"

"Just show me where the phones are located."

While he worked, I made myself a cup of coffee and again tried making a list of possible kidnappers. Detective Montgomery had suggested I think about workmen or delivery people who had been in our home recently. I drew a blank. Maybe Maureen had had someone in I didn't know about, but that seemed unlikely. The only name I could come up with was Wanda, our cleaning lady, who was in her fifties and a member of my father's church.

Someone we knew? It certainly appeared that Maureen had let her kidnapper into the house or had at least gone with him willingly. But again, I couldn't come up with a single name.

Hannah Montgomery had asked if Maureen could have been involved with someone. Not possible, I'd assured her. Not possible, I told myself now.

But I hadn't forgotten the unexplained e-mail address for Redhotsugarbear. Fairly paltry evidence of infidelity, but my mind had no trouble filling in the rest.

Less than half an hour after Murphy arrived, he poked his head into the kitchen to announce that he was done. "One of us will be here Monday, but we'll be monitoring calls in the meantime. If the kidnapper gets in touch when we're not here, just hit this button. It will alert one of us at the station."

My apprehension about involving the police returned. "I don't want you guys to do anything that might jeopardize my wife's safety," I told him.

"We're not going to do that."

"Not intentionally, maybe." I was wishing now I'd refused to let him in. "How much experience have you had with kidnappers, anyway?"

Murphy took off his glasses and cleaned the lenses with his shirt. "Me, personally, none. But the lieutenant's been around a long time, and Detective Montgomery worked a couple of kidnaps when she was with LAPD."

"A *couple* of cases?" If he'd meant to reassure me, he'd failed miserably. "What about the FBI? Shouldn't they be involved?" A minute ago I'd regretted ever breathing a word to the cops; now I was suggesting we bring in another layer of law enforcement. I didn't know what I wanted anymore.

"FBI doesn't ordinarily get involved unless we ask. I think the lieutenant doesn't feel the need." Murphy looked at me with sympathy. "I can only imagine how hard this must be for you. But we've got it covered. We're going to make it right."

* * *

When Brian Murphy left, I went to my dad's to pick up Molly. The two of them were in the living room watching a program on dinosaurs.

"You look like hell," Dad told me.

"I feel worse." I flopped onto the sofa next to them and gave Molly a hug.

"What's wrong—" Dad stopped himself and lifted his thick white eyebrows to give me an inquiring look. When I didn't respond, he turned to Molly. "Hey, why don't you go get that bowl of ice cream you were talking about earlier?"

She wavered, no doubt aware that she was being bribed. But the ice cream won out. When she was gone, Dad turned to me again.

"You weren't drinking, were you?"

"No." I looked at my hands. "But I came pretty close."

"Oh, Sam." His tone wasn't reproachful, but it was clear he understood how close I'd come to slipping up. "Why?"

"I don't want to talk about it."

"That's part of what got you in trouble before, you know. You kept everything locked inside you."

"I didn't take the fucking drink, okay? So forget it."

He shook his head. "Maybe you should call Jesse."

"Maybe you shouldn't give advice unless I ask for it!"

From the look on his face, I might as well have thrown a punch.

"I'm sorry," I told him. "I shouldn't take it out on you. It's just . . . just a bad time." I picked up a green corduroy accent pillow and punched it into shape.

"I know it's a bad time, Son. A terrible time. But you got the money delivered, right?"

"Yeah."

"And they gave you until Monday to get the rest of it?"

I punched the pillow again, harder. "I told the cops."

There was a moment of silence. My dad rubbed his jaw. "Well, that's good. The cops are good."

"The kidnapper told me not to."

"So, what do the police think?"

"They put something on my phone. If the kidnapper calls back, the cops will be able to trace the call."

"Cops are good," Dad said again. "Once the kidnapper gets his hands on the money, there's no telling . . ." He let the thought trail off. "You did the right thing, Sam."

"He told me not to tell anyone. First, I told you—"

"But I'm your father. Of course, you'd come to me."

"And I told the cops."

"Well, I don't think—"

"But I did something even stupider." I took a breath and told him about following the car last night and about the phone call when I got home.

Dad didn't say anything for a moment. Then he put a hand on my shoulder. "It's done, Sam. You did what you thought was right."

"But I—"

Just then Molly came back, spooning cookie-dough ice cream from an oversized plastic bowl. She sat down next to me and pulled my arm around her like a cloak.

"What are you guys talking about?" she asked.

"Grown-up stuff."

She gave a put-upon sigh. "You always say that."

I smoothed her hair. "Always?"

"Well, lots of times. I hate it."

There were times I wasn't too fond of *being* a grown-up.

"Was it about Maureen?" she asked after a moment.

"Sort of."

She set the spoon and bowl in her lap. "Did they find her?"

I shook my head. "Not yet."

"But they will, right?"

"I don't know, honey. They're doing everything they can."

"She has to be somewhere," Molly said with inescapable logic.

But was she alive? That was the real question.

CHAPTER 23

"That must be it," Hannah told Carla, pointing through the police car window to a weathered structure on their left. The building was about thirty yards from the road along an overgrown dirt drive. "Looks like a strong wind could knock it over."

Carla slowed the cruiser. "Lucky for us," she said, "it's a calm day."

Hannah detected a hint of sarcasm in the remark. She chose to ignore it. "We should park on the road so we don't disturb whatever evidence there is."

Carla tossed Hannah a disdainful look. "Gee, I'd never have thought of that myself." This time the sarcasm was thick enough to cut with a knife.

While Hannah wavered between *Can't we be friends?* and *Fuck off,* Carla pulled over to the side of the road and parked. From the passenger side, Hannah stepped out into a thicket of foxtails and burrs.

Nice move, Hannah thought. Ten feet ahead, the shoulder was clear.

"You're really good at this," Hannah told her.

"At what?"

"At whatever silly game it is you're playing."

Carla tucked the keys into her pocket and started across the road. "I don't know what you're talking about."

Bullshit, Hannah thought, shielding her eyes from the sun. But she certainly wasn't going to beg Carla for her friendship. Hannah wasn't even sure she liked the woman.

"Any idea what's up ahead?" There'd been a "no outlet" sign at the entrance, but Hannah knew it could be miles before the road ended.

"There's an old quarry up there," Carla told her. "It hasn't been used for years. I don't think there's much else."

"We'll take a look when we're finished here."

They stepped over strands of fallen barbed wire and followed the dirt drive toward the barn. Hannah's eyes caught a pattern of tire tracks in the dust. "These look recent," she said.

Carla nodded. "Just one set though. If they're Sam's, I wonder where the kidnappers parked?'

In her head, Hannah could hear Dallas taunting, *What kidnappers? It's just a story to send us on a wild-goose chase.* "Let's check inside."

The wide wooden door opened easily. The interior was dim despite the narrow rays of sunlight filtering through gaps in the roof and siding. Hannah pulled out her flashlight and made a sweep of the perimeter. The layout was what Sam had described. Except for some old machinery parts in the far corner, the place was empty. She turned the light to the hard-packed dirt floor. There were scuff marks and drag marks and occasional shoe treads. Impossible to tell how long they'd been there.

"You take the right," Hannah said. "I'll start on the left. Let's work in a vertical pattern, up and down, toward the center. We're looking for anything that might connect to the kidnappers."

She braced herself for a caustic comeback, but Carla

merely took out her own flashlight and moved to her side of the barn.

For several minutes, they worked without speaking. Hannah bagged a few pieces of debris—a cellophane wrapper of some sort, a penny, a film canister—but nothing that looked like it had been dropped in the last twenty-four hours.

"Come take a look at this," Carla called.

Hannah took the long way around the perimeter so as not to disturb Carla's search area. "What is it?"

"An opening to the outside. The boards are loose, just kind of lying against the wall. If you move them to the side like this"—Carla repositioned the siding panels—"you've got a rear exit."

It was narrow but large enough to allow access.

Hannah stepped through into the daylight. Carla followed. The barn was on a knoll, sloping down at the rear toward a family of gnarled oaks. Hannah scrutinized the ground. The brown grass was bent in places, but she couldn't be sure that human tromping was the cause.

"Let's see what's down there."

They started down the gentle incline. Where it leveled off at the bottom, they came to a dry creek bed and beyond that a rutted path.

Carla forged ahead down the path, nimble and sure-footed. "There's a dirt road up ahead," she called out. "Looks like a firebreak."

Hannah followed. Up close, she could see a pattern of overlapping tread marks in the soil.

"Off-roading," Carla announced. "Mostly motorcycles, I bet, but the road's wide enough that any vehicle with decent clearance, four-wheel drive, all-terrain tires, and skid plate could handle it."

"Skid plate?" Hannah asked. "How do you know all this stuff?"

"My kid brother is a big devotee."

Kid brother. This was the first remotely personal remark Hannah could remember Carla making. "Are there just the two of you?" she asked.

Carla shook her head. "There are three of us." But she didn't elaborate, and her tone didn't invite further inquiry.

Hannah turned to look back the way they'd come. "Relatively easy access to the barn."

"Yeah." Carla didn't seem much impressed. "I doubt this old fire road connects with El Dorado Avenue anywhere near where Sam was parked though. If the kidnapper took this way out, Sam wouldn't have seen him."

"No, probably not." But finding both a fire road and the obscured entrance at the rear of the barn raised questions in Hannah's mind. "You ready to head back?"

Carla nodded and once again took off in the lead, her long braid swishing rhythmically across her back with each step.

Hannah's mind was on Maureen Russell and the fast-approaching deadline for her ransom when something shiny in the dried grass caught her eye. She bent down to look more closely.

"What is it?" Carla asked.

"Looks like a decorative button. It's probably nothing, but let's bag it just in case. Doesn't appear to have been sitting out in the elements for very long." Hannah poked at the button with the tip of her pen. It was silver in color and stamped with some sort of geometric design. She slipped it into an evidence bag then passed it to Carla for inspection.

"It's not a button," Carla said. "It's more like a zipper pull from a jacket or purse."

Hannah looked more closely. "Or a gym bag, given the size of it." She labeled the bag and added it to her satchel.

Back at the car, Hannah waited until Carla pulled forward and out of the thick weeds before climbing in. They headed up the road toward the quarry.

Hannah surveyed the countryside, appreciating the bucolic setting and open vistas. "It's lovely out here."

"Won't be long before some developer turns it into cul-de-sacs with tiny lots and huge houses."

Hannah feared she was right. Even in the short time she'd been in Monte Vista, she'd seen gentle, rolling hills bulldozed to make room for so-called progress.

"Before you know it, we'll be just like Los Angeles." Carla's words carried such venom, Hannah was sure they were meant to be personal. As if Hannah had single-handedly brought the evils of Los Angeles with her to Monte Vista.

"Did you grow up here?" Hannah asked, determined to be pleasant.

"Santa Rosa."

"So what brought you here?"

"A job." There was that tone again. "Isn't that why you're here?"

"Pretty much." But Hannah knew that in her case, and maybe Carla's too, it was more complicated than that. She'd wanted out of Los Angeles, and she'd grabbed the first thing that came along. To say she'd been drawn to Monte Vista because of the job was misleading at best. Hannah simply didn't think she could handle the memories—sweet or bitter—that LA kindled. And she knew she didn't want to live anywhere near Claire. Ever again.

The job wasn't turning out the way she'd hoped though. She and Dallas were like oil and water, and it was becoming increasingly clear that the only other woman on the force resented her. Hannah had earned the wrath of a segment of LAPD by speaking out about the misconduct she'd witnessed—officers who felt the badge exempted them from following the law—but she'd also had friends on the force. Here she felt so isolated she might as well be a Martian.

"Must be quite a change coming from Los Angeles," Carla said.

"That was the plan." It was Hannah's standard response, one she hoped straddled the truth in such a way that she didn't have to elaborate.

They came to the end of the road and the abandoned quarry. Half the hillside had been cut away, exposing raw dirt and rock in place of rolling grassland. Hannah's hand brushed her chest. It was, Hannah thought, a scar not unlike the ugly slash of purple where her left breast had been.

"Guess nobody uses this place anymore," she said.

"Except kids who want a quiet place to drink and neck."

"One of the few good things about getting older."

Carla laughed. "Yeah, but it was sure fun at the time."

Fun wasn't a word Hannah would have used about her own memories. Insecurity, anguish, and heartache were more like it. But it was nice to hear Carla laugh for a change.

"Let's see if we can find where the fire road connects to the main road," Hannah suggested.

They turned and headed back past the barn and turned onto El Dorado.

"How is it partnering with Dallas?" Carla asked casually.

Hannah appreciated the friendly overture—it had been a long time coming—but she didn't want to bad-mouth Dallas, so she had to skirt the truth.

She shrugged. "We're doing okay."

"Meaning?"

"Meaning we have different takes on things, different approaches, but it works." *Most of the time,* she added silently.

Carla nodded. "Dallas is one of the best."

Hannah looked to see if she was joking, but Carla appeared serious. She also appeared to redden slightly. *So that's it,* Hannah thought. Carla harbored feelings for Dallas. She wondered if Dallas knew.

Monte Vista's "best" was waiting for Hannah when she returned to the station. He was on the phone at his desk, but he held up a hand and waved Hannah over.

"I appreciate it," he said into the phone. "Thanks again,"

and he hung up. He tore the wrapper off a Snickers bar and tossed it in the wastebasket.

"You've got something?" Hannah asked.

"Zippo so far on the licenses." He swallowed a bite of Snickers. "A seventy-year-old man, a couple of families, some dyke who raises wolfhounds . . ."

"She told you that?"

"Hell, yes. She's got a special kennel for them, better than my first apartment."

"I mean about being a lesbian."

Dallas smirked. "You can tell." He polished off the last bite of candy and wiped his hands on his pant legs. "But I've got two more to go. And I've just learned that one of them, Mitchell King, has a record."

Hannah felt a spark of excitement. "For what?"

Dallas smiled. "Sexual assault."

The Department of Motor Vehicle records showed Mitchell King as thirty-six years old and single. He was listed at six-two and two hundred eighty pounds. The man who answered the door was frail, balding, and close to seventy.

"We're looking for Mitchell King," Dallas said.

"You found him," the man said with a laugh.

Hannah and Dallas exchanged glances. "Do you own a dark blue Explorer?"

"Ah, you must be looking for my son. He's Mitchell King too. He drives an Explorer."

Hannah could never understand why parents did this to their children. She remembered once in high school working up her courage to call a boy at home, only to end up mistakenly talking to his father. She'd been so humiliated, she'd avoided the boy the rest of the semester.

"Is your son around?" Dallas asked.

"Afraid not."

"When will he be back?"

"Not for a month or so. He's in South Carolina, spending some time with his sister. What's this about?"

"We're looking for witnesses to an accident that happened last night. We have reason to believe a car like your son's might have been in the area."

King shook his head. "Couldn'ta been Mitch. He's been with his sister since February. He's helping them remodel their house."

"And the Explorer?" Hannah asked.

"It's in South Carolina too. He drove there."

"Can you give us a number where we can reach him?"

"Sure." Mitchell King gave them both his daughter's home number and his son's cell.

When they returned to the car, Dallas hit his hand against the steering wheel. "Well, that was a waste."

"Assuming the old man is telling the truth." Hannah's gut reaction was that he was, but they'd follow up on it just to be sure. "We've still got one more to check, right?"

"Sandra Martin. I don't think she's going to be our kidnapper." Dallas handed Hannah a sheet of paper. "There's the address and DMV information."

Sandra Martin was a forty-four-year-old hazel-eyed blonde who lived in a nice part of town. Hannah didn't hold out a lot of hope either.

Their knock was answered by a girl who looked to be about fourteen. She was wearing short shorts and a skimpy T-shirt that stopped short of her midriff. A fat white cat was cradled in her arms. The sounds of a cartoon program emanated from somewhere inside the house.

"Is your mom home?" Hannah asked.

"She's busy." The girl spoke with a faint British accent.

"We're with the police," Dallas said. "We need to speak to her."

The girl's eyes widened. She backed away a few steps then yelled, "Mum, it's the cops."

Seconds later a woman appeared behind the girl. She had a bandana over her head and her clothes were spattered with paint. "What is it?"

"Sandra Martin?" Hannah said.

"Yes."

"You drive a dark blue Ford Explorer?"

She nodded, hesitant. "Why?"

"We're investigating an accident that happened yesterday. We've reason to believe a vehicle similar to yours may have been in the area and witnessed the event."

"Yesterday? Where?"

"Along El Dorado Avenue."

She frowned. "I don't think I was . . ." She glanced at her daughter. "What did we do Saturday? We were shopping for shoes, weren't we?"

"The accident was at night," Hannah said. "Around nine."

The woman shook her head. "I'm sorry, it wasn't me. I went to a movie with a friend. She drove."

"What's the friend's name?" Dallas asked.

"Janet. Janet Langley."

"Where can we reach her?" Dallas wrote down the address and phone number.

"Does anyone else drive your car?" Hannah asked. The girl with the cat didn't look old enough, but Hannah had trouble judging. She'd seen fourteen-year-olds who looked to be twenty-one, and twenty-year-olds who could pass for twelve.

"No, my daughters are both too young, and my ex-husband lives in London."

Out of habit, Hannah gave her a card, noting that the woman's hand, like her clothes, was smeared with blue paint. "Looks like we got you in the middle of a project."

"One I'm beginning to think I never should have started.

But two walls are done, so there's no turning back. Not unless I want half-blue, half-beige."

Hannah smiled. "Good luck with it." She thought of the wall in her own bedroom with the collage of paint samples she'd tried. She understood the part about no turning back.

"That's it for the cars registered locally?" Hannah asked as they left.

"Yeah."

"Guess we need to broaden the search."

"Or forget it."

"Why would we do that? If we can identify the kidnappers before the second drop, we should do it."

"You really think some guy from out of town came all the way to Monte Vista to demand ransom money from Sam Russell?" Dallas shook his head in disbelief. "There are a lot of people with more money he could target."

"Unless it's personal. Some guy who's got it in for Sam and considers this payback."

"I still don't buy it."

"You should have heard him last night, Dallas. He was distraught."

Dallas huffed. "So? He knew we were on to him, and he was scared. He may have been drunk on top of it."

Hannah couldn't say if he'd been drinking, but Sam hadn't been drunk. Of that, she was certain. "There's a fire road that runs behind the barn," Hannah told him. "Carla and I discovered it when we were out there today. And some loose boards at the back that could make for a rear exit."

Dallas looked at her like she was crazy. "Are you suggesting the kidnappers used the fire road?"

"Not suggesting, just noting the possibility."

"Does it connect with the main road anywhere near where Sam was?"

Hannah shook her head.

"Then why would Sam tell us about the car?"

"I don't know."

Dallas let the silence stretch. "I don't understand why you want to be a cop, Hannah. You're afraid to believe the worst about people."

Hannah tried hard to be a good cop. But this wasn't the first time she'd been accused of being on the wrong side. "I am not. I just don't want to rush to a judgment that may be wrong."

Dallas regarded her critically. "We're a long way from rushing."

CHAPTER 24

May was a wonderful month in Boston. A flower-filled interlude between the cruel cold of winter and the sticky heat of summer. People emerged from the grumpiness of short, dark days and began smiling again, nodding to their neighbors, wishing them well. They were kinder, happier, more gregarious. The air buzzed with an energy that the bleak blanket of snow and ice all but smothered. Frank Donahue felt the difference himself.

That he was tilting at windmills by looking into a murder case the system had already chewed up and spit out didn't dampen the bounce in his step. In fact, being back on the job gave his spirits an added boost. Not that he was actually back on the job. He wasn't about to delude himself about that. He was a washed-up has-been of a detective who was still trying to feel important. Frank had seen it happen to other guys who retired. And he hadn't been above making a nasty crack or two at their expense. Now here he was, following in their footsteps.

Frank wasn't actually sure why he'd agreed to poke around Lisa Russell's murder again. Probably because it rankled him that his last big case had ended so badly. And maybe, on some level, he felt he owed it to the Pattersons. He'd been clear with them though that the odds were one in a million he'd ever find evidence to warrant a retrial, even if the DA were willing. The odds of him finding something that could help the Monte Vista police get Sam for his second wife's murder were almost as bad. But there was always that slim chance he'd come up with something.

He'd read through the case file—just obtaining permission and getting the thing released from storage had been a hurdle—and the trial transcript, but there was nothing that jumped out at him. Nothing he could use as leverage for getting the case against Sam reopened. And nothing that linked Lisa Russell's murder to the disappearance of Maureen Russell. Except Sam, of course.

All these years later, Frank still thought the case against Sam had been a good one. Sure, the defense had pointed out discrepancies and expounded an alternative-killer theory— that was what defense attorneys did—but Frank had trouble seeing how the arguments could have been persuasive.

All it took was one juror though, and Sam's attorney had managed to reach that one. Eleven of the jurors had decided the prosecution's version of events was correct. The hold-out—Eugene Titmus—had given the defense theory more credence. Frank wondered which aspect of the defense case Titmus had found most convincing.

Lacking anything else to work with, Frank had decided to speak with Titmus. He lived in Somerville now rather than Boston, but he'd agreed to meet Frank at a local coffee shop during his morning break.

Titmus was a UPS driver, and Frank spotted him immediately upon entering the shop because of the uniform. The man was slender, bony really, with a large Adam's apple, pointed chin, and thin mouth. He looked all of about twenty.

"Eugene?"

"You must be Detective Donahue."

"Retired," Frank said. "And call me Frank." He slid into

the booth and ordered coffee. Black. Then, spying Titmus's two donuts, ordered one for himself. Millie would never know.

"So, what can I help you with Detect—Frank? The trial was a long time ago."

Though his doctor disapproved, Frank had attended much of the trial. But he had focused on the witnesses, not the jury. He tried to remember where Titmus had been seated in the jury box and couldn't.

"I'm looking over past cases, trying to see what we can learn from those that don't end in conviction." It was a plausible explanation, and one Frank hoped wouldn't put Titmus on the defensive.

"Must be hard for you guys to see your hard work go down the tubes," Titmus said. There was no hostility in his tone but not much sympathy either.

"It's the system." Frank took a bite of donut. *Ah, heaven.* "Mind if I ask you how old you are?"

"Twenty-five next month."

"So you were, what, eighteen at the time of trial?"

"Yeah, my first call to jury duty, and I get picked. I couldn't believe it."

"How was it?"

Titmus shrugged. "I wasn't working then, so it wasn't a problem."

"Were you in school?"

"Nah, I never went beyond high school. But I was living at home still, trying to figure out what came next. Timing couldn't have been better from my perspective."

Frank knew that eighteen-year-olds fought in wars and gave their lives for the country, so he wasn't sure why jurors that age gave him pause, but they did. "So, what convinced you Sam Russell wasn't guilty?"

"Oh, I wasn't convinced he wasn't. But I wasn't convinced he was either. That homeless guy was pretty sure it was Russell he talked to that afternoon."

The homeless man, Ajar Mobje, was the only witness who corroborated Sam's story about biking the day Lisa disappeared. He'd been walking along the path near Concord where Sam was biking and had stopped to talk to Sam while he adjusted a gear on his bike. It was a short exchange of maybe thirty seconds, but Mobje had been sure it was Sam he talked to.

"The other jurors didn't pay much attention because the guy was a bum and foreigner," Titmus said. "His English was pretty bad. They figured he didn't really know what he was talking about."

"But you found him credible?" As Frank recalled, the man hadn't made a particularly strong witness. He'd done fine when questioned by the defense attorney, but the prosecutor had rattled him to the point where he admitted he could be mistaken.

Titmus crammed a quarter of a donut into his mouth and chewed it before answering. "He could describe the shoes Russell was wearing that day. Besides, why would he lie?"

"It didn't have to be a lie. He might just have been mistaken. And a lot of bikers wear biking shoes."

Titmus shrugged.

"Was that the only thing that raised doubt in your mind?" Frank asked. He took another bite of his own donut but didn't enjoy it as much as the first. He started thinking of how angry Millie would be if she knew. She worked so hard to keep him healthy. He pushed the rest away. He realized he ought to be worried for himself and not because his wife would be angry.

"No, there was a bunch of other stuff."

"Such as?"

"Well, there was that neighbor who'd seen a strange car parked near the house in the days before Lisa Russell disappeared."

Hardly anything out of the ordinary, Frank thought.

"And there were the two soda cans in the Russells' trash. One of them had prints that couldn't be identified."

"She might have drunk them both herself," Frank pointed out, though it hardly mattered at this point. "And the unidentified prints could have come from anywhere. Grocery clerks, customers, people not connected with the murder."

"Yeah, but her having a visitor makes more sense. And given the kind of woman she was . . ."

Frank frowned. "What do you mean?"

"You know, flirty, the kind that likes to flaunt her stuff."

"Where'd you get that impression?" Frank remembered testimony that Lisa Russell was friendly and outgoing, but nothing that indicated she was a tease. Had he missed something?

Titmus gave another shrug. "You can tell. Women who answer the door wearing practically nothing at all or come on to workmen. I'm not saying they deserve to die, but they take risks with that kind of behavior."

Frank frowned. "Has that happened to you?"

"Me?" Titmus looked embarrassed. "Whoa, that's a good one."

"That's a no?"

"I'm not the type."

Had Titmus's own insecurities colored his perceptions of Lisa Russell? Frank tried to remember the exact testimony from the trial, but it merged with what he knew of the victim from his own investigation. Lisa Russell was nothing like what Titmus suggested. Lisa was a devoted mother and wife and a trusted friend to all who knew her.

"So you think it was someone she flirted with?" Frank asked. He wondered if he and Titmus could actually have sat through the same trial.

"It's possible, is all. Maybe she got a delivery and invited the guy in for a soda. Things went from there. Even the missing ring sounds more like something a stranger would do than her husband. The husband would know people would be watching him. And an unusual ring like hers, an heirloom, it would be pretty distinctive. He'd have a heck of a time pawning it."

"That came out at trial? That it was an unusual design?" Frank was familiar with the ring from the investigation—it had been Lisa's grandmother's—but he remembered thinking the prosecution hadn't made much of it at trial.

"Must have." Titmus polished off his second donut. "I need to be getting back to work."

"Yeah, thanks for your time."

"Sure. Glad to help."

Good God, Frank thought. This . . . this kid had built a whole fantasy scenario about another killer, pulling interpretations about Lisa's character from thin air and mixing them with selected bits of testimony.

And it had been enough to let Sam walk.

CHAPTER 25

Not long after Molly and I arrived home from my dad's, Hannah Montgomery knocked on the door. It crossed my mind that she might have been following me, but I dismissed the notion as being overly paranoid.

"Did Officer Murphy get the phone tap set up?" she asked.

"First thing this morning."

"Good." She shielded her eyes from the sun and waited a beat. "Can I come in?"

I didn't see the point, but I could hardly refuse. I opened the door wider and stepped back. "I thought you guys were worried the kidnappers might be watching the house."

She nodded. "But we're also looking for a missing woman. If I suddenly *stopped* coming by the house, it might raise suspicion too."

"So that's why you're here? To make an appearance?"

"Sounds like you'd rather I wasn't." The detective brushed the hair from her face. She looked tired, but even tired she looked good. She had a nice smile: warm, friendly, forthright.

I shrugged. "What do you think?"

"I think you're understandably nervous."

Nervous was an understatement. But I knew I was acting like a jerk. "You want coffee or something, Detective?"

"It's Hannah. And a glass of water would be nice." She followed me into the kitchen. "How are you feeling?"

"Rotten, why?"

"You seemed pretty down last night."

It was a stupid comment, so I ignored it.

"The worry and waiting have got to be hard on you."

I handed her a glass of tap water. Normally, I would have asked about ice, but I couldn't muster the energy to care. Besides, a part of me blamed the detective for being at the bar last night when I was feeling vulnerable. There was no logic to it, but there it was. If she hadn't been there, I'd never have involved the police.

"I shouldn't have told you about the ransom call," I said. "The kidnapper specifically told me not to involve the cops."

She perched on a stool at the island counter and leveled her gaze at me. Her eyes were an unusual shade of green, almost emerald. It was the eyes that had gotten me in trouble last night, I decided. No way in hell would I have spilled my guts to Dallas.

She took a sip of water. "You think kidnappers ever say, 'Oh, and be sure to tell the cops'?"

"Funny."

"Let me tell you about a kidnapping case I worked in LA."

At least Murphy had been telling me the truth; she had experience with kidnappings. But I was in no mood to be mollified. "Why? So you can impress me with your superior knowledge?"

"It involved a young girl," she continued, as though I hadn't spoken. "Nine years old. She disappeared from in front of her house in a quiet, friendly neighborhood. The parents did everything the kidnappers said, including not involving us. They paid the ransom, which was sizable. They followed the instructions to the letter."

My throat constricted. Given her reason for recounting the story, there was only one possible outcome.

"Their daughter wasn't at the playground where the kidnappers told them she would be waiting after they picked up the ransom money. They never heard another word from the kidnappers, and they never saw their daughter alive. Some hikers found her body two months later in the canyons above Malibu."

"So it's a no-win situation? Damned if you tell the authorities, damned if you don't?"

Her expression was pained, like it had just dawned on her that instead of making me feel better, she'd made me feel worse. "All I meant was, telling the police is the right way to handle it. I could tell you about cases where we got the victims back alive."

"This isn't going to be one of them."

Her eyes narrowed, no longer friendly. "Why do you say that?"

"I just feel it, is all."

She seemed to be considering my answer. For all she knew, I'd already killed Maureen. For a moment, I'd forgotten I was still their number-one suspect.

"When they call," she said finally, "remember to ask for proof that Maureen is alive."

"Right, alive." No matter what Maureen's condition, I reminded myself, alive was better than dead.

"We'll have someone here with you and a team in the field. You'll have lots of support."

"What if they see you?"

"They won't." She pushed the water glass aside and set out four photographs. "Do any of these look like the vehicle you were following last night?"

They were all SUVs in different makes and models. "It

could have been any of them. It was dark. I wish I'd gotten a better look."

"You remember anything more about the license number?"

"Just what I gave you."

"Anything distinctive about the vehicle?"

I shook my head. "I've been wracking my brain trying to think of something. I should have paid better attention." Another way I'd screwed up. "I take it you haven't had any luck locating it?"

"Not yet. We're narrowing down the possibilities."

"To these four?"

"No. These are file photos from our vehicle-identification portfolio." She hesitated a moment before continuing. "We've pretty much eliminated the local cars that match."

"So you think it was someone out of the area?"

"You're sure the vehicle you saw turned onto El Dorado from Buckey?"

"Positive. I'd been waiting there for just that reason."

She put the photos away. "Your dad and brother—do they know about the ransom call?"

"My dad does. I had to ask him for money. But not Chase."

"Anyone else?"

"No. Except for the mess I made of last night, I've done everything they asked."

The detective tilted her head and looked at me. "How do you and your brother get along?"

"Fine."

"No tensions? Jealousies?"

"Not really."

"Even though you're a doctor and he's running a forklift?"

"He's doing okay." It suddenly dawned on me what she was getting at. I shook my head. "No way. Chase wouldn't do anything like this."

She seemed about ready to ask another question but in-

stead got up and refilled her water glass. The silence between us was broken only by the hum of the refrigerator and
the sharp staccato of a barking dog from outside.

"If the kidnapper contacts you and he's got her," the detective said kindly, "the chances are good we'll find her."

My ill-placed anger with her had faded. She was, after
all, doing everything she could to bring Maureen home
safely. What's more, I sensed her concern was genuine.
Hannah Montgomery was a hard woman not to like. But I
was too distraught to feel encouraged.

"I feel so helpless," I told her.

"You're doing all the right things, Sam."

To my mind, I'd done nothing right, starting with the moment I'd woken in my car with no memory of the previous
evening. Hell, even before that. I could see now that I hadn't
loved Maureen enough. Not in the way she wanted to be
loved. She'd told me once that Dr. Laura always said a loving
husband would swim through shark-infested waters to bring
his wife a lemonade. I'd made a joke of it, but I knew in my
heart what she meant, and I knew that if Lisa had asked me
to do just that, I would have. I think Maureen knew it too.

"I should have been a better husband," I protested. "I
should have made sure she knew how much she meant to
me."

"With luck, you'll still be able to tell her." Hannah placed
her glass in the dishwasher then turned to face me again.
"Regret is normal, you know. It's human. Don't let it get the
better of you."

There was so much she didn't know. Part of me wanted to
tell her, but I couldn't bring myself to do it. "So, what do we
do now?" I asked. "Just wait?"

"I'm afraid so." Her mouth twisted into the barest hint of
a smile. It lit up the soft green eyes. "You can't give up hope,
Sam."

I looked around the kitchen. Maureen's apron hung near
the stove; on the counter next to it rested the cappuccino ma-

chine I'd given her last Christmas. A photo of the two of us looked back at me from a magnetic frame on the front of the fridge. So many joyful memories. But all I felt was despair.

Hope didn't have a chance.

CHAPTER 26

The water was hot, almost scalding, the way Hannah liked it, leaving her skin crimson where the spray drummed against it. She turned her back to the shower and indulged herself for a moment longer before shutting off the faucet and stepping out into the cramped space of the bathroom. She grabbed a towel from the hook near the door and was drying her legs when Josh—the cowboy with the cute butt she'd met a couple of nights back—poked his head into the room. His gaze skimmed her nude body as he handed her the phone.

"Some guy. Says it's important." There was an emphasis on the *says*.

Hannah wrapped herself in the towel, pressed the phone to her ear. "Hi, Dallas."

"How'd you know it was me?"

"Who else would call me on a Saturday evening with something important?"

"You've got a problem, you know that? Your life's too predictable."

That was the least of her problems, Hannah thought. A rivulet of water ran down her neck and into the hollow of her spine. She hoped this call wasn't what she thought it was.

"Have I caught you in the middle of something?" Dallas asked. There was an unmistakable leer in the question.

Hannah glanced at Josh, who was standing in the doorway in his boxers, hair still damp at the ends. He wasn't Malcolm, but he was a step above what she usually dragged home. She'd been looking forward to the rest of the evening.

"We were just winding down," she said, ignoring the protest in Josh's expression.

"Good. We got a report of a body. Female."

Hannah's gut tightened. She had a bad feeling about this. "Maureen Russell?"

"I don't know, I just got the call. But it could be. Caucasian, late twenties, early thirties."

The feeling intensified. "Where?"

"A house out on Eagle Point."

An upscale neighborhood. "Whose house?"

"Guy by the name of Ben Albright," Dallas said. "He's in Europe. A lady friend of his discovered the body. She's staying there for a couple of days while her floors are being redone." There was a burst of static. "I'll pick you up in about ten minutes."

"Give me fifteen, okay?" Time for a touch of makeup—a necessity at her age. And for an apology of sorts to Josh.

Hannah dropped the towel and pulled on her underwear. "I've got to go to work."

"At this hour?"

"I'm afraid so."

He caught her waist as she walked by, pulled her close and nibbled playfully on her ear. "You didn't really think we were winding down, did you?"

She glanced at the rose hues of the western sky, heard the evening song of the crickets outside her window. A six-pack of beer was cooling in the fridge, and Josh's hands were warm against her skin. She knew the night had more to offer.

By way of an answer, she turned and brushed his shoulder lightly with her lips then headed for the closet.

Josh followed. He stood behind her and ran his hands over the contours of her body until she pulled away.

"I did warn you that I might get called out."

He grunted.

"Don't be a spoilsport."

Josh sighed, reached for his own clothes. "They ought to have a support group for guys who get involved with cops."

Involved. As if a few hours of meaningless, though admittedly very good, sex was the same as a relationship.

"You wouldn't get much of a crowd," Hannah told him. She pulled on a pair of tan slacks and the only clean white blouse in her closet. When she discovered a missing bottom button, she vowed anew to spend her next free day getting her wardrobe in order. Tonight she'd just have to make sure the blouse stayed tucked.

Back in the bathroom, she toweled off a spot in the steamy mirror and made a swipe at working magic with lipstick and blush. The hair she couldn't do much about.

Josh watched from the doorway. He slipped an arm into his denim jacket, squinted in her direction. "How do I know this Dallas isn't just some guy who's made you a better offer for the night?"

She grabbed her handbag and gun. "You don't," she told him with a grin.

Dallas was waiting when she got to the street. He handed her a large Styrofoam cup of coffee. She popped the lid and took a sip. It was flavorless but hot.

"So, who's the guy?" he asked, halfway into the next block. "Anyone I know?"

She shook her head.

"Anyone I'm going to know?"

"Probably not."

"Why all the secrecy?"

"It's called privacy, Dallas. Not secrecy."

He tapped a finger against the wheel. "You ever think about finding yourself one that's a keeper?"

"You're hardly one to talk." Dallas dated the way some people sampled chocolates—a quick taste and then on to the next offering. That's the way it seemed to Hannah, at any rate. She hadn't actually heard him mention anyone by name.

The corners of his mouth caught somewhere between a scowl and a smirk. He kept his eyes on the road and said nothing. *The double standard at play,* Hannah thought. *Different rules for men and women.*

"What do we know about cause of death?" she asked after a moment.

"No apparent gunshot wounds—that's all I know. The medical examiner is going to meet us there."

"Who's in charge of securing the scene?"

"Bauer."

Hannah groaned. "We might as well invite the whole town to tramp through."

"Give him a break, Hannah. He tries."

"*Tries?* That's not good enough, and you know it." Or maybe Dallas really didn't know the difference. "You saw what happened with Singer."

"So the evidence wasn't as rock solid as it could have been. The guy still ended up behind bars."

That was the difference between them, she thought. Dallas's world was painted in broad brushstrokes. As long as the picture looked something like a cow, it was good enough. Never mind that it had five legs and wings. Never mind that Singer should have received a life sentence and now would likely be out in seven years because evidence collected from the crime scene had been too tainted to stand up in court.

At least this time there would be no roommates trudging in and out. The damage Bauer could do here was more limited.

* * *

Half a dozen cars occupied the wide circular driveway when they arrived. The medical examiner's van was pulled in at an angle—the only way it could fit, given the crowded conditions. Two black-and-whites were parked on the street. Dallas pulled in behind them.

"Looks like a party," he said.

Hannah had the sinking feeling he was right. Literally. The house was ablaze with lights, and she could hear the soft hum of voices from inside.

Tony Bauer was at the door, speaking into his cell phone. He held up a finger as they approached, then hastily finished his conversation.

"Body's in the wine cellar," he said.

"A real wine cellar?" Dallas asked, sounding impressed.

Bauer nodded. "As big as my dining room."

Hannah eyed the house. It was one of the new, Mediterranean-style minivillas that had begun springing up on the outskirts of town. They were marginally better, she conceded, than the faux French chateaus, which were also quite the rage. All were large to the point of pretentiousness. Not to her taste at all.

"Who's been in there so far?" she inquired.

"The two of us who responded initially, plus Brian Murphy and Carla Adams, who are there now. And Joe Bones. I came out here to call the lieutenant. Can't get a good signal from inside."

Her gaze snapped from the house to Bauer. "What's Joe doing in there?"

Bauer looked at her like she was nuts for asking. "He's the medical examiner."

Joe Bones was his honest-to-God name. He was also staff physician at the Bellhaven Convalescent Hospital, where the patients he ministered to in life one week sometimes wound up on his steel autopsy table the next. Hannah wondered if the disconnect of his two roles didn't bother him at times.

"The detectives go in first," she reminded him. "We run the investigation."

Bauer shrugged. "Joe knows his business."

His business wasn't the same as theirs, however. It was a distinction that seemed lost on Bauer.

"What's with all the cars?" Dallas asked with a sweeping gesture of his arm.

"The friend who's staying here." Bauer checked his notes. "Woman by the name of Season Connell. She had a few friends over for dinner."

Hannah winced at what she knew would be coming. "How many of them have been in the wine cellar?"

"I'm not sure. I isolated them in the kitchen and told them they could go ahead with their dinner but they couldn't leave. Marsh is with them."

"Okay," Dallas said. "Better show us the body."

Bauer led Hannah and Dallas through the front door then down an interior stone stairway that descended from the left side of the foyer.

Carla Adams and Brian Murphy were standing in the hallway on the lower level outside an open door leading to the wine cellar. Hannah immediately felt a draft of refrigerated air. The closer she got, the colder the temperature. It felt more like a meat locker than a wine cellar.

Carla straightened her shirt and tucked a loose strand of hair into the clip at the back of her head. Her preening seemed lost on Dallas, who acknowledged her presence and Murphy's with nothing more than a curt nod.

"What have you got?" Hannah asked.

"No sign of a struggle in the cellar," Murphy replied.

"What about the rest of the house?"

It was Carla who answered. "The guests are upstairs in the kitchen-dining area. The woman who's staying here is using the bedroom to the top left of the stairs. It's a mess— all her stuff, she says. The rest of the house is neat as a pin."

Hannah stepped into the wine cellar. It was maybe twelve feet square, with a stone floor and lined with wine racks and bottles. The air was frigid and damp. Hannah ran her hands over her arms and wished she'd thought to bring a sweater.

"Whew," Dallas said. "This guy must like his wine chilled."

"It *is* colder than you'd expect, isn't it? Let's be sure to check the temperature setting."

Joe Bones was bent over the crumpled form of a woman. She was on her side, propped against the far wall.

"I haven't moved her," he said, turning to address Hannah and Dallas. "Haven't done anything really, except take a first look."

"And?" Dallas asked.

"From the ligature marks on her neck and the presence of petechial hemorrhages in the eyes, I'd say she was strangled." He stood up to give them a better look. "There are stab wounds present on her neck and chest as well though. I won't be able to say for sure what killed her until I get her on the table."

The body was female, fully clothed in cotton slacks, a gauzy blouse, and a boxy linen jacket. Her left foot was bare. On her right foot, she wore the sort of strappy, slingback sandal Hannah found impossibly uncomfortable. Height, build, and coloring were right for Maureen, but Hannah couldn't be certain. Even in the cold cellar, the woman's features had swollen and distorted with death. Her flesh was waxy, her eyes clouded. Hannah bit back the taste of bile. She'd never been good at this part.

"Looks like it could be her, doesn't it?" Dallas said.

Hannah nodded. She turned to Carla. "You find any ID?"

"Nothing. Not even any visible jewelry. I think Dallas is right though. The victim fits Maureen Russell's description."

"How long do you think she's been dead?" Dallas asked Bones.

"Hard to say, especially given the cool temperature."

"More than twenty-four hours?"

Bones nodded. "Definitely more."

Dallas turned to Hannah. "Doesn't exactly work with Sam's tale of a kidnapping, does it?"

She didn't like his tone, but neither did she like the fact that he was probably right. "We don't even know that it's Maureen Russell," she pointed out.

"Well, the sooner I get her out of here," Bones said, "the sooner I can get some answers. Do what you need to do and let me know when I can move her."

Hannah kneeled and forced herself to take a closer look at the woman. Bones had already bagged her hands to preserve trace evidence, but he'd assured them he'd left the body otherwise as she'd been found. Despite the wounds to the woman's chest and neck, there was relatively little blood. There was also dried blood near her temple and some scratches on her right arm.

"Did you check her pockets for identification?" Hannah asked Carla.

"Only the one I could reach without disturbing the body."

Hannah reached a gloved hand under the woman from the front and felt a scrap of paper in the obscured jacket pocket. She eased it out. Some kind of flyer on cheap yellow bond. A printed recipe for low-fat lasagna. On the back, someone had scribbled in pen:

233—160B

Dallas had been poking around the perimeter of the room. Now he peered over her shoulder. "What is it?"

"I'm not sure. Could be an identification code, a password, maybe a room number." She placed the paper in an evidence bag, though she wasn't sure how useful it would be.

Hannah lifted the woman's hair from her neck and noticed a purplish bruising along the back of her shoulders. "Lividity in the upper torso," she said.

Bones nodded. "Looks like the body was moved. Killed elsewhere and dumped here would be my guess."

Only not dumped in the usual sense, Hannah thought. If the killer had simply wanted to dispose of the body, there were many more-accessible places to choose from.

She stood up, feeling the strain in her back as she did. She'd gotten lazy about exercise, and it showed.

"Where's the photographer?" Dallas asked.

"Should be here any minute now," said Bauer.

Dallas bent down and, with a pair of tweezers, held up a piece of latex. Hannah first thought it might be a condom, but the shape was wrong.

"Looks like it might have come from a glove," Dallas said. He looked to Bauer. "Let's bag it."

Hannah turned her attention from the body. It wasn't going anywhere until they gave the word. The crime scene, on the other hand, was altered with every person who stepped near it. She pulled out her notebook and began recording her observations and impressions. If experience held, she'd end up ignoring most of it, but there was no telling which small detail might jog her memory or trigger a key thought later in the investigation.

She noted the placement of the body, the smooth cement floor, the walls lined with row after row of what she could only assume was premium wine. Not a lot of places for the killer to leave prints, even if he hadn't been wearing gloves. As crime scenes went, this one was practically antiseptic.

Hannah could only hope the forensics team would turn up something. But if the victim had been killed elsewhere, the odds of that were slim.

"Seen enough?" Dallas asked.

Hannah nodded, and they pulled back into the hallway. "I wonder what happened to her shoe."

"Maybe Sam's got a foot fetish."

Hannah glowered at him. "You're ready to pin this on him already?"

"It's pretty obvious, isn't it?"

"We don't even know the identity of the victim."

At the far end from the stairs they'd come down, there were two doors. "Where do those go?" she asked Carla.

"The one to the left is storage. The door to the right leads outside to the carport."

"Anyone dusted for prints yet?"

"Not yet, but we will."

Using a clean handkerchief, Hannah opened the door, revealing a wide, covered space that could hold three vehicles. There was a sports car parked in the far stall; the other two were vacant.

"Whose car is that?" she asked.

"Belongs to the guy who owns the house."

Hannah could see why the guests had chosen to park in the circular driveway. It was close to the front door, and it avoided having to climb stairs. She was thinking how inconvenient it would be to have to haul groceries in this back way.

As she turned to head into the house, she noted a tread mark on the concrete step by the door. A man's boot from the looks of it, and fairly fresh. She told Carla to be sure they got a photograph and measurements. Then she went back inside to find Dallas.

"Come on, let's go up and talk to Season Connell and her guests."

CHAPTER 27

Hannah followed Dallas upstairs, where they found six subdued diners gathered in the kitchen, sipping wine. The meal, which smelled divine, was still on the stove. One of the men, tall and rail thin, had spooned what looked like chicken breast with mushrooms and wine sauce onto a plate and was busily shoveling it in while the others seemed to have lost their interest in food.

The uniformed officer, Harry Marsh, stood at the door leading to the dining room, his hands near his weapon, as though the guests might be about to flee the scene. Marsh took his job seriously; Hannah gave him credit for that.

"None of them have left the kitchen in the time I've been here," Marsh said.

Hannah nodded. "Thanks. We'll take over here now. They might need you downstairs."

A heavyset redhead in a purple silk pantsuit stepped forward and introduced herself as Season, the hostess of the evening. "We decided to skip dinner," she explained. "But, given what's happened, we can clearly use the wine."

There was a murmur of agreement from the others and a shift of eyes toward the man with the plate of chicken.

"Hey, it's not that I'm callous," he protested. "Just hungry. I haven't eaten all day, and this stuff is too good to waste."

Season gestured to the wine and addressed the detectives. "Would you like a glass? Or maybe some coq au vin?"

"We're fine," Hannah said before Dallas had a chance to answer differently, "but thanks." She eyed the kitchen, which looked like a cook's dream. Two sinks, a big center island, granite countertops, professional Wolf range. "What's your relation to the owner of the house?"

"Ben and I have been friends for years," Season said. Her dangly silver earrings clinked melodically with each movement of her head. They reminded Hannah of fishing lures. "In fact, I sold him this house."

"It was yours?" Dallas asked.

Season shook her head, setting off an accompanying jangle from the earrings. "No, I'm in real estate."

"And what does Ben do?"

"He's a doctor. Anesthesiology. But his real passion is food and wine. It's a passion we share, only I'm not lucky enough to have a kitchen like this. Or a wine cellar like his." She grimaced. No doubt finding a body there had dulled her envy somewhat. "That's why he lets me use his place sometimes when he's away."

"Where is he?" Dallas asked.

"Italy. He's been gone two weeks already."

"When's he due back?"

"Next Friday." Season frowned. "I guess I should call him and tell him about this, shouldn't I? It's going to put a damper on his vacation."

Hannah pulled out her notebook. "It'll be better if we talk to him first. Do you have a number when he can be reached?"

While Season rummaged through the papers near the phone, a bearded man refilled everyone's wine glass. Hannah took the printout Season handed her and copied the relevant part of Ben Albright's itinerary.

"Tell us about discovering the body," she said, handing the paper back to Season.

"We went down to get wine."

"We?"

"Don and I." She pointed to the man who'd been pouring wine. "We spotted her right away. At first we weren't sure she was dead, though once we got a closer look, we could tell."

Don spoke up. "I felt for a pulse just to be sure. Then we called 911."

"Did you touch anything else? Take anything?"

"Of course not," Season huffed.

"So you left the cellar and didn't go back?"

"We went back later for wine," Don explained.

"You and Season?"

"Charlie and I." He gestured to the man who'd been eating.

"I wasn't going back into that cellar for anything," Season said, with a shiver. "One go-around with a dead body is enough for me."

A cell phone rang. One of the other women reached into her purse, checked the number, and then turned off the phone. "Do you need the rest of us to stay?"

"Were you in the wine cellar?"

"We all went to have a look," she replied, looking a little embarrassed. "But that's all."

Hannah groaned. Half a dozen additional people tromping through what little evidence there might be.

"Are any of you besides Season friends with the owner?" Dallas asked.

"I've met him," Don said. "Season brought me to one of his parties here. But can't say that I know him beyond that."

Dallas looked to the others, who shook their heads.

"Give us your names and contact information," Dallas said. "And then the others of you can go if you want."

While Dallas took down the information, Hannah resumed her questioning of Season. "You said Ben Albright has been gone two weeks. How long have you been here?"

"Just a couple of days. I'm staying here while the floors at my place are being refinished."

"Was this the first time you'd been to the wine cellar?"

"Right. Ben told me I could. Told me which section I could take bottles from and which I couldn't."

As if Hannah was there to investigate a stolen bottle of wine. "So you have no idea how long the body has been there?"

Season shook her head, looking a little green around the gills. "It's creepy to think I was walking around here, sleeping and eating, and all the while there was a dead body down there." Then another thought seemed to hit her. "The woman wasn't like . . . like being held prisoner there, was she?"

Hannah didn't think so, but she had to be careful what she said. "We're looking into everything."

Season reached for her wine glass and took a large swallow. "Sorry, I don't do well with stuff like this."

"Did anything seem off about the house during your stay?" Hannah asked. "Any sign of a break-in? Any indication that someone besides you had been here?"

Season shook her head. "I'm out during the day. But everything looked in order when I returned."

"How about today?"

She turned to Don. "You helped me carry the groceries in this afternoon. Did you notice anything unusual?"

"No, but I wasn't looking either."

Dallas had finished with the other guests and now rejoined the questioning. "Tell us about Ben Albright. Is he married?"

"Divorced. It's been a number of years. His ex-wife has remarried, I believe. She lives in Portland."

"Kids?"

"Two girls, both in college now. They lived with their mother growing up."

"But they might have a key to Ben's house," Hannah noted.

"I wouldn't know about that," Season said.

"You had a key?"

"Right. I've had one since he moved here. I sometimes come over and check the place when he's out of town for an extended period."

"Who else has a key?"

"His cleaning lady, I imagine. He told me not to worry about leaving everything spic and span because she'd be coming in to clean before he got home."

Charlie had picked up his plate again and was looking longingly at the food. "We going to be much longer?" he asked.

Hannah looked at Dallas. "I think we're about finished for now," she said. "Go ahead with your meal."

Season glared at him. "Honestly, Charlie, I don't see how you can even think of food right now."

Charlie winked at her. "It's your cooking, babe. It's irresistible."

Season turned to Hannah with a look of alarm. "You all, the cops I mean, you'll take the body tonight, won't you?"

"I imagine it's already out of there. If not, it will be soon."

"And do you . . . you know, clean up afterward?"

Dallas snorted.

"There's not much to clean up," Hannah said. "But I can give you the number of a place that specializes in crime-scene cleanup, if you'd like."

"There's such a specialty?" Season looked disgusted, but she took the number. "No way could I walk on that floor without having it cleaned."

The body hadn't, Hannah noted, kept her from drinking the wine.

* * *

"Do you suppose this Ben Albright had anything to do with it?" Dallas asked Hannah later when they were in the car.

"If the body is really Maureen Russell, he's been gone since before she disappeared."

"What about Season?"

"If she's a killer," Hannah said, "she's an awfully good actress. But it's worth looking into. We should also follow up on the ex-wife and daughters. Maybe one of them harbors a grudge against Albright."

"What's their connection with Maureen Russell though? Assuming she's our victim."

As Dallas approached the curve without hitting the brake, Hannah braced herself for a sharp turn. "It doesn't make a lot of sense, does it? But the killer had to have had a reason for dumping the body there. And it had to be someone who knew Albright was away."

Dallas nodded. "Sam would know. The medical community isn't that large."

"So would half the hospital staff, as well as neighbors, friends of the cleaning woman, and God knows who else."

"But none of them had reason to kill Maureen Russell."

"And Sam did?" Hannah couldn't keep the irritation from her voice.

"You said it yourself, Hannah. The killer had to have had a reason for dumping the body where he did. It wasn't a random thing."

"So?"

"Think about it. Why would he choose a wine cellar?" Dallas didn't wait for her to answer. "Because it's cool, right?"

"That's one reason." The cellar had been unusually cool, in fact.

"And a cool temperature will slow the process of decay." She nodded.

"Now ask yourself why someone might want to do that."
Dallas didn't wait for her to respond. "It makes perfect sense
if he wants to confuse us about time of death."

"Maybe the killer just didn't want the body to smell until
he figured out what to do with it."

"They go hand in hand, Hannah. Sam wanted us to think
she was killed after the ransom call. He was probably planning on moving the body in another day or two outside in the
elements. This whole kidnap thing is a ploy. You've got to
see that. As soon as it's clear we're looking at him as a potential suspect, he comes up with the kidnap story."

"But he didn't know he was going to run into me at a
bar," Hannah protested. "And I didn't get the feeling he'd
planned on telling me about the kidnapping."

"Maybe the timing was fortuitous. But Sam's been saying
all along that she was dead, don't forget." Dallas hit the brakes
for a stop sign. "You've got to admit that Sam looks good for
it."

Hannah silently conceded that he did, and she couldn't
figure out why that bothered her. "First things first," she said.
"We need to ID the body."

"We'll have Sam take a look. And if it's Maureen Russell,
we're guaranteed of getting our search warrant."

CHAPTER 28

Maureen was dead. Murdered. Another woman I'd loved, gone. My body was numb, but inside the pain was so raw it took my breath away.

Rain from a rare late-spring storm pounded the kitchen window. The wind whipped branches, and thunder sounded in the distance. Aptly bleak weather for my bleak mood.

The rain would pass. Maureen would be dead forever.

"You going to be okay, Sam?" My father stood behind my chair, one hand resting lovingly on my shoulder.

With my head buried in my hands, a minimal shrug was all I could muster. Besides, I wasn't sure how to answer.

For the moment, I was managing. Barely.

But when I looked beyond the present, either forward or back, I was so overwhelmed with despair I thought surely it would rip me in two.

Maureen was dead.

I'd known when Dallas and Hannah Montgomery showed up at my door shortly after ten last night. Before they said a word, I knew in my gut what they'd come for. Even when they said they weren't sure and needed me to identify her, I knew.

I'd accompanied them to the cool, dark basement of the morgue to make a formal identification. I rode in the backseat, fighting tears and nausea and praying for a miracle. Just as I had when I'd gone to identify Lisa's body a lifetime ago.

"Do you want to take a moment to prepare yourself?" Hannah asked before the coroner's assistant pulled open the drawer.

How could you possibly prepare for something like this? There was no way I'd ever be ready. I shook my head. The sooner I got it over with, the better.

The assistant wheeled a gurney out of storage, and Dallas pulled back the sheet to reveal her head.

There's nothing that brings home the harsh reality of death like standing next to the bloated, battered, and partially decomposed face of your wife. I felt lightheaded. Sick. Visions of Maureen, vital and animated, flashed in my mind then blended with those of Lisa, dead. A man should never have to witness a woman he loves so violated. And I'd had to do it twice.

The body on the slab was Maureen's, but I had trouble recognizing the woman I'd known and loved in life. And now this last image of her would be forever imprinted in my mind.

"It's her," I mumbled.

"I'm sorry," Hannah said.

I nodded numbly and managed to make it to the restroom before breaking down. Huge, shivering sobs racked my body until I could barely breathe. With the tears came a wash of guilt and self-loathing and a frightening black hole of unanswered questions.

I splashed water on my face. Studied my reflection in the mirror. It was my fault. I'd done everything wrong from the start. And there was no way to undo it now.

Dallas was waiting when I emerged. "We need to go over a few things."

I could barely think, much less talk. But I tried. *Yes, I knew Ben Albright. Our paths sometimes crossed at the hospital, and we'd served on an outreach committee together. No, I didn't know he'd gone to Italy, and I'd never met Season Connell. And yes, dammit, I was sticking to my kidnap "story."*

"You told us the last time you saw your wife was the Sunday morning she disappeared," Hannah said. "Is that true?"

I hesitated, but only for a second. If I started changing my story now, I'd be in deeper trouble than I was already. I nodded.

They'd finally driven me home, where only my father's vigilance kept me from drowning my pain in booze.

Now I sat at the kitchen table while the rain pelted the windows. My eyes were bloodshot and puffy, as much from lack of sleep, I suspected, as grief. I wondered if I'd ever be able to sleep again.

Molly and Chase were in the other room. He'd come last night with Dad to stay with Molly while I went to the morgue. She was already asleep by then, so I hadn't told her about Maureen until this morning. She'd taken the news quietly. I figured it probably hadn't fully sunk in yet.

For her sake, I vowed to be strong. But I wasn't doing such a good job of that today.

Dad refilled my coffee cup, though I couldn't remember drinking any. "You want some toast or an egg?"

I shook my head.

"You have to eat."

The thought of food turned my stomach. "Later," I mumbled.

Dad gave my shoulder another comforting squeeze. "God doesn't give us more than we can handle," he offered kindly.

Bullshit. The way I saw it, God had nothing to do with what life dealt, and people handled what they had to. Either that or they went off the deep end. I wasn't sure which was going to happen to me.

"It's my fault. If I hadn't followed the van, if I'd paid the full ransom—"

"You can't blame yourself, Sam. It was the kidnapper who took her in the first place. He's the one who killed her. You did everything you could."

I tried to laugh, but it came out more like a hiccup. "Tell that to the cops. They don't even believe I even got a ransom call. They think I made the whole thing up."

"They've told you that?"

"Not in so many words. But I know it's what they're thinking. They think I killed her."

Dad got that studied look on his face I remembered from when I was growing up. He was searching for a way to put my mind at ease. Finally, he said, "They can't have evidence of that."

But they might, and that terrified me.

The doorbell rang. Dad shot me a questioning look. "You think it's the press again?" He'd fielded several phone calls already that morning.

"It's not even nine," I pointed out.

"You want me to answer it?"

I wanted to ignore it, but I pulled myself to my feet. "I'll do it."

My gaze focused on the police cruisers in front of the house before it shifted to the three men at the door. Two uniforms and Dallas.

My gut clenched. They'd come after me already.

"We've got a warrant to search your house and car," Dallas said, forgoing any preliminaries.

I yanked the sheet of paper from his hands and scanned it quickly. "Not before I call my lawyer."

"Go ahead, call your lawyer. He's going to tell you there's not a damn thing you can do."

Jesse wasn't quite as blunt, but the message was the same. The cops were within their rights, and I couldn't do much except demand an inventory of what they took. An hour later it lay on the kitchen table, where my dad and I were again huddled, nursing cups of lukewarm coffee. Chase had taken a distressed Molly out for waffles when the cops arrived, sparing her the further upset of seeing them tear her home apart, and they weren't yet back.

I knew Hannah Montgomery had to be wrong in even thinking that Chase could be behind the kidnapping. Yet ever since she'd raised the possibility, I hadn't been able to push it completely from my mind. But I couldn't banish him from my life without explaining, and that was something I couldn't bring myself to do. Besides, if you couldn't trust family, whom could you trust?

Dad examined the inventory sheet. "It's pretty vague," he said. His tone made it clear he was hoping I'd dismiss the search as meaningless.

But I couldn't. "Yeah," I agreed. "It is." They'd taken some clothing—Maureen's and mine—some financial records, the computer, and stuff from the garage. "What's worse," I added, "is I don't know *why* they took what they did."

The cops had also swabbed the kitchen and bathroom drains and a hodgepodge of odd discolorations on the walls. Memories of the blood I'd washed away Sunday morning settled in my stomach like spoiled meat.

"When they don't find anything incriminating," Dad said, "they'll have to realize you had nothing to do with it. They'll be forced to look elsewhere."

But what if they found something? My memory of that Saturday was still blank.

"Maybe they'll look elsewhere. Maybe not. You saw what happened when Lisa was killed."

"Sam, you—"

I gave a humorless laugh. "It's déjà vu all over again."

Dad was quiet a moment. "Chase used to say that all the time when you two were kids."

"Yeah, I remember. I always thought it was stupid. Still do."

"Besides," he said, "this is different."

"How so?"

"They won't find anything that ties you to her murder."

"They'll make whatever they find fit their purpose. Believe me, I ought to know."

When I'd stood trial for Lisa's murder, the DA made a big point of the similarities between a coil of rope in our garage and the rope that bound Lisa's hands. He presented expert testimony to back up his argument that the frayed ends of the two samples matched. The DA also found a witness who testified she heard harsh words just before she saw Lisa and me leave the house the day she was killed, though I hadn't been anywhere near the house. And, of course, there was the testimony of Lisa's mother regarding the bruises on Lisa's arm.

As far as I was concerned, it was all a crap shoot. I'd gotten off once, but only by a lucky fluke. There was no guarantee I'd get off a second time.

"You need a lawyer," Dad announced. "Not Jesse. A real lawyer."

"Jesse was a real lawyer. A damned good one too."

"*Was,* Sam. You need someone who's a lawyer right now."

"I'll get some names," I said just to mollify him. How the hell was I going to afford a private defense attorney?

I stood up and rinsed my cup in the sink.

Dad drummed his fingers on the table. "What are you going to do about a funeral?"

"I don't know." I was still having trouble absorbing the

fact that Maureen was dead. I hadn't begun to think beyond that.

He cleared his throat. "I don't want to sound hard-hearted, but there are practical matters that need to be dealt with. If you'd like me to help—"

"A memorial service rather than a funeral," I told him. "And she wanted to be cremated."

We'd discussed this only once, in passing, on a drive that took us by the cemetery outside of town. We'd been headed into the country for a picnic, and death was the last thing on our minds. But Maureen said the idea of being buried gave her goosebumps. She'd rather be cremated, she'd said, and her ashes scattered. It wasn't much to base plans on, but it was the best I had.

"Any idea where you'd like to hold it?"

I shrugged.

"The pastor at the community church is a good man."

"I'll think about it."

Dad looked at his hands. His tone was hushed. "Do you know when they'll release the body?"

The body. An image of Maureen's distorted features flashed into my mind. "The autopsy is set for tommorrow," I said, "so probably in a couple of days."

"We could plan a service for late in the week then. There'd be time to get the word out."

I nodded without enthusiasm. When Lisa died, her parents took over making all the arrangements. Maybe it was because they still considered her to be "their baby." Or maybe it was because they'd hadn't really liked me from the start, and knowing that the cops regarded me as a potential suspect didn't exactly win them over. Bottom line was, they never consulted me about any of it. Funeral, burial, obituary, they ignored me and handled it all. It rankled at the time, but now the idea of planning a service seemed overwhelming to me.

"It doesn't have to be elaborate," Dad said, as if he'd been reading my mind. "Chase and I can help."

"Thanks. I don't know that I'm up to doing it myself."

"You going to notify her folks?"

"I probably should." Maureen might have been estranged from them, but they *were* her parents. There was a bitter irony in the fact that my first contact with them would be word of her death.

"They must be mighty terrible people for a daughter to cut them out of her life that way."

"Not everyone's as lucky as me and Chase." I patted my father's gnarled hand. He put his free hand on top of mine and held it there for a moment.

"Do you even know how to reach them?" Dad asked.

"Not directly, but I might be able to track them down." I didn't know where Maureen's parents lived, or if they were even alive still. But I did know she'd gone to high school in Rochester, New York, and that her father's name was Ted. It was someplace to start.

"Why don't you do it now and get it over with," Dad suggested.

I nodded half-heartedly.

Because the police had confiscated my computer, I was stuck calling long-distance information. There were no listings for Ted, Theodore, or Edward Brown, but I did get numbers for two T. Browns.

That was the easy part. I stared at the telephone for a long time, rehearsing what I would say. How did you introduce yourself to your father-in-law and in the next breath tell him his daughter was dead? Even a mighty terrible person, to use my dad's phrase, would have difficulty receiving a call like that.

Finally, I took a breath and dialed the first number. A woman picked up. I asked for Ted.

"There's no one here by that name."

"I'm trying to locate a Ted Brown who had a daughter by

the name of Maureen." When she didn't jump in, I added, "Are you by any chance related?"

"Afraid not. I'm Tina. My dad's Bob, and my brother is Hank. No Maureen in our family."

I apologized for bothering her and tried the second number. I got an answering machine that told me I had reached the Brown residence. I hung up then thought better and dialed again. This time I left my name and number with the message that I wanted to speak to Ted Brown on a matter of some urgency.

CHAPTER 29

Hannah craved a cigarette. Quitting was a good idea in theory, but what difference did it really make? If she didn't die of lung cancer or breast cancer, she'd die of something else. Maureen Russell hadn't smoked, and she was dead, wasn't she?

Hannah was reaching into her desk drawer for the pack of Marlboros when Dallas looked up and addressed her across their abutting metal desks. "Let's have him take a lie-detector test."

"Sam Russell?"

"No," he replied, laying on the sarcasm, "the pope."

She glared at him. "You expect me to read your mind?"

"There are times it would be helpful." He gave her a cocky grin. "And times it would definitely *not* be a good idea."

"We discussed this already. The results wouldn't be admissible in court. We'd still have to put together a case."

"It might turn the pressure up a bit," Dallas said. "Maybe force a confession or make him nervous enough he'd trip himself up."

Hannah clutched the cigarette pack longingly. Her mind

was already halfway out the door. "What if he sailed through with flying colors?" she asked.

"You think that's what would happen?"

Hannah wasn't sure anymore. Wasn't sure why there was a part of her still wanting to believe Sam was innocent.

"What did you learn from Ben Albright?" she asked instead. Dallas had finally gotten through to him that morning.

"The Russells have been to his house a couple of times—hospital events with a lot of people in attendance. Albright says he and Sam Russell are colleagues but not friends. Different interests, different circles, that sort of thing. He saw Maureen only at social functions and couldn't recall that he'd ever had a real conversation with her. Lots of people knew about the wine cellar, he said. Every time he had a party, he'd have to give a tour of it."

"Poor guy."

Dallas laughed. "That was my feeling. He struck me as a bit pompous. Turns out we were right about the temperature, by the way. The setting was lower than Albright left it. He seemed as upset about that as the body."

"What about access to the house?" Hannah asked.

"Except for Season and his cleaning lady, he can't recall anyone who would have a key, especially not his ex-wife. Not his daughters either. But he's got a spare in his desk at the hospital and another hidden in the garden. Both accounted for, but that doesn't mean they weren't borrowed. And when he changes into his scrubs for surgery, he leaves his whole danged key ring in his trousers pocket in the locker room."

So Sam might have had access to a key, Hannah thought, but he wouldn't be the only one. "Anything on Albright or the dinner guests?"

"Carla's following up on that. So far, nothing that raises suspicion. Oh, and none of them were down in the carport, so we can eliminate them as sources for the shoe print."

"It's not Sam's size either," she pointed out.

Dallas nodded but didn't seem much interested.

Hannah was tempted to press him about Carla—what, if anything, was going on between the two of them?—but just then the lieutenant's administrative assistant, Jolene, appeared at their desks. "Morrissy wants to see you two," she said with a smack of her ever-present chewing gum. "Now."

Hannah reluctantly relinquished her grasp on the pack of Marlboros. *Damn.* If Dallas hadn't interrupted her with that business about the lie-detector test, she'd be outside right now enjoying a smoke. Their meeting with the lieutenant would just have had to wait.

Or he'd have talked to Dallas without her, which was not a reassuring thought. She respected the lieutenant's judgment, but if he had input only from Dallas, he wouldn't get a clear understanding of the case.

Hannah sighed, reached for her notebook and pen. "Shall we?"

Lieutenant Morrissy was seated at his desk, phone pressed to his ear, but he waved them into his office and gestured for them to have a seat.

He was in his late forties, only ten years older than Hannah, but she thought of him as being of another generation. He had two grown daughters and a grandchild, with another on the way. His head was mostly bald, his face was ruddy, and his middle thick enough that his shirt pulled at the buttons.

Hannah imagined that at one time he'd been an excellent cop, and he was still a fair and reasonable supervisor. But he liked things quiet and orderly. These days he seemed more comfortable in the world of community relations than heavy crime.

"Yes, absolutely," the lieutenant said into the phone. "Will do." He hung up and turned to glower at Hannah and Dallas. "Well?"

He'd called them there, Hannah thought. Shouldn't they be the ones throwing the *Well* in his direction?

"You wanted to see us," Dallas offered.

"The Maureen Russell case. Are we anywhere close to making an arrest?"

"No," Hannah said, at the same time as Dallas said, "Yes."

Morrissy groaned. "Christ, don't tell me it's one of those. It hasn't even been forty-eight hours since the body was discovered, and already I've heard from the chief, the DA, and half a dozen of the local media. Craig Jones from the *Monte Vista Monitor* has been practically sitting on my desk waiting for a statement. Some television station out of San Francisco even wanted a live interview."

Hannah had caught the story on a radio broadcast out of Sacramento, and she'd skimmed the newspaper accounts, which made the front page both yesterday and today. Word had finally gotten out not only about Maureen Russell's death but that she was the second of Sam's wives to have died under suspicious, and similar, circumstances. It was the kind of story reporters loved, even if it meant rehashing the same stuff over and over.

"I'm scheduled to go on vacation in ten days," Morrissy grumbled. "Hawaii. Beth will have my hide if I don't make it."

His phone rang. He picked up the receiver and punched the intercom. "Hold my calls, will you, Jolene? Yes, even the ones on my private line." He slammed the receiver back into its cradle. "Well," he said again, more calmly this time. "What do we have?"

"The husband looks good for it," Dallas said.

Morrissy turned to Hannah with an inquiring look.

"With all due respect," she said, "we only found Mrs. Russell's body Saturday night. We're still in the early stages of our investigation."

Dallas rested an elbow on the arm of his chair. "He was guilty before; he's guilty now. Nobody's unlucky enough to lose two wives to chance murders."

"You're passing on the party guests?" the lieutenant asked. The light on his phone blinked. He ignored it.

"For the time being."

"She'd been dead for a couple of days by the time they found her," Hannah added. "And none of them except the hostess of the party even knew the owner."

"She's the one with a key, isn't she?"

Hannah nodded. "But in terms of a suspect, she's not even close."

For once, Dallas agreed with her. "The woman's got a solid reputation and no ties to either of the Russells."

"She's a real-estate agent. She's got access to lots of houses."

Morrissy eyed the red light on his phone. It was blinking again. "What does Bones say?"

"Officially, nothing yet," Hannah reported. "The autopsy was only this morning." One advantage of a high-profile case was that the medical examiner handled their requests promptly. Under other circumstances, they might have had to wait several more days.

Hannah had forced herself to attend the autopsy because she'd learned over the years she could sometimes pick up details that never made it into the written report. And she got the information sooner too, which was an advantage in itself. But watching took its toll. It wasn't so much the snipping of flesh and sawing of bone that got to Hannah, though the physical details sometimes made her queasy. What weighed on her had more to do with the metaphysics of life and death, and the fine, ephemeral line between them.

"Bones is estimating she died anywhere from four to eight days ago," Hannah told the lieutenant. "It's difficult to be more precise because of the cool temperature in the cellar. Still, there was significant decomposition. She'd been dead some time."

Hannah's mind flashed on a vision of Maureen Russell's bloated and lifeless body laid out on the stainless-steel autopsy table. "Bones says she was killed somewhere other than the cellar, then moved."

Dallas rolled his shoulders. "The timing puts a total kibosh on Sam Russell's kidnapping story."

"Sam could be the victim of a hoax," Hannah said. "It wouldn't be the first time some lowlife took advantage of news about a missing person to extort money."

"He claims to have talked to her on the phone on Friday." Dallas looked from Hannah to Morrissy. "Kind of hard to do if she was dead."

"Could have been a tape. Or someone who sounded like her. Or possibly Bones is mistaken about the timing." Although Hannah doubted that. Despite his nonchalant and sometimes irreverent manner, Bones knew his business.

"How'd our victim die?" Morrissy asked.

Hannah answered. "She was strangled. Looks like the killer used something soft. Bones thought maybe a necktie or scarf. There were lacerations on her throat and chest, apparently inflicted post-mortem. And trauma to the left side of her head, like she'd been hit with a blunt object. That happened while she was still alive."

"Defense wounds?"

Hannah shook her head. "Fingernail scrapings were clean too."

"Anything useful from the scene itself?"

"A couple of acrylic fibers on her sweater," Dallas said. "Navy blue. The kind that might have come from a fleece jacket or blanket."

"Any blue fleece turn up in your search of the Russell house or car?"

"No, but Sam wouldn't keep something like that around," Dallas pointed out. "He'd know it would link him to the murder. We found a handwritten note in Maureen Russell's pocket. Some numbers—maybe an apartment number or something. Could have been there for ages and have nothing to do with her murder."

"There was also a recent footprint in the carport by the door leading into Albright's house," Hannah added. "Appears to be a man's boot, size eleven. Sam's a size ten, and so is Albright, the guy who owns the house."

"Anything that ties the print to the killing?" Morrissy asked.

"No, but the carport is the most direct way to get to the wine cellar from outside. And none of the house guests entered or left that way."

Morrissy rubbed his fleshy cheek. "Do we have *anything* useful?"

"We found a towel in Sam's laundry with what looked like blood on it. Forensics team is on it. They're also going over the items we collected, both at the scene and as a result of our search of Sam's house and car," Dallas said. "The car alone had enough odd and ends to keep them busy for a bit. Point to note though: he had it washed right after she disappeared."

The lieutenant frowned. "What do we have on him?"

"The marriage might have been headed south," Dallas explained. "We suspect the wife was in touch with a divorce attorney. And Sam's story doesn't add up. Says he last saw her Sunday morning when he left for the hospital, but no one remembers seeing him there. He bought flowers Sunday morning at a place that's on the other side of town from the hospital and his home. What's more, the house where the body was found belongs to one of the other doctors at the hospital. Sam's been to the house in the past and could get access to a key through the doctors' locker room."

"Nothing that ties him directly to the crime though?"

"Not directly, no. We're hoping there'll be something yet in the items seized during the search."

"Is the flower stand anywhere near Albright's place?" Morrissy asked.

Dallas shook his head. "Albright lives out beyond the hospital."

"So according to your theory, Sam is no more likely to have been there Sunday morning than at the hospital?"

"Sam and his wife were no-shows for their dinner reservation Saturday night," Dallas pointed out. "Sam says they changed their minds about going out, but it seems to me there's a good chance whatever happened, happened Saturday evening, not Sunday."

Morrissy looked about to speak when Dallas continued. "Rick Thompson from the canine unit thinks Maureen Russell last left the Russell residence through the garage. My theory is she and Sam drove off together, then he whacked her."

"But why?" Hannah asked. She'd kept quiet as long as she could. "Except for one possible visit—and I stress possible—to an attorney who handles divorces, we haven't seen anything to indicate the marriage was less than solid."

Dallas continued as though she hadn't spoken. His voice grew more animated as he expounded on his theory. "He dumps her in Albright's wine cellar—he knows the guy is in Italy and the body's not going to turn up. He reports her missing because that's what a good husband does, right? As soon as he sees we're looking at him, he concocts this intruder story. Then he comes up with the kidnap idea. He feeds you the story of the ransom call, Hannah, and figures in a couple of days he'll collect the body from the wine cellar and dump it somewhere in the hills. He's hoping by the time she's discovered, we'll have a hard time proving when she was actually killed."

He paused for a moment, cracked his knuckle, and smiled. "Might have worked if the dinner guests hadn't gone looking for wine."

"If he planned it so carefully," Hannah asked, "why did he fail to pick up his daughter Sunday morning? And why back himself into a story about being at the hospital if he wasn't?"

Morrissy looked to Hannah. "What do *you* think happened?"

"I haven't worked out a detailed scenario the way Dallas

has." She didn't want to sound antagonistic, but she was afraid the words came out that way. "I agree that Sam isn't being totally honest with us, but given what happened with his first wife, it's understandable."

"To the contrary," Morrissy said. "I should think that if he's innocent, he'd want to cooperate fully and clear his name."

"Not if he was also innocent the first time," Hannah pointed out. "He was one juror away from conviction. That's got to shake his faith in the system."

Dallas crinked his neck. "And if he was guilty then?"

"Then why risk killing a second wife?"

"Because he *did* get away with it before."

Morrissy's phone light was blinking again. He glanced at it, then at his watch. "Anything else?"

Neither Dallas nor Hannah spoke up.

"Okay, I think we've about covered it for now. We're getting a lot of scrutiny on this one. Let's make sure we move with care. But I'd like to get it wrapped up too. If the husband's our guy, let's bring in the DA and see if we can put together a case. Dallas, that's your thought, right?"

"Right."

"Hannah?"

She hesitated. "If you look only at the evidence, I agree, he looks good for it."

"*Only at the evidence?* What else is there?" It was Dallas who spoke, but from the look Morrissy gave her, it was clear he was thinking the same thing.

There's instinct, Hannah noted silently. But she'd been wrong before, with people she thought she knew a whole lot better than Sam Russell. "I just don't want to make a mistake," she said.

Morrissy narrowed his gaze. "Good. Neither do I."

* * *

Hannah slipped the pack of Marlboros into her purse and headed outside. Her plan was to sit on the edge of the concrete planter in front of the building, have a smoke, and soak up some soothing sunshine while mulling over what they had on Maureen Russell's murder. But the bench was already taken by the desk sergeant and one of the uniformed cops. Smokers' camaraderie aside, she had no desire to join them.

She had a better idea anyway. She got into her car and, once she was safely on the road, called Dallas and told him she was going to talk to Ben Albright's neighbors.

"We covered that," Dallas said.

"I'm covering it again." In fact, they hadn't covered it—patrol had. And while Hannah could only assume they'd done a fine job, she preferred interviewing potential witnesses herself.

Half an hour later, she'd tried the five closest neighbors. No one was home at two of the houses, and she learned nothing useful from the three people she managed to talk to. The houses along that stretch of hillside were far apart and strategically placed to offer views of the valley rather than the street. None of the people she'd spoken with had even known Albright was away.

Hannah perched in a spot of shade on the rock wall that abutted Ben Albright's driveway and pulled out another cigarette. So what if she was a few hours short of the prescribed time for her next one. Regimented smoking wasn't very satisfying, which of course was the point, but Hannah no longer cared.

Hannah watched a hummingbird hovering near an overgrown honeysuckle bush that climbed the side of the carport. The air was pleasantly warm and fragrant, the silence soothing.

She could probably afford better than the cottage she was currently renting, she thought. Nothing as elaborate as Ben

Albright's, but with the proceeds from Malcolm's life insurance, she had enough for a down payment on a house. You'd think after what he'd done, she'd be happy to spend the money on herself. Instead, it sat in the bank, untouched. As though by not actually using the money, she could distance herself from the hurt and betrayal.

Hannah finished her cigarette and headed for the car. Suddenly, the roar of a leaf blower shattered the silence. A gardening truck was now parked in the driveway of the house directly across the street.

Well, why not? Hannah thought. *I'm here anyway.* She approached the man with the blower. He was young and thin, with a scraggly goatee. With the noise of the blower, she had to walk into his line of sight to get his attention. He finally saw her and turned the thing off.

Hannah showed him her badge. "I'm investigating the murder of a woman whose body was found across the street," she explained.

"Yeah, I read about that. Dr. Albright's house, right?" He set the blower on the ground. "That will put a crimp in his vacation to Italy."

"You know him?"

"I do some gardening for him on occasion."

"Have you seen any activity around the house while Dr. Albright's been gone?" Hannah squinted into the sun. "Delivery truck perhaps? Workers or visitors?"

The man fingered his goatee, thinking. "There was a woman. Drives a big red SUV of some sort."

That would be Season. "We know about her," Hannah said. "She's a friend of Dr. Albright's."

"There was a silver car there too. About a week ago."

Albright would have been in Italy by then. "Do you remember the day?"

"It had to be a Monday or a Thursday, 'cuz those are the days I work here. I'd planned to go over to Albright's to do some pruning, but his ladder's at the back of the carport and the car was blocking it."

"The car was in the carport?" Hannah asked. From what she'd seen, most visitors, including Season Connell, parked in front and entered that way.

The man took a handkerchief from his pocket and mopped his brow. "Yeah. Albright's got a second car parked to the right, but he mostly uses that section of the carport for storage, so it was odd seeing a car there."

"What time was it?" she asked.

"Early afternoon sometime."

"Do you remember anything distinctive about the car? What make it was? Old or new?"

"Newish. A sedan. Fancy. I couldn't say for sure what the make was."

"Was it there long?"

The young man shrugged. "It was there when I left, is all I know."

A lot of people drove silver sedans, Hannah reminded herself. And Sam Russell was one of them.

CHAPTER 30

Dallas wasn't at his desk when Hannah returned to the station. She was grateful for the reprieve. She knew the look he'd give her when she told him about the silver sedan the neighbor's gardener had spotted parked in Ben Albright's carport. She wouldn't even have to remind him the description matched Sam's car.

Hannah poured herself a cup of coffee from the communal pot of sludge in the break room. It was pretty awful stuff, in part because nobody ever really washed the pot. Its redeeming quality was that it was quick and convenient. Carla was standing by the fridge talking to one of the other uniformed officers, but she broke away to speak to Hannah. She was holding a cup, which Hannah knew would contain tea, not coffee—peppermint from the smell of it. Carla kept a personal cache of herbal teas in her desk.

"I put my report on Dallas's desk," she said. "Nothing more on the SUV Sam claims to have seen the night of the ransom drop."

"Dallas thinks he made the whole thing up."

Carla ran a hand through her bangs. "It strikes me as a

pretty fair assessment. There's also a preliminary report from the lab on that towel with blood spots found in Sam's laundry. The blood type matches Maureen's."

Hannah absorbed the shock. Could she really have been so wrong about Sam? "Any indication how old it is?"

Carla shook her head. "Didn't *look* like it had been there forever though. Oh, and I put the detailed inventory from the search of Sam's house and car on Dallas's desk too."

"Anything significant?"

"Nothing like a murder weapon, if that's what you mean." She blew on her tea to cool it before taking a sip. "There's one thing though. Among stuff they found in Sam's car was a small silver buckle."

"You think that might be important?"

"The shoe Maureen Russell was wearing when we found her body, didn't it have a buckle?"

Hannah couldn't remember. "I'll check on it, but she undoubtedly rode in the car many times, so finding anything of Maureen's—hair, clothing, a buckle—it doesn't mean much."

Carla cocked her head. "Except it was found in the trunk of Sam's car, not the interior."

Back at her desk, Hannah put the coffee aside. It was worse than usual. Maybe tea wasn't such a bad idea.

She reached for the inventory report and glanced over it quickly then headed downstairs to the evidence room. She signed in and asked to look at the items taken from Sam Russell's car. She dumped the contents of the bag on the table and found the buckle. It was delicate and maybe a quarter of an inch square.

Next she asked to see the clothing taken from the body. Hannah found the shoe Maureen Russell had been wearing. It had a heel strap with a buckle. To Hannah's eye the buckle on the sandal and the one taken from Sam's car were identical. There were arguably any number of ways it could have landed in Sam's trunk, but she knew Dallas would see it as further evidence of Sam's involvement.

Hannah had to admit it didn't look good.

She took the opportunity to again examine the cryptic notation on the back of the recipe flyer she'd found in Maureen's pocket. *233—160B.* Sam had affirmed that the handwriting appeared to be his wife's but said he had no idea what it referred to.

Hannah could imagine Maureen reaching for whatever piece of paper was handy to scribble down a reminder to herself. Hannah often did the same thing. Shopping lists, phone numbers, addresses, directions, web sites, names of songs—if there wasn't a notebook handy, and there usually wasn't, she'd grab an envelope, a mailer, the back of a sales receipt, even the deposit slip from her checkbook. Her jacket pockets and the front seat of her car were littered with such scraps of paper, many of them quite old.

Likely that was the case here as well. A notation about an event or meeting long since past. Something Maureen had jotted down in a moment on the move, something that had nothing whatsoever to do with her abduction or murder.

But it *might* be related. The possibility kept buzzing in the back of Hannah's mind. Trouble was, the notation was vague enough that Hannah didn't know where to go with it.

Since she was there already, Hannah also asked for the box that contained the items she and Carla had collected from the barn and surrounding area. She looked them over again, one at a time. Nothing that shed any light on the identity of the kidnappers or even confirmed Sam's story about the ransom drop. She examined the object she'd picked up behind the barn, the one Carla thought might be a zipper pull. The geometric design looked like a logo of some sort, one that was vaguely familiar, but Hannah couldn't say from where.

She took the plastic pull to the desk clerk and showed it to him. "Do you recognize this logo?"

He glanced at it then back to her. "Sure, it's from that Indian gaming casino a couple of hours north of here."

Once he said it, Hannah recognized the logo herself. She'd never been to the casino, but she'd seen the ads. It was a popular place, and they probably sold, or gave away, all sorts of promotional items. She swallowed her disappointment. The pull wouldn't help them identify the kidnappers, even if they knew for sure it was connected to them, which they didn't.

She returned the evidence to the box, and the box to the clerk, then climbed the two flights of stairs to her desk.

Half an hour later, she remembered she'd promised to call Frank Donahue, the Boston cop who'd worked the case of Sam's first wife. She dialed the number, noting too late that, with the time difference, she might be catching him in the middle of dinner.

He answered on the second ring and assured her dinner was long past. "We eat early since I retired," he said. "Early and light. My wife watches me like a hawk." The words were delivered with an affectionate chuckle.

"We found Sam Russell's wife," Hannah told him. "She was murdered."

"Oh my." Donahue was silent a moment. "You think Sam killed her?"

"That's what we're trying to determine. Anything you can tell me about the murder of his first wife that might help us in that regard?"

"I doubt it. How did she die?"

"She was strangled," Hannah explained, "but there were stab wounds to the neck and chest."

"Like Sam's first wife."

"The coroner thinks the killer used something soft, like a scarf or necktie, to strangle her." Hannah fiddled with a blue plastic paper clip from her desk. "You mentioned last time we talked that they found rope in Sam's garage similar to the stuff Lisa was strangled with."

"Right. Common cotton rope, the kind you can buy at any hardware store."

"So it's not exactly the same."

"Not exactly, no."

She slipped her thumbnail under the inner band of plastic. It looked like her nail was bright blue. "In our case, the ME thinks the lacerations were inflicted postmortem."

Donahue was silent a moment. "Lisa Russell was still alive when her throat was cut. The theory was he strangled her first, to subdue her. Or got impatient when she wouldn't die."

Hannah cringed and again stumbled in trying to reconcile the evidence with the man.

"Maureen Russell was wearing only one shoe when we found her. Does that mean anything to you?"

"No. Lisa's body was fully clothed, including both shoes." He paused. "What about her ring?"

"What about it?" The paperclip broke, and Hannah tossed it into the trash.

"Was she wearing her wedding ring?"

Hannah tried to recall. She'd just looked through the box of personal items taken from the body. She didn't remember seeing a ring. "I don't know," she told Donahue. "Why?"

"Lisa's ring was missing. At trial, the defense argued that the missing ring pointed to a stranger having killed her. I didn't see it that way myself. A smart man might take the ring to make it look like someone else did it. Or he might take it because it was valuable."

"Was it? Valuable, I mean?" Instinctively, Hannah ran her thumb along the base of her own ring finger. She'd gotten married with a simple gold band and the promise of a diamond. The diamond had never materialized.

"Yes, in fact it was," Donahue said. "It belonged to Lisa's

grandmother. It was appraised at the time of the wedding at twenty thousand dollars."

"Wow, that's some ring."

"You can see why Sam might have removed it before dumping her body."

Or why a killer might have wanted it. "You're convinced he killed her, then?"

Donahue didn't answer at first. Hannah thought he might not have heard her. Or perhaps he'd found the question insulting.

"I thought Sam looked good for it," Donahue said after a moment. "I wouldn't have taken it to the DA so quickly though without pressure."

The unspoken message being he was something short of *convinced*. "What pressure?" Hannah asked.

"The chief. He and Lisa's father were old friends." Donahue hesitated again. "I think the rush may have had something to do with Sam's walking. We left holes in the case, and the defense ripped into them."

Hannah knew that was always a dilemma. If you waited until you had an airtight case, you'd never close any of them. "You think I could get a copy of the file?" she asked.

"Going through channels could take a while. Let me see what I can do for you."

"I'd appreciate that."

"I'm sort of re-examining the evidence anyway," Donahue added.

Hannah was confused. "The case is active still?"

"Not officially. But Lisa's parents asked me to look into it."

"They think their daughter's killer might have been someone other than Sam?"

"Not at all. They want to make sure Sam gets nailed for the current murder." He paused before continuing. "They're also worried about their granddaughter."

"Worried how?"

"Her being around Sam. They had custody while he was on trial. Now they'd like permanent custody."

A mental picture of Sam and Molly flashed into Hannah's mind. It had been readily apparent that the bond between them was strong and genuine. Hannah's heart immediately went out to the little girl. She'd already lost a mother and a stepmother. How awful to lose her father too.

"You think they stand a chance?" she asked.

"If Sam's arrested, it will be a slam dunk."

Hannah flipped on the evening news while she chopped mushrooms and onions for the omelette that would be her dinner. She knew she should fix a green vegetable too, but there was nothing in the house except an open package of frozen peas, heavily discolored by freezer burn.

There'd been a time when Hannah took pride in her cooking. She'd bought cookbooks, clipped recipes, shopped for the freshest ingredients, and delighted in fixing meals Malcolm loved. She'd stopped cooking during chemo, in part because she didn't have the energy and in part because food lost its taste. Now she'd simply lost interest. What was the point anyway in cooking for yourself?

Hannah put the skillet on the burner. She was already on her second glass of wine. She'd have to watch it or she'd be loopy before she finished dinner. She admired Sam's resolve in pulling himself together and quitting. It couldn't have been easy for him. She knew how hard it was trying to give up smoking.

The television coverage switched from national politics to local items. Maureen Russell's murder remained a top story, in part, Hannah thought, because of what had happened with Sam's first wife. A photo of Sam and Lisa in happier times flashed on the screen. Hannah wondered how they'd gotten hold of it. In light of what Frank Donahue had told her, she had an idea who had provided it. Details about

Lisa's murder might not be admissible in a court of law, but the court of public opinion was another matter. If Sam were to stand trial for Maureen Russell's murder, the defense would have a hard time finding jurors who hadn't heard about the first trial.

The news piece wrapped up with a short sound bite from Morrissy, who announced that the department was making good progress in the investigation into Maureen Russell's murder. *Thanks for the added pressure, Lieutenant.* When the reporter asked if Sam was a suspect, Morrissy offered his standard response—those closest to the victim were always under close scrutiny.

With good reason, Hannah acknowledged. There were basically only two scenarios when it came to homicide. The victim was either random or targeted. And in the second situation, more often than not the killer turned out to be a family member, spouse, boyfriend, or the like. Maureen's murder bore none of the earmarks of a random killing; that left them with someone she'd known. By default, her husband would naturally be a serious suspect. What's more, they'd yet to come up with any potential suspect besides Sam.

The other component in Maureen Russell's murder was that the killer was somehow connected to Ben Albright. He, or possibly she (Hannah tried to be evenhanded), had been familiar with the climate-controlled wine cellar and had known the house was vacant. Sam could have known, though he was hardly alone in that regard. Even the neighbor's gardener was aware that Albright was away.

Who among them though would have a motive for killing Maureen?

Hannah turned the omelette out on her plate and sprinkled it with Tabasco. She ate standing at the counter, her mind again locked onto the building evidence.

Maureen's blood on the towel with Sam's laundry. The bruise Hannah had noticed on Sam's face the evening he reported his wife missing. The buckle from Maureen's shoe

found in Sam's trunk. The car like Sam's the gardener had
seen at Albright's house. The missing wedding ring—she'd
checked after talking to Donahue, and Maureen's ring was
missing from the body just as Lisa's had been. The pieces of
Sam's story that didn't add up.

Sam. It always came back to Sam.

It angered Hannah to think she'd believed in him.

She poured herself a third glass of wine and felt the sting
of tears in her eyes. How could she be sad over someone
who'd killed his wife?

But it wasn't really about Sam, was it? Hannah was feeling sad for herself. For believing in jerks, which she did far
too often. For being attracted to men who would betray her.
For all the things she wanted out of life that seemed forever
to elude her.

CHAPTER 31

"I could use a drink," I told Jesse as we stepped from the cool interior of the church into the bright afternoon sun. Now that the memorial service was over, I faced the rest of my life. I wasn't sure I was up to the task.

Jesse pulled on a pair of dark glasses. "Too bad, you aren't going to have one."

"Why not?"

"Jesus, Sam."

"Give me one good reason."

"Because you've got too much riding on *not* drinking," Jesse snapped.

"Not anymore." I'd lost a second wife, and the odds were good that I'd once again be charged with murder. What did it matter if I took a drink?

Jesse draped an arm around my shoulder and pulled me aside. "Look around you, Sam. These are people who love you. You want to let them down?"

"It's *my* life."

"And Molly's."

"Sometimes I think she'd be better off without me."

He dropped his arm in disgust. "Wait until she's all grown

up before you piss away everything you have going for you, okay?"

A man with a camera—one of the anonymous press hounds—jumped in front of us and snapped a couple of photos before I had time to react.

"Dr. Russell," he called out. "Quite a coincidence that both your wives have been murdered, don't you think?"

"Get the fuck out of here," Jesse shouted.

The photographer stepped away, but he didn't let up. He raised his voice. "Is that a 'no comment,' Dr. Russell?"

Several of the other mourners turned to watch. I could hear a buzzing in my ears.

"This was a private service," I yelled. "Have you no sense of decency?"

As soon as the words were out of my mouth, I knew exactly what he'd fling back.

"Perhaps you should ask yourself the same question, Dr. Russell."

I lunged toward him, but Jesse grabbed me and dragged me to his car. It was parked at the curb, and he more or less shoved me inside. "Don't make it worse," he muttered.

"Is that possible?"

"Snap out of it, Sam." He wasn't about to feed into my self-pity. He turned back toward the church. "What about Molly? Shall I get her?"

"She's going to ride with my dad and Chase." In fact, I could see my dad's Buick up ahead, already pulling away from the curb. I was glad they'd missed the scene with the reporter.

But the rest of the small gathering hadn't. Even from inside Jesse's car, I could sense their discomfort. I wasn't sure if it had to do with the reporter's intrusion or the unspoken allegation in his remark. Despite the outward show of support, I knew that privately many of them were wondering what I'd done.

My picture had been on the evening news several nights in a row, as well as on the front page of several local papers. The tragedy of Maureen's death had become the real-life equivalent of a soap opera. And I had the leading role.

I leaned my head back against the seat and pressed my palms to my forehead. "Shit, Jesse, what am I going to do?"

He handed me a Reese's peanut butter cup. I waved it away. "I don't mean about the drink, I mean about my life."

"Same as with the drinking," he said, starting the engine and putting the church behind us. "You're going to keep going forward, one day at a time."

AA had stood me in good stead, but sometimes I got sick and tired of their homilies. "The cops think I killed her," I said. "It's only a matter of time before they arrest me. Dallas is practically salivating at the idea."

"Dallas doesn't run a one-man show."

I started to protest. Jesse held up a hand. "I know you two have issues . . ."

"He has the issues, not me."

"So you've said. All because he was an insecure kid and you some small-town baseball star." Jesse unwrapped the peanut butter cup I'd declined and popped it into his mouth. "That was high school, Sam."

I nodded glumly. Jesse was smart, probably one of the smartest people I knew, but he'd grown up in Chicago and gone to a high school that served close to three thousand students. Growing up in Monte Vista was different.

"It's more than just that," I explained, not for the first time. "My dad was a doctor. My mom a teacher. Dallas never knew his dad, and his mom scraped by working in the school cafeteria." And the petty meanness of teenage boys was not a pleasant sight. While I never initiated any of the teasing and taunting, I never rose to Dallas's defense either.

Jesse shrugged. "My dad was no prince. I'd have been

better off *not* knowing him. But there's no one from high school I even care about anymore, much less have it in for."

"That's because even if your dad wasn't a prince, you are."

Jesse grinned, flashing his gold front tooth at me.

"History or not, Dallas thinks I'm guilty." I closed my eyes. "Hell, maybe I am."

"Don't even go there, Sam." His voice was sharp.

"Why? Because as an attorney you don't want to know the truth about what I might have done?" I'd known that much from watching television, but until I stood trial for Lisa's murder, I'd never fully understood how circumscribed lawyers were about what they wanted to know.

Jesse shook his head. "Because I'm your friend, and I know what you *didn't* do."

"Hell, even I don't know what happened that night. You can't be sure of anything."

"If you killed her, how do you explain the ransom call?"

"Some opportunist who saw Maureen's disappearance as a chance to get his hands on easy money."

"But you heard Maureen's voice when the kidnapper called, right?"

In hindsight, I was having trouble remembering what I'd heard. "It could have been a recording."

"How would a random opportunist get a recording of your wife begging for your help?"

"I don't know. Maybe it was someone who sounded like Maureen. It was only a second or two, not a real conversation. And I was already a nervous wreck. I could have heard what I wanted to hear." I pressed my palms to my forehead, exhausted by trying to make sense of it all.

"Possibly. But I think the kidnapper is somehow implicated in her murder." He turned in my direction. "Which means you aren't."

"Doesn't matter. I can't prove any of it."

"Well, in theory, the cops are the ones who have to prove something."

"That's a crock, and you know it." They'd almost been able to prove I killed Lisa, which showed how far off base they could be. "I wish I knew what happened that Saturday."

"If you didn't suddenly fall off the wagon," Jesse reasoned, "and I can't see why you would, then someone either got you drunk or drugged you."

"Unless the amnesia stemmed from head trauma."

"Bottom line is, you're not at fault for Maureen's death."

I stared out the window at the familiar sights of my hometown. Growing up, I'd sometimes yearned for the glamor and action of a big city, but I'd come back from Boston four years ago longing for the quiet refuge of home. Now even that was denied to me.

"I'm thinking of sending Molly east to see her grandparents," I told Jesse.

He gave me a sideways glance. "I thought you were afraid they'd try to regain custody."

"She's interested in knowing her mother's side of the family. Hell, she might be better off with them. She lived with them, you know, during the trial and after, while I had my head in the toilet."

"You're not going to get me to feel sorry for you, Sam. I've been there too, don't forget."

"They're not warm people," I told him, "but they seemed to do a fine job raising Lisa."

"Except that Molly is *your* daughter."

"Which is why I need to do what's best for her."

Jesse shook his head. "Jesus, talking you out of taking a drink was a piece of cake compared to talking you out of this pit of self-pity."

My dad had invited mourners back to his place for coffee and dessert following the service. Several of the neighbors had pitched in, and the food was already set out by the time Jesse and I arrived. It was a small gathering—Ira and Debbie, of course, along with a few of the other doctors in town and a handful of women Maureen knew, mostly mothers at Molly's school.

I didn't feel much like coffee or dessert, nor was I in the mood for comfort and sympathy. What I really wanted was a dark corner to myself and full bottle of scotch. Which may have been the real reason my dad had organized this gathering.

I was standing apart, leaning against Dad's fireplace, when Sherri approached and handed me a cup of coffee. "I'm so sorry," she said. "If there's anything I can do, just ask."

I nodded. "Thanks."

"I was so hoping she'd turn up alive."

The sentiments were echoed by another woman, who took Sherri's place at my side when she left.

"Thank you," I said again.

And again and again as each of the guests offered condolences. Not a single one even mentioned the article in yesterday's paper that named me as a "person of interest," which is legally cautious jargon for "potential suspect."

Finally, Ira made his way over. "This has got to suck," he said.

"Big time."

He was wearing a dark wool suit that had to be too heavy for the warm afternoon. His face was flushed, and he looked miserable. "How are you holding up?" he asked.

"I feel like I'm in some fog-shrouded alternate universe. I keep hoping I'll wake up and find it was all a dream."

"I gather the cops have their sights on you."

"Afraid so."

"Have they said why?"

"Aside from the fact that I'm her husband, and I seem to make a practice of killing my wives?"

He wiped his brow and gave me a look of pained commiseration. "For what it's worth, I know you didn't have anything to do with it."

Ira and I were partners and had been best friends in high school. What else was he going to say? Still, I was touched. I felt myself choke up. "I appreciate that."

He shuffled uncomfortably. "Well, it's the truth."

I saw that Chase had found a beer somewhere, probably the back of his own car. I was tempted to ask for one for myself, but if I was going to blow it, I wanted better than one of his cheap beers.

I turned back to Ira. "I appreciate your picking up so much of my load at the office. I know it's not easy for you."

He looked a little embarrassed. "No problem. I'm glad to do it."

"I'm going to start carrying my weight again. I mean, if I'm in jail there won't be much I can do—" I tried to make light of it and failed. "But short of that, you can count on me. And as soon as this thing is over, I'll cover your patients while you take that two weeks in Hawaii you've been talking about."

"Yeah, sure." His voice lacked enthusiasm.

"I mean it."

"Thanks." He looked at his feet. "In the short run though, maybe it would be better if you . . . well, if you stayed away."

"You mean not come to the office at all?" I stared at him, dumbfounded.

"Just until all this blows over." He cleared his throat. "Or whatever. The patients are uncomfortable with all that's going on. You can't blame them really."

But I did. I felt utterly betrayed.

These were people for whom I'd gotten out of bed at two in the morning. I'd given up my weekends, cut dinners short, left in the middle of movies, all to attend to their fevers and pains. They knew me.

"They've said as much?" I asked.

"A lot of them, yes. The others, well, I can tell."

"Is that what *you* want?"

"Don't put words in my mouth, Sam. I mean, there is the

practice to consider. We need to be realistic about that. But I should think you'd want some time away regardless. You've got more important things to deal with right now than sore throats and stomachaches."

Just then another neighbor appeared to offer her condolences. When I looked for Ira again, he was nowhere to be found.

It was only five o'clock by the time everyone had gone home, but I was beat—and beaten. I declined Dad's offer of dinner and company and took Molly home. We made toasted cheese sandwiches and crashed on the sofa to watch a rerun of *The X Files*.

"Do you think Mom and Maureen will be friends?" she asked during a commercial break.

"Friends?" I was lost.

"In heaven. Since they were both part of our family. It's weird, don't you think?"

I didn't put a lot of stock in heaven, especially not the "happily ever after with angels and clouds" kind of heaven that Molly had in mind. But what she needed right then was comfort, not a diatribe about life after death.

I put an arm around her and pulled her close. "I don't see why they wouldn't be friends. They've both loved us, after all. And we loved them."

"But wouldn't that make them jealous of each other?"

I gave her a hug. "Not in heaven. It's different there."

I didn't check the day's phone messages until Molly had fallen asleep on the couch. There were three. One was a hang up, one was from a reporter, and the third was from Ted Brown, the man I was hoping was Maureen's father.

It would be almost eleven in New York, but I decided to call anyway. It might well be his daughter we'd buried that day.

Taking a deep breath, I picked up the phone and dialed. I

was about to speak for the first time to a man who could be my father-in-law.

He answered on the second ring. It didn't sound as though I'd woken him, for which I was grateful.

"Mr. Brown? This is Sam Russell. I appreciate your getting back to me."

"I was out of town for a while or I'd have called sooner. Your message said it was urgent. What's this about?"

"I know this is out of the blue, but I . . . we . . ." I took another breath. "Do you by chance have a daughter named Maureen?"

I could feel the winds shift. His tone became decidedly cool. "Who are you?"

"I'm a doctor in California, sir. I'm married . . . was married, to Maureen Brown of Rochester, New York. I'm looking for her father."

There was a moment's silence. "I don't know what the hell kind of scam you're pulling here, but I'm not interested. I've had enough of your type to last me a lifetime."

He hung up on me.

I was stunned. Estranged from her family, indeed. With good reason, from the sound of it. But I wasn't about to give up. I dialed the number again.

"Mr. Brown, please. Just give me a minute. It's about your daughter."

He waited in silence.

"Maureen *is* your daughter?"

"Was my daughter."

"Whatever might have happened between you . . . well, I loved her. We got married two years ago." I was rambling, trying to convince him I was legit and maybe putting off delivering the bad news as long as I could. Not that I expected him to care. "She's really a wonderful wom—"

"My daughter is dead," he said, interrupting me. "She died eleven years ago at the age of seventeen."

I felt as though the air had been knocked out of me. For a

moment, I couldn't even think. Then my brain kicked in. His daughter would have been twenty-eight now. The age was about right.

"What was your daughter's birthday?" I asked him.

"September fifteenth."

"That's my wife's birthday."

"Whoever you married, Mr. Russell, I can promise you it wasn't my daughter."

CHAPTER 32

I played the words over and over in my head all night long, trying to make sense of them.

But there was no sense, and no sleep.

My daughter died eleven years ago at the age of seventeen. Whoever you're married to, it isn't my daughter.

I was beyond stunned. It was as though science had just discovered that the Earth was indeed flat or that the sun occasionally rose in the west.

If my wife wasn't Maureen Brown of Rochester, who was she?

Why was she using Maureen's name?

Did her true identity bear on her murder?

The questions were clear. What I was feeling was not nearly so coherent or focused. A whole cast of emotions vied for center stage: hurt, betrayal, confusion, grief.

First thing the next morning, I called Ted Brown again. When he didn't answer, I left a message. As the day progressed, I tried several more times. He never picked up, and he didn't return my calls.

While Sherri took the girls to the local pool, I spent the day sifting through Maureen's—my wife's—closet and bureau drawers, her papers, books, files, everything I could get my hands on. I found nothing I hadn't seen before. But I saw with clarity what I'd so blithely glossed over during the two years of our marriage. There were no mementoes, photographs, letters. No hint of her life before she'd moved to Monte Vista.

Why hadn't I been more curious? I had asked, of course, but I'd been ready enough to move on when she changed the subject, explaining that the past was too painful to dwell on. In truth, and it embarrassed me now to acknowledge the fact, I *wasn't* all that interested. We both came to the marriage with what psychologists are fond of calling "baggage," and I could barely handle the weight of my own.

But I did try sometimes. I remembered we'd been driving past the high school once when I started to reminisce about my youth. We were living in my hometown, after all, and I wanted her to understand a little of what my life had been growing up.

"Ira was a wild man then," I told her. "I was a wimp."

She gave me a playful poke in the ribs. "You were never a wimp."

"I was. I would have been a total washout without Ira's prodding. He was always the one who got us the six-pack or the grass. I only cut school when Ira tempted me. And the time we got caught TP-ing the algebra teacher's house—"

"You really did that?" She laughed.

"Well, he *was* a pretty awful teacher. He never explained anything, just gave us assignments and sat at his desk reading the newspaper while we worked. But it was Ira's idea. And he tossed most of the toilet paper. I didn't even get through a whole roll. I was too afraid of making a mess."

"Sounds like you had a good time in high school."

It hadn't always seemed like fun at the time, but looking back, I remembered those years fondly. "Yeah," I told her. "I liked high school. What about you?"

"I hated it."

"Why?"

She shrugged. "You know, dull. So you and Ira have been friends practically forever?"

"Since grammar school, though we aren't as close as we used to be. I miss it sometimes, the 'best friend' thing, I mean."

We'd continued to talk about Ira and my youth, and I'd never learned why she'd hated school.

Now I sat down on our king-sized, cherry-frame bed—the one my wife had picked out and adorned with colorful comforter and pillows—and thought about what I did know. Maureen (it was the only name I'd known her by) was by nature aloof, but she could be warm and affectionate and kind. She worried about her weight—unnecessarily, in my opinion—loved romantic comedies and anything with Johnny Depp. She was terrible at spelling, terrified of rollercoasters, and dreamed of renting a house in Italy someday. She had a lovely voice and a sense of humor, though as I thought about it now, I realized it had been dormant these last few months. She'd brought joy into my life at a time I'd pretty much forgotten there was such a thing. Despite the tensions in our marriage, I'd loved her.

But I hadn't really known her.

Finally, I got tired of waiting for the phone to ring and went to see Jesse at the nursery. Maybe my brain was so rattled I was missing something obvious. Something Jesse would see straight off.

I found him watering the roses on display. The sweet fragrance of the blooms took me back to my childhood, when my mother tended to her rose garden as if it were her third child.

"You sure there's not some mistake?" he asked when I told him about my conversation with Ted Brown.

"Not likely. Her date of birth, her father's name, the city where she went to high school, they all match."

He whistled softly. "Wow."

"Why did she lie? If she loved me, why couldn't she trust me?"

"Maybe it wasn't a matter of trust."

"What do you mean?"

"Why do people use false identities? Usually because they're in hiding, right? Maybe they've got money problems, or a deranged ex, or they're being stalked." He paused. "Or maybe they're hiding from the law."

I shook my head. "A crazy ex-boyfriend I'd buy, but not the law. Maureen wasn't like that."

"But she wasn't Maureen either," Jesse pointed out, not unkindly. He shifted the soaker nozzle and pulled a couple of dead leaves off one of the plants. "It could be something innocuous like bad debts."

"That's innocuous?"

"Relatively speaking. Have you told the cops?"

"Not yet."

"You going to?"

"I don't know. They're closing in on me, Jesse. It's only a matter of time before they arrest me."

"At least they stayed away from the memorial service."

I nodded. I'd been sure they would show up, if only to rattle me. Although they never came out and said in so many words that I was their prime suspect, the fact was apparent to anyone who listened to the news.

"I guess I'd like to know a little more about what's going on first," I said.

"Smart move. You don't want to dig yourself into a deeper hole."

"That's for sure."

"On the other hand, this might get you *out* of the hole."

I nodded. "Trouble is, at the moment I don't know which it is."

Jesse moved the hose again. Surprisingly, for a Sunday, the nursery was quiet. There was only one customer that I could see, and she was over by the annuals, slowly making her way down the aisle of pansies and impatiens. I hadn't known Jesse when he was a public defender, and I couldn't imagine him in any work environment but this.

"I've got to unravel this soon," I told him.

"Yeah, I think you do."

"If I don't hear back from Ted Brown tonight, I'm going to Rochester myself."

"What if he still won't talk to you?"

"I guess I'll have to make sure he does."

Molly was thrilled at the prospect of staying at my dad's— a special treat given that it was a school night. And Dad, needless to say, was equally thrilled.

"I'll call you when I get there," I told Molly. "I'll only be gone a day or two."

"Why do you want to meet Maureen's father, anyway?"

I'd debated how much to tell her. I didn't want to lie, but I didn't want to confuse her either, especially not until I got it sorted out myself. "I want to know more about her," I said. "Her childhood, her family. You sure you're okay with my going?"

"I'm going to be staying with Grandad." Her tone made it clear I shouldn't worry.

I gave her a hug. "Don't wear him out. Remember, he's not as young as me."

She laughed. "Dad!"

I caught the first flight out the next morning, walking past a Boston-bound plane in its final stages of boarding on my way to the gate. As I settled into my seat, a wave of bitter-sweet nostalgia rolled through me.

Boston. Lisa.

God, I missed her. I missed our quiet talks, the way she ran her hand through the hair at the back of my neck, the scent of herbal shampoo in her hair. The way she understood what I was thinking and feeling, even when I didn't. She'd helped me grow in so many ways.

I remembered again that I'd been dreaming about her that Sunday morning two weeks ago when I'd woken in my car, lost in the hills, and returned home to find Maureen gone. Why had I dreamed about her then, when I so rarely did anymore?

Coincidence? Or was it because I knew deep inside that Maureen and Lisa had suffered similar fates?

I hadn't killed Lisa. I knew that. And I was hoping—no, I was reasonably confident—that I hadn't killed Maureen. But I was a link between the two murders. Had I inadvertently caused them? Was someone deliberately trying to cause me pain? Or maybe there was no connection at all.

I leaned back in my seat and closed my eyes as the plane taxied down the runway. If my wife wasn't Maureen Brown of Rochester, finding out who she really was had to be a step in the right direction.

Having subjected my stomach to a soggy airline omelet and bitter coffee on the first leg of the trip, and pretzels on the second, while my rather large seatmate snored in my ear, I arrived in Rochester feeling queasy and exhausted. I thought about checking into the hotel and calling on Ted Brown in the morning. But I was too antsy to wait any longer.

With the aid of a street map I picked up at the airport newsstand, I found the Browns' house with little difficulty. It was an older, two-story brick structure of modest size in a neighborhood of similar houses. None of the properties was run down, but they all showed their age.

It was only eight-thirty in the evening, but because of the northern latitude the sky was lighter for the hour than it would have been in Monte Vista. Still, it wasn't the best timing for calling on a stranger.

I rang the bell, my stomach in knots. The man who answered appeared to be in his fifties. He was solidly built, with bushy eyebrows that formed a prominent ridge across his forehead.

"Mr. Brown?"

His scowl deepened. "Do I know you?"

"I'm Sam Russell." I'd have offered my hand, but the screen door prevented me.

"Russell . . ." His face pinched in thought. "You're the one who keeps calling about Maureen."

"I'm sorry to bother you, sir—"

"I don't want to talk about it. Whatever it is, it doesn't concern me. Maureen's dead."

"May I come in? Please. I'm as confused as you are, and it's important. I flew here from California just to speak with you."

"Then you wasted your time."

I wasn't going to take "no" for an answer. "Someone claims to be your daughter, and you aren't even curious?"

The eyebrows furrowed again. "Your wife really told you she was my daughter?"

"My wife and your daughter had the same name and birth date, and both went to the high school here in town."

"Where was she born?" he asked.

"New Orleans." It was what she'd put on our marriage license.

His bushy brows knit together into a single line. "She told you I was her father?"

"She said her father was named Ted."

He didn't respond one way or another.

"And her mother's name was Annette."

His face registered surprise. His shoulders slumped, and his eyes closed momentarily. Then, with a sigh, he unlatched the screen and stepped back. "Might as well come in. Looks like you won't leave me alone otherwise."

"Thank you." I stepped inside. The house was comfortable but dated. Like my dad's house. The carpeting was kelly green, as were the two recliners in front of the television. The couch was a brown and green plaid. Above it was a gilded frame holding a reproduction of Van Gogh's *Sunflowers*.

"What is you want from me?" he asked.

"To start, I was hoping you could tell me about your daughter. Maybe that will help me figure out why my wife took her identity."

"Why not ask her yourself?"

"She's dead. She was murdered almost two weeks ago."

He drew in a breath then gestured to the sofa. "Have a seat. I'm sorry about your wife." He picked a framed photograph off the mantel and handed it to me. "That's Maureen at fourteen, with her mother. Both of them gone now. There's just me left."

The photo showed a young girl with wispy blond hair and a round, cherublike face. She bore a striking resemblance to her mother. Neither of them looked anything like my wife.

"She was lovely," I told him. She was, in an all-American, girl-next-door way. I knew also it was something he'd want to hear, and I wasn't above using whatever means I could to gather information.

"She was the light of our life."

"How did she die?" I asked.

Ted Brown shook his head slowly, like he didn't relish going there again, even in his mind. "In an auto accident." His voice was tight. "A boy was driving. Someone we didn't even know. He'd been drinking."

Every parent's nightmare. "I'm sorry. I've got a daughter myself. I can't imagine anything worse."

"She'd been at a party. We thought she was spending the night with a girlfriend." His eyes grew moist, and he turned away, replacing the photo on the mantel. "Would you like some coffee?" he asked after a moment. "It's decaf. I was just about to pour myself some."

My stomach hadn't fully recovered from the coffee I'd had on the plane, and what it really needed was something solid, like dinner. But I didn't want to appear ungrateful. "Thanks. Just black."

Brown excused himself to the kitchen and returned a short while later with two cups of coffee. China cups with saucers, not the earthenware mugs I was used to.

I showed him a photo of my wife that I'd brought with me.

"She doesn't look anything like my daughter," he said.

"No, I can see that now. There must be some connection though."

He set the photo on the coffee table in front of us. "How long were you married?"

"Two years. My first wife died when my daughter was a toddler. Maur . . . my second wife told me she was estranged from her family, and I never pushed the matter. I guess I wanted to look forward instead of backward."

"So what led you to me?"

"Our marriage license listed her parents as Ted and Annette Brown, and she mentioned going to high school in Rochester. It was pure luck that you still live in town."

Brown pressed his fingers together then glanced down again at the photo. He picked it up and studied it. "You know, your wife looks a little like a friend of my daughter's. A girl by the name of Eva Flynn."

A tingle of excitement worked its way across my shoulders. A dead friend was the near-perfect identity if you were going to assume one other than your own. Eva would not only have known Maureen's vital statistics but also her personal and family history.

"Eva's the one who got Maureen hooked up with the wrong crowd," Brown added. His eyes bored into me. "If it hadn't been for Eva, Maureen would be alive today."

I wasn't sure how to react. It could well be my wife he was talking about. "Eva was a bad influence?" I asked lamely.

"The worst." Brown's tone was bitter. "She was a schemer

and a manipulator. The only person she cared about was herself." He paused. "Does that sound like your wife?"

"Not at all." But the little voices inside my head were already taunting me. She'd managed to deceive me, hadn't she? How could I say what she was really like?

"Were they good friends?" I asked. "Eva and Maureen."

"They spent a lot of time together, but like I said, Eva didn't think about anyone but herself. Maureen didn't have many friends. She was a quiet girl. Shy, unsure of herself. We moved around a fair amount while she was growing up, and she never really had a chance to build relationships with her peers. When we moved here, Eva took my daughter under her wing. For the first time in her life, Maureen was part of a crowd. We, my wife and I, didn't know the kids at school very well, and we were glad Maureen had friends. When we began to see what was going on, we tried to keep Maureen away from them, but it was too late. She fought us and went behind our backs."

"It's hard with teenagers." Another lame response. I felt slightly nauseated, whether because I'd skipped dinner or because of what I was hearing, I wasn't sure.

"There was a little group of them. They spent a lot of time at the house of one of the boys. He lived with his older brother. No adult supervision at all." Brown's expression was pained. "There was lots of drinking, partying, some drugs. All the things you don't want for your child. We'd forbid Maureen to go there, but she'd go anyway."

"What about Eva's family? What were they like?"

"They seemed like decent enough people, but I think they'd more or less given up on being parents."

"Eva was that difficult?" I asked.

"I imagine she was, but that's not what I meant. Her parents were older. I thought at first they might be her grandparents. The father was a respected businessman, and the wife was quite active socially. Their names were often in the paper in connection with civic events and charitable affairs.

But I don't think they gave their daughter much supervision. I'm not even sure Eva graduated from high school. There was some talk about trouble with the law, as I recall. This was after Maureen was gone. I wasn't much interested in keeping up with her classmates."

"Do Eva's parents still live in town?" I asked.

"I have no idea. You thinking about going to see them?"

I nodded. "Since I've come this far, I might as well. I have to say though, Eva sounds nothing like my wife."

"They had a house on Brookdale," Brown said. "A big yellow house on the corner where Brookdale intersects Meadow."

"Do you recall their first names?"

"The father was Lou, I think. Or Len. Something like that. I can't remember the wife's name."

"Thanks." I rose to leave. "I appreciate your seeing me."

"I could be wrong, you know," Brown said. "About the photo. There was just something about the eyes that made me think of Eva."

I wasn't sure whether I wanted him to be right or not.

CHAPTER 33

By the time I finished talking with Ted Brown, it was almost ten o'clock. Too late to go knocking on the door of strangers, even if the strangers turned out to be my in-laws.

I drove to a local hotel, ordered a club sandwich from room service, then called my father and talked to Molly. They'd just dished up sundaes with my father's special hot-fudge topping and real whipped cream, so our conversation was brief.

"How was your day?" I asked her.

"Terrible."

The word every parent dreads. "What happened?" When she didn't respond, I tried again. "Are you upset about Maureen?"

"No. It's not that."

"Is it about school?" Molly thrived on school. For reasons I couldn't understand, she even looked forward to spelling tests and book reports.

"Not really."

"What was it then?"

"Nothing." She sounded exasperated.

"Honey, it can't be nothing if it ruined your day."

"I'll tell you later. I don't want my ice cream to melt."

I felt bad not being there. Maureen's death had to have upset Molly. Maybe she was worried about losing me too. That was why I'd made the trip, I reminded myself. Left to their own, the police weren't going to look any further than me for their killer. I needed to point them in a different direction, and in order to do that, I had to know who it was I'd been married to.

"Try not to worry," I told her. "I'll be home tomorrow. And you've got my cell number. You can call me anytime."

Silence.

"I love you, Sweetpea."

"Love you too."

My father came on the line, and I could hear him move to a different room. "Did you reach Ted Brown?" he asked me.

I told him about my conversation with Brown and how he thought my wife looked a little like his daughter's high-school friend Eva. "I'm going to contact Eva's parents tomorrow. I suspect they'll tell me their daughter is married and living in Connecticut and that they talk to her once a week."

"Then what?"

"I don't know." If the lead to Eva didn't pan out, I wasn't sure how I'd ever figure out who my wife actually was. "I suppose anyone could go through the obituaries, find a name, and then order a birth certificate. From there, I guess you could build a new identity without too much trouble."

He mumbled agreement. "All you'd have to do is find someone about the right age."

I rolled my shoulders to relax the tension between them. "Do you have any idea what happened with Molly at school?"

There was a moment's silence. "It's the other kids. You know how they can be."

Petty, mercurial, and sometimes cruel. But Molly was surprisingly immune to stuff like that. "Someone was mean to her?" I asked.

Dad lowered his voice. "They're saying things about you, Sam. You know how the media's been with stories about Lisa's murder and your trial. And Maureen."

"Jesus." Parental guilt rocked me like a punch in the gut. My daughter was an outcast at school, and it was my fault. "They're only in fifth grade. How do they even know?"

"I'm sure they pick up most of it at home."

"It's okay with me if she wants to skip school tomorrow," I told him.

"We'll see. You don't want her to think running away from problems is the right way to handle them, do you?"

Sometimes it wasn't such a bad idea. "But if she's un-happy . . ."

"Molly's tough, Sam. She's not going to let a bunch of snotty-nosed kids get to her."

I hoped he was right. But my heart ached for Molly and the trouble I'd caused her.

When I hung up, I searched the hotel-room drawers for the local phone book. There were three listings under Flynn that caught my eye. One for a Lloyd and one for a Larry, both on streets other than Brookdale, and one for an initial *L* with no address listed. I jotted down the numbers so that I'd be ready to call first thing in the morning.

When my sandwich arrived, I ate hungrily then found the vending machines and bought a pack of M&M's for dessert. Keyed up as I was, I expected to have trouble falling asleep. Instead, I dozed off in front of a made-for-television movie about drug running.

By seven the next morning I was showered, shaved, and dressed, impatient for the day to get started. It was, of course, too early to be making phone calls. I drove to the corner of Brookdale and Meadow, where Brown had said Eva's family lived, simply to get a feel for the area. There was no guarantee they still lived there.

Of the four corner houses, none was yellow. But they were all well kept. The homes in this neighborhood were larger and more stately than Ted Brown's.

Which one was the Flynns'? I tried to imagine my wife growing up in each of them. Tried to picture her here as a semisophisticated girl of sixteen. Which of the many upstairs windows had been her bedroom? On which of the wide front porches had some boy stolen a kiss? What had she felt each day coming home from school?

Were Eva Flynn and my wife even the same person?

I waited until the respectable hour of eight, then pulled out my cell phone and called the number with no address listed. A woman answered.

"I'm looking for Lou Flynn," I told her, ready to jump in with Len or other similar-sounding names if she told me I had the wrong number.

"He passed away three years ago," she said.

"Are you his wife?"

"Yes." Her tone was hesitant. "I'm not in good health, however. I don't want to buy whatever it is you're selling."

"I'm not selling anything. I'm calling about your daughter."

I heard a sharp intake of breath. "Eva? How is she?"

I'd found the right Flynn at any rate, and it didn't sound as though mother and daughter were close. There went my lives-in-Connecticut-calls-home-once-a-week scenario.

"Could I come by and speak to you in person? I think it would be best. I'm actually close to Brookdale."

"Brookdale . . . We sold that house a number of years ago. I'm in North Gardens now."

"How about I come there, then?"

She hesitated. "Who did you say you were?"

"A friend of your daughter's."

"Did she tell you to call me?"

"Not in so many words."

"But you've talked to her recently?" Mrs. Flynn sounded hopeful.

"Yes," I said, knowing full well my answer was misleading at best.

"Give me your name, and I'll leave it at the gate. They'll direct you to my unit."

North Gardens was, I learned from the large sign at the entrance, an adult retirement community. The grounds were lovely—common areas of green with borders of colorful flowers. The red brick condos were grouped in clusters about a central area. The first-floor units had small patios, while those on the second story had balconies.

Mrs. Flynn—Sonia Flynn, according to the mailbox outside the elevator—was in 108C, in the assisted-living wing of the largest building. I was greeted at the door by a woman whose right side appeared to be partially paralyzed, giving her a lopsided look. A stroke, I guessed. She used a walker and kept her head turned slightly to the side. It took me a minute to figure out she probably had lost the sight in her right eye.

I looked for any likeness to Maureen and saw none. Mrs. Flynn had sharp, almost rodentlike features and a thin mouth which she'd painted a garish coral color. Her bony fingers were heavily laden with rings.

"Please come in, Mr. Russell. I'm sorry I don't have anything to offer you. My maid hasn't been to the store for a few days."

It wasn't clear if she was referring to a personal aide or the assisted-living staff. Or if she was totally daft.

She shuffled to an upholstered chair and pointed to another for me. The room was cluttered with knickknacks, but

I could tell they were expensive ones. A crystal vase, a porcelain plate on a stand, cut-glass candy dishes. The remnants of a well-to-do life.

"You said on the phone you had word of Eva?"

"I . . . I might," I told her. "I'm not sure the woman I'm inquiring about is actually your daughter."

I showed her the photo of my wife.

And then I held my breath.

Mrs. Flynn angled her head and stared at the photo with her good eye. She picked up a pair of spectacles, put them on, and studied the photo further. "It could be her," she said finally. "Her hair's shorter; she's a little heavier than last time I saw her." She raised her eyes to look at me. "You said you'd seen her recently."

This was a quandary. I hated to lead off by telling her the woman in the photo was dead, and I was still far from convinced my wife and her daughter were the same person.

Instead, I asked, "When did you last see your daughter?"

"Oh, four years, at least. Maybe longer." Mrs. Flynn folded her hands in her lap. The skin was loose, darkened with age spots. "She calls though. Used to call every February twelfth. That's her birthday. But lately it's just whenever."

"Have you talked to her, say, within the last year?"

"I could have." She gave an apologetic laugh. "When you get older, it's difficult to keep the years straight."

Would there ever come a time when I couldn't remember talking to Molly? I doubted it. "What was she doing at the time?" I asked. "Where was she living?"

"Out west somewhere. No snow. Eva always hated the snow."

Maureen wasn't fond of the cold either. "She didn't say where in the West?"

Mrs. Flynn shook her head. "Eva's never stayed in one place for very long." She hesitated. "I thought once my husband passed, Eva might come see me more often."

"Eva and her father didn't get along?" I remember Maureen telling me once, *I didn't really have a father.* Is this what she meant?

Mrs. Flynn's mouth worked as though chewing on her response. "Our daughter was a disappointment to him," she said at last.

"In what way?"

She gave a brittle laugh. "In what way was she not? The ultimate blow came when Eva had some trouble with the law her senior year in high school. Lou thought it was better we not get too involved."

Not get involved? What good were parents if they weren't there in your moment of need? Then, with a pang of guilt, I thought of Molly and the taunting she was taking from the kids at school. I couldn't help feeling I'd deserted my own daughter in her moment of need. Maybe I shouldn't be so quick to judge.

Mrs. Flynn again picked up the photo I'd brought. "When was this taken?"

"Last year."

"She looks good, doesn't she? Where was she?"

"California."

Mrs. Flynn's mouth drew to a pucker. "That would suit Eva. She hated growing up here. Hated everything about the place, as far as I could tell. She was a most ungrateful child."

There was not a spark or warmth or motherly affection in her remarks. I felt myself growing protective of Eva, regardless of whether she'd been my wife. "If you wouldn't mind, I'd appreciate hearing what you could tell me of your daughter's life since high school."

"I thought you were here to tell *me* about Eva."

"I'm not sure this woman"—I gestured to the photo—"is actually your daughter. She changed her name."

"That doesn't surprise me." Mrs. Flynn settled back a bit in her chair. "Eva always had a flair for the dramatic."

"What else?" I waited while Mrs. Flynn searched her mind for a place to start.

"Eva was a good student. A real whiz at math."

I hadn't noticed that numbers were a particular strength of Maureen's, but I wasn't sure it would ever have come up either.

"She had lots of potential," Mrs. Flynn continued. "That's what angered Lou. Eva never lived up to it. Never even graduated. Well, technically she did, but she left home before the graduation ceremony."

"Why?"

Mrs. Flynn's hand fluttered to her throat. "She got in such a snit about . . . about something of no consequence. She absolutely refused to see our side of it. She and Lou had words, and well . . . she took off. Like I said, dramatic and impulsive. She was all too happy to use our money, but not to abide by our rules."

Mrs. Flynn's face clouded. "We never got to see her in her cap and gown. All those years of hard work raising them, you want to see them accomplish something. Graduation, marriage, the birth of a grandchild—milestones that make you proud. But Eva denied us all of them."

"So she never married?"

"If she did, I never knew about it." Mrs. Flynn sounded bitter.

I felt the need to speak up in my wife's defense. "If your daughter is the woman in the photo, she married me."

Mrs. Flynn gave me the once-over with her good eye. "Why are you asking me all these questions then?"

"She never talked a lot about her past, and now . . . now she's . . . disappeared."

"What do you mean, 'disappeared'?"

I still wasn't ready to lay out the entire story. Not that I expected Mrs. Flynn would spend a lot of time grieving. "She went missing about ten days ago," I explained.

Her mouth twitched. "Have you been in touch with the authorities? Do they suspect foul play?"

"The police are working on it. But I'm . . . looking into what happened as well."

She took a moment to digest the information. "And you think your wife, the woman who disappeared, might be my daughter?"

"Right. So anything you can tell me—"

"Do you have children?"

"I have a daughter by my first marriage."

She frowned. "That's too bad."

I wasn't sure if she was referring to a prior marriage or to the lack of children from my current one.

"When Eva was young, she used to talk about having a big family. She hated being an only child herself. But when she got older, she never talked about having children at all. I think she realized how they tie you down."

I'd been keeping a running checklist in my head without even realizing it—in one column, the ways Eva and Maureen were alike. In the other, the ways they were different. I didn't know what to do with this latest information.

Maureen tried very hard—too hard, I thought sometimes—to win Molly's affection. I told her it would take time, but she was impatient. It was as though she saw *family* as a role she could slip into rather than a relationship built through shared experience. But I think she'd also have been happy if Molly wasn't in the picture.

I mentally started a third column for details that could go either way and moved on. "When Eva left home after high school, where did she go?"

"We suspected she was living on the streets or staying with anyone who'd let her. She never called us, although she did send a postcard from Florida a few months later to say she was okay. Lou thought she did it just to taunt us."

I was beginning to see why Eva might have wanted a

fresh start with a new identity. Maybe being Eva Flynn was just too painful.

"She did ultimately find work," Mrs. Flynn hastened to add. "I don't want to make it sound like she stayed homeless. She'd get a job, drop us a line, and then by the next postcard she'd be living somewhere else, with a new job. It wasn't what you'd call a stable life, but she must have been doing okay for herself. It sounded that way, at any rate. She'd tell us about the places she'd been and the restaurants she'd eaten at, the fun things she was doing. Not that we necessarily believed all of it."

"Can you give me names of her high-school friends, people who might have stayed in touch with her?"

"Her closest friend died when they were still at Holbrook, the high school. It was an automobile accident, very sad. Maureen, the girl who died, was a mousy little thing. I never understood why Eva hooked up with her. Now, Darla Winfield, she was popular with the other kids, and very pretty. She was homecoming queen senior year. They were neighbors of ours on Brookdale. Her mother and I were in the Opera Guild together. I tried to encourage Eva to be friends with Darla, but she never listened to me."

"How about other friends? A group that she hung around with, maybe."

Mrs. Flynn thought a moment. "There was that boy, Danny Vance. The kids used to hang out at his place. He wasn't Eva's boyfriend or anything. Kind of a gangly boy, with a bad case of acne. He lived with an older brother, and I don't suppose either of them ever thought to consult a dermatologist. And Melody Lucas, she was part of that group as well."

"Are they still in town?"

"Danny is, or was several years ago. He managed the gas station on Lakeview, over by the Sears store."

"And Melody Lucas?"

"Oh, yes. Her name is Hughes now. She married a very successful dentist. They've got two boys and a lovely home on the outskirts of town. She's done very well for herself."

As poor, disappointing Eva hadn't.

CHAPTER 34

I wasn't convinced Eva Flynn was the woman I'd been married to, but it struck me as a real possibility. My conversations with Ted Brown and Mrs. Flynn had been productive. In terms of gleaning information, in fact, I was on a roll. That is, until I tried to reach Danny Vance at the service station he managed. He was on a camping trip and not expected back until Wednesday.

Next I tried Melody Hughes and got an answering machine.

Undaunted, I decided to dig a little on my own. I started with Holbrook High School, which Mrs. Flynn had said Eva attended, pulling my car into an empty *visitor* parking space.

A walkway led from the lot to a traditional two-story brick structure with wide front steps—obviously the original school—which was flanked by two newer single-story buildings, also in brick. I could see a sports field and a gymnasium beyond.

This was where Eva had gone to school. Where she'd mingled with friends, worried over tests and papers, maybe walked hand in hand with some special boy. Was it also the school my wife had attended? I tried, as I had earlier that day while parked near the house that might have been her child-hood home, to imagine Maureen in these surroundings.

She'd told me very little about her life growing up, but I'd somehow envisioned a less comfortable environment than what I'd seen today. Of course, a teenager with a barren home life would hardly feel comfortable.

With the help of the high-school librarian, I found a copy of the yearbook from the year Eva graduated and turned to the senior photos. The names were listed, along with school activities and interests. While some entries ran half a dozen lines or more, Eva's noted only that she'd been a member of the glee club her freshman year.

I counted three photos in from the left and found hers. Despite the sullen smile and impenetrable eyes, Eva Louise Flynn had been a pretty girl with a heart-shaped face and dark coloring that were nothing like her mother's. But very much like my wife's. In fact, the similarity was striking enough to make me catch my breath.

And that's when it hit me. Eva Louise Flynn—E.L.F. The locket Maureen had given Molly was engraved with her real initials, not her nickname. For the first time, I allowed myself to believe that my wife was indeed Eva Flynn.

I felt momentarily light-headed. I took what I now knew of Eva and superimposed it on a mental image of my wife. It cast her in a whole new light. One that in some ways made me feel closer to her—I knew something of her family, of the town where she'd grown up—but at the same time made me feel I'd been married to a stranger. When had Eva taken Maureen's name, and why? And why had she kept the truth from me, her husband?

The librarian who'd help me locate the yearbooks was much too young to have been at the school ten years earlier. I asked her if there was anyone still on the faculty who might have been here then.

"Why don't you talk to the assistant principal, Ms. Parker," she suggested. "She was a physical education teacher here before she became an administrator. She's been here practically forever."

She directed me to the assistant principal's office, which was not unlike the one I remembered from my own school days. Ms. Parker was with a student, the secretary informed me, but if I cared to wait she'd see me when she could.

I waited, but not long.

"Mr. Russell? I'm Joyce Parker." She held out a hand.

Tall and broad-shouldered, Ms. Parker held herself in an erect, almost formidable posture. She reminded me of someone central casting would tap for the role of assistant principal. Unfortunately, she had little to tell me about Eva Flynn.

"The name's familiar," she said, "but beyond that . . ." She shrugged. "As a physical-education teacher, I had classes of sixty to seventy girls at a time. Over the years, that's a lot of girls."

"How about Maureen Brown?"

"Maureen, I remember. But only because of what happened. You knew she was killed in an auto accident the beginning of her senior year?"

"Yes, I heard. Tragic."

"It was. I'm sorry to say she's not the only student we've lost over the years either. But kids, they think it's never going to happen to them."

"What can you tell me about her?"

"She was young for her age. Lonely. One of those kids who grabs your heart, kind of like a stray puppy." Ms. Parker stopped. "Oh wait, Eva Flynn was a friend of hers, right? I remember her now."

"What was she like?"

"Eva was . . . sassy. A bit of a handful, but that's not all bad, in my opinion."

"Wild?"

"I'd say not so much wild as rebellious."

"Her mother indicated to me that she'd gotten into trouble her senior year. Do you have any idea what it was about?"

"Nothing that rings a bell with me now."

I could sense that my time was about up. "Do you know what she's been doing since high school?"

The assistant principal shook her head. "She's not one of the ones I've kept in touch with. You can check with the main office. They try to keep an up-to-date alumni roster, but it's far from complete."

I thanked her and made my way to the other end of the lobby and the school registrar's office. The last known address for Eva Flynn was the house on Brookdale.

When she'd rolled out of Rochester at seventeen, Eva had obviously not looked back.

CHAPTER 35

My return flight was scheduled for six o'clock that evening. When I hadn't heard back from Melody Hughes by three, I dialed her number again. And again got the answering machine. With about an hour before I had to head for the airport, I figured my only chance to speak to her in person would be to catch her as she returned home. It was a long shot, but there was nowhere else I needed to be right then. I could kill time in Melody's neighborhood as well as anywhere.

The Hughes home was farther from town than the area where Eva had grown up. The homes were newer and more pretentious, with lots of rock work on the facades, and gabled roofs that must have driven the builder crazy.

I'd just pulled into a spot across the street from the Hughes house when a new-model Lexus SUV pulled into the driveway. Two young boys, maybe five and seven, emerged from the backseat, followed a moment later by a woman who got out of the driver's side. She was wearing a yellow sundress and carrying an assortment of shopping bags. I recognized "Chico's" and "Ann Taylor," but the other names meant nothing. She was slender and tanned, with shoulder-length blond hair and a full mouth.

I approached her. "Mrs. Hughes?"

She turned, looking more annoyed than surprised. I couldn't say that I blamed her.

"I'd like to speak to you about Eva Flynn."

"Eva—from high school?" She gave a breathless laugh. "That was a while ago."

I nodded. "It won't take long."

The boys were playing a game of bumping shoulders, knocking one another off balance. "Mark and Lawrence, please, watch out for the flowers." She turned back to me, pushed a wave of silken hair from her face. "Why are you interested in Eva?"

"She was my wife." The words came naturally though unintentionally. "She was murdered not too long ago."

"How terrible. I'm so sorry." Melody frowned, still watching the boys out of the corner of her eye. "What is it you want from me? I haven't seen Eva in years."

"I'm trying to find links to someone who might have."

Another breathless laugh. She shook her head as if distancing herself from the question. "That's a part of my life best forgotten."

"Why?"

She shrugged. "I didn't always make the right choices. I'm just grateful I had the good luck not to get sucked in the way Eva did." She stopped abruptly, looking genuinely chagrined. "I'm sorry, that just slipped out."

"It's okay. As you said, it was a long time ago." But that was exactly why I wanted to talk with her. "In what way did Eva get sucked in?" I asked.

"It was just petty stuff, really."

"Such as?"

Another shrug. "We liked to party, all of us."

I waited.

"Booze, guys . . . drugs. Nothing serious."

"Eva took it further though?"

"It was like she had to prove herself." Melody seemed to regret having gone down this road. "She was really needy, but what she showed to the world was how tough she was. Her parents were a big part of the problem. She had a father she couldn't please and a mother who was jealous of her."

"Jealous?"

"Of Eva's youth, her looks. I don't know how all this psychological stuff works, but I do know it wasn't a loving family."

I showed her the photo I'd brought with me. "Would you recognize her?"

Melody smiled. "Yeah."

My heart skipped a beat. I no longer had any doubt. I'd been married to Eva Flynn.

"She looks so happy," Melody said. "She turned out all right, huh?"

I nodded. I wasn't sure I trusted myself to speak right then. Not about Maureen, at any rate. It was one of those moments when tender memories of our life together collided with the ache of missing her.

"I'm really sorry to hear she died." Melody's boys began arguing, and she called out a quick reprimand to them. Then she turned back to me, sounding almost wistful. "Those were good times. Maybe we did do some stupid stuff, but life felt real then. Exciting and full of possibilities. I miss that freedom sometimes. Did you guys have kids?"

"No, but I have a daughter from a previous marriage."

"I have a hard time picturing Eva with this—" She held out her arms. I wasn't sure if she meant the shopping bags, the boys, or maybe all of it. She laughed. "Of course, back then I wouldn't have imagined myself here either."

"When were you last in touch with Eva?"

"Not since high school. She left before school was actually out. Just up and left home."

"Do you know why she ran away?"

"I think she was sick of taking crap from her parents. She got picked up for shoplifting, and they went totally nuts. And there was something else she was upset about too."

Eva's mother had said the same thing. "What was it?" I asked.

"I never knew. I don't think it was anything important, but it sort of was the final straw."

"Any idea where she went?"

Melody shook her head. "Sorry. I wish I'd been better about staying in touch. I liked Eva."

"Are you still in touch with Danny Vance?"

"You've been digging, haven't you?" She looked amused. "Danny's still in town, as you probably know. I've run into him a couple of times, but that's all. He turned out okay too. I mean, he's just a mechanic, but all things considered, Danny's done pretty well."

"Eva used to spend time at his house?"

"Yeah, we all did. He lived with an older brother. At the time we thought it was cool not having parents around. We thought Danny was so lucky."

"Where were his parents?"

"His mother died when Danny was a freshman. I don't know where the father was. They never talked about him."

The younger of Melody's boys tugged on her hand. He whined, "Mommy, I'm hungry."

"Okay, just a minute." She turned back to me. "In his own way, Eric tried. I mean, he was far from perfect, but he held a steady job, made sure Danny went to school and had a roof over his head. It couldn't have been easy for him. He was only five years older than we were."

"Eric?" The name rang a bell with me. I poked around my memory for a clue as to why.

"Danny's brother," Melody said.

Then I remembered. The man who'd broken into my home had told me he was a friend of Eric's. A coincidence? I didn't think so.

"Where's Eric now?" I asked.

Melody shook her head. "Jail, maybe. Or maybe he turned out okay too."

"Why would he be in jail?"

"I'd heard that he was, but that was a while ago." She gave me a long look, seemingly weighing her response. "We all skirted the rules," she said at last. "Eric and Eva, they went a little further than some of us."

"In what way?" I had trouble imagining anything Eva had done more than ten years ago coming back to haunt her now, but Eric's name *had* come up.

"The shoplifting thing with Eva. And Eric was . . . I don't know, someone who seemed to have his fingers in a lot of pots." Melody nodded to her son, who was still tugging at her hand. "I'm sorry I can't be of more help," she said, turning to go into the house. "I haven't thought about any of those people for years."

It appeared I'd learned as much as I was going to from Melody Hughes.

On the flight home, I sank back into my seat, physically and emotionally exhausted. Tension knotted the muscles in my shoulders, and my head throbbed. I now knew Maureen's identity, which was more than I'd dared hope only two days ago, but I didn't really have answers.

I mulled over what I'd learned, dissecting the information bit by bit. Eva Flynn—my wife—had been a rebellious and troubled teen raised in a loveless home. As teenagers were inclined to do, she pushed the rules—partying, which no doubt involved booze, drugs, and sex, as well as a good time. And shoplifting. Not sterling behavior certainly, but in the scheme of things, nothing so terrible either. In fact, Ms. Parker, her PE teacher, appeared to recall Eva with a certain fondness.

She'd left home at seventeen after an argument with her

parents. *The straw that broke the camel's back*, Melody Hughes said. *Something of no consequence*, Mrs. Flynn told me. But Eva had put up with her parents for years. Whatever it was that happened, it was important to her.

I felt I knew something, however limited, of her life growing up. And being married to her, I knew the woman she'd become. But the years in between were a void. What sort of life had Eva carved out for herself after leaving home? Had she taken Maureen's name because she'd envied her friend or because she was desperate for a new identity? And where did Eric fit in?

I thought back to the early stages of our relationship. I'd like to say the first time I met my wife was a moment forever seared in my memory, but that would be a lie. It had been like that with Lisa—our eyes locked, she smiled at me, and I felt as though a wave had knocked me off my feet. But I was younger then, and circumstances were different.

With Maureen, I had only a faint recollection of our early exchanges, and I feared even those were colored and embossed by the subsequent life we'd built together.

I know Ira and I both spoke with her when she applied for the receptionist position, but since we'd delegated hiring to Debbie, the interview was brief and strictly pro forma. Leaning back in the narrow airplane seat, I closed my eyes and tried to bring that first moment with Maureen into my memory. But I couldn't recall anything about it except relief that we'd found someone to step in so quickly. For the first few weeks she worked for us, I passed by her desk several times each day and spoke with her regularly about patient charts, lab results, medication orders, and the like. Yet I'm not sure I would have recognized her if I'd passed her on the street.

Maureen was competent and pleasant, and that was all I cared about.

Then one day, after she'd been there a month or two, we happened to leave the office at the same time. On the way to the parking lot, we talked, and I discovered that she had a wonderful smile, an even better laugh, and a way of looking at me that sent my pulse racing. I thought initially it was because she reminded me a little of Lisa, but gradually I came to see that she was an appealing woman in her own right. Over the course of the next several months, we spent more and more time together. I was flattered by her interest and energized by her companionship. And the sex was good. For the first time since the ordeal of Lisa's death, I was beginning to feel like a whole person again.

I hadn't questioned her extensively about her background, and in return, she hadn't pressed me about Lisa. We talked, of course, but our focus was on who we were now, not who we'd been. She was clearly interested in me. I liked that. I liked feeling like somebody again.

I took everything she told me at face value. Why would I have reason to do anything else? I'd gotten the impression she'd been living in Seattle before coming to California, and before that, somewhere in the South. She led me to believe she'd left Seattle because of a bad personal relationship, but she was reluctant to talk about it, and I didn't push.

Besides, when it came to personal baggage, I was well over the norm.

But I wished now I'd shown more interest in learning about hers.

CHAPTER 36

Hannah reached into her purse for a cigarette. The guy seated next to her at the bar—Jake or Jack or whatever his name was—pulled out a lighter and lit it for her.

"Thanks," she told him.

"My pleasure." His smile was a bit intense, like something copied from the big screen.

He'd bought the beer she was drinking and had spent the last ten minutes trying to impress her with the fact that he drove a Lexus and owned a powerboat. He was in his mid-to-late forties, with a high forehead and a mouth too wide for his face. Not unattractive, but not someone who sent tingles into her toes either. Still, he'd spotted her from across the room and come to claim the empty seat to her right. That counted for something. Or would have if she'd been interested in being picked up.

But if she'd been in that kind of mood, she'd have chosen a bar somewhere farther from home.

"Mind if I have one?" he asked.

She handed him the pack of Marlboros. She shouldn't have come out, she decided. Beer and television in her own living room, a hot bath and bed. That's what she was in the mood for, not some carpet salesman who was soft around the edges.

But she'd felt a need to shake off the prickly irritation of the day.

She and Dallas had met that afternoon with Assistant District Attorney Lon Mitchell to discuss the case against Sam Russell. Mitchell wanted time to study the evidence and confer with his boss before giving them the go-ahead, but Hannah knew they'd moved beyond the stage of conducting an open investigation. Sam was their target. Instead of looking for a killer, they'd focus on culling the evidence that supported Sam's guilt.

It made sense. There were too many holes in his story, and no other viable suspects. Still, the meeting had left her with an uneasy feeling she hadn't been able to shake.

Or maybe it was tomorrow's mammogram looming on the horizon that made her anxious. She knew it was only a matter of time before another lump would be detected.

Jake-or-Jack touched her knee. "Hey, you look lost. What are you thinking?"

She shook her head. "Nothing."

"You can't think about nothing." He leaned close, his tone playful.

But Hannah didn't feel like playing. She turned back to her beer.

"You want another?" he asked.

"I'm fine, thanks. I need to get going anyway."

"Aw, come on. The night's still young."

The night's young, but I'm not. It was something Malcolm used to say when she wanted to stay out and he was eager to head home. He hadn't been old—younger than Jake-or-Jack and certainly better looking. But there was a serious streak to Malcolm that she suspected had been there from the day he was born. Serious and steady. They were qualities she'd admired.

Malcolm was the last person in the world she'd have suspected of cheating. And that made it doubly painful. How desperate he must have been.

Someone put money in the jukebox, and the Beatles started singing "I Want To Hold Your Hand." Hannah's foot tapped out the beat.

"Come on," her companion said. "Let's dance."

"Really, I need to be—"

"One dance before you leave."

She relented, and they joined the throng of sweaty bodies on the tiny dance floor. It wasn't easy to find space, but it felt good to move, to get her blood flowing. Even though Hannah wasn't a great dancer, she loved the feeling of moving to the rhythm of music. And after a beer or two, she didn't care what she looked like.

The music ended and another song came on. One dance became two, then three. The third song was a slow ballad, and Hannah closed her eyes, let herself lean into the solid bulk of her partner. There was something comforting about being in the arms of a man, even a stranger she wasn't ga-ga about.

When the song ended, she pulled away. "Now I really am out of here."

He held onto her hand. "No." He was teasing again.

"Yes." She wanted to sound strong but hiccupped at the same time she spoke. "Truly, I need to get home."

"I'll walk you to your car."

He slipped his arm around Hannah's waist and held her close as they moved through the crowded room.

"Where are you parked?" he asked as they stepped outside into the cool night air.

"Over there." She pointed to her old Camry. Thankfully it was not off by itself in some lonely corner of the lot.

At her car, he kissed her, pressing himself hard against her. The first kiss was urgent and forceful, but when she pulled away, he became more gentle. His features were blurred by the dark of night, allowing Hannah full rein with her imagination. She gave herself a moment to enjoy the physical contact.

He slipped a hand under her blouse. His fingers were soft but cold on her skin. She shivered.

"Hey, what this?"

"A prosthesis," Hannah told him. And then held her breath.

"A pro what?"

"A fake boob."

His hand touched her other breast, and she felt an effervescent tingling sensation all the way down to her toes.

"This one's real," he said. "I can tell."

"So what do you think?"

"I like the real one better."

"So do I," she said.

Maybe he wasn't a prince, but he'd passed the first test. She slid her hands up his chest and then down his back. He had a small layer of fat around his middle. Her standards were slipping something terrible.

"Breast cancer?" he asked.

She nodded.

"How long's it been?"

"Three years." Not even long enough for the oracle of medical wisdom to declare her free of the disease. And tomorrow might just break her three-year run of good luck. She felt panic grip her.

"Bummer," declared her man of the hour. As far as he was concerned, the subject was closed. His fingers went back to exploring the flesh under her blouse.

Hannah wished she could silence the tapes in her head as easily. *Just a small spot, probably nothing. But the radiologist would like a few more films.*

The man nuzzled her neck. "Do you really have to go home? Why don't you stay at my place?"

He wasn't her type, and she hadn't been looking for action. But he hadn't freaked at her lopsided chest, and once he'd lightened up on the kissing, he'd done okay.

Besides, this wasn't a good night to be alone.

"How far is it?" she asked.

"About ten minutes." He stroked the back of her neck, and Hannah shivered with pleasure.

"Okay," she said after a moment. "You lead, and I'll follow you."

The instant she was alone in her own car, Hannah regretted her words. Going home with this guy would be a big mistake. She wasn't really attracted to him, and he lived in the community. She'd made that one of her ground rules— no one she might run into when she was on duty. Sort of like not soiling your own nest, she supposed.

As Hannah pulled onto the main road behind him, she considered the best way to extricate herself—head straight home or follow him and explain.

She was weighing the alternatives when a blue Explorer passed her going the other direction. She caught only a fleeting glance at the license plate, but the first digits matched what Sam had reported seeing the night of the ransom drop.

Hannah made a quick U-turn and followed the SUV. In her rearview mirror, she saw Jake-or-Jack slow then turn to follow her. *Damn.*

She caught up with the Explorer and followed it for about a quarter of a mile. There were two people inside. The driver was taller than the passenger, and slender. That fit the description Sam had given them.

Hannah pulled close enough to read the whole license. It sounded familiar, but she couldn't remember off the top of her head if it was one they'd already checked.

Only one way to find out.

Hannah rolled down her window, reached through, and planted a flashing red light on the roof of her car.

The Explorer slowed then sped up again.

She gave the Camry gas and followed.

The SUV made a sharp right. So did Hannah. She reached for her cell phone and called in her location. With luck, there'd be a patrol car close by.

Within minutes, she heard the wail of a siren ahead of her then saw the bank of flashing lights.

Hannah held her breath. Would the driver of the Explorer stop, or would he plow through and lead them on a full-fledged chase?

The Explorer braked sharply, swerved to the right, and stopped.

The uniforms—Carla and Brian—approached the vehicle from the front. Their hands were on their guns. Hannah came at the vehicle from the rear.

"Let's see the registration," Brian barked.

Hannah was even with the car now. She could see that the driver was male, in his late teens.

Her companion from the bar had screeched to stop behind her and scrambled out of his car. "What's the matter?" he yelled.

"Stay back, Jack."

"Jake. It's Jake."

Well, at least that mystery was cleared up. "I'm a cop. Everything is under control."

"A cop, wow. You're on duty?"

"Just get back in your car and go home."

"I thought you were coming back to my place with me."

Jesus. Hannah looked to Carla to see if she'd heard. She couldn't tell. "Please, Jake. This is police business. Go on home."

"Will I see you again?" When she didn't respond, he yelled, "I'll be at the same spot tomorrow night."

Carla shot Hannah a quick look. There was nothing of the smirk in it Hannah had expected.

"Leave now," Carla said to Jake, "or I'll arrest you for interfering with a police officer."

Hannah walked toward the Explorer. Brian was still dealing with the driver. "What do you mean, you don't know where it is?"

"I just don't," the driver replied.

"Hey, hope to see you again," Jake called out.

Hannah heard Jake's footsteps retreat and the engine start. He took off with a squeal of rubber on asphalt, and she began to breathe easier. What had she been thinking, anyway? Maybe it was time to put an end to this stupid, self-destructive behavior of hers.

"Is this your family's car?" Hannah asked the driver of the Explorer.

He was just a kid, maybe seventeen, who looked scared half to death. He answered her question with a shake of his head.

"Get out of the car," Brian told them. "Both of you. Keep your hands where we can see them."

The boy opened the door and emerged with his hands in the air. His left arm was heavily tattooed. He was joined moments later by a girl in a scanty tank top and short shorts.

"It belongs to my mother," the girl mumbled. Her voice had a faint British lilt.

It sounded familiar. Hannah shone the light near the girl's face. It was the young girl with the cat in her arms who'd answered the door when she and Dallas had been checking SUVs that fit Sam's description.

"You're Sandra Martin's daughter."

"You know her?" Brian asked.

"We talked to her mother when we followed up on the plate Sam gave us." Hannah had a sudden, uneasy thought. "Does your mom know you have her car?"

The girl started to cry. "Not really. She's out with a friend. But Ethan's got his license and everything."

"Shut up, Sally. You don't have to answer their stupid questions." The kid was trying hard to impress the girl, but Hannah could see that his hands were shaking.

"Why didn't you stop when you saw my flashing red light?" Hannah asked.

The boy shrugged, trying to appear nonchalant.

Carla leaned out from the passenger side of the car and held up a baggie. "Probably because there was grass in the car."

Sally started crying harder now. Ethan looked like he might be sick to his stomach.

"Is this the first time you've taken the car?" Hannah asked.

Neither of them said anything.

"Did you borrow it a week ago Friday?"

"We don't have to answer that," Ethan said with bravado that rang false.

Hannah turned to the girl. "Your mom said she was out that night. But you were home. Did you and Ethan take her car?"

"Don't answer," Ethan said to her. "You've got a right to ask for a lawyer."

Sally ignored him and addressed Hannah instead. Tears streamed down her face. "You said you were looking for a car that witnessed an accident. We didn't see any accident."

"But you were on El Dorado," Hannah said with sudden certainty. "And you went through a red light at the intersection of Mills Landing."

Ethan jerked his head in her direction. "How'd you know about that?"

"We got scared," Sally whimpered. "There was this car following us. We wanted to get away. That's all."

"What were you doing out there?"

"We'd been to the quarry," Sally said. "We just wanted someplace to be alone. We weren't doing anything wrong."

Except taking her mother's car without permission and maybe smoking some grass. Could they have been involved in the ransom demand as well?

"What did you do with the money?" Hannah barked.

They both spoke at once. "What money?" The looks on their faces registered genuine surprise.

"You think we should take them in?" Carla asked.

Ethan looked confused. "Take us in? For what? It's only a little grass."

"Did you see anyone else that night?" Hannah asked. "Any other cars on the way out to the quarry?"

"It was dark," Ethan said. "We weren't paying attention."

"A car parked on the side of the road maybe, or by the barn as you come in?"

"No, nothing," Sally said. "We just wanted someplace quiet to talk. We've never seen another car up there."

"That Friday night wasn't the first time, then?"

She was sobbing now. "My mom is going to kill me when she finds out."

Hannah left Carla and Brian to deal with the unauthorized driving. She'd follow up on the kids' story, though from their reactions, she could only assume they knew nothing about the ransom call.

But their account of the evening corresponded almost exactly with Sam's.

The uneasy feeling that had been with her all day gripped her tight like a steel band. It appeared Sam had been telling the truth about following the SUV. Could it be that he was telling the truth about everything?

CHAPTER 37

The guy sitting at Frank's old desk at the station was a young black man he didn't recognize. Looking around the once-familiar room that had been like a second home to him, Frank was hit with the reality that he was now an outsider. He'd been back after retirement but not in the last couple of years. Mostly he met with the guys for a beer after work. With both horror and relief, Frank realized that time had moved on. In his heart he'd been pining for something that no longer existed.

He found his old partner, Wade Cushing, in the file room.

"Hey, Frank, what are you doing here? Millie kick you out of the house for the day?"

Frank laughed. "In a manner of speaking."

"I got two more years, then I'm outa here myself. We can finally get us a daytime bachelor pad and leave the ladies to their dusting and whatever the hell else it is we get in the way of. Big-screen TV, top-notch sound system, maybe even a pool table. A fridge full of beer."

It was a fantasy they'd woven together over years of grueling hours investigating crimes, and Frank was somewhat surprised to discover he no longer found it so appealing. "I don't know, Wade, life changes when you retire. You see things differently."

"Don't tell me you've found God!"

Well, in a way, he had. But it had been the heart attack that ushered in those feelings, not retirement. "We'll talk about it when you're closer to retirement," Frank offered.

"So what brings you here?"

"I'm doing a little follow-up on the Lisa Russell murder."

"Follow-up? That one's dead and gone."

"Don't I know it. Case files had to be dug out of storage. But Lisa's parents keep hoping something will turn up that Sam won't be able to wiggle out from under."

"Ain't going to happen."

"Yeah, I know." Frank brushed a streak of dust from his sleeve. He'd forgotten how dusty the file room was. "But Sam Russell and trouble have crossed paths again, this time in California."

Frank had Wade's full attention now. "He got remarried and his new wife was murdered," Frank explained.

"Whoa. They think Sam did it?"

"That's one theory. Anyone here assigned to Lisa's murder still?"

"I don't think so. As far as the department is concerned, it's closed. We got our man. But funny you should ask, because we got a call last week. A young woman, says she was related to Lisa. She wanted to talk to someone in charge. It wound up on my desk. I haven't had time to follow up. Not a high priority, with the active cases we've got."

"Mind if I talk to her?"

"Be my guest. I'll get you the contact info."

Wade took the file he'd pulled and headed back to the squad room. Frank followed. While Wade rummaged through the stack of message slips on his desk—some things never changed—Frank looked around.

"Who's the guy at my old desk?"

"Jeff Monroe. A little wet behind the ears, but he's a good

guy. I mean, he's black but green." Wade rolled his eyes. "Here it is . . ." He pulled a pink message slip and handed it to Frank. "I'd better keep the slip, but you can copy the information."

Frank reached for a piece of blank paper and wrote down the woman's name—Annalise Rose—and the phone number.

"Thanks," he said. "You remember anything about Lisa Russell being a . . . I don't know, someone who'd come on to deliverymen and the like?"

Wade shook his head. "Why, is the second wife like that?"

"I don't know. But I talked to the holdout juror a while ago, and he said that was a big factor in his decision to give Sam the benefit of the doubt."

"It's been a long time, but that sure isn't the impression I got."

"Me either."

"What a system we got, huh? We bust our butts to haul in the bad guys, and then one kook like that can throw a monkey wrench into the whole system."

CHAPTER 38

Hannah turned from the radiology reception counter and surveyed the packed waiting room, looking for an open seat. She was about to head into the hallway, where she'd noticed a bench earlier, when a technician summoned the next patient for her appointment. Hannah made a beeline for the now-vacant seat.

The woman seated to her right was checking messages on her cell phone. To her left, another was chatting in Spanish to her companion. They were both laughing. Hannah wondered if she was the only one in the room with butterflies in her stomach.

Until three years ago, she'd diligently, and complacently, shown up for routine mammograms when her doctor ordered them. She considered the appointments a nuisance—one more demand on an already tight schedule—but she'd never given them a thought beyond that. She tossed the follow-up postcard that gave her a clean bill of health with the same offhand disregard she showed for junk mail.

Then came the call that started the avalanche that knocked her off her feet.

There was a spot on one of the films, the nurse had told her. It was probably nothing, but the doctor wanted to take a second set of films just to be sure. And with the second set of films, the spot became a lump. A tiny lump, which the doctor assured her would probably turn out to be nothing. But the biopsy showed it to be a definite something, after all. The tiny lump, which only a week earlier had been only an ambiguous spot on the X-ray, was suddenly a frighteningly aggressive strain of cancer. Medical appointments were no longer simple annoyances; they became the milestones in her battle. Surgery, chemo, radiation, tests. More tests. Even now, with a precarious three-year streak of good luck, she was terrified that the next test would send her headlong into another cavern. And that this time she wouldn't have the strength to climb out.

The technician called two more names. The woman with the cell phone stood, as did an older woman across the room. Their seats were quickly grabbed up by others. Hannah counted twenty people in the waiting room. Twenty mammograms an hour, roughly, six hours a day. And most of them were clean.

It was like flying, Hannah told herself. Despite occasional horrific crashes, statistically speaking, airplanes were safe. She needed to take comfort in remembering the odds were in her favor. But they weren't as good as if she'd never had cancer.

Hannah picked up a magazine from the table, flipped through pages of makeup tips and fashion advice without focusing on any of it.

Finally, her name was called. The technician handed Hannah a scratchy paper gown.

"Opening goes in front," she said. "Leave the door ajar when you're ready."

The gown provided no warmth and would be useless for modesty once they got down to business. Nonetheless, Hannah pulled the flimsy paper tight around her and wrapped her arms across her lopsided chest.

The technician reappeared and began setting the machine's controls. Then she positioned Hannah, sandwiched her breast between the acrylic plates that pinched her flesh until it was pancake thin.

"Don't breathe," the tech said.

As if I could, Hannah thought.

"You get off easy having only one breast. Half the torture." No doubt she thought she was being funny. "They ought to give you a discount. They don't, do they?"

Hannah had no idea. Her insurance paid for the mammograms, and since she'd never considered losing a breast to cancer as being advantageous, she'd never checked. In any case, she didn't appreciate the chummy humor.

The woman repositioned Hannah so she felt like she would topple. Another bout with the vise-like machine, and the tech said, "Let me check these. I'll be right back."

The room was freezing. *Right back* took ten minutes. Hannah could hear conversation and laughter in hall. She was sure one of the voices belonged to her technician.

Finally the woman returned. Hannah tried to anticipate what her exact words would be. *There's a spot here that's suspicious, I'd like to take a couple more films.* No, not *suspicious*—that was too emotionally laden. *Unclear* or *blurred.* Or maybe she'd just say, *We need another few shots.*

When she announced that Hannah was free to go, it took Hannah a moment to understand. She dressed in record time, took the sheaf of papers and cards that she'd accumulated since checking in, and fled.

Now the real waiting would start. It took even longer to get the radiologist's report here than it had in LA.

Safely back in her car, Hannah lit a cigarette. The irony of it wasn't lost on her. A cancer stick to still the terror of finding cancer. Or maybe it was just sheer recklessness. Isn't that what the shrink had suggested? A way to get back at Malcolm, though Hannah never did understand how that was supposed to work.

Well, she was quitting, wasn't she? Today she'd exceeded her limit, but tomorrow she'd smoke fewer cigarettes to make up for it.

Her cell phone rang. She flipped it open and answered. Myrna Edwards, the divorce attorney who'd been less than helpful the last time they'd spoken, was on the line.

"You were asking about Maureen Russell," she said.

"Yes. And you claimed confidentiality."

"Now that she's deceased, I suppose I can talk to you. I'm not sure I'll be of much help though."

Hannah was tempted to point out that if she'd talked sooner, her client might have lived, but it probably wasn't true. "So Maureen Russell *did* make an appointment with you?" she asked instead.

"Just one. She wanted to ask about a prenuptial agreement."

"Hers and Sam's?"

"Right. She didn't have an independent attorney at the time she signed it, but it didn't sound like she was coerced or misled either. I told her I wanted to see a copy of the document before giving a final answer, but based on what she told me, I thought it would be binding."

"She was planning on divorcing him?" Hannah asked.

"She must have thought about it, or she wouldn't have asked me about the prenup. When she never made a return appointment, I figured she either decided to tough it out or found another attorney who gave her an answer she liked better."

"Why'd she agree to it in the first place?"

"People in love have trouble imagining a future where the love has turned. Even without the prenup, she'd have had a hard time laying claim to money he'd had coming into the marriage, though divorce is messy business, so you never can tell. She'd probably have been able to leverage something from him." The attorney paused. "The news makes it sound like you're focusing on her husband as a suspect."

"He's someone we're taking a close look at," Hannah replied. "Did she say anything about arguments or threats?"

"No, nothing like that. I prodded her a little too, thinking maybe I could find some wedge that might get her a better settlement. I got the sense that she just didn't want to be married anymore."

"After only two years?" It hadn't taken Malcolm much longer, Hannah reminded herself. Only instead of ending their marriage, he'd simply taken his love elsewhere.

Myrna Edwards chuckled. "In my line of work, I've seen people come to that conclusion after only two weeks."

Hannah thanked the attorney for getting in touch then spent a few minutes thinking about what she'd learned. Not a lot. She'd pretty much assumed that Maureen had at least considered leaving Sam, though having testimony to that effect would help at trial. The prenup was interesting, but if anything, it undercut Sam's motive for killing his wife. Not that money was the only issue where love was concerned.

Slipping her phone back into her bag, Hannah accidentally scattered the various papers that had been forced on her during her medical appointment. She was gathering them into a pile when she noticed a single-page flyer—a recipe for heart-healthy lasagna. Just like the one she'd found in Maureen Russell's pocket with the cryptic *233—160B* jotted on the back.

Hannah took the paper and returned to radiology registration.

"Name?" The clerk behind the counter spoke without looking up.

"I just completed my appointment, but I have a question."

"Medical questions, you'll have to talk to your doctor. For

billing questions, go to room 216, east wing by the eleva-
tors." She was already looking over Hannah's shoulder at the
next patient in line.

"Not those kind of questions." Hannah showed her the
recipe flyer. "You gave me this?"

"It's part of the hospital's community outreach.
Everybody gets one; it's nothing personal."

"Is this the only department that hands them out?"

Irritation flickered crossed the clerk's face. She clearly
found Hannah's inquiries annoying. "They're available all
over the hospital, as well as on-line. There's a new one each
month."

"New when? At the beginning of each month?"

"The first Monday of the month." Her tone was curt. "Now,
if you'll step aside, I need to check in the next patient."

"Just one more question," Hannah said. "Would a doctor
or someone from the hospital have access to the flyer prior to
the first Monday?"

The woman looked as though she might be about ready to
call security. Hannah was reaching into her purse for her
badge when the woman sighed. "I suppose the printer would
have them beforehand, but they're delivered here on
Monday. Nobody gets the inside track for our heart-healthy
recipes." The last was delivered with a caustic smile.

First Monday of the month. Hannah bit her lip and
headed back to the parking lot. Maureen had disappeared on
Sunday the fifth. The flyer wouldn't have come out until
Monday. So how had it ended up in her pocket with her
handwriting on the back?

Hannah hadn't made it back to her car when her phone
rang again. This time it was Dallas.

"You sprung from your appointment yet?"

"Just. I'm on my way." They'd planned to meet at the DA's
office.

"Change of plans. I just got a call from the station.

There's a guy there by the name of Ed Phipps who wants to talk to us."

"Who is he? Does he know something about the Russell murder?"

"Maybe. He's apparently with the FBI."

CHAPTER 39

Even if Dallas hadn't told her, Hannah might have guessed Special Agent Ed Phipps was with the FBI. Like other agents she'd known, he had *that look*: closely cropped hair, squared shoulders and rigid posture, shiny black wing tips, and eyes that took in the whole room at once.

"Detective Montgomery," Phipps said, extending a hand. He looked to be in his early forties, with sharp features and a hawk nose.

Hannah acknowledged the greeting then looked at Dallas. "What's this about?"

"Agent Phipps is interested in talking to us about Maureen Russell." Dallas's voice was noncommittal. If he was sending Hannah any silent cues, she wasn't picking up on them. But she knew her partner well enough to know that he must be bristling at having an outsider stepping on his turf.

"Is there somewhere private where we can talk?" Phipps asked.

Dallas led the way to the smaller of the two interrogation rooms. He gestured to a chair for Phipps, the seat usually reserved for their suspects. Hannah smiled to herself. Men and their pissing contests.

She and Dallas took their regular positions on the other side of the table.

"What's your interest in Maureen Russell?" Dallas asked.

Phipps smiled thinly. "I'm afraid I'm not at liberty to say."

"I see." Dallas stretched his legs out nonchalantly under the table. "We scratch your back, but you keep your hands in your pocket. Is that what you mean?"

"Detectives, surely you—"

"She was murdered," Hannah said. "Did you know that?"

Phipps hesitated. "Yes. Though I didn't find out until I arrived in town."

"Which was when?" Dallas asked.

"This morning."

"What office are you out of?" Hannah asked. She'd assumed he was from the Sacramento field office, or maybe San Francisco, but his comment about arriving in town made her wonder.

"Las Vegas." He crossed his arms over his chest. The body language said it all—he was keeping as much to himself as he could.

Hannah flashed on a mental picture of the old "Spy vs. Spy" cartoon from *Mad* magazine. Dallas and Phipps, each protecting his territory.

"We're working an active homicide," she said. "Anything you can tell us your interest in Maureen Russell could help."

Phipps fidgeted in his chair. Hannah didn't blame him. It was straight-backed and hard, and the seat height was two inches shorter than standard. She wondered if he realized what Dallas had done in seating him there.

"Any suspects?" he asked finally.

"Her husband," Dallas said, and Hannah winced inwardly.

The fact that Sam had been telling the truth about following a dark-color SUV the night of the ransom drop hadn't changed Dallas's mind. He'd dismissed it simply as proof that Sam had planned his story carefully.

"Her husband," Phipps repeated. "Are you talking in terms of a general pattern, or do you have evidence against the guy?"

"Both."

Phipps laced his fingers and frowned. "Tell me about her murder."

Dallas shook his head. "First you tell us why you're interested."

"I can't—"

"And neither can we," Dallas retorted without letting Phipps finish.

"Fine. I can get the details of the crime other ways." Phipps pushed back his chair. "If you're not going to cooperate . . ." He started to rise.

"What brought you to Monte Vista?" Hannah asked. She sided with Dallas in expecting cooperation to be a two-way street, but she didn't think it had to be paved with hostility. "You didn't know Maureen was dead until this morning, yet you came here from Las Vegas looking for her."

Phipps sat down again, but he didn't respond. The expression on his face was that of an exasperated parent.

"Maureen Russell was murdered," Hannah said, with impatience of her own. "Last time I looked, run-of-the-mill homicide wasn't a federal crime. If you've got some other interest in her, we're not going to take that away from you. We might even be able to help you."

"It came to my attention she was missing," Phipps replied after a moment.

"Her name showed up in the FBI database?"

He hesitated. "Her photo."

Hannah was confused. "That still doesn't explain why

you were looking for her." When the FBI got involved in a missing persons case, it was at the request of local authorities. And there'd been no request from Monte Vista.

Phipps pursed his lips. "She was a possible witness."

"Witness to what?" Hannah and Dallas asked in unison.

"It's an FBI matter."

"But it might also be the key to our homicide case," Hannah pointed out. She knew the FBI liked to play things close to the vest. They wanted to call the shots, and they weren't happy about sharing. Still, most of the agents she'd dealt with in the past were reasonable people. "Surely you can tell us something."

He sighed. "It involves drugs. Now that we've tossed the ball back and forth a couple of times, what can you tell me about her murder? I'll help you to the extent I can once I get a fuller picture."

Dallas looked to Hannah. She shrugged. It might be their only chance to hear what Phipps had to say, and he *could* get the information on Maureen Russell's murder without them.

"Her husband reported her missing a week ago Sunday," Dallas said, taking the lead.

"He wasn't convinced foul play was involved," Hannah added. "Not at first. There seemed to be some possibility she'd simply taken off."

Dallas leaned forward, resting his arms on the table. "But he was uncooperative from the start. Wouldn't let us search the house or car, gave evasive answers to questions that should have been straightforward. Then he comes up with a story about a kidnapping. He claims to have gotten a ransom call, during which he heard his wife's voice over the telephone. Two days later, her body turned up in the wine cellar of a house owned by a colleague of his."

"This colleague—"

"Is out of the country," Dallas said. "He let a friend use his house, which is how the body was discovered when it was. Otherwise, we'd still be looking for her."

"How was she killed?"

"Strangled, and there were stab wounds to her chest. According to the coroner, she'd been dead for more than two days, which means the husband's story about a kidnapping is nothing but a crock. My bet is she was already dead when he reported her missing."

Hannah bit back the urge to speak up about the flyer. You didn't broadside your partner in front of the FBI. There would be time to tell Dallas later, in private. Still, she found herself feeling oddly protective of Sam. "We haven't ruled out the possibility that the ransom call from the kidnappers was unrelated to her murder," she said.

Phipps got up from his chair and walked to the other side of the small room. "Who's the husband?"

"Sam Russell," Dallas said. "He's a doctor. This is where it gets even better. He stood trial in Massachusetts for the murder of his first wife."

"But he wasn't convicted," Hannah pointed out.

"When was this?"

"She was killed seven years ago."

Phipps frowned. "What were the circumstances in that case?"

"He'd been out biking for the day," Dallas said, "and arrived home to find his wife missing. Her body was discovered a few days later in the woods outside of town. Manner of death was the same as with his current wife."

"What about motive?" Phipps asked.

"Not clear." Hannah spoke up before Dallas could. It wasn't clear which case Phipps was inquiring about at this point, and Hannah didn't care. She was tired of the focus on Sam. "Now, why don't you tell us why Maureen Russell's photo sparked your interest. Surely not every missing housewife garners the interest of the FBI?"

Phipps ignored the question. "I'd like to look at the case file," he said.

"Not so fast." Dallas left his chair and stood in front of

the agent. They were evenly matched in height, but Phipps was broad and muscular and must have outweighed Dallas by fifty pounds. "We've answered your questions. Now it's your turn. Tell us what this is about."

Phipps glowered for a moment then walked back to the table, reached into his briefcase, and pulled out a photograph. It was grainy, in black and white, and the light was poor. It showed Maureen Russell and a dark-haired man stepping into a cab.

"Where did that come from?" Dallas asked.

"Las Vegas."

"That's hardly an answer." Hannah supposed Phipps was enjoying this, but from her perspective, the game was growing tiresome. "Who's the guy?"

"Someone we've been keeping an eye on. We think she may have ties to organized crime."

Hannah looked at him. Was he joking?

"Sam Russell's wife in the mob?" Dallas sounded skeptical as well. "Are you shitting us?"

"No, it's the truth."

But not all of it, Hannah guessed. She waited for Phipps to continue. He didn't. "I don't know how we can help," Hannah said. "Maureen Russell is dead."

"And you suspect her husband of having killed her. Maybe you're right. But maybe not. A woman with connections—"

Dallas put his hands on the table and leaned closer. "You'd better not say that outside of this room," he warned. "That's the kind of remark defense attorneys dream about."

Phipps gave Dallas a disgusted look. "Do you think I'm petty enough to screw up your case intentionally, or just stupid enough to do it by mistake?"

Hannah jumped in and addressed Phipps. "So, what's your theory?"

"No theory, just questions."

"You're barking up the wrong tree," Dallas said. "Ours is a simple homicide. Everything points to her husband."

Phipps crossed his arms again. "Then why haven't you arrested him?"

Hannah and Dallas exchanged looks. In her mind, everything *hadn't* pointed to Sam. And now, with what Phipps had told them, the realm of possibilities had expanded considerably.

Hannah turned back to Phipps. "You're probably wasting your time, but it's yours to waste. I'll get you the file."

As she left the room, she could feel Dallas's eyes like daggers on her back.

CHAPTER 40

Wednesday morning, I set my alarm for five-thirty. With the three-hour time difference, I was hoping I'd be able to catch Danny Vance in Rochester at the beginning of his work shift. I made myself a cup of strong coffee then dialed the number for the service station.

"This is Danny," he said when he came to the phone.

I could barely contain my excitement at finally reaching him. I introduced myself and told him I'd gotten his number from Melody Hughes. "I wanted to talk to you about Eva Flynn," I told him.

"What about her?" He didn't sound particularly surprised to hear her name.

"You were friends in high school?"

"We were part of a group that hung around together. She was actually closer to my brother Eric than to me."

"Have you talked to her recently?"

"Not in years. Like I said, there was nothing special between us."

"Do you know if Eva and Eric have stayed in touch?"

Danny hesitated. "What's this about? Are you a friend of hers?"

"I'm her husband."

"Wow." It sounded like he wasn't quite sure what to make of that. "How long have you been married?"

"Two years."

"Wow," he said again. "That's great, I guess." There were voices in the background competing for Danny's attention. He covered the mouthpiece and said something to one of his companions. "Sorry," he said, speaking into the phone again. "I don't have a lot of time to talk."

"Eva was killed not too long ago," I told him. "Murdered. For reasons too complicated to go into right now, I've reason to believe her death might be tied to . . . to her past." I wasn't about to tell Danny that his brother might be somehow involved.

"Murdered? Jesus, I'm sorry to hear that." His voice registered real regret.

"Where's Eric now? I'd like to talk with him."

Danny hesitated. "Last I heard, it was Las Vegas."

"When was that?"

"About a month ago. In fact, he mentioned Eva. Said she'd gotten in touch with him."

I felt my pulse quicken. "Did he say why?"

"No. It was just something he mentioned in passing. You in Phoenix?"

"Phoenix?"

"A few years back, Eric told me Eva was living in Phoenix."

"California," I said, trying to remember if my wife had mentioned ever living in Phoenix.

"Never been there. I've heard it's nice."

"Some parts are nicer than others." I took a sip of my coffee. "You don't happen to know what she was doing in Phoenix, do you?"

He seemed taken aback by the question. "I thought you were married to her."

"We didn't talk much about the past," I explained. A gross understatement if there ever was one.

"She was working at a bookstore, I think. We got a laugh out of it because in high school Eva hardly knew what a book was."

I'd filled in another piece of the puzzle that was my wife's life. "She turned into quite a reader," I told him. She read mostly romances, but she'd gone through them at a rapid clip. "I think she probably changed quite a bit since her teens."

"We all have, I hope." There was more jumbled background conversation, and I heard Danny speak away from the phone. "Okay, I'll be right there." Then he said to me, "Sorry, I've got to go."

"How can I reach Eric?"

"I can give you his number, but I don't know if it will do any good. I've been trying to get hold of him, and all I get is his voice mail."

"Do you have an address in Las Vegas?" I wanted to talk to Eric badly enough that I'd fly there if I couldn't reach him by phone.

"Afraid not," Danny said. "He moves around a lot."

"Does he have a job?"

"One of the casinos."

"Which one?"

"Vegas is another place I've never been, so the names don't mean much to me. I got the feeling it wasn't one of the glitzy ones."

Just as I was about to hang up, I thought of something else. "Danny, one more question. Does Eric use the e-mail name, Redhotsugarbear?"

"Not that I ever heard. Doesn't sound like something Eric would come up with."

I thanked him for talking to me, left my number, and asked him to have Eric call me if he got in touch.

When I hung up, I made myself a second cup of coffee, which didn't help my already jittery nerves. Eric knew Eva. He'd talked to her in the last month. The intruder had used

Eric's name. *You don't want to follow Eric.* And now Eva was dead. I was on to something, I was sure of that. Something that would help me understand my wife and might even help me find her killer. But I wasn't sure where to go with it.

I tried the cell number Danny had given me for Eric and was connected to voice mail. I left my name and number then called Las Vegas information, asked for Eric Vance, and got nothing, not even an E. Vance. Next I tried a few casinos and again struck out.

I checked the Internet for bookstores in Phoenix and printed out the pages of addresses and phone numbers. If I could find someone who'd known my wife in Phoenix, maybe I could get some answers that way.

By the time I'd finished my coffee, I'd decided that the kind of information I wanted was better obtained in person than by phone. I called Southwest and booked a flight for Phoenix for tomorrow and Las Vegas the day after. Both flights were short enough that I could spend the day and be home by dinnertime. Molly would hardly know I was gone.

At seven, I woke Molly and made French toast and bacon for both of us.

She eyed the plates suspiciously. "Is it a holiday or something?"

"Why?"

"We usually eat cereal during the week."

When we'd first moved to Monte Vista, I made Molly French toast or scrambled eggs almost every day. But after I married Maureen . . . Eva, the pattern had changed. Maureen didn't eat breakfast, and somehow cooking a big meal and leaving her out felt funny.

"I decided we deserved something special," I told Molly. "Because you're so special."

She gave me an unconvincing smile. "You're trying to make me feel good, aren't you?"

"There's something wrong with that?"

She shrugged, and we ate in silence for a while. If only protecting Molly were as easy as making a home-cooked breakfast. Hell, I'd have baked the bread from scratch and cured the pork myself if that's all it took.

Finally, I asked, "Are you going to tell me what happened to upset you at school the other day?"

She put down her fork and stared at the table.

"Are the kids giving you a hard time because of me?"

Her bottom lip quivered and tears welled up in her eyes.

"Oh, honey. I'm sorry."

"I don't care what they say. They don't know anything."

I smoothed the back of her head with my hand, wishing with that simple gesture I could brush the whole experience away. "I know it's hard, Molly. And I feel terrible about being the cause of it."

"It's not your fault."

I wondered if she really believed that. I hoped so. "If you'd rather not go to school for a bit, we could do lessons here at home."

"Grandad says that would be letting them win."

"What do you think?"

"He's probably right," she said, sounding less than convinced. "It's better just to ignore them."

"But that's not always so easy to do, is it?"

She was quiet for several moments, staring at her plate. "Are they going to send you to jail?" she asked finally, her voice barely above a whisper.

The twin blades of worry and guilt twisted in my gut.

Being a parent is never easy, but there are times it's harder than others. This was one of the hard times. Was it best to offer false assurance or give her an honest answer? I opted to do both.

"I don't think that will happen, honey. I'd like to promise you it won't, but it's not something I have control over. The police want to find the person who killed Maureen, and there are some things that make them think it might have been me."

She kept her eyes on her plate.

"They are wrong. You know that, don't you? You know that I had nothing to do with the terrible thing that happened to her?" Until that moment, I'd never considered that Molly might have her own doubts about my involvement.

She nodded then looked at me. Solemn and trusting. "I know you didn't, Dad."

I prayed she was right. "Good. I think the police will figure that out pretty soon too."

"Like they did with Mom?"

"Right." Only it hadn't been the cops who figured it out then but one lone juror. It took my breath away every time I considered how close I'd come to being convicted. "I don't want you to worry about it, okay?"

She nodded unconvincingly.

I took a bite of bacon, though I no longer had the stomach for it. "So what about school? You want to stay home or stick it out?"

She sighed. "I'll go."

I usually dropped Molly off at the school crosswalk and went on my way. But today I felt the need to get out of the car and go with her to the playground gate. Nobody pointed at us or called out names, which I'd feared might happen. I felt modestly reassured. Maybe it was only a small group of kids who were giving Molly a hard time, and by now they'd even forgotten why. At their age, scandals were generally short lived.

I knew better than to hug her good-bye in front of her friends, but I squeezed her shoulder. "Have a good day, Sweetpea." Then I mouthed the words, "I love you."

"Me too." And she ran off to join a group of girls.

Two or three of the faces were familiar, but the only one I actually recognized was Heather Moore. She gave the others in the group that vapid, rolled-eye expression pre-adolescent girls were so good at, and, as if on cue, the girls turned their backs on Molly and walked away.

I bit my lower lip and willed myself not to go after her and drag her home.

Molly looked after them a moment then squared her shoulders and marched off toward the classrooms. She reminded me right then so much of Lisa it brought an ache to my chest. *You'd be proud of your daughter*, I told her. *So very proud.*

As I turned to head back to my car, I caught sight of Sherri, who was getting out of her car with another mother. They were struggling with several boxes and bags. Roommother stuff, no doubt. I went to see if I could help.

"You need an extra pair of hands?" I asked.

Sherri looked up at me. Her expression, which had been animated in talking to her friend, turned flat. "Hello, Sam."

"Want me to help carry stuff?"

The other mother backed away slightly. She looked uncomfortable.

"We're fine," Sherri said curtly.

"I don't mind."

"Really, we're fine." Sherri and her friend hurried across the street, still struggling with their load but eager to put as much distance between themselves and me as possible.

As I watched their retreating forms, I thought of Molly's squared shoulders and rigid chin and felt the rising tide of despair. Dear God, how had things turned so badly?

CHAPTER 41

Although Ira had suggested I stay away, I went into the office that morning. There was paperwork I needed to deal with. Since I'd be in my own private office with the door closed, I figured the patients wouldn't even know I was around.

I caught Ira at his desk before the morning rush started and explained.

"That's fine, Sam. Whatever works for you. I was only thinking it would be best all around if you didn't have to see patients."

"You managing okay on your own?" I asked.

"It's hectic, but it keeps me out of trouble." He was sorting through a stack of message slips but looked up to offer me a forced smile. "How are you doing?" His tone was perfunctory.

"I have my ups and downs."

"Are the police making any progress finding Maureen's killer?"

Part of me wanted to tell him about Maureen being Eva, but I held back. Until I knew the full story, the less said, the better. Besides, I was hurt by how quickly Ira had turned his focus from my pain to the well-being of the practice. But then, Ira probably harbored his own doubts about my innocence.

"They don't keep me in the loop," I told him.

"No, I guess not." He put the messages aside. "I'm sorry for all you're going through, Sam. It's gotta be rough."

"Yeah."

He wet his lips. "They can't pin it on you if you didn't do it."

I wasn't sure if Ira meant he didn't believe I'd killed Maureen or only that if I hadn't, I'd probably be okay. Suddenly, I didn't really want to know which it was.

"Thanks," I said blandly. "And don't worry about this morning. I'll keep out of your hair."

It was almost noon when I finished up. I took my files and correspondence to the front desk. As I approached, Debbie slid the glass partition shut and lowered her voice. "I was just coming to get you," she said in a stage whisper. "You've got visitors."

Visitors, not patients. "Who?"

"The police."

The blood in my veins went cold. I gave half a thought to dashing out the back door. "Did they say what they wanted?"

"To talk to you."

Talk. Of course they'd say they wanted to talk. They'd hardly storm into my reception area waving their handcuffs.

The moment of my arrest seven years earlier flashed through my mind. I'd been at work then too. At the hospital, where I'd just delivered good news to an overweight man who'd thought he was having a heart attack—merely indigestion—and was reading through the chart of an elderly woman who'd presented with a case of severe nausea. I could recall with frightening vividness the green of the walls, the cloying mix of hospital food and stale air, the buzz of conversation at the nurses' station, and the heavy, unexpected footsteps of men on a mission. The suddenness of it all, coming when I least expected it. The humiliation of being dragged off in handcuffs. The total disconnect between my life up to that point and what was unfolding in the moment.

I didn't even get to say good-bye to Molly.

"Show them to my office," I told Debbie. I swallowed hard, hesitated, and then said, "And if I end up . . . going with them, call my dad and have him pick up Molly, okay?"

Debbie put a reassuring hand on my arm. She had the same soft, velvetlike skin my mother had had. "It's going to be okay, Sam. You had nothing to do with what happened to Maureen. Everyone who knows you, knows that."

"Thank you." Her simple vote of confidence brought tears to my eyes. I tried for an upbeat smile, but I could feel my mouth quiver. "Give me a minute, then show them to my office."

There were three of them—Hannah Montgomery, Dallas, and a broad-shouldered man I didn't recognize. None of them was smiling, but I didn't see any handcuffs.

I leaned back into the plush leather of my chair and watched them file in.

With three visitors, my office was crowded. Okay by me. There was plenty of room on *my* side of the desk.

I asked Debbie to find another chair for the visitors.

"Don't bother," Dallas said. "I'll stand." Hannah took a seat. The stranger elected to stand also.

It made me uncomfortable to have both men standing, but I figured that was the point.

"This is Agent Phipps," Hannah said when the four of us were alone. "With the FBI."

"The FBI?" I knew they sometimes investigated kidnappings, but the consensus seemed to be that Maureen hadn't actually been kidnapped. Did his presence signal a change of heart about that?

Phipps pulled a photo from his satchel and set it on the desk in front of me.

It was a picture of Maureen and a man. They were getting into a cab, and the man had a hand on her shoulder. He was about her age, with a full head of dark, wavy hair. He wasn't particularly attractive, but he had the kind of craggy look a lot of women went for.

"Is this your wife?" Phipps asked.

I nodded and felt an irrational eddy of jealousy in my gut. I wasn't normally the jealous type, but there was something oddly intimate about the moment captured on film.

"Do you recognize the man?" Phipps asked, almost accusingly.

It took a moment to find my voice. "Never seen him before."

"You're sure?"

"Of course I'm sure." I'd taken an instant dislike to the man in the photo, probably because he was with my wife and I knew nothing about it. "When was this taken?"

"A couple of weeks ago."

A couple of weeks? The eddy of torment inside me intensified. I'd been hoping it was a piece of her missing past. I looked to Hannah Montgomery. Was this the man she'd hinted that Maureen had been involved with?

Hannah's eyes were, as always, a warm, soft green. I thought I might have seen sympathy in them, or pity. But her expression was impassive.

"The afternoon of April twenty-ninth, to be exact," Phipps added.

"That's—"

Phipps nodded. "Seven days before your wife disappeared."

Before she was murdered, I amended silently. "What's it mean?"

"You tell us."

"I have no idea. Why don't you ask the guy?"

"He's dead."

Dallas grasped the back of the empty chair and rocked it toward him. I resisted the urge to tell him to put it down and turned back to Phipps. "What's your interest in this anyway?"

"Vance had some information we wanted. Your wife was the last person we know to see him alive."

I opened my mouth, but no words came out. "Vance," I said at last. My voice sounded like sandpaper. "Eric Vance?"

Phipps crossed his arms and regarded me intently. "So you *do* know him."

"It's a long story," I croaked.

"We've got time."

Hannah Montgomery's face registered surprise. "Eric. Isn't that the name that came up during the break-in of your house?"

I nodded.

Dallas let go of the chair, and it settled back onto all fours with a bang. "I thought you didn't know anyone named Eric."

"I didn't. Not then, anyway."

"I'm waiting," Phipps said. "How do you know Vance?"

I looked across my desk. Six eyes stared back at me. I'd thought I had the roomy part of the office, but now it felt like the hot seat. I realized I was in way over my head.

"I want to talk to my attorney," I told them.

CHAPTER 42

Jesse's strength, one of many, was his patience. I don't know what he was like before—when he was an overworked public defender and a heavy drinker—but now he almost never became ruffled or excited. And when he gave you his attention, it was as though he had all the time in the world.

He was sitting across from me now in a private interview room at the police station, calmly listening as I brought him up to date on everything I'd learned, including the current kicker—the photograph Agent Phipps had showed me. Jesse had arrived about thirty minutes after I called him, still dressed in the cargo pants and boots he wore for work at the nursery. He'd brought us each a large cup of coffee from Starbucks' chief competitor in town, the locally owned Daily Grind.

"When are you going to get yourself an actual attorney?" he asked.

"They'll appoint one if I'm arrested, won't they?"

"Not one you're going to want."

"You were a public defender."

"Proves my point." He flipped the lid from his cup. "But since I'm here now, bring me up to speed."

When I finished telling him what I knew, he took a few more sips then set his cup down on the table. "The standard legal advice is, the less said the better."

"Not tell them about Eva, you mean?"

"There's just too much we don't understand at this point."

"But they think I killed her!"

"They haven't arrested you yet," he pointed out.

"It's only a matter of time."

"You think just because you tell them your wife wasn't Maureen Brown but Eva Flynn, they will suddenly slap their heads and say, 'Gee, Sam must be innocent after all'?"

"It opens up other possibilities."

"But it doesn't impact motive or evidence against *you*. Hell, it could even make you look guiltier."

"Is that possible?" I tried for a humorous tone, but the words came out flat.

Jesse smiled, revealing his gold tooth. "Don't tempt fate."

"She's been involved with Eric Vance since high school. Don't you think they need to know that?"

"Sam." He shook his head in disbelief. "Like everyone else who's innocent, you think if you spill your guts, you're home free. Examples of that working against you are legendary."

"But she was using an assumed name. And now, with the FBI interest in Eric Vance, they've got to see that I had nothing to do with her murder."

"Or maybe you found out the truth—whatever that is—and killed her in anger. Or maybe you are all three part of whatever the FBI is investigating. In fact, I'd guess that's their working premise." Jesse drummed his fingers on the tabletop. "My advice, Sam: Tell them nothing."

I shook my head. "Jesse, you're one of my best friends. You've given me strength when I needed it most. But I can't go back in there and tell them I'm refusing to talk. I need to set the record straight."

Another smile. "I didn't think you'd take my advice, Sam."

"Then why'd you give it?"

"Because it's good advice." He frowned and leaned forward. "But watch what you say. Tell them about Eva if you must, but not *everything*."

"About not remembering, you mean?"

He nodded, then whispered, "And the shoe."

"I'll be careful."

"I hope so." Jesse stood. "Okay, let's go get this over with."

"So what's your connection to Vance?" Phipps asked when we were again all together.

Jesse held up a hand. "Not so fast."

Phipps regarded him with the politely disguised aversion one might show a host's mangy, old dog. How much of it had to do with Jesse's appearance, and how much from his being a lawyer, I couldn't tell.

"Sam's learned some things this last week," Jesse continued. "Things which he's under no obligation to disclose. But because he's as interested as you are in finding his wife's killer, he's willing to share them with you." Jesse looked at each of the three in turn before speaking. "First off, he discovered that his wife wasn't the woman she claimed to be."

"What?" The reaction was unanimous.

"Maureen Brown, with the same birth date and birthplace as claimed by his wife, and the same parents, has been dead for ten years. Her high-school friend, Eva Flynn, was using her name when she met and married Sam."

"Of all the—" Dallas bit back the rest of the remark. "Why?"

Jesse shook his head. "Sam has no idea why. That's one of the things he'd like to know himself. Eva grew up in Rochester, New York, as did Eric Vance. They were friends in high school, and she's apparently stayed in touch with him. Sam didn't know anything about this until a few days ago. He's been trying to trace her activities since high school, when she left home, until he met her."

Phipps wrote something in his notebook.

Hannah addressed me directly, pleasantly. "What have you learned?"

"She was living in Phoenix right before she came to Monte Vista," I said. "Her mother is still in Rochester and hasn't seen Eva in years. Her father's dead. I got the impression it wasn't a happy family."

"Your wife never said a word about any of this?" Phipps asked.

"No. She didn't want to talk about her past."

"You didn't think that was odd?"

I sighed. There was no way to make them understand, when I wasn't sure I understood myself. But at the time, I'd been all too willing to go along. Maureen loved me and I loved her. My heart, which had been ravaged with grief at losing Lisa, was slowly healing. The last thing I wanted was to force an issue that might break it again.

"In retrospect," I said, "it raises big-time questions. But at the time . . . I was in love, and I know . . . I can understand how a person might want to put the past behind them."

"You would know about that, wouldn't you?" Dallas said pointedly. "Having been there yourself."

I fought the urge to get up and leave right then. Instead, I looked Dallas in the eye. "Yes, Detective Pryor, I have been there. You obviously haven't. The pain of losing someone you love is unbearable."

I caught a flicker of empathy in Hannah's expression, but Phipps ignored the exchange altogether.

"What about the photo?" he asked. "Did you know your wife had been to Las Vegas?"

I shook my head.

"Isn't that something you'd know?"

"Not if she just went for the day. It's only an hour's flight. I've checked the schedule."

Dallas narrowed his gaze at me. "Why'd you check? You said you didn't even know about the photo until today."

Maybe this was what Jesse meant about it being easier to say nothing. But I knew that fudging and backtracking were worse still. "I knew Eric Vance was in Las Vegas because his brother told me. He said Eva had recently contacted Eric."

They waited.

"And I booked myself a flight there. And to Phoenix."

This time all the eyes in the room were aimed my direction, including Jesse's. And the look in them was identical.

"Jesus." Phipps tugged at his ear.

"Stay out of this," Dallas warned, directing his comment to me.

Even Jesse felt obliged to weigh in with advice. "Not a good idea, Sam."

"This is my *wife* we're talking about. I have to know what she was doing."

"Let us handle it," Phipps said.

"Are you going to stop me?" I looked at the faces around me. No one spoke. There seemed to be a lot of silent dithering going on.

Finally, Jesse spoke up. "Are you telling Sam he is not free to travel within the U.S.?"

Instead of answering, Phipps looked at the photo again. "You're saying that you don't know anything at all about Eric Vance?"

"From talking to his brother, I know he works at a casino. And I gather he has a record. He raised his brother, who is

Eva's age, after their mother died. That's the sum total of my knowledge."

"What's the FBI's interest in him?" Jesse asked. "Was he under investigation?"

Phipps pressed his palms together. "At one point. Most recently he was cooperating with us. He had information we need to go forward."

"To go forward with what? What was he involved in?" Jesse's tone had become more clipped. He sounded more like a lawyer than an easygoing garden enthusiast.

"I'm not at liberty to say."

"How'd he die?"

"Cerebral hemorrhage." Phipps said. "Blunt trauma to the head."

"Accidental death or murder?"

Phipps hesitated. "We're not sure."

"When?"

"Shortly after this photo was taken."

I felt a new stab of worry. "You don't think my wife had anything to do with it, do you?"

"We don't think she was with him at the time."

It wasn't a decisive answer, but it was more reassuring than not. At least they weren't ready to pin a murder on her.

Jesse straightened, hands on the table. "It's obvious," he said, "that Sam's wife had a secret life and was possibly involved in something criminal. A few days after she disappeared, an intruder broke into Sam's house with a message about Eric. You can't at this point still be thinking Sam had anything do with her murder."

Dallas flashed a mocking grin. "Mr. Black, you know better than that. We have only Sam's word about the break-in and his ignorance of his wife's activities. Don't tell me you never met a suspect who twisted the truth to work in his favor."

"You can't—"

"And if Sam only recently learned about Eric and Las

Vegas . . ." Dallas shrugged. "Jealousy, anger, revenge—seems to me I've run into them all before. As motives for murder."

I didn't even have to look at Jesse to know he was giving me the I-told-you-so look. The look that said *This is why I told you not to talk to the cops.*

CHAPTER 43

Frank traded calls with Annalise Rose for a couple of days before he finally reached her. When Wade Cushing first handed him the name, Frank had held out some small ray of hope that she might have pertinent information. But she sounded young, and Frank figured she just wanted to hear about the case firsthand.

"You said you wanted to talk to someone about the Lisa Russell murder," Frank said when she came on the line.

"Right. She was my cousin."

Frank explained he'd gotten her name from Detective Cushing, that he was now retired but had been the lead detective on the case at the time of Lisa's murder.

She cut him off. "Can we talk later? I'm on my way to class."

So she *was* young. "You in school?" With cell phones, you never knew where you'd catch the person you were calling.

"I'm a freshman at MIT. It's a ninety-minute class. Can I call you back when I get out?"

"How about I meet you there instead. Tell me where."

"You know the campus?"

"Somewhat."

"How about right outside the union. How will I recognize you?"

"I'll be the old guy."

Frank hadn't been to Cambridge for years, but it hadn't changed much, including the difficulty of finding a parking spot. He finally got lucky then sat on a bench outside the union to wait for her.

All that youth, he thought as he watched the throngs of students pass by. Most walked, but many rode bicycles or skated by on Rollerblades. A few had scooters. He hoped they appreciated their youth, though he was sure they didn't. That was one of life's ultimate ironies. Youth was wasted on the young.

It was almost exactly ninety minutes after his phone conversation with Annalise Rose that he was approached by a girl—young woman was the proper term, he'd been told—with dark hair pulled into a pony tail and snug jeans that were cut below her navel. She had rosy cheeks and a perky spring to her step.

"You must be Detective Donahue," she said, sitting down next to him.

"*Old* must have been a pretty good description."

She laughed. "There are lots of *older* people on campus, but you're the only one who looks like he's waiting for someone."

Frank appreciated the *old/older* distinction. He offered a hand. "Call me Frank. I'm retired, so I no longer hold the title of detective."

She dumped her backpack on the bench between them and shook his hand. "Pleased to meet you."

"So, Lisa Russell was your cousin?"

"Right. Our mothers are sisters." She rocked forward. "I feel sort of stupid calling the police at this point, but I decided I needed to. I overheard my mom talking to Aunt Sylvia, Lisa's mother. Aunt Sylvia said the police were reexamining the evidence and that there might be a new trial."

So much for Frank's careful admonition about the odds of success. The Pattersons had heard what they wanted to hear. "Not officially," he told Annalise. "But your aunt and uncle asked me to take another look, and I agreed."

"They were pretty upset when Sam got off."

"So was the DA," I reminded her. "And so were we."

She looked as though she hadn't thought about it from that angle before. "Yeah, I guess that makes sense. I was only twelve at the time, so nobody ever told me anything outright. It was just what I picked up here and there."

Like most kids, she probably picked up a lot. Parents weren't usually aware how much kids knew.

"How well did you know Lisa?"

"She was older than me, obviously. But in some ways she was like a sister. Both of us were only children, and our mothers were sisters. I was a flower girl in her wedding, and I used to hang around with her and Sam, and then with the baby. They were both, Sam included, really nice to me."

She played with the strap of her backpack for a moment. She seemed on the verge of continuing, so Frank waited.

"It's bothered me all these years that I never said anything."

"About what?"

"Lisa wasn't her usual sunny self in the weeks before she was killed. She seemed agitated and worried."

Frank nodded. "Her mother testified to that at trial. She thought Sam and Lisa were having marital problems."

"They might have been. But Lisa also talked about a monster."

"A monster?"

"Not a wild beast. And not Sam. I'm sure she didn't mean that. No, there was someone bothering her. I thought maybe an old boyfriend or something. I talked to her the day before she was killed, and she told me she was going to get rid of the monster."

"She said that?"

"I *think* she said it just like that, but I'm not sure anymore. I know that was the impression I got. I was what's called a mother's helper, only it wasn't a formal job or anything. I'd just hang around and help out playing with Molly while Lisa did chores or took a little time for herself. I remember Molly and I were playing Chutes and Ladders, which if you haven't played it in a while I have to tell you is the most boring game invented, when Lisa came into the room and announced she was going to get rid of the monster."

"What did you think she meant?"

"Molly thought it was a game. And Lisa turned it into one. I figured she'd just decided she wasn't going to let whatever was bothering her get to her anymore. And after she died, when everyone was sure it was Sam who killed her, I sort of forgot about it. Nearer to the trial I remembered and told my aunt, who said not to worry."

"So why contact the police now?"

"I wouldn't have, except that you guys are looking into it again and I figured it might be important."

"An old boyfriend is what you think?"

"That's what I thought then. At twelve, pretty much everything was about boys. Now, I don't know. I remember there was some friend Lisa was mad at, so I guess it could have been her. Or something else entirely."

"Do you know the friend's name?"

"No. I only saw her once." Annalise waved to a group of students. "My mom says Sam's second wife was murdered too. Do you think Sam did it?"

"I don't know. There are certain similarities."

"Poor Molly. It must be hard on her knowing her dad might be a killer. Aunt Sylvia and Uncle Hal want to bring her to Boston to live with them."

Frank nodded. They'd already spoken with an attorney about the best way to proceed. "We'll have to see what develops with the investigation. But I appreciate your getting in touch."

CHAPTER 44

I got to the airport in time to get the first boarding group on a Southwest flight to Phoenix. Since the airline didn't assign seats, getting there early was important if you wanted to avoid sitting in the middle. I took a window seat near the front of the plane, and an older woman sat on the aisle. I was hoping the flight wouldn't be full.

As I settled in, my mind was struggling to make sense of what I'd learned. Why had Maureen gone to Las Vegas? Why hadn't I known?

April 29 was a Monday. I'd have been at work, Molly at school. I'd checked the calendar at home. There was nothing noted for the day. But then, she'd hardly have written *Meeting with Eric in Las Vegas*. Had I gotten home late that evening? Had Molly been with a friend? I tried to reconstruct that Monday, but in my memory it was a day like any other. I examined Maureen's behavior the last few weeks through the lens of new information, but again, nothing jumped out at me.

I leaned my head back and closed my eyes, trying to evoke the memory of my wife. But her newly unveiled duplicity was so tangled with the image of the Maureen I'd known, I had trouble remembering. Lies and half-truths didn't always spell trouble, I reminded myself. Sometimes they were a necessary part of avoiding trouble.

But either way, there was a whole dimension to Maureen I knew nothing about. That hurt. It also frightened me.

The conversations of other passengers floated past me. I heard the flight attendant helping a child with her seat belt. A man struggled to find an open bin for his carry-on luggage. And then I felt someone slip into the middle seat.

I opened my eyes, sat bolt upright when I saw who it was. Hannah Montgomery.

"What are you doing here?" I asked. Or rather, snapped.

"I'm going to Phoenix."

"I figured that much. It's where the plane is headed." I looked down the aisle to see if Dallas was on board as well. I didn't see him.

Hannah ignored me and settled in, stuffing bottled water and a paperback novel into the seat pocket.

I didn't like the feeling of this. "Does it mean I've got a police escort?"

"Do you mind?"

Of course I minded. All I could think of was the handcuffs she probably had hidden in her carry-on. "Is it an official police escort?"

She smiled. Her green eyes, accentuated by the laugh lines at the corners, twinkled. "No," she said. "It's just me tagging along for the fun of it."

"You really expect me to believe that?"

"No, but it's the truth."

"So I can ignore you?"

"If you'd like." She looked amused. "But remember that I can follow you, or worse yet, beat you to the answers. And since we're both after the same information . . ." She spread her hands. "Well, it might be easier to cooperate."

Unless the information was something I didn't want to share with the cops. I was willing to bet they weren't sharing everything with me either. And I didn't take kindly to the notion of having a babysitter along. I liked Hannah Montgomery, probably more than was wise under the circumstances, but she was still a cop.

On the other hand, did I really want her digging up information on *my* wife before I got to it myself?

At least it was Hannah accompanying me and not Dallas.

I closed my eyes again and kept them closed for the duration of the flight.

We ended up sharing a rental car. Rather, I did the renting and she rode along. She didn't exactly insist, but her earnest smile and green eyes were hard to resist. I reminded myself it would be easier to keep tabs on her that way.

"Do you know which bookstore your wife worked at?" she asked as we pulled out of the rental car lot and onto the wide boulevard leading to the highway.

"No."

"But you've got a plan?"

I handed her the pages I'd printed out from the Internet. "There are eighty-three bookstores listed, but if you eliminate the religious stores, the adult places, and specialty stores like metaphysics, it's a manageable list."

"Why eliminate those?"

"They don't seem the kind of places my wife would work."

Hannah raised an eyebrow in my direction. I knew what she was thinking—that I hadn't really known very much about my wife at all.

"At least we should save them for last," I told her.

"So what have we got?"

"Close to forty, and that's not counting the outlying areas."

"That's a lot of stores."

I handed her the phone. "You want to start calling while I drive?"

"I've got my own phone."

"Ask about both Maureen Brown and Eva Flynn." After I said it, I realized she'd probably have known that on her own.

Hannah responded with an indulgent smile.

It was a warm day. Hot, in fact. The car's thermometer registered the outside temperature at ninety-nine. By Phoenix standards it wasn't a scorcher, but compared to Rochester, where the air had been decidedly cool even in the sun, the difference was staggering. Eva's mother had said that Eva hated the cold. Phoenix would have suited her well in that regard.

I drove while Hannah made calls. The city spread out on all sides, flat and open, with outcroppings of dry, rocky hills. I've never been drawn to desert living, maybe as a result of growing up in the forested foothills of the Sierra, but I could understand how some people might like it.

"Which direction?" I asked as we approached a freeway divide.

"I don't know where we're going yet."

"How far through the list are you?"

"Only about a third down."

I took the next off-ramp, pulled to the side of the road, and took out my own phone. While Hannah continued to call from the top of the list, I started from the end. On the fourth try, I got lucky.

"The name Maureen Brown doesn't mean anything," the woman who answered told me, "but Eva Flynn worked here."

I felt a rush of blood pounding in my chest. Here was someone who'd known my wife in the not-too-distant past.

"Is this about a reference?" the woman asked.

"Not exactly. It might be easier if we spoke to you in person."

"Sure. I'll be here until three. My name's Cathy. And you're . . . ?"

"Sam," I told her. "We'll be there in about half an hour."

"You hit gold right off," Hannah said, sounding mildly piqued. "You must have the magic touch."

"Only in Phoenix." The rest of my life seemed shadowed by a black cloud.

I pulled out a map and found the address. The bookshop was in an outdoor mall, flanked by a Mexican import place and a clothing store. The store was small, but it had an inviting feel. In addition to books, there were displays of cards, notebooks, hand creams, stickers, and gift items. There was only one customer, a woman at the back with her nose deep in a paperback.

The woman at the register was a plump redhead with a round face and dimples. She reminded me of the girl in the old Campbell Soup ads.

"Cathy?"

"You must be Sam." She looked at Hannah, who nodded but said nothing. "So, why are you asking about Eva?"

I took a lesson from Phipps and ignored the question. "How long did she work here?"

"About eighteen months. She was a good employee."

"Are you the owner?"

Cathy smiled. "Yep. It was my mom's shop, and I took over when she died. I have a seven-year-old son, so it's a perfect job for me. I don't have to work full-time, and I can bring him with me in a pinch."

"When did Eva quit?" I asked.

"Almost three years ago." Cathy squinted. "Why all the questions?"

Hannah spoke up and handed Cathy her business card. "I'm a detective out of California. Eva was murdered not too long ago."

"My God!" Cathy's face registered shock. "How did it happen?"

"We're not sure, but we've reason to believe it wasn't a

stranger who killed her. We're looking for any information that might lead us to the perpetrator."

Cathy shook her head. "You think it's someone from here in Phoenix?"

"Did you know her well?" Hannah asked.

"Sure, we were friends. I mean, I had a kid and she was single, but we got along. We liked the same books, laughed at the same stuff." Cathy was quiet a moment, then she pointed to a photo collage on the wall. "Top left. That's the two of us stuffing ourselves at the store's tenth anniversary party. We had about ten authors and a good crowd of customers."

The two women mugged for the camera, their cake-laden forks raised in a toast. I moved closer and studied the photo. It certainly looked like Maureen . . . or rather Eva, though there was something disorienting about it too. Maybe it was the shorter hair or the impish look on Eva's face. Or maybe it was simply getting another peek at my wife's life before my time.

"When did you last hear from her?" Hannah asked.

"Not lately. I used to get an e-mail now and then. But you know how it is. You get wrapped up in your own existence, and old friends kind of move to the back burner."

"Where'd she go when she left here?"

"Someplace in Mexico. She'd broken up with her boyfriend and wanted a change. She had a little money saved up and figured it would go further there than in the States. Eva was always a day behind and a dollar short. But I had no complaints about her performance on the job."

"She was in Mexico last time you heard from her?" I asked.

"I assumed so, but I could have been wrong. She had one of those free web-based e-mail accounts that you can pick up anywhere." Cathy smiled. "Redhotsugarbear. I always thought that was cute."

I felt the air leave my lungs. Redhotsugarbear. The name I'd discovered in our address book. Not a lover, but my wife's own private e-mail address. The one she probably used to communicate with Eric Vance and everyone else who knew the real Eva. A world she'd kept secret from me.

Hannah was playing with the magnetic paper clips near the register. "Did Eva ever mention the name of Eric Vance?"

Cathy nodded. "They knew each other growing up, back East."

"Were they . . . lov . . . involved romantically?" I asked. It was probably irrelevant, but I had to know.

"They may have been at one time, but not when I knew her," Cathy said.

May have been at one time. Maybe they'd hooked up again. Was that why she'd flown to Las Vegas to see him?

Hannah turned her attention from the paper clips. "What can you tell us about Eric?"

"Not much. I only met him once. He seemed like a nice enough guy, but a little weird."

"Weird how?"

She shrugged. "A little jumpy. Not much of a sense of humor. Ralph took an instant dislike to him."

"Who's Ralph?" Hannah and I both asked.

"The boyfriend I told you about. The one Eva broke up with. I thought he was a bit of a prick."

"What's his last name?" Hannah asked.

"Nash. Ralph Nash. He was always putting Eva down. He wanted to dictate what she wore, who she saw, where she went."

"Do you know where we can reach him?"

"He worked at a gallery out in Scottsdale," Cathy said. "Very upper end. But he lost that job, which was part of the problem, I think. He took out his frustrations on Eva. That's when she decided she'd had enough. Broke up with him and took off for Mexico."

"Any other friends who might still be in touch with her?"

Cathy thought a moment then shook her head. "Ralph might know. But like I said, he was pretty possessive. I suspect he smacked her at least once, though she made up some lame excuse about running into a door. He didn't like Eva going out with friends without him."

Hannah and I exchanged glances. "Thanks," she told Cathy. "Sounds like it might be useful to talk with him."

CHAPTER 45

We stopped at a Coco's restaurant to look for a phone book and get a bite to eat. It wasn't my favorite kind of place, but it was convenient, quick, and air-conditioned. We were able to find a listing for Ralph Nash, complete with address.

"A possessive ex-boyfriend," I said while we waited for our Cobb salads. "That might explain why Eva was using Maureen's name." Although it didn't explain why she'd kept the truth from me.

"It might," Hannah agreed, sounding far from convinced. Her eyes met mine. "This must be hard for you, discovering you were married to someone you didn't really know."

"Harder than you can imagine." Harder still because now that she was dead, I could never ask her why.

Hannah hesitated. "I think I have some idea how you must feel."

There was something about her tone that conveyed more than the words suggested, but I wasn't sure what. I took a sip of my Coke. "You're married?"

"I was." She looked away. "My husband died three years ago in an automobile accident."

I felt a surge of sympathy. "I'm sorry. I know how devastating it is to lose someone you love."

She emptied a packet of artificial sweetener into her iced tea. "And I understand what it's like to feel betrayed by that person."

"Your husband?"

She stirred the tea with a straw. "We'd only been married two years. A month after he was killed, I found out that he'd been having an affair with my sister."

"Ouch. Doubly betrayed."

"I was undergoing treatment for breast cancer at the time. Already feeling vulnerable and sick and ugly and unlovable." Her voice faltered.

"How terrible." The words seemed inadequate. I could imagine the emotional blow must have been crushing.

She gave me a sad smile. "More terrible than you can imagine."

"I appreciate your telling me. It helps explain . . ."

"Explain what?"

I shrugged. "I don't know. You seemed to have some feeling for what I'm going through."

"That's the hardest part of my job sometimes. Witnessing the pain and hurt, and"—she paused, looked at her hands— "and feeling a degree of empathy with *all* the parties involved."

Even the ones who might be guilty was what I presumed she meant.

Our salads arrived, and for a while we ate without talking. Then Hannah asked, "Why were you surprised when Cathy mentioned Eva's e-mail address?"

"Was I?" It was disconcerting to know that Hannah had picked up on it. I wondered what else she might have observed about my behavior.

"You had a visible reaction. Redhotsugarbear must mean something to you."

"It was a private e-mail address my wife used. I only discovered it by accident after she was gone."

"You should have told us about it."

That and several other things. But for reasons of my own, I hadn't. "If we can gain access to her account," I suggested, "we might learn something about Eric Vance."

Hannah speared a piece of hard-boiled egg. "It will take a court order to get access, and I don't think that's going to happen."

"Maybe the FBI can help."

"Phipps hasn't exactly been bending over backward to cooperate with us."

"What's his interest in Eric Vance, anyway?"

She studied her salad a moment then shook her head. "I don't know any more than what he told us yesterday. My guess is that they had something on Vance, and if he's an ex-con they'd have plenty of leverage. They were probably using him to get to a bigger fish."

"And it was the bigger fish who killed him."

"Phipps didn't rule out accidental death."

"You believe that?"

"No."

"Maybe the same big fish killed my wife. Whoever it was that broke into my house certainly knew about Eric."

Her eyes met mine. They weren't quite as warm as they'd been earlier. "Whoever killed your wife also knew about Ben Albright's wine cellar."

To that pointed observation, I had no response. We finished eating in silence.

Ralph Nash lived in an upscale, two-story apartment complex on the east side of the city. It was landscaped with the customary crushed rock and cactus and looked to be only a couple of years old.

The heat, as we stepped from the car, was like a blast furnace. The temperature had risen probably five degrees since we'd arrived that morning. "It's unlikely he'll be home in the middle of the day," I said.

Hannah agreed. "But maybe one of his neighbors will be."

We found his name on the lobby roster and took the elevator to the second floor. I rang the bell and was surprised when the door was answered almost immediately by a blond woman in her early twenties. Her hair was piled on top of her head in an artfully casual ponytail and held in place with a bright pink band that matched her pink lips. She was dressed in Lycra exercise clothes, skintight, and carried a gym bag and bottled water.

"We're looking for Ralph Nash," Hannah said.

"He's not here." She examined her nails, which were the same flaming pink as her mouth.

"Are you his wife?"

She looked uncertainly from Hannah to me and back again. "Fiancée," she said finally.

"Do you know if Ralph used to work at a gallery in Scottsdale?"

"A long time ago. What's this about?"

Hannah displayed her badge. "We'd like to talk to him about someone he used to know. Where could we find him?"

"He's at work," she said. "The Hilton. He's their events liaison." She gave us the address.

We parked in a spot reserved for registration and again stepped from the air-conditioned cool of the car into an oven. Thankfully, it was a short walk to the hotel entrance.

At the front desk, we asked for Ralph Nash. He appeared a few minutes later, sporting a gold watch, gold neck chain, and diamond pinky ring. And a leg cast and crutches.

"Motorcycle accident," he explained, extending a fleshy hand. "I've learned my lesson. It's been two months, and I'm just now able to hobble around."

I couldn't imagine what Eva had seen in him.

Hannah introduced herself then asked him about Eva.

"Yeah, we dated," he said.

"Was it serious?"

He shrugged.

"Why'd you break up?"

"Eva got cold feet." Ralph leaned on one of his crutches. "Turns out her leaving was the best thing that ever happened to me. You've met Cindy, so you know what I'm talking about. Eva is . . . well, a bit of a flake."

I remained silent, but inside I bristled in defense of my wife, who was in no way a flake.

"Eva was fun," Ralph continued. "But she couldn't follow the simplest direction. Screwed up everything. She'd make meatloaf and forget the catsup. Or she'd show up an hour late for a date because she wrote the time down wrong."

Somehow I couldn't see Cindy making meatloaf at all. And I'd never known Maureen to be late for anything.

"When did you last talk to her?" Hannah asked.

"The day we broke up. She moved not long after that. Couldn't take the painful memories, I guess." Ralph flashed a smug grin.

"When was it you broke up?"

"About three years ago. Just after Christmas. Why are you asking? Is she in some kind of trouble?"

Hannah ignored the question. "What about Eric Vance? Do you know him?"

Nash grimaced. "That low-life friend of hers from when she was growing up? I've met him." He snapped his fingers. "I get it. She's involved in something with Vance. Doesn't surprise me that *he's* in trouble. He's an ex-con, you know."

"What kind of lowlife?"

"Scams, forgery, gambling. She never actually said, but I could read between the lines. So what is it this time?"

"Murder," Hannah said. "They're both dead."

* * *

When we returned to the car, Hannah turned the air-conditioning to high and leaned into the draft like a dog panting for fresh air. "How can people live in this climate?"

"I guess you get used to it."

She closed her eyes. "Not a particularly useful day, if you ask me."

"I didn't. I didn't even ask you to come along."

She turned to me and smiled. "You do the warm, fuzzy stuff so well."

"You think Nash was telling the truth about not having seen Eva since they broke up?"

"I don't think he killed her or Eric Vance, if that's what you mean. Not with a broken leg and restricted mobility. Besides, he didn't come across like a vindictive ex-boyfriend."

"He came across like a jerk."

The corners of her mouth twitched. "No argument there." She sat back in her seat and adjusted the air vents. "You aren't seriously thinking about doing this again in Las Vegas, are you?"

"It sounds like Eric Vance is the key to this. I want to know why my wife was meeting him there."

"You're not going to find out by knocking on people's doors."

"I'm not going to hear it from Phipps either."

She started to say something then seemed to think better of it. She nodded instead. "You're probably right about that."

CHAPTER 46

By the time I got home from Phoenix that evening, Molly was already in bed. I stopped in to kiss her good night, and she opened her eyes.

"Go back to sleep, honey. I just came to check on you."

"Did you find out anything?"

"Not really." I'd given her a bare-bones account of wanting to meet with Maureen's friends and had told her that Maureen's real name was Eva. We'd looked at the locket together, confirming that what Molly had first read as *ELF* was really the initials E.L.F. I'd explained that her murderer might be someone from her past. But I'd stepped gingerly around the many questions for which I didn't have answers.

Molly was not easily put off, even half-asleep. "You didn't even learn why she changed her name?"

"No. But she was using the name Eva when she lived there."

"Did you talk to her friends?"

"A couple of them. How was school today?"

Molly pulled the covers under her chin. "It was okay. Mary Louise got suspended for throwing paint at Ida."

"I should think so. Why did Mary Louise throw paint?"

"Because Ida told everyone about Mary Louise's mother."

"Told what about her?"

"That she's sleeping with Mr. Brand."

"The principal?" I knew that some parental wisdom was probably called for at this juncture—I was shocked that *sleeping with* was even part of Molly's vocabulary—but I could think of none to impart right then. Mostly I was relieved to hear that my daughter's classmates were focused on something other than my supposed guilt.

"Good night, Daddy."

"'Night, Sweetpea. Sleep tight."

Chase had left work early to pick Molly up from school and stay with her while I was gone. He was in the living room watching some sitcom on the television.

"There's leftover pizza in the fridge," he said. "And Coke. The real stuff, not that diet crap you're so fond of."

"Thanks. Everything go okay with Molly?"

"Just fine. Dad stopped by for dinner before he took off for his bridge game." Chase picked up the remote and turned down the volume. "How was your trip? Productive?"

"We talked to a woman who worked with Eva, and to an ex-boyfriend. I have a better feel for what was going on in her life, but I can't say we learned anything specific."

"We?"

I opened a can of Coke. "Big surprise. Monte Vista's finest decided to go to Phoenix today too."

He made a face. "Dallas?"

"Not as bad as that. Hannah Montgomery."

"Bummer. So you had a cop on your tail the whole time?"

I had, but it hadn't felt like that. "It worked out okay, actually. Being a cop is a good way to get people to talk."

"Don't go falling for the old 'good cop' trick, Sam. They're trying to pin your wife's murder on you."

I knew Chase was right, but I wanted to believe differently. I remembered the kindness in Hannah's eyes the night of the ransom drop when I'd run into her at the bar. The empathy I'd felt today over lunch. If she was playing a role, she was damn good at it.

"Nothing we learned gave her more ammunition," I assured him. "You want another slice of pizza?"

"Sure, thanks."

I got napkins and carried the pizza box into the living room, where I set it between us on the coffee table.

"I'm glad to be seeing bits of Eva's life," I told him. "But it's weird to have been married to someone and only now be figuring out things you should have known all along."

"Must be."

Chase had never warmed to Maureen, although he'd generally been polite. I wondered if he now felt somewhat vindicated. "Remember when we used to watch home movies of Mom and Dad before we were born?" I asked him. "We thought it was like eavesdropping on family secrets."

Chase laughed. "Even though they were the ones showing us the movies. I still remember the one Aunt Marge took of Dad kissing Mom by the Christmas tree. You'd have thought we were watching a bedroom scene the way we squirmed."

"That's what it feels like learning about Maureen's . . . Eva's past. I'm seeing her in a whole new light, and I feel something like a Peeping Tom. Why did she have to pretend to be someone different?"

"Maybe she was afraid you'd find out about Eric."

Unless she was actively involved in something criminal though, I didn't understand why she'd hesitate to tell me about him or share her true identity. Could Maureen have been on the wrong side of the law? I'd mourned my wife's death, and now I was beginning to mourn the loss of her memory as well.

"So it's Las Vegas tomorrow?" Chase asked.

"You still up for staying with Molly?"

"Yeah, we have a good time. And I'm always happy to have an excuse to take time off from work."

I'd given Chase a hard time in the past about what I saw as a lackadaisical attitude about his job. Now I was sheepishly grateful. I vowed to be more supportive in the future.

Chase turned up the volume on the television. I tuned out the program and let my mind drift back over the events of the day. I tried to picture Eva with Ralph and couldn't. I reminded myself that, in the end, she hadn't been able to either, and she'd left. On the other hand, I could easily see how she and Cathy would have gotten along. I felt a little envy, in fact, that the sparkle I'd seen in her expression in the photo was not something I'd seen much of in person.

And then suddenly it hit me why the photo had appeared off balance.

I choked on the pizza in my mouth and had to spit it out into a napkin.

"What is it?" Chase asked.

"Maureen was right-handed."

He gave me a funny look. "So?"

"Cathy, the woman who owns the bookstore where Eva worked, she had a photo of the two of them eating cake."

"And?"

"And Eva was eating with her left hand."

"When it comes to cake, some people aren't particular."

"No, you don't get it. She was holding a fork in her left hand. Maybe you'd pick up a slice of pizza with either hand, but when you eat with a fork, you use your right hand, don't you?"

Chase pantomimed eating. "Yeah, I guess I do. Holding a fork in my left hand would feel really strange."

I felt a sweat break out on my forehead. I thought maybe I was going to be sick.

Suddenly Chase understood what I was getting at. "You're saying Eva wasn't Maureen? I mean, that the woman who was your wife wasn't Eva Flynn after all?"

That's what I was saying, but it seemed impossible. Everyone I'd asked had seen the photo I'd shown them and agreed it looked like Eva.

I went to the phone and called Cathy. I didn't expect her to be there still, but she was. "I was just catching up," she explained. "My son and his dad have T-ball this evening."

"I've got what's going to sound like a dumb question."

"There are no—"

I didn't even let her finish. "Do you recall, was Eva left-handed or right-handed?"

"Left-handed," she said. "She had this thing about sitting on the left so we wouldn't always be bumping arms."

There were lots of things about a person that might change over time, but which hand was dominant wasn't one of them. My wife wasn't Maureen Brown, but she hadn't been Eva Flynn either.

CHAPTER 47

It was way past midnight in the East. Much too late to call, especially someone I barely knew. But I did it anyway. Mrs. Flynn answered after several rings. It was clear I'd woken her.

"I'm sorry to bother you," I told her.

"Do you know what time it is?" I had a vision of the partially paralyzed woman, her tight curls flattened by sleep, clutching the bedside phone in her frail hands.

"I do know, and I wouldn't call if it wasn't important. It's about Eva."

"I already know." Her voice sounded thin and vaguely accusing. "There was a detective who called me this morning. He told me."

"Told you? What did he say?"

"Well, he asked me a lot of questions, then he said . . ." She took a breath. "He said Eva had been murdered." Mrs. Flynn started crying softly. "You didn't tell me she was dead. You only said she was missing."

"Was your daughter left-handed?" I asked.

She was clearly perplexed by the question. "Yes, of course."

"I don't want to get your hopes up, Mrs. Flynn, but it may

be that your daughter isn't dead after all. I thought my wife and Eva were one and the same, but my wife was right-handed."

"But the photo you showed me . . ."

"I know. And I saw her yearbook picture as well. The similarity is striking."

The silence on the other end of the phone stretched long and heavy. I thought maybe she'd hung up. "Mrs. Flynn?"

"The detective said she was using the name Maureen Brown."

"Right."

"Maureen was a friend of Eva's from high school. Your wife has to have been my daughter." Mrs. Flynn's voice was insistent and oddly hollow. "She . . . she has to have been."

My chest felt as though it were wrapped in wire. "Was Eva your only child?"

"Yes, just her." The same flat tone that made Mrs. Flynn sound as though she were talking through a wall of fog.

"How about cousins? Any of them girls about her age?"

Mrs. Flynn hesitated again. "I . . . We . . ." She sounded like she was having trouble breathing.

"Mrs. Flynn?"

"Eva was adopted," she said, her voice breaking. "We adopted her as a baby. Raised her as our own. That was the last big fight we had before she left home. She found out and got angry at us for keeping it from her."

Adopted. I could hear my pulse pounding in my ears. "What about her birth parents. Do you know who they are?"

"I wanted to know as little as possible."

"But surely you—"

"You've no idea what it's like not to be able to have a child of your own. All my friends were having babies, and there I was with nothing. Nothing. It was so unfair. Then we got Eva. She was only ten days' old. We moved here to Rochester, and I tried to forget she wasn't really mine."

"You must know *something* about the birth parents."

She hesitated. "Only that the mother wasn't married. There was no father listed, so I suspect she got herself pregnant on some one-night stand. The name on the birth certificate was Wycoff. We had it changed, of course."

"Which agency handled the adoption? Was it through the state?"

"It was private, through an attorney who was a friend of my husband's."

My heart was pounding, my throat dry. "What's his name?"

"Why is any of this important? It's frankly none of your business."

I took a breath. *Slow down,* I told myself. *Don't antagonize her.* I wished we'd had this conversation earlier, when I could have pled my case face-to-face.

"I'm not trying to pry, Mrs. Flynn. Or to create problems." I tried not to let my impatience show. "It's possible the woman who was murdered was not your daughter but someone related to her. Don't you want to know if your daughter is dead or alive?"

There was a long silence, and again I thought I'd lost her. Finally, she said, "Dunbar. Robert Dunbar. That's the name of the attorney."

"Do you know where I can reach him?"

"He was in Atlanta. I don't know if he's still there, or even if he's still in practice."

I took a deep breath. "Thank you."

"You'll let me know what you learn?"

"I will. Right away."

CHAPTER 48

Hannah was exhausted. For reasons she didn't understand, flying did that to her. Even a short, easy trip like today's left her feeling drained. And the Phoenix heat hadn't helped. She was a wimp about the cold, but Hannah hated really hot weather just as much. As Malcolm had pointed out to her on more than one occasion, she was not easy to please.

She stepped out of her sticky clothes and into the shower, letting the warm, pulsating spray dissolve the tension in her neck and shoulders along with the day's grime. She wasn't convinced the trip had been a good use of her time. Except, of course, that she'd enjoyed being with Sam, something she'd never admit out loud. She'd gone along to keep an eye on him and learn what she could about Eva Flynn, not for her own gratification.

Hannah couldn't help thinking though how pleasant it would have been if the circumstances had been different. She was reminded of the Sunday mornings early in her marriage when she and Malcolm would get into the car and take off for the day. Sometimes they'd drive up or down the coast, and other times they'd head into the mountains. It wasn't the destination so much as the journey itself. She loved that it was just the two of them alone in the car—her whole world in a bubble.

Was it that memory that had prompted her to tell Sam about Malcolm and Claire? She hadn't meant to and now regretted it. There were very few people with whom she'd shared that humiliation.

Hannah stepped out of the shower, dried herself with an oversized terry towel, and slipped into jeans and a T-shirt. She grabbed a beer and a wedge of cheese from the fridge. The tiny bag of peanuts she'd eaten on the plane hardly constituted a meal, but she didn't have the energy to prepare something more.

She checked her phone messages—her mother and Dallas. The earmarks of a pathetic social life.

Her mother didn't like to be called after seven in the evening. Thankfully, Hannah could put that task off until tomorrow. She punched in Dallas's number. He must have been clutching the phone, because he answered right away.

"How was Phoenix?"

"Hot as Hades."

"I can get a weather report off the Internet, Hannah. Was Sam nervous having you tag along?"

She knew Dallas was hoping that was the case. Killers weren't comfortable with police scrutiny, and their uneasiness sometimes led them to make mistakes.

"He wasn't happy about it at first," Hannah said, "but it worked out." Far better than she'd expected. "I can't say that he was really upset though."

"You're set for Las Vegas in the morning?"

"Seven-thirty flight. Phipps isn't going to be happy if he finds out we're messing in 'his' case."

"Screw him. He's messing in ours."

A point on which Hannah and Dallas agreed.

"What did you learn today?" he asked.

"Not much, I'm afraid. We found the bookstore where Eva worked. She was using her real name at the time. The owner says Eva left town a couple of years ago after breaking up with her control-freak boyfriend."

"Left for where?" Dallas asked.

"Somewhere in Mexico. She didn't remember the town. We paid a visit to the boyfriend. He's happily engaged to someone else now and seems to be well over losing Eva. He's also been in a cast and on crutches for the last couple of months, so it's unlikely he has anything to do with her murder."

"And Vance?"

"The bookstore owner met him. Says he was a bit 'weird,' but she couldn't be more specific. The boyfriend called Vance a lowlife, which sort of fits with what Phipps has told us. But neither one said anything that would explain why Eva went to see him a week before she was killed, or why she was using an alias when she married Sam."

"And you really think Sam didn't know anything about this until the other day?"

Hannah had asked herself the same question. She didn't want to think her personal attraction to Sam had clouded her judgment. "I really think he didn't."

"Sam's motive in killing her might have nothing to do with her past," Dallas pointed out.

"Or maybe Sam didn't do it."

"Hannah, the evidence says he did."

She opened the fridge and cut off another hunk of cheese. "What about your day? Any luck?"

"I talked to Eva Flynn's mother. Like Sam told us, she claims not to know where her daughter has been or what she's been up to. She didn't know Eva had been killed. Sam told her Eva was missing."

Dallas lacked finesse in delivering bad news under the best of circumstances. Hannah could imagine that from three thousand miles away, and with his own agenda, Dallas hadn't offered much in the way of sympathy.

"I ran Eva's name through the system," Dallas continued.

"She's got a poor credit history, four outstanding parking tickets in Phoenix, but nothing downright criminal. It might not be the kind of reputation you'd brag about, but nothing so bad you'd hide it from your husband either."

And yet she had. There must have been a reason. "Anything more on Vance?"

"Phipps isn't talking, but I have a friend at the agency. He tells me Phipps is part of a team trying to break an international drug ring."

"And Vance was part of it?"

"Or peripherally connected. They apparently had him on a fraud charge then cut a deal to get the goods on whoever they were after."

Hannah's conjecture to Sam that afternoon had been close to the mark. "What goods?" she asked.

"That I don't know. Information of some sort. I'd guess the guys he was turning on got to him first."

Like the gang culture Hannah was familiar with from her days in Los Angeles. If word got out you were about to rat on your buddies, you died. Sometimes your family and loved ones died as well. That might explain Eva's death. But it was a stretch.

On the other hand, if Eva was part of the network . . . "Whoever broke into Sam's house was looking for something connected to Vance," Hannah pointed out. "They must have thought Sam's wife had the information."

"That's a possibility."

"What the hell was Sam's wife doing involved with the mob and drugs?"

"And where does Sam fit in?"

They were back to that again. "I can't believe he was part of it," Hannah said.

"Maybe, maybe not, but I think Phipps is working under the assumption that they were both involved. If Sam wasn't part of it though, and found out what was going on," Dallas said, "well, that might show motive for murder."

"But if she was alive on Monday, after he reported her missing—"

"Based on what? That recipe flyer you got at the hospital?" His tone was impatient. "Any number of people would have had access to that before it showed up in hospital clinics, especially a physician. In fact, the company charged with distribution picks them up at the printer Friday afternoon."

It was like talking to a wall. "With all we've learned, you still really think Sam killed her?"

"There's something he's not telling us, Hannah."

"There may—"

"And whoever our killer is, he knew about Ben Albright's wine cellar."

She sighed. "I know." That was a sticking point Hannah had yet to resolve.

The next morning, Hannah was at the gate an hour before departure time. No sign of Sam yet. She got her boarding pass, bought a cup of coffee and a newspaper, and sat down to wait.

At seven-ten, the plane pulled into the gate. Sam hadn't arrived. Thinking she might have missed seeing him come in, Hannah walked around the lounge area looking for him. She watched the men's room for a full five minutes.

Still no sign of Sam.

Where *was* he?

The gate agent was beginning the loading process. With a niggling sense of alarm, Hannah went to the desk and inquired about her traveling companion.

"Can you tell me if he's checked in yet?"

"Sorry," the agent replied. "I can't give out that information."

Hannah pulled out her badge. "This is police business."

Frowning, the woman checked the computer monitor. "No, not yet."

Hannah used her cell phone to call Sam. He didn't answer.

She didn't want to board until she was sure Sam had made it. She'd already passed up the opportunity for a window or aisle seat. She wasn't going to lose anything by waiting longer.

Her chest tight with anxiety, Hannah paced the now empty boarding area. Why wasn't Sam here? Had he decided to flee? And following that line of thought, Hannah couldn't help asking herself if Dallas might not be right, after all. Was Sam actually guilty of murder?

The final boarding call came, and Sam still hadn't arrived. The agent was closing the door to the runway when Hannah called Dallas.

CHAPTER 49

First thing Friday morning I was on a plane to Atlanta, having used the last of my frequent-flyer miles to book the flight. I'd been hoping to accrue enough points to take a family vacation to Hawaii, but vacation plans were a low priority right then. Besides, there would be no vacation at all if I was in prison, which was where I was likely to end up if I didn't get some answers soon.

And I wanted to digest those answers myself before I shared them with the police. I felt more than a twinge of guilt at not telling Hannah about my change of plans, but I needed to do this alone.

I'd considered simply telephoning Robert Dunbar, the attorney who'd handled the adoption, but I knew he'd probably refuse to talk to me. I wasn't sure how I was going to convince him to do so once I was there either, but my chances of success, if not high, had to be higher in person than over the distance of three thousand miles.

The flight was delayed, and I worried I wouldn't arrive in time to see Dunbar that same day. I paced impatiently at the gate, checking the monitor every few minutes for updates. Would I get to his office before he'd gone for the day? I didn't relish the idea of spending any more time away from home than was necessary.

Once, my phone rang. When I saw that it was Hannah Montgomery, I ignored it. Another pang of guilt twisted inside me. I knew she was probably in the next terminal, pacing as impatiently as I was. Only she was waiting for *me*.

Finally, we were allowed to board, and the plane took off. Keyed up and restless as I was, it felt like a very long trip.

I stepped out of the terminal building at the Atlanta airport into a wall of steamy heat. Arizona had been hot. Georgia was sweltering. By the time I made it to the Hertz lot, my shirt was soaked with perspiration.

The air-conditioned interior of the rental car was heaven. I remembered Hannah sticking her face in front of the air vents of our car in Phoenix and experienced a moment's regret. There was a part of me that would have liked to have her along.

Robert Dunbar was in solo practice with an office in the southwest part of Atlanta. I'd checked the location last night on the Internet. Out of curiosity, I checked the yellow pages of the phone book at the airport. His listing noted only *attorney at law;* no specialities.

I took the elevator to the third floor of a faceless concrete building and followed the brown linoleum maze of corridors to room 338. From the outdated look of his reception area, I was willing to bet Dunbar's clients weren't among the rich and famous.

His secretary, a middle-aged Latino woman, looked up as I entered.

"May I help you?" she asked.

"I'd like to see Mr. Dunbar."

She frowned. "Do you have an appointment?"

"No, I'm afraid not."

"But he's expecting you?"

I shook my head. "I'm in town only today, and it's important."

The frown again. "Just a moment." She picked up the phone then addressed me. "Your name?"

"Sam Russell. I'm a doctor." I had no idea why I added the doctor part, but sometimes it helped.

It seemed only to make receptionist more wary. She spoke into the phone softly. "I'm sorry to bother you, Mr. Dunbar. There's a gentleman here to see you. A Dr. Russell. He says he's only in town for a day." She turned back to me. "What's this concerning?"

"An adoption." Terse. I figured the less said, the better my odds of not tripping myself up.

She relayed the message to Dunbar. I must have passed some unwritten test, because she showed me to his inner office.

It was dingy without being actually dirty. Cigar smoke hung in the air, and there were papers stacked everywhere— on Dunbar's desk, a chair, the top of the file cabinet, the floor. They had the look of having been there awhile.

Dunbar looked close to sixty. His fleshy face was framed by thinning hair he'd combed in a wide swath over the bald crown of his head. He'd removed his suit jacket and rolled up the sleeves of his rumpled cotton shirt. There was a spot of grease by the open collar.

He gestured me to a chair.

"What can I do for you, Dr. Russell?" His manner was pleasant and upbeat. "You have a patient who would like to place a baby for adoption?"

"No, it's not that." I realized he'd misunderstood my explanation to his secretary and that it had probably worked in my favor. I'd gotten in to see him, after all. I doubted he'd be as receptive to the actual reason for my visit.

"It's about an adoption you handled a number of years ago."

As I expected, his expression became more guarded.

"Twenty-eight years ago," I continued. "The birth mother was named Wycoff. The baby was adopted by Lou and Sonia Flynn."

He shook his head. "I'm afraid I can't help you."

"But you were the attorney—"

"It was a long time ago, and the information is confidential."

"My wife was murdered recently," I told him, leaning forward slightly. "She looked very much like the woman known as Eva Flynn, Lou and Sonia's adopted daughter."

"I'm sorry, but I don't see how—"

"Mrs. Flynn was the one who gave me your name."

"That doesn't change anything." Dunbar had lost interest. His gaze drifted to the papers on his desk and, surreptitiously, his watch.

I'd come this far. I wasn't going to be turned away. In desperation, I did something I'd never done before in my life. I reached for my wallet, pulled out five twenties, and set them on his desk. Dunbar eyed them, not without interest, then looked away again with studied boredom.

"You can call Mrs. Flynn and ask her for permission to talk to me." I wasn't at all sure she'd give it, but I was grasping at straws.

Dunbar eyed the money again. "That may not be necessary . . ." He drummed his fingers on his desk.

I pulled out another hundred.

He waited expectantly.

I cleaned out my wallet. Another hundred and twenty. "That's all I've got," I told him.

He picked up the bills, folded them neatly, and stuck them in his desk drawer. "What is it you want to know?"

"Tell me about the birth parents."

"Generally, that's not done."

I thought about counting the change in my pockets. Or maybe he'd take Visa.

"But since Eva already made contact with the family—"

"Eva contacted them?"

He nodded. "When she was eighteen. She'd found out she was adopted. Her parents, the Flynns, I mean, hadn't told her. It apparently caused a major blowup."

No kidding. "How did she find out?"

"I'm not sure of the details, but somehow she came across records with my name on them and came to see me. I contacted the birth mother, Helen Wycoff. She gave permission for Eva to contact her."

"What happened then?"

"I don't know. I merely gave Eva the information. Later she wrote a short note to thank me. That was it."

"How can I reach Helen Wycoff?"

Dunbar spread his hands on his desk. "Dr. Russell, I've already told you more than I should."

And been well compensated for the information, I added silently. "You gave Eva the address. I can't ask her myself, because my wife is dead." I was fudging the truth, since Eva wasn't my wife after all, but I didn't care. I'd have lied through my teeth if I had to.

It didn't matter. Dunbar wasn't talking.

Then I remembered the hundred-dollar bill I kept folded in my wallet under my driver's licence. For emergencies. Bribery wasn't what I'd had in mind at the time, but I was learning that emergencies came in all flavors.

I pulled the hundred out and put it on the desk. Dunbar reached for it, but I covered it with my hand.

"When you've answered my questions," I told him.

He sighed. "I don't know how to reach her. I have the address and phone number I gave Eva. I'm not sure they're current."

"Good enough. What about the birth father?"

"Unknown."

I remembered Mrs. Flynn's comment about the birth mother and a one-night stand. "Is that common?"

He thought I was doubting him. "It's the truth," he said.

"Sometimes the woman really doesn't know how to reach the man she slept with. Other times, she doesn't know which of several men might be the father."

"Which was it in this case?"

Dunbar shook his head. "I don't honestly know. Helen Wycoff worked as a legal secretary, which is how I happened to hear of her. Not my secretary," he hastened to add, lest I jump to the wrong conclusion. "But the legal world is in many ways a small one. All I knew was that she had a newborn she wanted to place for adoption."

"And the Flynns?"

"I knew Lou at Cornell. He let it be known that he and Sonia were looking to adopt and hadn't had any luck. Babies generally go to younger couples." He offered an apologetic half smile. "It's a competitive market," he explained, as if I'd protested the unfairness of it. Probably a number of his clients did.

"Helen Wycoff didn't care that they were older?"

"She chose the Flynns," was all Dunbar said. But he looked uncomfortable.

I had the sudden realization that it might not have been as straightforward an adoption as it appeared on the surface. Maybe Lou Flynn was the biological father. Or maybe more money exchanged hands than was legal. None of it was germane to my purposes, however.

"Did Helen Wycoff have other children?" I asked.

Dunbar pressed his fingertips together. "None that I knew about. But like I said, Eva sent me a note after she met with Helen. She thanked me for allowing her to know her mother and sister."

Sister. That was just the information I was looking for. I'd been married to someone who bore a strong resemblance to Eva Flynn. Sister fit the bill.

"What do you know about the sister?"

"Absolutely nothing, Dr. Russell. Now, if you'll excuse me . . ."

Dunbar found the address and phone number he'd had on file for Helen Wycoff. He gave it to me, and I released the hundred-dollar bill.

Thank God, the address was here in Atlanta.

"You understand," he said as I left, "that this conversation never happened."

I was so eager to get on with finding Helen Wycoff that it took me a moment to understand what he was saying. But it wasn't a problem. All I wanted was the name.

"Right," I said finally.

CHAPTER 50

The phone number Dunbar had given me was no longer in service. I checked the phone book and didn't find a current listing for Helen Wycoff, so I drove to the address he'd given me.

It was a small tract home in an older subdivision that had seen better times. The woman who answered the door when I rang the bell had moved in three years earlier. She didn't recognize the name Helen Wycoff.

"You might try Doris Jones two doors down," the woman suggested, pointing to a saltbox house with a sagging porch. "She's been in the neighborhood a long time."

Doris Jones was in her early fifties, with unnaturally yellow hair and a jowly face etched by hours in the sun. She seemed thrilled to have someone to talk to.

She stepped out onto the porch. "Helen Wycoff. Of course I knew her. Our daughters were friends."

I held my breath. "Your daughters?"

"Her Andrea and my Jennifer. All the way from Girl Scouts through high school. Are you a friend?"

"We have a mutual acquaintance," I explained. "I was hoping to talk to her. Do you know where she moved to?"

Doris grimaced. "Helen passed away eight years ago. Lung cancer. She never even smoked. It doesn't seem fair."

My heart sank. I had my own reasons for thinking her death unfair.

"Come in, why don't you, where it's cool." She stepped back to invite me in. "I just got home from work and was going to fix myself a drink. Can I get you one?"

I was tempted. To have Helen Wycoff snatched from me at this point was almost more than I could bear. "Uh, just water. Thanks."

"Sure." She led me into the kitchen, where she poured water from an iced pitcher into a glass for me then made herself a tall glass of vodka and grapefruit juice. "Let's go into the den."

The den was a step-down addition to the house with cheap wood paneling and a big ceiling fan. The fan felt good.

"This mutual friend of yours," Doris asked, "one of her exes?"

"No, a woman. Someone Helen befriended a long time ago." More poetic license with the truth. But it wasn't actually a lie. "You mentioned exes. She married more than once, then?"

Doris laughed. "I was referring to live-in boyfriends. There were quite a few."

"Her daughter, Andrea . . ." I repeated the name in my head. *Andrea. My wife?* "Was she the only child?"

"Yep. It was just the two of them."

"What about Andrea's father?"

Doris took a long drink from her glass before setting it on the coffee table. "I never knew him. Helen didn't move into the neighborhood until Andrea was five, and by then he wasn't part of the picture. She never said much about him."

I wondered if Helen had made a habit of one-night stands, or if Andrea's father, unlike Eva's, had been someone she'd hoped to build a life with.

"Helen didn't have an easy life," Doris continued. "No husband, not much money, not a lot of common sense sometimes either. But she tried to be a good mother."

"Tell me about Andrea."

"She was a bright girl but not a happy one, I'm afraid. A bit of a dreamer. Always seemed to have a chip on her shoulder. She and Jennifer drifted apart in high school because of that. Jennifer's a very upbeat person."

"Do you know what's happened to Andrea? Where she is now?" My voice wavered with emotion, but Doris appeared not to notice.

"She was attending the local community college when her mother died. I think she stuck it out for the rest of the semester then moved north, where she had family. We pretty much lost touch."

I did the math in my head, and my heart skipped a beat. If Andrea was in college eight years ago . . . "How old is Andrea?"

"Same age as my Jennifer. Twenty-eight. Jennifer is a preschool teacher. Has a little girl of her own and another on the way."

Twenty-eight. The same age as my wife.

And the same age as Eva.

I could feel my pulse racing. "Do you recall Andrea's birthday?"

"Not the exact date, but February. Jennifer was an April baby and always hated that she was younger than Andrea."

February. The same month as Eva. The same year.

I could feel the rush of blood like wind in my ears. My throat was tight. I showed her the photo of my wife. "Does this look like Andrea?"

Doris nodded then smiled. "I haven't seen her recently, of course, but it sure looks like her."

I could barely breathe. Eva and Andrea weren't just sisters: they were twins.

"Do you recall, was Andrea right-handed?"

"Yes, she was. Why?"

I ignored the question. "You said she moved north, where she had family. Do you know where?"

"My Jennifer got a card from her . . . somewhere in New England, if I recall. It didn't make sense to me, because Helen didn't have any family. Both her parents were killed when she was quite young, and she was raised by a single aunt who died not long after I met Helen. I figured maybe it was someone on her father's side."

Doris lifted her eyes from the photo to meet mine. "You must know Andrea, then. What's she doing these days?"

Her question barely registered. My mind was doing somersaults.

When I didn't answer, Doris asked again. "How do you know her?"

"I was married to her."

"Was?"

I took a breath. "She died a couple of weeks ago."

"Oh dear. I'm so sorry for you. An auto accident? Cancer?"

I shook my head. "She was murdered."

"How awful. How did it happen?"

"She was abducted," I said, keeping the story simple. "They found her body a week later."

"You poor man." Doris placed a hand gently on my shoulder. "I lost my Harry five years ago. I understand."

I nodded, numbly.

She gazed at me with sympathy for a moment, then rose. "I'll be right back. I still have a box of things that belonged to Andrea. She asked to store them here temporarily when she moved north, but then she never told me where to send them. Let me get them for you."

Doris was gone maybe five minutes, during which time I collected the bits and pieces of what I'd thought was real and reassembled them. The world through yet another turn of the kaleidoscope.

Doris returned with a file-drawer-sized cardboard storage

box. I wasn't sure how I'd get it on the plane, but I figured I'd manage somehow.

"After Helen died, Andrea had to move. She sold most of Helen's stuff. Didn't get much for it, I'm sure. She went into the dorms where space was tight and asked me to hold this for her."

"What is it?"

"Memorabilia. Old photos, letters, financial papers. I almost tossed it a couple of times, but then I thought, well, Andrea's still young. I'm not sure my Jennifer would know what to do with my old letters at this point either. But someday she might like to look them over."

Doris set the box on the cushion next to me. "Of course, now Andrea's gone, and you never knew Helen . . . How long were you married?"

"Two years. No children." My voice broke.

I'm sure Doris thought it was grief at having lost my wife. She wasn't all wrong, but it was so much more.

CHAPTER 51

I caught a red-eye flight and arrived back home in the gray light of morning, feeling fatigued, confused, and not a little anxious. The sun wasn't fully up, and except for the occasional jogger and dog walker, Monte Vista was steeped in weekend quiet. I headed straight for Jesse's without even stopping by my own house first. I knew Molly would be asleep for hours still.

Without my untimely intrusion, Jesse might have enjoyed an extra hour or two in bed himself. As it was, the doorbell shattered his sleep.

I could see him lift the blinds in the bedroom window and peek outside. I stepped into the open so that he could see it was me. Several minutes later, still blurry eyed and wearing mismatched sweats he'd clearly pulled on in haste, he opened the door.

"Jesus, Sam. Where have you been?"

I'd expected him to yell at me for waking me up at an ungodly hour. Instead, he seemed relieved to see me. "Atlanta," I told him.

"Georgia?"

I nodded. "It turns out the woman I was married to wasn't Eva Flynn after all."

Just saying the words aloud helped ground me. My brain had been spinning in a mental fog during the whole flight home. I no longer knew up from down.

He stared at me open-mouthed for a moment then stood back. "Come in. I can tell I'm not going to be able to follow this without coffee. Strong coffee."

While Jesse heated water and pulled two bagels from the freezer, I told him what I'd learned.

"Twins, huh?" He rubbed his bristly cheek.

"Mirror twins. Andrea was right-handed, Eva left-handed. I was married to Andrea."

"So all that stuff about Eric . . ."

"That was Eva." Much to my relief. I couldn't imagine my wife involved with the mob, and I didn't want to imagine her involved with Eric. "Phipps saw the missing persons photo of Maureen and assumed that she was the woman they'd seen with Eric."

"Confused your wife for her twin, in other words?"

"Right." I took the coffee Jesse handed me. "Unfortunately, now that Eric and his criminal connections are out of the picture, I'll again be the prime suspect in Maureen's death. Not that Dallas ever considered me anything else."

"Not so fast." Jesse poured heavy cream and two teaspoons of sugar into his coffee. It was, he said, an indulgence he allowed himself for staying off the booze. "Why would Andrea use Maureen's name if Maureen was Eva's friend?"

"The two sisters knew each other. Eva must have told Andrea about Maureen."

"And why use a false name at all?"

That one I couldn't answer.

"Your wife also had Eva's childhood locket, don't forget."

"Eva could have given it to Andrea or left it with her at one time. It's not anything valuable. They were still in touch, you know. The Redhotsugarbear e-mail address is Eva's."

That had also been a relief. Yes, my wife had been carrying on a clandestine correspondence, but it wasn't with Eric or any other man. It was with her sister.

As if Jesse's train of thought had followed my own, he asked the question I was stumbling with myself. "Why would your wife not tell you about her sister?"

"I don't know. Maybe she was embarrassed about having a twin who'd been adopted out." It seemed like a pretty weak reason, but it was the only one I could come up with. "I wish I knew where Andrea had gone after leaving Atlanta."

"Have you tried sending Redhotsugarbear an e-mail?" Jesse asked. "Finding Eva might help clear things up."

I nodded. "I sent a message as soon as I realized my wife might not be Eva. No response yet. At this point, Eva may not want to be found. Her friend Eric is dead and the FBI is on her tail."

"What about the box of Helen's stuff her neighbor gave you? Have you looked through it?"

"Briefly, as soon as I got back to the car after leaving the neighbor's. It's just family photos, cards, a couple of child's drawings. There's nothing like an address book or diary or anything that jumps out as being significant."

I broke off a piece of bagel and chewed on it while I thought about what I was going to say next. "What if my wife's killer mistook her for Eva? Phipps thought she was Eva; the guy who broke into my house must have thought so too. So why not the killer?"

Jesse frowned. "Okay, so Phipps and your intruder ended up here because they saw Maureen's photo in the news after she disappeared. How would the killer have known about your wife? There would have had to be something *before* her disappearance that caught his attention."

Half-asleep or not, Jesse was a logical thinker. "You're

saying it's not likely Maureen's killer confused her with Eva then."

"I'm saying we shouldn't jump to conclusions, Sam."

"Then we're back to her being killed by her kidnappers." *Or me,* I added silently. I knew Jesse wouldn't consider that as a real possibility, but I hadn't completely ruled it out. If only I could remember what happened that Saturday night. I was no closer to coming up with an answer now than I had been at the time.

"The killer was someone who knew about Ben Albright's wine cellar," Jesse pointed out. "And knew that he was away. So it has to be someone with ties to both you and Albright."

I shook my head. "Ben and I barely know one another."

"I'm not sure that's relevant." Jesse got up to pour more coffee. "I wonder if Ben is in any way connected to Eric Vance."

"Seems highly unlikely." I declined a second cup of coffee and pulled myself out of my chair. "The cops are currently operating under the assumption that I was married to Eva Flynn. I need to set them straight."

"They came looking for you yesterday," Jesse said. "You were supposed to fly to Las Vegas with Detective Montgomery."

"Yeah, well that was before—"

"They were highly suspicious, and more than a little pissed, when you didn't turn up at the airport."

"It wasn't as if we'd made plans to travel together," I protested. "It was her idea to tag along."

"Semantics," Jesse said, walking me to the door. "She expected you, and you weren't there. No one knew where you'd gone."

"Chase knew."

"Chase wasn't talking."

That had been my doing. "I guess I told him to keep it quiet."

"And you didn't return phone calls," Jesse pointed out.

At the time, I'd been focused on getting answers, but now that I was no longer pumping adrenaline, I was ready to concede I'd been shortsighted. "So, have I made things a whole lot worse for myself?"

"I don't know, Sam. I sure hope not."

CHAPTER 52

Hannah patted the soil around her newly planted petunias. Eighteen of them. It had seemed like a lot when she bought them at the nursery, but the bed looked skimpy now that the plants were in the ground. They'd grow and fill out over time, she told herself. Still, she should have bought double the number. Maybe she'd go back and get some taller plants for the back of the border.

Gardening had never been her strength. Surprisingly, it was Malcolm who enjoyed working in the garden. He could spend hours amending the soil, pinching back buds, feeding and spraying. Her friends, with husbands who balked at even mowing the lawn, were envious. They shouldn't have been. Malcolm knew how to nurture plants, but he hadn't known how to do the same for a wife.

She stood slowly, easing the creaks from her knees, and turned on the hose. Around her, the neighborhood was beginning to stir. Hannah had woken early after a fitful night's sleep. She'd been hoping her work in the garden would provide a diversion. But it hadn't. The troubling questions were right there still, churning away in her mind.

Where had Sam gone yesterday?

Was Phipps right in thinking Sam had ties to organized crime?

If his wife was involved, could Sam really not have known?

And when he reported her missing, had he suspected all along that her disappearance was mob related? It might account for his evasive behavior. The theory did not sit well with Hannah, but it did make sense.

Her phone rang. Hannah dropped the hose, stripped off her gloves and shoes, and dashed for the house. She picked up on the fourth ring.

"Hannah? It's Sam." A pause. "Sam Russell."

She'd recognized his voice straight off, but the call was so unexpected it took her a moment to respond. "Where are you?"

"Home. I'm sorry about standing you up on the Las Vegas flight."

She bit back a few curt responses. She was angry at being lied to and manipulated. But he'd called, and she wanted to know why.

Aloud, she asked, "Where were you yesterday?"

"It's a long story. Easier to explain in person than over the phone."

"I can meet you down at the station."

"I'd rather we met somewhere else. Somewhere we can talk in private."

Jesus, was he going to confess? "Sam, if you've done something—"

"No, not that. I just have some new . . . new background information."

"About Eva? Eric?"

"Sort of."

He was being intentionally vague. It annoyed Hannah. Especially after the way he'd blown her off yesterday. "I'm a cop, Sam. This is official business. You can't tell me things and expect them to stay confidential."

"I know that. I know you'll have to tell Dallas. I just don't want to be there when you do."

In spite of her irritation, Hannah was intrigued. "Where do you want to meet?"

"How about the city park near the sports field. Half an hour?"

Time enough to get the mud washed off. "See you then."

She considered alerting Dallas then decided against it. She'd hear what Sam had to say first.

Hannah spotted Sam seated on a bench in the shade near the bandstand at the center of the park. He was slumped forward, elbows on his knees, but sat up as she approached. There were dark circles under his eyes, and his mouth drooped at the corners. For all that, Hannah still experienced a rush of pleasure at seeing him and was annoyed with herself for it.

He nodded a greeting. "Thanks for meeting me here."

She took a seat beside him. "What's up?"

There was a moment's silence. "The reason I didn't go to Las Vegas," Sam said finally, folding his hands on his knees. "I went to Atlanta instead."

"Why?"

He ran his fingers through his hair, leaving a tuft at an odd angle to the rest. Hannah found it oddly appealing. "Remember that photo Cathy showed us when we were in Phoenix? The party at the bookstore?"

Hannah nodded.

"I thought at the time that something was a bit off about it. It wasn't until I got home that night that it hit me. The woman in the photo—Eva Flynn—was holding her fork in her left hand. Maureen . . . well, my wife was right-handed."

Hannah was confused. "You said your wife *was* Eva Flynn."

"She looked just like Eva. But I checked with Cathy and then called Mrs. Flynn. Eva was left-handed."

"Your wife could have been ambidextrous."

He shook his head. "I asked Mrs. Flynn about sisters or cousins, and that's when she told me Eva was adopted. I talked to the attorney who handled the adoption; he's in Atlanta. I managed to learn the birth mother's name."

Had Sam dragged her down here to feed her some house-of-mirrors line to further muddy the waters? Hannah studied her hands. There was dirt from the garden under her nails still.

"Let me guess," she said. "Eva has a sister who looks like her."

"A twin."

Twin. Hannah hadn't expected that. Wasn't sure she actually believed it. "Are you saying the twins were adopted by different families?"

"Not quite. Eva was adopted by the Flynns. My wife, Andrea, was raised by their natural mother, Helen Wycoff."

"Good God. She had twins and adopted one out while keeping the other?"

Sam nodded. "Having met the attorney, my guess is she received more than the customary expenses in return."

"She sold the baby, in other words."

"That's my take on it. She was a single mother, probably struggling to make ends meet. I'd guess the idea of being responsible for two babies overwhelmed her, both financially and emotionally."

"Go on."

"Helen Wycoff died when Andrea was nineteen. A neighbor said that after her mother's death, Andrea moved north to be near family. But the neighbor was also under the impression that Helen didn't have any family."

"Andrea did have a twin though." Hannah kicked the grass with her toe. "Did the girls know about each other growing up?"

"I don't know about Andrea, but I doubt it. I mean, would you tell your kid that she had a twin you'd given away?"

Hannah shook her head. She couldn't imagine doing what Helen had done. No matter what the going price for a baby.

"Eva didn't even know she was adopted until she was a senior in high school," Sam said. "I think that's what precipitated the big fight that caused her to leave home. The attorney told me Eva contacted him about that time, and she eventually met her mother and sister."

"What a shock to discover at the age of eighteen that you have a twin."

"The bottom line is that my wife was Andrea, not Eva. Andrea wasn't involved with organized crime. She didn't even know Eric, much less go to see him right before she disappeared."

Hannah hadn't forgotten Phipps's warning that Sam and his wife might be part of a crime ring. "The man who broke into your house said something about Eric though."

"He must have made the same mistake as Phipps," Sam told her.

"Mistaking your wife for her twin sister."

He nodded. "That could be the reason she was killed too. The real target may have been Eva."

Hannah frowned.

"There would have to be some reason the killer even knew to look for my wife in the first place, but I'm thinking maybe Eva pointed him our way to get herself off the hook."

"Set up her own sister, you mean?" Hannah shouldn't be shocked, she supposed. She and Claire had been on good terms, and look what Claire had done to *her*. Eva and Andrea hadn't even known about each other until late into their teens. If there'd been bad feelings between them, and there might well have been . . .

"What about Ben Albright's wine cellar?" Hannah asked. "How would the killer, a mobster from Las Vegas in your scenario, know about the wine cellar?"

Sam shook his head. "I don't know. But a person interested in pinning this on me could probably have found out."

"And why would a person from organized crime be interested in setting you up to take the fall for your wife's murder?" Hannah tried not to sound overly cynical, but she was sure her skepticism showed.

Sam's shoulders dropped. "It doesn't make sense, does it?"

Part of her wanted to put a hand on his and offer comfort, but that side of her didn't belong here. Still, Hannah wasn't ready to buy Phipps's conspiracy theory. It would take an amazing actor to fake the anguish she saw in Sam's eyes. And by telling her about Andrea, Sam had actually made his own case worse, assuming the whole preposterous story was true.

"When we were operating under the theory that your wife was Eva," Hannah said, "it seemed logical to think her murder might be tied with the crime ring. Now, despite your mistaken-identity hypothesis, it's more of a stretch."

"I'm aware of that. And I know Dallas is convinced I killed her. Maybe you are too. But stretch or not, I have a feeling Eva and Eric are implicated in my wife's death."

This time Hannah did reach out, tentatively and very lightly, to brush Sam's hand with her own. "I want to believe you, Sam. But parts of your story just don't add up."

She waited a moment for him to respond. When he didn't, she continued. "No one at the hospital remembers seeing you the Sunday morning your wife disappeared. And the flower stand where you bought her flowers—it's on the other side of town from the hospital."

She expected a rebuttal, a defense of some sort that explained away the discrepancies. Instead, he looked at her then away. His expression was drawn. "The truth is, I woke up Sunday morning out in the country with my car in a ditch and no memory of what had happened."

"No memory? You mean now you're claiming amnesia?" The breeze fluttered the leaves in the trees above them. Their shadows flickered across Sam's face, making his expression difficult to read.

"Not just claiming; it's the truth. At first, when I got home and Maureen wasn't there, I figured she was just angry at me. I didn't even think of calling the cops. It wasn't until later that I got worried, but by then I'd already told Sherri Moore I'd gone to the hospital that morning." He smoothed his hands along his pant legs. "Past experience taught me that telling the truth is no guarantee people will believe you, so it wasn't such a big deal at first. Then one thing led to another, and pretty soon I was tangled in a lie."

Hannah was still reeling with Sam's revelations. "What *do* you remember?" she asked.

"Not much between Saturday and Sunday mornings, but I was apparently at work Saturday."

"So the last time you saw your wife was Saturday morning rather than Sunday morning?" Hannah wasn't sure what difference it made, but she was trying to get a clear picture in her head.

"Right. Though Sherri saw her Saturday afternoon when she dropped Molly off for Heather's slumber party. When Sherri called me Sunday morning, it was because she'd been unable to reach Maureen."

"What do you think caused your lack of memory?"

"At first, I thought maybe I'd blacked out from drinking or hit my head in an accident."

Hannah remembered what Dallas had said about Sam's drinking. "You're an alcoholic, aren't you?"

He nodded then looked her in the eye. "But I've been sober for five years. Besides, I don't think it was drink, and I don't think the amnesia was trauma induced. I think I was drugged."

"So that the killer, who is a member of organized crime and has mistaken your wife for her twin sister, could pin the murder on you?" Hannah's voice was veined with sarcasm. She hadn't intended that, but the story was so far-fetched she couldn't help it. She wanted to believe Sam, did believe him on many levels, but this hypothesis strained her credulity.

Sam didn't say anything.

"Drugged you how?" Hannah asked.

Sam lifted his hands helplessly and again said nothing.

"If you don't remember what happened," Hannah pointed out, "you could have killed her."

"I loved her. Why would I hurt her?"

Would Sam have told Hannah about blacking out if he thought there was a chance he'd killed his wife? Probably not. But his *thinking* he had nothing to do with the murder didn't make it so.

"Remember the flyer in your wife's pocket?" she asked. "You told us it was her handwriting on the back. Is that true?"

"It looked like hers." He paused, thinking. "That was before I knew she had a twin, but I doubt their handwriting would be that similar. Especially since Eva was left-handed and Andrea right. Why?"

She hesitated. "The flyer was one those monthly recipes handed out at the hospital. It didn't officially come out until Monday. The day after you reported her missing."

Sam's face drained of color. "You mean she was alive on Monday?" Sam looked like a man reeling from confusion.

"That's one explanation. It's also conceivable that someone in the medical profession could get his hands on the flyers before Monday."

"Me, in other words."

Hannah got to her feet. "I want you to come down to the station so we can write up exactly what did happen. The truth this time."

She had the feeling it wasn't going to make things any clearer, but at least they'd have the right pieces of the puzzle to work with.

CHAPTER 53

Dallas looked bored. It was clear he wasn't buying my explanation.

We were back in the interview room where I'd been questioned earlier. Only this time, I felt the walls closing in on me. My palms were sweating and my throat was dry.

Hannah had given him a brief rundown of our conversation in the park, and then I'd told it again in my own words. As far as I could tell, Dallas hadn't listened with anything approaching an open mind.

"Bull," he said now, stabbing the table with his index finger.

"My wife had a twin," I told him. "You can check it out for yourself." Of course the attorney, Dunbar, might not speak as freely to a cop as he had to me. But there'd have to be a birth certificate, wouldn't there?

Dallas wasn't impressed. "So what if she *was* a twin? I'm willing to accept that it was Eva and not Andrea who was in Las Vegas, but none of that has any bearing on who murdered your wife. The evidence is there, Sam. It all points to you."

"It can't. I didn't kill her."

"You don't *know* what you did, Sam. You just admitted you don't remember a thing between Saturday and Sunday mornings."

Anxiety squeezed my gut. Why hadn't I listened to Jesse and kept my mouth shut? "I know I didn't kill her," I said with newfound conviction.

"The evidence," Dallas asked, waving his hand in the air like a butterfly, "it was arranged just to frame you?"

I didn't answer. I wasn't going to rise to the bait.

"And the guy who killed your wife and tried to frame you is a member of organized crime? Someone who came all the way to Monte Vista and happened to stumble upon a woman who was the spitting image of Eva Flynn, a woman he was looking to murder?" Dallas turned away from the table with an incredulous shake of his head.

"The man who broke into Sam's house did mention Eric's name," Hannah pointed out.

Dallas looked at her. "I can't believe you buy this."

"I'm not *buying* anything, Dallas. But Sam has brought us new information we need to follow up on."

"This is Monte Vista, for Chrissakes. We don't have mob murders here, but we damn sure have husbands who kill their wives."

"Even if my wife's murder had nothing to do with Eva," I said, "you need to keep looking. Because it wasn't me."

Dallas narrowed his eyes at me. "We're going to let you go today, Sam. But I promise you, it's only a matter of time before we arrest you. You're not going to get away with murder a second time."

CHAPTER 54

Annalise Rose watched the collage of brightly colored sails dancing along the Charles River outside her dormitory window. A lot of the MIT dorms were located on Memorial Drive paralleling the river, but only the south-facing rooms had a view. She counted herself lucky to have ended up with such a choice location, but there were times, like today, when it made studying difficult. With a final on Monday, no matter how inviting the afternoon, she was stuck inside.

And she'd be stuck inside all summer too. Not even doing something challenging like research for a professor or interning with a company she might be interested in working for after graduation. Instead, she'd be holed up in the back room of a bank, pushing paper for Uncle Hal. At least the job paid well, which was the only reason she'd taken it.

Her cousin Lisa had worked at the bank too. Three summers in a row when she was in college. Annalise had been too young at the time to pay any attention, but Lisa had told her about it later, when Annalise was twelve.

It was summer, and she was being shipped off to camp, when what she really wanted was to stay home with her friends. Lisa told her summer camp was a whole lot better than working, so she should count herself lucky. Coming from anyone else, the advice would have sounded preachy. But Lisa wasn't like that. She didn't lecture the way Annalise's parents did when they gave their you-don't-know-how-lucky-you-are speeches. And she didn't consider herself superior because she was older. Lisa had been like an older sister, a wonderful sister, wise and generous. She gave Annalise advice about makeup and clothes and even boys. They laughed that their parents had given them similar names. Lisa. Annalise. It was like they really were sisters.

And little Molly was so cute. Annalise had helped Lisa out after school, and she babysat if Lisa and Sam weren't going to be out too late. Annalise smiled at the memory. She'd had such a crush on Sam. An innocent crush, but she'd dreamed of growing up to be just like Lisa, with a husband like Sam and a darling baby girl. When Lisa was murdered, Annalise felt like her whole world had been torn apart.

After Sam was arrested, Lisa's entire family, her parents included, wanted nothing to do with him. Annalise had been too young to attend the trial, and she hadn't seen Sam since the funeral. But she'd seen the grief in his eyes that day, and she'd never been able to reconcile that anguish, and the memory of the gentle man she'd known, with the image of a husband who'd murder his wife.

It all seemed like such a long time ago. She hadn't thought much about it until the other day, when she'd overheard her mom and Aunt Sylvia talking. It brought Annalise up short to realize Molly would be only a year younger now than Annalise had been then. Uncle Hal was talking about bringing Molly home to stay with them for good. Annalise supposed it might be fun to be a big sister, the way Lisa had been to her, but the circumstances were kind of strange. Besides, she didn't see how Uncle Hal could just take the kid away from her father.

Annalise didn't know whether it was good or not that the cops were still looking into Lisa's murder. What would happen if Sam was arrested a second time?

She was glad she'd told the detective about "the monster" who'd been bothering Lisa. It was probably nothing, but it had weighed on her mind ever since she'd heard Aunt Sylvia tell her mother that Sam's second wife had also been murdered. In a tone that implied, *Sam's done it again.*

Annalise's roommate, Becky, picked up her Rollerblades and backpack. "Catch you later," she said.

"You off to the library?"

"I should be, but Aaron and I are going to the afternoon concert in the park instead."

"Have fun." With a pang of envy, Annalise turned back to her problem sets. Boring.

She got up and closed the blinds. Maybe studying would be easier if she wasn't looking out at the beautiful day she was missing. Halfway through a long calculation, her computer beeped, announcing an instant message from a friend. Glad for the reprieve, Annalise responded. They commiserated at being stuck with finals. When the friend signed off, Annalise went to Google and typed in Sam Russell's name.

Until Aunt Sylvia mentioned him the other day, Annalise hadn't thought of him for years, but now she was curious. She was hoping she'd find a newspaper story. She wanted to see what he looked like now. And to know what had happened to his second wife.

There were quite a few hits. Some were medical associations and such, but there was a lot of news coverage too. She read through several articles. Sam had reported his wife missing and then she'd turned up dead.

Strangled and stabbed, just like Lisa.

Annalise felt a shiver work its way down her spine.

She clicked on a related link and jumped to another screen revealing a photo of Sam. She enlarged the picture.

He looked just like she remembered. Those soft crinkly eyes that seemed to laugh even when he didn't. He'd been so kind to her, hadn't treated her like a kid at all.

Another link. Another photo of Sam. And next to it, a photo of his missing wife.

Annalise drew in her breath sharply and again enlarged the image.

Could it be?

But it made no sense.

Studying forgotten, she fumbled through her backpack for the card Detective Donahue had given her.

CHAPTER 55

I called my dad from the police station so he wouldn't worry that I was stuck in Atlanta. Instead, he worried that I was with the cops. He and Chase and Molly were waiting the minute I walked into the house.

"What happened?" Dad asked. "Why did they need to talk to you again?"

"I'm the one who called them," I explained. Well, I'd called Hannah anyway, which somehow made it more palatable. But it hadn't stayed that way for long. Now I regretted the whole thing.

"Why'd you call them?" Chase asked.

"There's a new twist I thought they should know about."

"About the adoption? Were you able to talk to the attorney who handled it?"

I nodded. We sat around the kitchen table, where the others had just finished a breakfast of waffles and bacon, and I told them what I'd learned about Eva and her twin, Andrea Wycoff.

Dad scratched his head. "Maureen was Andrea?"

"Right."

"Why was she so secretive about her family?"

"I'm not sure. Probably because she didn't have any real family left, aside from Eva. And telling me about Eva would mean talking about the adoption."

Molly touched the locket Maureen had give her. "You mean this isn't even Maureen's? It's her sister's?"

"It looks that way."

"Why did she give it to me?"

"I don't know. I guess she thought you'd like it." But Molly was a sentimentalist. I knew the locket had lost much of its meaning for her.

"None of this gets the cops any closer to finding her killer," Chase pointed out.

"I know."

We tossed around theories and possible explanations for a bit, then Chase headed home. Suddenly I hit the wall of exhaustion.

"I need to take a short nap. Are you okay with that, Molly?"

She nodded unconvincingly.

"I'm sorry, honey. I'm just beat."

"I'll stay a bit," Dad said.

"You're not going to leave again, are you?" Molly asked me.

"No. I'm home to stay. We'll rent a movie tonight and have takeout Chinese food for dinner." Usually, a winning combination as far as Molly was concerned.

She wasn't so easily placated today. But after a moment, she gave me a hug. "Sleep tight, don't let the bedbugs bite."

"I'll try."

My sleep wasn't tight or restful. I tossed and thrashed, jolted awake what seemed like every few minutes by nonsensical and exhausting dreams. Lisa and Maureen, Eva and Andrea, Hannah and Phipps, and even Eric Vance—they all made repeated appearances as I climbed endless stairs and raced to find the right room for a big test.

I didn't sleep soundly, but I did sleep much longer than I'd intended. When I got up, it was three o'clock and the house was quiet. I found a note on the kitchen counter from Dad.

Molly and I have gone to play miniature golf. Back by four.

I showered, which cleared a few of the cobwebs from my head, and then tackled the job of cleaning up the kitchen. Dad and Chase were great with Molly, but neither of them paid much attention to things like bread crumbs and bacon grease.

Although I'd given the box of mementoes Andrea's neighbor had given me a cursory run-through in Atlanta, I wanted to go through it again in more depth. I figured the free afternoon was a perfect opportunity. I was hoping I'd find some clue that would help me understand the woman I'd been married to and hadn't known at all.

The phone rang just as I finished loading the dishwasher.

"Hi, Sam. It's Ira. You got a minute?"

"Sure." I found Ira's affable voice reassuring. Maybe we weren't as close as we'd once been, but Ira was familiar and comfortable the way only an old friend can be. "Molly's off playing with my dad," I told him, "and I'm here cleaning. I feel like Cinderella."

"Great. I mean, not about your cleaning, but that you're free. You think you could come by the office for a few minutes?"

"What's up?"

"Just a few papers we need to go over."

It wasn't strange that Ira was doing paperwork on the weekend. He was a stickler for administrative stuff and was always trying to squeeze the last dollar out of the business.

But that he'd want my input, especially now, was curious. For a brief instant, I experienced a glimmer of hope that he wanted me back in the practice on a regular basis. But I realized it was more likely there was some egregious error that was all my fault.

"Sure. I can be there in fifteen minutes."

"I appreciate it, Sam."

In case my father and Molly got home before I did, I left a note saying I'd gone to the office.

Our practice was located on the ground floor of a building with one other tenant, an orthodontist who didn't work weekends. Parking was never a problem. Still, when I pulled into the reserved spot in the back lot, I was glad to see that Ira hadn't given my space away.

Ira was at his desk. He pushed back his chair and gave me a friendly cuff on the shoulder. "Thanks for coming on such short notice. How are you doing?"

I made a gesture with my hands. "So-so."

"You want a Coke or something?"

"Sounds good."

He left and returned a few minutes later with a glass of soda for each of us. "I've been thinking," he said. "I feel like a real heel asking you stay away from the practice."

My heart lifted. Maybe he really did want me back. "It's okay," I told him. "I understand." It wasn't really okay, but given how little time I'd had to focus on anything but my wife's murder, it was probably for the best. At least that's what I'd tried to tell myself.

I took a gulp of Coke. It was cold and refreshing.

"The patients ask about you. They miss you."

"I'm glad to know I'm missed." I wondered if Ira was softening me up before he dropped the bombshell. After all, it was supposedly the patients' suspicions and discomfort that had made him ask me to stay away in the first place.

"Do you think the cops are making any headway toward solving the case?"

"It's gotten very complicated. Now the FBI is involved."

"The FBI?" He looked startled. "What for?"

"I don't understand all that's happening." I didn't have the energy to go through it all again. "What papers did you want me to look at?"

"You sure you're up to it? We can do it another time."

"No, now's fine." I felt suddenly lightheaded. Despite my nap, jet lag and lack of sleep had caught up with me. I guzzled more soda then held the icy glass to my forehead.

Ira shuffled through some files. "Mr. Langley's ulcer is acting up again."

"Really?" Was that what Ira wanted to talk to me about? Had I misdiagnosed a condition? I tried to remember Langley. I knew he was a patient, but my head was swimming and I felt woozy.

"You okay, Sam?"

"Just a little dizzy. I didn't sleep well last night."

"Have more soda. Maybe you're dehydrated."

I took another gulp. I could feel perspiration beading on my forehead. Was I having a heart attack?

"Sam?"

Ira's voice sounded far away and muddied. The room began to spin.

A female voice off in the distance. It sounded like Maureen. God, I *was* having a heart attack. Or a stroke. Or something. I gripped the desk for support.

"Can't you just give him a shot like last time?" the voice that sounded like Maureen's said.

Last time?

"He's got to be conscious to sign his name."

My mouth was dry. It felt as though it were filled with cotton. "Sign what?" The words came out garbled.

Ira put a typed page in front of me. "We just need your signature, Sam." He put the pen in my hand.

"Whasssss thiis?" I tried to read it, but the words blurred.

"Don't worry about it, Sam. Like I said, just some paperwork."

I shook my head, tried to focus on the page. Odd words here and there were all I could make out. *Distraught. Sorry. Guilty.*

"Just sign it. Then we'll let you get some sleep."

Sleep sounded wonderful. I gripped the pen. Slowly signed my name.

"Is he done?" The woman's voice again. She came into view.

Not my imagination.

"Maureen?"

"Hi, Sam."

Tears pricked my eyes. "You're alive?"

"I am."

"But the body . . . the wine cellar . . ."

"My sister, Eva."

With my head spinning, it was hard to hold onto any thought at all. "She was . . . wearing . . . your jacket."

"We wanted people to think it was me. But it was Eva. She's the reason this has gone all wrong."

"Whadda ya mean?"

Maureen sat on the edge of the desk and crossed her legs. "It was a simple plan. All we wanted was the ransom money."

I shook my head, trying to clear it.

"The marriage wasn't working, Sam. I gave it a shot, but it wasn't . . . what I expected. I couldn't just divorce you though. Your money is all tied up in trust. I'd never get my hands on it."

I looked at Ira, my friend since fourth grade. I wanted him to tell me I was delirious. I wanted him to reassure me. But he was busy folding the paper I'd signed.

"Ira helped me with the kidnapping," she explained. "He

needed money too. And now he's going to get the practice for himself. Eva made things worse for you, Sam. But actually it worked out for everyone else."

Maureen took a sip of Ira's Coke. "Eva was a spoiled brat. Always had been as far as I could tell. Just like Lisa."

Lisa? What did she have to do with this? But I couldn't wrap my mind around the question.

"You killed your sister?" The words were slurred, but Maureen seemed to decipher them.

"She was going to ruin everything. She was going to tell you what was going on. She backed us into a corner—we had to kill her."

"It still might have been okay," Ira said. "The body wasn't supposed to be discovered at Albright's. We figured we'd dump it someplace obvious after we got the rest of the ransom money. That way Maureen wouldn't need to get a divorce, because everyone would assume she was dead. As soon as those guests of Albright's discovered the corpse, everything changed. We thought about framing you right then."

"We should have framed you, Sam. It would have been better for you. You might have gotten off at trial like you did last time. But now the cops know about Eva, so you've got to step up to the plate."

Ira pushed back his chair. "Now that you've confessed to her murder, you're going to take your own life."

"No!" I tried to stand. My legs wouldn't hold me up. In fact, I had no feeling at all in them.

Ira opened the bottom drawer of his desk and pulled out a syringe, which he filled from a small glass bottle. "We'll make it easy on you, Sam. You're going to drive off the bridge, but I'll make sure you've got enough drugs in you first that you won't know what hit you."

"You can have the money." I struggled to make them understand, but neither of them seemed remotely interested.

Using a tissue, Maureen picked up the envelope with my signed confession. "I'll put this on his desk."

Ira nodded and flicked the syringe with his finger to remove the air bubbles.

"Just hold still, Sam. You'll hardly feel it."

CHAPTER 56

Hannah hung up the phone. "He's not home," she told Dallas. "His father said he went into the office. Let me try that number."

A recording greeted her. "Our office is currently closed. If this is an emergency . . ." She turned to Dallas. "Let's just drive over there."

"You tried his cell?"

She'd tried that first. "He's not answering."

Dallas grabbed the car keys from his desk. "You sure that Boston cop knows what he's talking about?"

"No. I've only spoken with him a couple of times. But Lisa's cousin called him after seeing Maureen's photo on the Internet. She says Sam's wife looks like the woman Lisa argued with only days before she was killed."

Dallas whistled under his breath. "Eva or Andrea?"

"Good question." Hannah had assumed it was Andrea, Sam's wife. But she didn't have any real grounds for that.

"Did the cousin say what Lisa and the woman argued about?"

"Something about Molly. The woman was apparently talking to her, and Lisa went ballistic."

"For talking to her kid?"

"Donahue only gave me the short version, but he thinks Andrea might be 'the monster' Lisa talked about. It sounded like the woman was stalking her. Trying to steamroll her way into Lisa's life for some reason."

"Didn't Lisa report her?"

"Apparently not. This was the first Donahue had heard of it. The cousin was a twelve-year-old kid at the time. She says she told her parents, but the family was so convinced Sam was involved they didn't pay much attention. The bruises Lisa's mother noticed on her arm and thought came from Sam could actually have come from the stalker."

"Why was the woman stalking Lisa?"

Hannah shook her head. "Some sort of psychotic crush on Sam maybe?"

"Do you suppose Sam and Andrea were having an affair? Maybe they were in this together from the beginning."

The thought had crossed Hannah's mind. But if that was so, they'd waited a long time to pick up again. "Maybe. Let's see how Sam reacts to this latest information."

Dallas turned into the parking lot behind the medical building and pulled into a parking spot reserved for patients. There were only two other cars and a motorcycle in the lot. Hannah recognized one of the cars as Sam's Audi.

"We're in luck," she said. "It looks like he's still here."

Dallas put the cruiser into park and opened the door. Hannah was still mentally sorting out the cars. Suddenly her pulse kicked into overdrive.

"Whose motorcycle is that?" she asked.

"Ira's, I think. He's got one like it, at any rate. Why?"

The information dropped like a lead weight in Hannah's stomach. "Look at the decal on the rear fender," she said, forcing her voice to remain calm.

Dallas peered at the bike. "It's from the Indian gaming casino north of Sacramento."

Her mouth was dry. "It's the same symbol as on the metal pull Carla and I found behind the barn."

"So?" But even as he spoke, Hannah could see Dallas making the connections himself. "Holy shit. You think Ira's part of this?"

"I think it's time we found out," Hannah told him.

"Maybe we should run the plate first." He was already heading back to the cruiser.

Just then, there was a loud crash from inside the building. Hannah could hear raised voices, but she couldn't make out the words.

She and Dallas raced for the entrance.

"How are we going to play it?" Dallas asked.

"By the seat of our pants, I'm afraid."

CHAPTER 57

During the long, hard months following Lisa's murder, I spent a lot of time thinking about death. Hers, of course, but my own as well. I'd lie on the thin, hard mattress of my jail cell, sometimes imagining my final moments on death row but more often agonizing over not being alive to see Molly grow up. The idea of missing all that wonder was as painful to me as the loss of her mother had been.

I mourned my own demise for months on end.

But now, facing imminent death, I didn't think at all. When Ira flicked the syringe with his fingernail, panic and rage propelled me into mindless action.

Though I was weak and dizzy, I somehow managed to get to my feet.

Ira put a hand on my chest and pushed me back into my chair. "Don't fight me, Sam. It will only make things worse."

I sucked in gulps of air, trying desperately to clear my head. Raised an arm to fend him off. Ira brushed it aside.

"You can't do this," I told him. "Please . . . don't do this."

He readied the syringe to plunge into my arm. My eyes focused on the needle and the drop of serum that glistened on the tip.

"Just hold still, Sam. It won't hurt as much." He reached for my wrist.

At the last minute, I slumped forward and rolled onto the floor, hitting Ira in the midsection and knocking him off his feet. The syringe went flying.

"Goddam it, Sam." He clambered to all fours.

I managed to drag myself to the corner between Ira's credenza and the wall. While he was righting himself, I stuck a finger into my throat, making myself gag and then vomit. Whatever Ira had given me was already at work in my system. But the less of it I had in me, the better.

Maureen rushed back into the room. "What's all the racket?" She looked at the mess on my clothing. "Jesus, Sam."

Ira lunged toward me. I pulled the cord of the table lamp and sent it toppling to the floor. The ceramic stand shattered.

Ira kicked at the fragments.

Between the pounding of my heart and the commotion in the room, I was only dimly aware of the pounding on our outer door.

"Police. Open up."

Maureen's face froze. She turned to Ira. "What do we do now?"

Hannah pounded on the door.

"Stand back," Dallas told her. Gun drawn, he kicked in the door and entered first. Hannah could hear voices from one of the inner offices.

"Sam's office is at the back," she whispered. "Ira's is to the left."

"Go around to the rear of the building," Dallas barked. "Make sure any exits are covered."

Hannah nodded. "I called for backup. Don't do anything foolish."

"You'd care?"

Surprisingly, she realized she would. For all her complaining, she'd sort of settled into working with him. "Of course," she barked.

Then she hustled around to the back of the building, where she'd noticed an unmarked door leading to the garbage bins at the left of the parking lot. She'd barely gotten into position when it flew open. Ira and a woman who looked like the photos she'd seen of Maureen Russell careened through the door.

"Police," Hannah shouted. "Get your hands above your heads."

CHAPTER 58

Never in my wildest dreams could I have imagined being so happy to see Dallas. He stood at the doorway with his gun drawn.

"Don't shoot," I called to him. "It's me."

He slipped inside, keeping his back to the wall, his eye on the hallway. "Are you hurt, Sam?"

"I was drugged, but I think I'm okay." I tried to drag myself to my feet and couldn't. I was still weak and woozy, but I felt more clear-headed. "They went out through the rear door. To your right."

"Patrol should be here any minute, along with an ambulance. You sure you'll be okay?"

I nodded. "It's Ira and Maureen. Don't let them get away."

As Dallas disappeared, I could hear the whine of sirens in the distance.

Despite my protests, I was carted off in an ambulance. A female cop in uniform rode with me and took my statement. At the hospital, I was checked out and finally released to my worried dad and daughter. I assured them repeatedly that I was fine, but we all knew that *alive* and *fine* were not quite the same.

When I got home, I called the police station. I couldn't get anyone there to answer my questions, but Hannah called about seven that evening to ask if I was okay.

"I'll live," I told her. I had a pounding headache and a gut that felt like it had been trampled on by a herd of elephants. But the truly battered parts of me weren't physical.

"Have they confessed?" I asked. "They told me they killed Maureen's sister, Eva."

"I can't talk right now, Sam. I just wanted to be sure you were in one piece."

"Thanks. I'm grateful you and Dallas showed up when you did this afternoon." For once, fate had gone my way.

"I'm glad it worked out. Tomorrow, I'll want to go over your statement. I'll tell you what I can then. In the meantime, get some rest."

It wasn't until that night, after Molly was in bed and I was finally alone in the house, that I was finally able to really look through the cardboard box Andrea's neighbor had given me. I cleared the kitchen table of fortune-cookie crumbs—earlier in the evening Molly and my dad had eaten Chinese food while I sipped hot bouillon—and started sorting through the papers and photos in the box.

It was a disappointing collection. There was a handful of photos of a young girl I presumed was Andrea, whom I'd known as Maureen. In a couple of them, she was with a woman I took to be her mother, Helen Wycoff. Helen was a good-looking woman with the same coloring as her daughters but a fuller figure.

There were also school papers and drawings, a news clipping about Andrea's appearance in the high-school production of *Fiddler on the Roof*, a slightly grimy but much loved stuffed bear. The sort of things that had meaning, maybe, for the person who collected the items, but little beyond that.

The truth was, I really didn't care anymore.

I started taking items out, leafing through them and stacking them on the table, only half paying attention to what I was doing. Then I came to an envelope inside a larger manila envelope. I emptied the contents on the table.

My heart skipped a couple of beats.

Two photos. Both showed Helen with the same man. A man I recognized.

My former father-in-law, Hal Patterson.

It was no wonder my second wife had reminded me of Lisa, I realized with a jolt. They had the same father.

CHAPTER 59

Dallas was getting a candy bar from the machine when Hannah joined him in the break room. She was tired and she was hungry, but the pitiful offerings of the machines didn't appeal to her.

"You get anything from Ira?" she asked.

"He's not talking, which isn't surprising. There's not much he can say about what happened today that will help him. As for Andrea's murder . . . right now all we have is what they supposedly told Sam. It's their word against his."

Hannah experienced a flash of anger. "Surely you don't still suspect Sam!"

Dallas stepped back as if she'd slapped him. "Jesus, I know you don't like me much as a partner, but do you really think I'm such a lousy cop as that?" He held up a hand. "Wait, don't answer. All I meant was, from Ira's perspective it's smart to see what we've got on him before he opens his mouth."

Hannah was stung by his assessment. She hadn't much like being partnered with Dallas at first, but it embarrassed her to know she'd made it so apparent. Especially now that she was beginning to appreciate Dallas's good points. She'd focused on the annoyances without giving him credit for his strengths.

"How do you know what I think of you as a partner?" she asked.

"You've made it pretty obvious."

And yet he hadn't turned against her. She, it seemed, was far more petty than Dallas. "I think you're a fine cop," she told him, truthfully. "It's just that we have different styles." She was beginning to see that wasn't always a bad thing.

"We do sure do. But it's a useful balance." He grinned. "Most of the time."

He tore open the package of M&Ms and offered her some.

"No thanks," she said then thought better of it. It wasn't candy; it was a peace offering. "Well, maybe just a few."

Carla pushed open the swinging door.

"How is he?" Hannah asked. Carla had ridden with Sam in the ambulance to the hospital.

"Pretty good, all things considered. They aren't even keeping him overnight."

Dallas offered her some M&Ms, and she took a handful with a grateful—and, to Hannah's mind, coy—smile. It went straight over Dallas's head. Hannah wanted to shake him.

Carla shot Hannah a look—a woman-to-woman look that said *what am I going to do about this guy?* It was a very small gesture, but one that made Hannah think the two of them might yet be friends.

"Good work, you two," Carla said. "Incredible timing. Any later and Sam would be dead."

Hannah shuddered to think how close Sam had come to being killed. How close, in truth, he'd come to being arrested for his wife's murder.

Dallas must have been thinking the same thing, because he turned to Carla. "It was Hannah who kept saying we shouldn't be so ready to pin the murder on Sam. Guess she was right."

"His own wife and his medical partner trying to bilk him out of money," Carla said. "That's sick."

"And that's just the tip of the iceberg."

"Do you think you'll ever get it sorted out?"

Hannah and Dallas nodded in unison. "They'll end up talking," Dallas said. "Both of them. And eventually we'll get the answers we need."

"Some of it we've already figured out," Hannah said. "The notation on the back of the recipe flyer from the hospital, for instance. It turns out to be an item number from a clothing catalogue. Nothing relevant to our investigation, except for the flyer itself, which wasn't available until the day after Maureen disappeared."

The three of them hung out a bit longer in the break room. Then Carla went to type up her report. Hannah and Dallas were going to question Maureen. Hannah had trouble thinking of her as Andrea.

Dallas offered her the last M&M, and she took it. They walked a few moments in silence.

"Carla has her eye on you," Hannah told him.

"On me? Why?"

"I imagine she thinks you're hot."

"Oh God."

"What's wrong with that? She's an attractive woman."

He looked at her like she'd just spoken gibberish. "I thought you knew."

"Knew what?"

He reddened and turned away. And in that moment she saw something she hadn't before.

"Dallas, are you gay?"

For a moment, he said nothing. "It's a small town," he mumbled finally. "I grew up here—"

"Is that a *yes*?"

"I figured that's why you didn't like working with me."

Hannah laughed. "I didn't like working with you because

I was a pompous jerk and you were pigheaded about going after Sam. It had nothing to do with sexual preferences."

He smiled. "And because we have very different styles of working."

"That too."

CHAPTER 60

Despite being up half the night, Hannah was at her desk bright and early the next morning. She had a meeting with Phipps later in the day and mounds of paperwork to get through before then. In addition, the lieutenant had a press conference scheduled for that afternoon, and she knew she'd be called upon to give a brief statement.

Still, when Hannah got word that Sam was at the station wanting to speak with her, she put the papers aside and went to greet him. He looked wretched. The dark circles under his eyes had deepened, and his skin seemed to have lost elasticity overnight. Her heart ached for him.

"How are you feeling?" she asked.

"Rocky." He smiled. "But it could be worse."

"It was close."

"I want to see her," he said.

Hannah assumed "her" meant Andrea, whom she still thought of as Maureen. "She's under arrest."

"The jail has visiting hours, doesn't it?" When Hannah didn't respond, he continued. "I'm her husband. Don't I have a right to visit?"

She took his arm. "Let's go somewhere more private to talk. Can I get you anything? Coffee? Soda?"

"No, I'm fine." He laughed humorlessly. "Well, not fine really. I'm a mess. But coffee and Coke won't help. Especially not Coke. I may never drink it again."

"I'm sorry, Sam. Truly sorry." She couldn't imagine what he was going through. She'd suffered enough from Malcolm and Claire's betrayal. Adultery was child's play next to murder.

The small interview room was vacant, and she ushered him in there. It was the same room where they'd first questioned him, but there weren't a lot of options.

"I need to talk to her," he said again.

"Are you sure you really want to?"

He nodded. "I've also got one last bit of information for you." He slid a photo onto the table. A man and woman.

"Who are they?" Hannah asked.

"The woman is Helen Wycoff, Andrea's and Eva's natural mother."

"And the man?"

"I presume he's their father. He's got the same mouth they do. His name is Harold Patterson."

"Patterson?" She looked up. Lisa's maiden name.

"Right, my former father-in-law."

"Oh my God. So that's what—"

"What do you mean?"

Hannah knew she was about to violate some basic tenet of investigation, but she thought Sam deserved to know. "Did Lisa ever talk to you about someone stalking her?"

"No."

"She never mentioned 'the monster'?"

Sam shook his head.

"You know Annalise Rose?"

"Lisa's cousin? Sure. She used to visit us a lot, help out

with Molly. Cute kid. Kind of like Lisa's little sister. Why?"

"She remembers a woman stalking Lisa. Your wife called her 'the monster.' Annalise saw an Internet photo of your wife and identified her as the stalker."

Sam looked ill. "She was in Boston?"

Hannah nodded. "Around the time of Lisa's murder."

"My God, are you saying . . ."

She leaned closer. "If I get you in to see your wife, would you be willing to wear a wire?"

He didn't even have to think about it. "You bet."

I stared at the woman in the orange jumpsuit seated across from me and felt nothing but anger. She was my wife, and at one time I'd loved her, but at that moment I couldn't recall why.

"What are you doing here?" she asked.

"I wanted to see you."

"Here I am. Not a pretty sight, is it?"

"Why did you do this, Maureen?" It was simplest to call her by the name I'd known.

She shrugged.

"Didn't you care about me at all?"

"It wasn't supposed to turn out the way it did, Sam. You're a nice man. But being married to you wasn't what I thought it would be. I wanted out."

I was tempted to argue. I knew our marriage had problems, but I thought we could work through them. Obviously, I'd been wrong.

"Most people who feel that way get a divorce," I said.

"I needed money. You had money. You wouldn't touch it when we were married, and you sure as hell weren't going to give me any of it in a divorce." Her tone was so cold and flat, I cringed.

"It wasn't mine; it was Lisa's. And now Molly's."

Maureen gave me an exasperated look then spread her hands. "It's all my sister's fault."

"Tell me about her." I wasn't entirely sure which sister she was talking about at that point.

"Eva?" She laughed bitterly. "Until I was eighteen, I never even knew I had a sister. Then Eva came to Atlanta and looked us up. I was blown away. Not only did I have a sister, I had a twin. I was shy, but she was spunky and lively. We looked exactly alike but were so different in many ways." She paused, seemingly lost in thought. "Our upbringing was different, you know. Eva's parents were rich. They gave her things. I was jealous of that."

"Eva wasn't very happy about it, was she?"

Maureen made a dismissive gesture. "What did she know? If she'd been the one our mother kept, then she'd know what a truly shitty home life really was. We never had enough money. My mother was an alcoholic who hooked up with one abusive man after another. Eva had the life that could have been mine, and she didn't even appreciate it."

"But the two of you remained close."

She shrugged. "It's funny about twins. There was definitely a bond between us, but not always a loving one. Eva showed up when she needed something. I was the good girl, boring and shy, but responsible. She was a flake. I rescued her time after time. I told her not to come to Monte Vista, but she came anyway." Maureen huffed. "That's so like her. Thinking of no one but herself. If she'd been seen around town, it would have ruined our ransom plan, so I set it up for her to stay with Ira. To keep her hidden for a bit."

Maureen examined her nails and made a face. "They don't even have hand lotion in here." She looked up. "Anyway, Eva didn't like being confined to Ira's. She threatened to tell you what was going on. She and Ira got into a fight, and he killed her. I don't think it was on purpose, but there it was. When life gives you lemons, make lemonade. Right? We had a body that looked like me, so we decided to use it."

I'd never heard Maureen speak with such cold-blooded indifference. It raised goosebumps along my arms. "What about the Saturday night of our anniversary?" I asked.

"Ira gave you a drug of some sort, a couple of them, in fact. So you wouldn't remember what happened. We didn't want to hurt you, Sam."

Right. If I'd been hurt, I couldn't gather up the ransom money.

"You put up quite a fight, though. You clawed at my arms and whacked me so hard with your arm you gave me a bloody nose."

So that's where the blood had come from. "What about Eva's shoe? How did it get into my trunk?"

Maureen smiled. "Nice touch, huh? We knew you would doubt yourself because you couldn't remember what happened. We thought the confusion would keep you from going to the police."

"What happened to the money?"

"Ira picked it up at the barn. With his motorcycle. I was waiting down below on the main road. I saw you take off after that SUV, Sam. That was pretty stupid, you know. If it actually had been kidnappers in the SUV, you think they wouldn't notice you? When I told Ira, he got the idea of leaving a message on your answering machine. We wanted to make sure you didn't try something like that again. Not until we had the rest of the money."

"And Eric? Where does he play into this?"

She made a face. "Eric got himself caught up in a big one this time. Eva went to Las Vegas thinking she could help him. He said he was in trouble with the law and she shouldn't stick around. That's why she came here. Whatever troubles he has, they're his own."

"But Eric's friends thought Eva had something of his."

"Really?" Maureen didn't seem interested. "That's Eva's problem. Was her problem."

There was not an ounce of feeling in Maureen's voice. I wondered how I could have been married to her and never seen this side of her. If I hadn't needed to hear what she would say about Lisa, I'd have gotten up right then and walked away.

Instead, I leaned back, trying for a relaxed posture. "What about your father? Did you ever know him?"

There was a moment's hesitation and a flicker of emotion in her eyes. "Not while I was growing up," she said.

I showed her the photo of Helen Wycoff and my former father-in-law.

She looked at me. "You know, then. My mother was his secretary. They had an affair. How clichéd is that?"

When I didn't respond, she continued. "He was married and had a child. There was no question he would leave his wife. My mother claims she never even told him she was pregnant. She left Boston and moved to Atlanta. I didn't know anything about this growing up, but when she knew she was dying, Mom told both Eva and me his name. Eva went to see him, hoping, I guess, for some sort of Hallmark Channel–type reunion. Instead, he denied everything. He wasn't interested in his twin daughters. He didn't even care that Mom was dead."

"She went to see Lisa too, didn't she?"

Maureen looked at me a moment then nodded. "Lisa wasn't interested either. She was a bitch, Sam, not the kind, loving wife you think. She wouldn't hear of her dad doing wrong. She warned Eva to stay away from her mother too. Eva wasn't interested in causing problems; all she wanted was to be part of the family. She wanted to be Lisa's friend. Her sister." Maureen's eyes flashed. "Do you know what Lisa did? She offered Eva a thousand dollars to leave them alone. A fucking thousand. It was like pennies to her. It was an insult."

"So what did Eva do?" I had trouble getting the words out.

"She killed Lisa." Maureen sounded triumphant.

"You knew about this when you married me?"

Maureen's face softened. "Don't you see? I was trying to make it up to you. I was going to be a good wife to you, a good mother to Molly. I'm sorry it didn't work out."

"I was arrested for Lisa's murder. I could have spent the rest of my life in prison. I could have been executed."

"I made sure you weren't. Don't you see how I've taken care of you, Sam? I scoped out the jury and found the easiest mark. A young, geeky guy who'd never had a girl in his life. Eugene Titmus. It was like taking candy from a baby, he was so easy to mold."

The horror of knowing how close I'd come to being convicted rocked me. "You influenced a juror?"

"Well, I slept with him. And I told him about the kind of woman Lisa really was. Stuff that never came out at trial. I don't really know if I influenced him. He may have seen through the prosecution's case on his own." She leaned forward. "Sam, I really wanted our marriage to work. I'm sorry it didn't. And I'm sorry about trying to trick you out of your money. It was just that I was desperate. I had no choice."

Even with her apology, there was a harshness about Maureen now that I had been blind to earlier. I couldn't believe that this was a woman I'd held in my arms and promised to love and honor.

"Maybe when I get out of here, we can still be friends."

"I don't think so, Maureen. And I wouldn't count on getting out any time soon."

She shrugged. "Not real soon, maybe. But a faked kidnapping—what are they going to give me for that? Especially if I agree to testify against Ira." She smiled. "And you can't testify against me, Sam. You're my husband."

As I got up to leave, the guard came to escort Maureen back to her cell.

"Just a minute," I said as she was walking away.

She turned back, and I tossed my car keys to her. She reached for them instinctively.

With her left hand.

CHAPTER 61

Five Days Later

Hannah felt a funny but familiar flutter in her belly when she spotted Sam. She slid into the worn wooden booth across from him. "Sorry, I'm late."

"You're not late. I was early."

She studied the menu. "What's good?"

"Pretty much everything. I'm going with the avocado and sprouts on rye with a side of potato salad."

"Sounds like a winner. I'll have the same. And iced tea." She closed the menu and smiled at him. The dark circles were gone from his eyes, and the taut, wary expression had relaxed. "Funny, I wouldn't have taken you for an avocado and sprouts kind of guy."

"Don't tell me you were thinking cheeseburger and fries," he said in mock horror.

"No." She studied him through half-closed eyes, pretending to size him up. "More like grilled chicken on whole wheat. With coleslaw." She was well aware that her tone was flirtatious, and she didn't try to rein it in.

He grinned at her. "Well, that's a favorite of mine too." He leaned forward. "At least you never took me for a killer. I appreciate that."

"To be honest, Sam, there were moments I wasn't convinced you *weren't*. It's just that I never actually believed you were."

"Well, that's something, I guess."

The waitress brought their drink orders. When she left, Hannah said, "You were right. It's Eva, not Andrea, we arrested." She paused. "Your wife is dead, Sam. I'm sorry."

"Why did Eva tell me she was Andrea?"

"To save her own skin. You are her husband, so there's a limit as to what you could testify about. There's also the issue of Eric Vance and the mob."

"Eva is really connected?"

"Maybe. But Eric clearly was. And she can identify his killers. I think she thought she was safer being Andrea than Eva."

"The man who broke into my house, he was mob connected too?"

"We don't know who it was, but I'd guess that's the case. Someone who followed Eva here."

"What about the rest of her story?"

"Well, it's taken a while to sort it out—Ira and Eva are so busy pointing the finger at each other, we're still not sure about some of the details. Most of what she told you is true, in essence. But the particulars are very different."

Hannah hesitated. Sam had to know, but she hated to be the one to tell him. "It was Andrea who killed Lisa. The Boston cops were able to match her prints to those lifted from the soda cans at your house when Lisa disappeared."

He looked as though he'd been stabbed. "My wife killed Lisa?"

Hannah nodded. "For all the reasons Eva told you. Andrea grew up poor, with a mother who wasn't much of a mother. Then she discovered she had a twin, someone who by pure luck had been given a golden life. She was jealous and bitter because it could have been her instead of Eva who'd been adopted out."

"So she took it out on Lisa?" Sam's voice cracked.

"Andrea wanted to be part of a family. The Pattersons rejected her. That's how she saw it anyway. Lisa's offering her money to go away was the last straw. Andrea flew into a rage and killed her."

Sam's eyes were hollow.

"Andrea tried to make sure you weren't convicted," Hannah said. "That part is true. She did her best to influence one of the jurors."

"And then she married me."

Their sandwiches arrived. Sam only stared at his. Hannah took a small bite before continuing.

"Eva says Andrea married you with the best of intentions. I believe that. It was the life she'd wanted all along, remember. But the reality didn't quite live up to the fantasy."

"So she faked her kidnapping in the hopes of getting her hands on Molly's trust money."

"She wanted out of the marriage, and she wanted money. Eva's timing in coming to visit couldn't have been worse. Andrea and Ira had their plan in place. It worked well because Molly was going to be at Heather's sleepover that Saturday night. They didn't want to risk putting it off."

"But murder . . ."

Hannah brushed bread crumbs from her lap. "I don't think murder was part of the original plan, but it worked well for them. Andrea would get her share of the money with no need to go through the pain of a divorce, and Ira would get the medical practice. It apparently riled him that he spent all those years working with your father, and you waltzed back in and got half the business."

"Andrea was the one who ended up dead though."

"Eva claims she killed Andrea in self-defense, but that will be up to a jury to decide. Myself, I don't buy it."

"Did Ira know?"

"He says he helped move the body but that he had nothing to do with the murder itself. Didn't even know about it until after the fact." Hannah paused. "He also claims he was under the impression that it was Eva who was killed, and the only reason he went along with keeping it quiet was because he thought he was protecting Andrea, his co-conspirator."

Sam looked forlorn. His face was slack, like a balloon that had lost most of its air. "Ira and I have been friends since grammar school. How could he do this?"

"Money. Ira has a lot of gambling debts. And resentment about the medical practice. It was a double whammy."

"I feel utterly betrayed. I can't even remember what it felt like to love my wife."

"I know the feeling." Hannah laced her fingers around her iced-tea glass. "I loved my husband. I was devastated when he died. But when I found out about the affair . . ." She bit her lip. "I can't remember what love felt like either," she said softly.

Their eyes met and held. Then Hannah looked away. Until recently, she'd been sure she'd never know love again. Now she was beginning to think maybe she did have it in her, after all.

"Why did Andrea use Maureen's name?" Sam asked. "Did Eva explain that to you?"

Hannah nodded. "She was afraid to use her own name because Hal Patterson would recognize it. Or recognize Wycoff at any rate. And she'd heard Eva talk about Maureen. It was an easy identity for her to assume."

Sam ate in silence. "I should be happy. I'm no longer a suspect in my wife's death, and I am cleared of Lisa's murder. I don't *feel* happy though."

"No, I imagine not. I do have one bit of actual good news for you though."

"What's that?"

"We recovered the ransom money. Most of it, at any rate."

"Hey." He offered a forced smile.

"It will get better, Sam. You have Molly, and your father and brother. You aren't alone."

"You were? After your husband, I mean."

"My mother tried. But mostly she wanted me to forgive Claire and move on."

"And you couldn't do that?"

"Well, I have moved on with my life, I guess." It was true, she realized. She'd sworn off one-night stands and cigarettes. She'd planted petunias, made peace with Dallas, begun to create a real home here in Monte Vista. "Maybe one day I'll get around to forgiveness too."

"No children, though?"

Hannah hesitated. She'd never told anyone but Malcolm. "I was three months pregnant when I was diagnosed with breast cancer. I wanted to wait until the baby was born to start treatment, but the doctors recommended against it."

"You had an abortion?"

Hannah nodded. Tears stung her eyes. "The chemo would have killed the baby anyway. But I keep wondering if maybe I should have waited until after it was born." Maybe if she had, Malcolm and Claire would never have happened. She sometimes wondered if Malcolm hadn't been secretly punishing her. On the other hand, if she'd waited, maybe the cancer would have spread, and she'd be dead.

Sam peeled her hand from the glass she was gripping and held it in his own. "Isn't there a saying that life isn't so much about beginnings and endings as it is about muddling through the middle? I guess in a sense that's what we're all doing."

Hannah smiled to herself. She'd certainly muddled through the last few years. But she had an inkling that might be changing.

"I think there's also a saying," she told him, "about end-ings being new beginnings."

"Sort of like today being the first day of the rest of your life?"

"Sort of."

He grinned. "Well, having lunch with you is a good start."

Enthusiastic fans of Jonnie Jacob's thrillers know what they're getting in bestseller after bestseller: riveting suspense, knockout writing, and a smart, world-weary heroine who can kick butt and take names when she needs to. Now Jacobs delivers another gripping tale of sex, lies, secrets, and murder whose razor-sharp twists and turns don't let up until the very last page is turned.

A body count that's rising. A lone witness on the run. A killer who'll do anything to buy silence. It's the most dangerous case of attorney Kali O'Brien's career—and it's hitting way too close to home.

The last time Kali spoke to her brother, John, he was desperate to tell her something but too drunk to get it out. Now he's dead, an apparent suicide by overdose. That would be shocking enough, but the cops have more bad news: John was also the lead suspect in the recent double homicide of two women in Tucson. The victims include the wealthy heiress of the corporation John worked for and Olivia Perez, a pretty college coed whose family is determined to make someone pay for the crime, and Kali's at the top of their list—if she can't clear his name first. It's a tricky case that's about to get even trickier.

Kali didn't know her brother very well, and in death, the only clue he's left behind is as damning as it is mysterious. Hidden in the pages of his dictionary is a photo of three attractive young women. One is Olivia Perez. One is a street-tough runaway named Crystal. The third woman—a strip club dancer and porn actress—has just been found in a ditch, the victim of a brutal slaying. As shocking as the woman's death is her connection to Kali's brother. How did they know each other? What was John trying to tell Kali the night he died? And would someone kill to keep him from saying it? Suddenly her brother's suicide is starting to look a lot like murder.

Kali's only hope for solving the case lies in finding the last girl in the picture—a witness who knows far more than she should, maybe too much to live—and Kali has to get to her before the killer does. It's a search that will plunge her into the secrets and lies of her own family and deep into the sex industry's hidden underworld of going-nowhere-fast girls looking for easy money, where fantasies can be had for a price, blackmail is deadly, and silence can be bought with blood. And if Kali isn't careful, she could lead a cunning killer straight to the last target while putting herself in line to be the next victim. . . .

**Look for THE NEXT VICTIM
coming in hardcover in February 2007!**

CHAPTER 1

The call came a little after two in the morning and pulled Erling from a particularly pleasant dream. As a homicide detective with the Pima County Sheriff's Department, he was used to being awakened at odd hours, but engaging his brain was always a struggle. He remained blurry-eyed, clinging to the remnants of sleep, until the dispatcher read off the address of the crime scene—one that was painfully etched in Erling's memory.

Instantly, he was fully alert.

His pulse quickened and an involuntary cry escaped from his lips, waking Deena, who had long ago learned to sleep through the intrusion of middle-of-the-night calls. She shot him an inquiring look, which he pretended not to see.

"Sorry, honey," he said instead. "I've got to go."

"What is it?"

"Just work."

"Figures." Deena sighed and rolled over, turning her back to him.

A shaft of moonlight illuminated her form and Erling took a moment to study the familiar curves of her body, the splash of auburn hair streaked with gray. There were times he could still see in her the playful and sexy woman he'd married twenty years earlier. What he saw more often though, or rather felt, was an aloofness tinged with reproach. It had been that way for four years—since their eleven-year-old son, Danny, had died in a skateboarding accident. Erling could never decide whether the tragedy had caused the problems in their marriage or simply exacerbated existing ones he'd been blind to at the time.

Erling headed for the bathroom, where he showered quickly before pulling on slacks and a collared knit shirt. Before leaving the house he gently shook Deena.

"Don't forget, Mindy needs to be up by seven in order to study for her sociology test." At eighteen, their daughter still had trouble getting out of bed on her own.

"I'll make sure she's up."

He kissed Deena on the cheek. "Have a good day."

"I'd tell you the same but I guess a dead body kind of precludes that."

Especially given the address, Erling thought with an ache in his gut.

There was no mistaking that the large, tile-roofed house on Canyon View Drive was a crime scene. Half a dozen patrol cars were parked in front. The coroner's van and mobile crime tech unit sat in the driveway. Yellow police tape cordoned off the house entrance and part of the yard. Already, a news helicopter was circling over head.

As he passed under the tape and through the front door, Erling felt a tremor of longing and sadness. Please, he whispered silently, don't let it be her.

Inside, the evidence of carnage was everywhere. A blue hand-blown glass vase had been knocked from the library table, one of the floor lamps had been overturned, and the rocking chair lay on its side. Bits of flesh and brain matter were splattered against the cherry cabinets. Dark, sticky blood pooled on the terra cotta tile floor. Erling had trouble breathing.

Across the room, he could see a female form crumpled against the wall. Olive-toned skin. Wavy black hair, long enough to fall below the shoulders. Erling felt a surge of relief. Definitely not Sloane.

"Other one's over there," the uniformed officer told him, pointing in the direction of the fieldstone fireplace. An image flashed in Erling's mind—Sloane in front of a blazing fire, facing him and slowly unbuttoning her blue silk blouse. Don't think about it, he told himself. Stay cool and don't think.

"It's pretty awful," the uniform warned. "I couldn't do more than take a peek myself."

Erling glanced over and saw a woman's leg and sandaled foot protruding from behind the sofa. Female also, but fair. He didn't recognize the shoes but that didn't mean anything. He hadn't seen Sloane in five months.

He said a silent prayer as he moved closer. The body was sprawled on the floor, arms and legs akimbo, the face largely blown away. Erling's gut rumbled and churned.

It might not be her. No way to know for sure without a formal ID.

But in his heart, he knew. The curve of the neck, the mole on her shoulder, the jade-and-silver ring on her right hand. Swallowing hard against the bile that threatened to rise in his throat, he crammed his shaking hands into his jacket pockets, hoping no one would notice, and closed his mind to the memories.

Erling experienced a familiar tug of anger and sadness at the senseless loss of life. The feelings came with the job, he supposed. Only this time the glaze of professional distance failed him. This wasn't just another victim, this was a woman he'd held and kissed, and laughed and loved with. This was Sloane.

Michelle Parker, his partner of six months—a younger detective with the tenacity of a bulldog—had been talking to the responding officers when he arrived. Now, notebook still in hand, she crossed from the wall of windows in the living room to join Erling by the kitchen archway.

Michelle brushed a wisp of chestnut brown hair from her forehead. "What a way to start the day, huh?"

"It's what we do," he snapped. His chest was so tight he could barely breathe.

Michelle's face registered surprise at the curt response. A moment of hollow silence followed while she regarded him thoughtfully. "Some of us do it in better humor than others," she said finally.

The sudden, if subtle, hint of tension in the air jolted him like the snap of a rubber band against his skin. *Get a grip, Shafer. You want the whole damn world to know?*

"So, what've we got?" he asked, more hospitably.

Michelle glanced at her notebook. "Call came in just after midnight. A neighbor noticed the lights had been on all day and the morning paper hadn't been picked up. She called the house and when no one answered, came over and rang the bell. Then she went around the side and peeked in the window. She saw a body on the floor and called 9-1-1."

"Do we have an ID on the victims?"

"Nothing positive. Best guess is that the older one is Sloane Winslow. This is her home."

Older one. Erling cringed. Sloane was only forty-one, two years younger than himself, and much too lovely to be called *older*.

"Her maiden name was Logan." Michelle paused. "As in Logan Foods."

When he didn't respond right away, she added, "The grocery chain."

Erling whistled softly. It bought him a moment's time. "You know anything about the family?"

"I didn't even know it was a family business until the neighbor filled me in. Do you?"

The moment of truth.

Or not.

Erling knew he should remove himself from the investigation. He had personal connections to one of the victims. Emotional connections. Big-time emotional connections. Department policy dictated he step aside and let someone else handle it.

But he couldn't do that. Not without explaining. Word would get around. Eventually it would get back to Deena. His stomach clenched. He couldn't. He simply couldn't take that chance. Not after Danny.

Besides, he wanted to personally nail the creep who'd done this. He needed to do it—for Sloane even more than for himself.

Michelle gave him that curious look again. She was still waiting for an answer.

"Only what I read in the papers," Erling said. The lie burned his tongue. Maybe, just maybe, they'd find the killer and wrap this up quickly.

"So, tell me."

"The grandfather started the business right here in Tucson. Sloane Winslow and her brother, Reed Logan, have controlling interest, though it's Reed who actually runs the company. Winslow lived in L.A. with her husband. It wasn't until she divorced and returned to Tucson a few years ago that she got involved in the business at all."

"Local gentry, local money." Michelle frowned. "I guess this one's going to be in the headlines."

"Afraid so." They looked at one another and Erling voiced what they were both thinking. "The lieutenant will put our feet to the fire if we don't hand him a suspect in short order."

"Can we do that?"

"You tell me. How's it look?"

Michelle flipped to a different page in her notebook. "Crawford's here from the medical examiner's office. His initial estimate is that they've been dead twenty-four to thirty-six hours. Both were shot at close range. The older woman in the head. The younger one in the chest and right leg. Weapon appears to be a shotgun."

Again Erling felt the tightness in his chest. Sloane moved with grace. A woman completely comfortable in her own skin. He couldn't imagine the terror she must have felt when she saw the gun in the killer's hands. His mind flashed on an vision of a Sloane trying frantically to fend off the inevitable. For a moment, he couldn't breathe. Then he shook his thoughts clear.

"We have the weapon?" he asked.

"No." Michelle paused and glanced around the room. "Looks like they put up a fight, doesn't it? But even with two of them, they'd be no match for a sleazeball with a gun."

Erling grunted agreement. "Any ID on the second victim?" he asked, moving in to take a closer look. She appeared to be in her late teens or early twenties. The *older woman* comment made sense to him now.

"The neighbor who called it in is a regular verbal fountain. Says there was a young woman living here with Winslow. Olivia Perez is the name. She was a student at the university."

"A relative?" Last Erling knew, Sloane had been living alone.

"A boarder, I think."

"A boarder?"

"I know, it doesn't make a lot of sense. The Logans must be loaded."

Certainly not in need of taking in boarders. "What do we have in the way of trace evidence?" Erling sent a silent prayer to the heavens for a dumb perp. One who'd left fingerprints and fibers, maybe even his driver's license.

"We won't know until the techs have finished going over the place. But there's an old guy a couple of houses down who gave us the description of a car he saw out front Tuesday night. A silver Porsche with a broken taillight. If Crawford's right about the time of death, that would put the car here near the time of the murders."

An eyewitness wasn't as good as a dumb perp, but Erling would take it. At least a Porsche wasn't your average, run-of-the-mill kind of car. "Did the old guy see anyone?"

"He thinks the driver was male, but can't say for sure."

"What about other neighbors?"

"Nothing so far. The houses are pretty far apart and private."

That was one of the things Sloane had liked about living in this part of Tucson. It wasn't as affluent as some of the newer gated communities, but the houses were all set on large lots, many of them an acre or more, and the neighborhood landscaping had matured to the point where plantings provided a screen. They'd made love one night out in the yard under the black, star-speckled sky. Erling remembered the soft breeze that grazed their skin, the lilac scent of Sloane's hair, and the rough texture of the nubby blanket beneath them.

The crime scene photographer reached into his equipment bag. "I'm about done here unless there's something in particular you want."

"You get both stills and movies?" Erling asked. His voice was gruff with the invasion of memories.

"Right. And I checked with Crawford about shots of the vics."

"When do you think you'll be able to get us prints?"

"Later today good enough?"

"That the best you can do?" Erling asked.

The photographer capped his camera. "Afraid so."

"I guess it's good enough, then." He turned to Michelle. "Anyone notified next of kin yet?"

"Boskin and Dutton are on their way to the brother's. Maybe he can give us more on the girl."

"Let's hope so."

Independently, Michelle and Erling walked the crime

scene, taking their own measurements, making their own sketches. Erling pulled out his palm-sized digital camera and shot the room from a dozen angles. The crime scene photographers did a terrific job, but he liked to have his own pictures, too, because they sometimes jogged his memory and filled in the details of his sketches.

"What's your take?" Erling asked as they worked. "First impression."

Michelle rocked back on her heels and frowned. She was wearing dark, form-fitting slacks and a cream-colored silk shirt that draped softly over the swell of her breasts—her standard uniform for the job, even when she was called out in the middle of the night.

He'd initially resisted being partnered with her because he'd considered her a lightweight, or worse. But Erling had come to see that despite the eye-catching body and head of soft, brown curls, she was an earnest and intense as anyone he'd worked with before. A little too intense sometimes.

"I'd say there's a good chance the killer was someone Winslow was familiar with," Michelle replied. "Either that or she was comfortable enough with what she saw that she had no qualms about letting him in. There's no sign of forced entry, and both victims were dressed in street clothes, so it's not like they were rousted from bed in the middle of the night. The lights are on, there's an open bottle of brandy on the counter."

Had she been entertaining a new lover? Erling wondered. But the girl, Olivia, was in the house. He doubted Sloane would bring a man home under those circumstances.

Michelle gestured toward Sloane's body. "Looks like the killer went for her first, and while she was trying to fend him off, the younger woman surprised them. He got Mrs. Winslow in the head, probably standing close to her. The girl . . . my guess is that the autopsy will show she was hit from farther away."

"Not a bad for someone who's only worked a couple of

homicides," Erling said. Michelle had worked vice in Phoenix before moving to Tucson and signing on as a detective with the Sheriff's Department.

She acknowledge the compliment with a slight twist of her head. "Doesn't mean it's right."

"No, it doesn't, and it's good to remember that."

"You get locked into in a midset too sooon," she said, parroting one of Erling's favorite adages, "and you'll miss the important stuff."

"Guess I've hammered that one home.'"

"You might say that." This time there was a faint hint of a smile. "Shall we check the rest of the house?"

Erling took a deep breath to still the pounding in his chest. Sloane's house. Sloane's things. Rooms charged with bittersweet memories. He wasn't sure he could manage it.

Finally he nodded. "Now's as good as time as any."

A canvass of the home was standard procedure for detectives in instances like this. The techs processed the actual crime scene, but careful inspection of a victim's personal possessions revealed alot about his or her life. Some of it interesting, most of it dull and irrevelant to the murder. Sometimes, though, they got lucky. A receipt, a phone number, a photo, some small tidbit that would eventually lead them to the killer.

But normally the detective and the victim were strangers.

Erling and Michelle spent the next forty minutes going through dressers, files, desk drawers, wastebaskets, and medicine cabinets. He was half-afraid he'd find something that marked his own previous presence in the house, and equally fearful of discovering that Sloane had obliterated his memory entirely. He almost smiled when he found the copper and bronze pendant he'd bought her for Christmas last year laid out on the velvet lining of her jewelry drawer.

"Looks like she was astylish woman," Michelle said at one point.

Erling shrugged. "I wouldn't know about that."

He paused at a familair photo on Sloane's bureau—a framed picture of Sloane and her brother, Reed, taken during a family barbeque. Her skin was virtually unlined, her blue-green eyes sparkling with humor. And often Erling recalled, with mischief. He felt an ache in his gut, a longing some-where deep inside him that was less about her dream than his own loss.

It had been a brief affair—six months and fourteen days, to be exact. Over since early May. Him like a panting mon-grel around a pedigreed bitch in heat. Her words, but they resonated as much as they stung. His behavior was nothing to be proud of. Erling had known that even then. Still, he'd wanted to hate her for ending it. There were times he'd come close. But he'd certainly never wished her dead.

By the time he and Michelle finished their canvass of the house, the sun was just rising over the hills near Sabino Canyon. Morning was Erling's favorite time of day. Blue, cloudless sky, wide and open, the air soft, just beginning to build to the blinding heat of day.

Leaving the house, he saw that the media were already out in force. A cameraman from one of the local news chan-nels shoved a camera in his face. His cohort held a mic.

"Detective Shafer," the reporter shouted, "what can you tell us? We understand there's been a homicide inside. Two victims. Was one of them Sloane Logan Winslow?"

"We're not prepared to make a statement at this time," Erling barked.

He could only hope Boskin and his partner would be able to notify Sloane's family before they learned about her death live on television. Erling figured the murders would be the lead story on the morning news.

More Books From Your Favorite Thriller Authors

More Thrilling Suspense From Your Favorite Thriller Authors

If Angels Fall by Rick Mofina	0-7860-1061-4	$6.99US/$8.99CAN
Cold Fear by Rick Mofina	0-7860-1266-8	$6.99US/$8.99CAN
Blood of Others by Rick Mofina	0-7860-1267-6	$6.99US/$9.99CAN
No Way Back by Rick Mofina	0-7860-1525-X	$6.99US/$9.99CAN
Dark of the Moon by P.J. Parrish	0-7860-1054-1	$6.99US/$8.99CAN
Dead of Winter by P.J. Parrish	0-7860-1189-0	$6.99US/$8.99CAN
Paint It Black by P.J. Parrish	0-7860-1419-9	$6.99US/$9.99CAN
Thick Than Water by P.J. Parrish	0-7860-1420-2	$6.99US/$9.99CAN

Available Wherever Books Are Sold!

Visit our website at **www.kensingtonbooks.com**